For those who live in the shadows,

it's time to embrace the darkness within.

CHAPTER 1
HAPPY BIRTHDAY

Larissa

It was my own screams that startled me awake, and it was always the same dream. The man in the black cloak, with his face shrouded in darkness. A woman's shouts echoed through the room. The sound of 'shhh' filled my ears as the voices stopped. I held my head in my hands and tried to remove the image of the glowing golden eyes that glared me into submission. They were eyes I could never forget, the face always blurry but the eyes I could not mistake. I wiped the sweat from my face as I lifted my head to look around my room. A green balloon bobbed on the dresser near the bed. My mother had obviously snuck in and planted it while I slept. I reached over to my side table and grabbed my phone. I took one of my anxiety pills to bring down my racing heart rate and the feeling that I was being watched. My twin, Lucianna, had sent me a text:

LUCIANNA

Happy Birthday sis, FYI I have already pissed off mummy dearest.

I sank back into the pillows. Luce tended to piss off our mother and I always had to deal with the repercussions. Despite only being three minutes older, I had the role of big sister. Luce was the free-spirited baby—she did what she wanted while I had to be the responsible child. I took a calming breath as I sat up in the bed and texted her back.

ME

> Happy Birthday Luce! I assume you told her you were leaving?

As I locked the phone, I changed into my matching black yoga pants and crop top before I snuck out of the house for my morning run, avoiding our mother. Winter was fast approaching—the leaves were turning from their lush green to orange, and some had already fallen from trees. I worried about what Mum would be like when I got home. She had guilted me into staying home rather than getting a job in London when I finished my degree two years ago. She cried for days on end when she forbade me from leaving. Lucianna took her time changing between her degrees before she finally finished it and now, she had secured a job doing what she wanted. I envied her free spirit; she did not care what anyone thought of her. She was always the most popular in school, while I was only popular for being her twin. I wanted nothing more than to read in school, always absorbing information on any topic.

I ran into town as people waved and said, "Good morning." I smiled and nodded my head at them in response. My mother was well known, as she owned the only café in our small town of Shaftesbury and had served every resident. I stopped in at her café to pinch a bottle of water and saw the television turned to the news channel.

"Today is the 50th anniversary of the end of the war. The day the world stopped fighting and peace ensued." I shook my head and took a gulp of the water. It was 2070 and they were *still* talking about how society had been destroyed in 2020.

"If only they told the whole truth. But this is the world we live in." Sam broke my focus; he always had the morning shift at the café. This gave him time to go to our local college to study for his accounting degree. His mousey brown hair was pulled back into a ponytail and his horrible mustache was overgrown and untamed. I knew he did it as a screw you to my mother. She may have been well-known, but she also had a reputation of being a bit of a bitch, which was the truth.

"Morning Sam, we both know that lies are easier than the truth. We must only be grateful for what we have today." I smiled at him cheekily.

"If only we were born earlier." He cleaned the table and walked to the counter as I followed to pay for the bottle of water.

"I am glad that I was not. I cannot imagine what it would have been like to see the whole world change. We deal with the repercussions of the bombs being dropped, and that is enough for me." The door chimed to alert us that someone else had entered the café, Sam looked over and shook his head.

"Here are our repercussions now." I knew he was referring to Richard or Valerie, our town vampires.

"Morning Richard." I turned to greet him. He tipped his head at me and smiled. He always wore a suit and today was no exception; this time, it was navy. Richard's slightly greying hair curled above a distinguished handlebar mustache, hinting at a heritage not in this century. As I watched him, I could not help but speculate about his age.

I disliked vampires because of their control over our world. They had a superiority and authority that I did not believe they deserved. It all started fifty years ago, when North Korea finally followed through on their threat to bomb America, except it was not just a bomb; rather a nuclear bomb. The leader at the time did not care about what had happened at Hiroshima or Nagasaki or what happened at Chernobyl. The use of nuclear power and weapons was one of humanity's biggest mistakes. After they attacked, those that remained in America launched their own weapons at Korea. This affected multiple countries within Asia and made China retaliate against Europe. The nuclear aftermath caused ripples that still affected everyone today. It was important not to be outside during a thunderstorm unless you wanted to be burnt by acid rain. There were various foods that we could no longer eat due to the radiation damage.

Luckily, England had not been bombed, and we were far enough away that the whole country could still run as it normally did. Mainland Europe, Australia, Asia and America took the brunt of the radiation damage. After the mainland was attacked, the vampires showed themselves and took over. They said humans were not fit to ensure their own survival, and they pushed our leaders out. We let it happen. They still ruled us, and the humans did not have the power or the guts to overthrow them. We just dealt with it now. I had no love for vampires, but I was polite to the only two that I knew. They were our local sheriffs, so they ruled Shaftesbury. A vampire ran every town to guarantee a peaceful community. Being in a small town helped, as we rarely had any issues.

———

I reached my street with the perfect, idyllic houses; all made of weatherboard but each a different colour. Every house had the typical picket fence and perfectly manicured garden, filled with roses or coloured flowers, all bursting with aromas. I stopped outside our gate and put my hands on my hips to catch my breath. I reached over and opened the white picket fence only to cut my finger on the latch. I sucked on it to stop the bleeding. I barely took note of my surroundings as I walked up the stairs to our olive-green door.

"Happy Birthday, baby girl!" My mother threw her arms around my neck and smothered my face in kisses.

"Mum, I am no longer a child," I said as I tried to avoid her smooches. I turned twenty-five today.

"You will always be my baby." She let me go but held my face in her hands. I pulled them away and kissed her palm before I made my way to the kitchen. I could almost taste the freshly cooked French toast and bacon as I entered. Mum had the table set and a freshly brewed cappuccino ready for me. I knew what this meant. I sat down to eat and cut into the toast. I could feel my mother's green eyes staring at me as she sat opposite me. She reached over the table.

"You need to eat more. You are getting too skinny with this new running regime." I glanced down at myself. I was barely skinny. I had lost about ten kilos and most of my fat had turned into muscle. I felt refreshed during a run, more myself. The days were clearer, and my brain was less muddled. I put my cutlery down and looked up at Mum, her wavy red hair was pulled into a perfect bun. Lucianna inherited the same red hair as our mother but mine was dark chocolate. If it were not for the same green eyes, I would assume that I was adopted.

"What is it, Mum?" I asked her as I crossed my arms to show I knew what she was up to. She sighed and put her coffee down on the table.

"Did you know?"

"Know what?" I thought it best to play dumb.

"Rissa, do not play dumb with me." Her voice was stern. I shook my head in annoyance. Here I was again, cleaning up my sister's mess.

"Yes, of course I knew, Mum. She is my sister. Why does it matter? She has a job, for which she was headhunted by Google for her vast knowledge in computer programming. Any other mother would be proud that her daughter has secured a job from her college degree. Why would you care? You guilted me into staying here to help you with the café. You do not need both of us. Let her go and live her life."

"I want to keep my girls protected," she mumbled as her cheeks were beginning to match the colour of her hair.

"There is a difference between protection and control." My voice came out a little more aggressive than intended, and my mother flinched.

"The world is a dangerous place, Larissa. You need to understand this," she pleaded with me, but I had heard it way too many times.

"We would not know that because you keep us trapped in a bubble. We cannot do anything without *your* permission. Is it any wonder Lucianna does what she does? She wants nothing more than to be free from the constraints that you have put on us. Why else do you think that she would sneak out at night and go off with boys?" I snapped at her; I was proud of my sister.

"You never did." She crossed her arms over her body smugly, her mouth tipping up in a smirk.

"I did not, but only because I was trying to keep her safe from you and the repercussions of what she was doing. I am so goddamn proud of her. Why are you not?" She stayed silent as she looked away, while holding back tears and possibly holding back what she really wanted to say.

"Larissa—"

I put my hand up to stop her from her usual tirade about how we should be grateful that she provided us with so much when others went without, how she kept us safe from the vampires that constantly threatened us, which was not true.

"Just stop, Mum. Thank you for breakfast, but I have a shift at the café. Bye." I stood up and put my plates away in the tiny cottage-style kitchen before I headed upstairs to change into my boring work attire.

I came back down in my uniform. The black pants and a beige shirt that had the name *Lizzie's* written in red across the pocket.

"Larissa." I stopped in the doorway and waited for her to say something. "I love you." My shoulders relaxed as I looked back at her.

"I love you, too." Despite how much I hated her control, I did love my mother. I walked to work as I usually did. Once I was clear from her eyesight, I called my sister to vent to her about our mother and to yell at her for doing this on our birthday. Lucianna never was the best at picking the most appropriate times to do things. The typical baby sister, if only by a few minutes. I reached the café and Sam smiled and waved me in.

"You are early. You do not start until lunch; it isn't even ten."

"I am here to do paperwork. Just leave me alone in the office please." Sam knew what Mum was like. After all, he worked with her as well. He smiled as I strolled into the tiny office that barely had space for a chair to sit in. I flicked through our expenses and our ordering sheets as Sam brought me a coffee. I smiled as he leant against the doorway.

"What is it, Sam?" I turned towards him, noticing his arms were crossed. This meant one of two things with Sam—concern or anger.

"I need to ask you a serious question." I knew where this may be going, and it worried me.

"Can I leave early?" I was stumped. Sam had always been rather flirtatious with me, but it seemed I was wrong.

"Oh, how early?" He scratched the back of his neck this was his nervous tick. I had read him completely wrong from earlier.

"About an hour. I have a date tonight." For some reason that stung a little bit. I had only had one boyfriend and he only dated me to get closer to my sister. I was the perfect nun; I had not bothered to date because most of the men here had been with my sister in some way, shape, or form. It was hard to find one who hadn't, so I just never bothered. Sam knew this, and he had always been super sweet, but that was just his personality.

"Yeah, ah…of course. Have fun," I said awkwardly. I finished cleaning up the paperwork before I moved to busy myself with another task. Instead of walking away, he stepped into the office.

"Are you upset?" My cheeks flushed at his question.

"No, why would I be?" He sighed as he ran his fingers through his hair.

"Larissa, you said you never wanted to be with a man who had been with your sister. I assumed that meant I was out of the picture." His shoulders slumped, and anger and frustration filled my belly.

"What? When?" I yelped and took a step back.

"A couple of months ago."

THE WHISPERS SERIES BOOK ONE

WHISPERS

in the

BLOOD

S.K MAY

I shook my head. She did it on purpose. She knew I liked him and had sought him out. I should not have asked, but I was upset. I shook off the anger.

"Sam, that is fine. Sorry for kind of losing my temper. I just…" I trailed off, not knowing what to say. He strode over and rubbed my arms.

"Don't worry about it, I get it. You shared everything growing up and you don't want to share men. If I was not so intoxicated, I wouldn't have. I like you better than Luce." The comment made me smile but did not help the fact that he was now another man I could not have.

"Come on, we need to get ready for the lunch rush," I said with a smile as I changed the topic, walked out of the office, and chose the first menial task I could find. I started checking the salt and pepper on the tables.

I was grateful for the lunch rush, as it was a literal rush. We were busier than normal, and a lot of locals had brought in gifts for my sister and me. It was nice, if not a little annoying, that I would have to carry all of them home. Sam left not long ago after he had helped with closing. I just had to do the final wipe down, restock the tables, and count the till before I left. The door chimed and I turned to see Richard and Valerie walking in.

"Are you closing, Larissa?" Valerie asked as she looked me over with her typical disdain.

Richard had always been nice, but Valerie must have lost her humanity when she converted because she was nasty. Her black hair was pinned back off her face and she wore a grey pinafore layered over a blue top. She had a unique sense of style. There was no mistaking which era Richard came from as he always wore a beret, which became popular in the early nineteen hundreds in France. Richard had a slight accent, but I could never place it. Valerie, on the other hand, was English to the core. My guess was that in her life before she transitioned, she was a whore. It was hard to explain how, but there were just vibes. I did not know what Richard saw in her, she was not as kind as him.

"Yes, just finishing with the tables. Can I help you with anything?"

Valerie scoffed and Richard glared at her, his eyes flashed red. I had never seen anything like that.

"Do your eyes always turn red?" I stared at him curiously before his eyes turned back to their hazel colour. He beamed at me.

"Only when we are hungry, angry, or experience any intense emotions. We just wanted a drink and some cake, if possible?" he asked in his usual polite tone.

"Huh. Interesting! Yes, of course, just your usual bloodcinos? Which cake would you like?" I made my way behind the counter to prepare their order.

"Red Velvet, please." I internally rolled my eyes, of course they wanted a red velvet. Not only did I have to make them a cappuccino with blood and milk mixed in, but I would now have to go to the fridge to get their cake. I stood behind the coffee machine and mixed their drinks before I cut the slices and took them over. Richard put his nose in the air and sniffed before he grabbed my hand.

"You need to clean that." I took my hand back forcefully. "Oh sorry, I did not mean to. I can smell the infection setting in."

"Wait, you can smell that?" I questioned as he smirked at my ignorance.

"Yes, it is hard not to notice with your blood." Valerie kicked Richard under the table.

"My blood?" I questioned, feeling vulnerable. I rubbed my hands, close to my chest. Valerie spoke in another language, which prompted a rather abrupt response from Richard. It was unlike him. He had always been so polite. He turned to me.

"Every person has a particular smell, as you well know. We smell what their blood could almost taste like. It is how we pick our meals, so to speak. You are a rare treat with your blood." A coldness shivered through my body at the thought.

"Pardon?" It almost felt like an insult.

Valerie rolled her eyes. "We can smell that you are a virgin. For us, the purity within your blood is one of a kind. As well as your rare blood type, O negative, it makes you…" She stopped as her eyes flashed with delight, which prompted a growl from Richard.

"You would be like a drug to any vampire. I understand why your mother wanted to keep you at home. If you moved to London, you would either be dead or a blood slave."

"A blood slave?" I questioned.

Valerie chuckled. "What, are you interested?"

"Valerie!" Richard slammed his fist on the table. "Phoenix, remember?"

"What is Phoenix?"

Richard drank the rest of his coffee and stood up. "Thank you for the coffee, Larissa. Enjoy your birthday night." He grabbed Valerie's arm and lifted her from the chair. I had never seen him act that way before, it was odd.

CHAPTER 2
BLOW OUT THE CANDLES!

Larissa

I WAS DISTRACTED ON MY WALK HOME, AS I THOUGHT ABOUT MY conversation with Richard and Valerie. I rounded the corner into the dark street that was lit only by the tall streetlights that needed a serious update. I swear, they were probably the same lights since electricity was first invented. I heard raised voices in the distance and recognised who they belonged to. I opened the gate and walked in to see my sister and mother fighting in the window of our house. I approached slowly and heard them yelling.

"You cannot keep me here forever!" Lucianna shouted at the top of her lungs. I sat on the step outside, knowing better than to get involved. Lucianna stormed outside, the door slamming behind her.

"You didn't think to help? Some sister you are," she grumbled as she saw me on the step. I stood up.

"Hey, do not take your anger out on me!"

She instantly settled and took a breather. I walked over to her and pulled her into my arms—one of the perks of being taller than my sister. She snuggled in as I heard her soft cries.

"She is impossible." Her voice was a whisper as I squeezed her tighter. I searched for my mother and saw her watching us silently through the window. Her arms were crossed, and her forehead creased with worry.

"I know, but she loves you and does not want to see you hurt. You will be fine, and she knows it, but it does not stop her worrying." My mother left the window and ran to the kitchen. I watched as she ran back with tears on her face. She put her hand against the glass and closed her eyes, just as the flames started behind her.

"LUCE!" I shouted, turning her around to block the blast that I knew was coming.

I felt the warmth before the pain in my back as we were pushed over by the force of the explosion. I landed on top of her as the flames surrounded us. I did not burn, though. The fire burned out as I rolled off Lucianna and I looked her over as she did with me. She held my face.

"Are you alright?" I could not hear myself speak, but Luce nodded her head. We frantically searched each other for any signs of injury.

"Are you?" Her voice was barely audible as the ringing in my ears drowned out all other noises. She nodded; we knew what we were asking even if we could not hear each other. I stood slowly, my body aching. Flashes of light appeared. Fire and ambulance had arrived. How much time had passed for them to be here already? The firefighters ran past us with their hoses as the paramedics ran over to us. The male paramedic grabbed me and helped me to the van, while my sister remained on the ground. I saw the concern on his face, his brow creased. I reached up and touched my forehead, my fingers were wet as I pulled them away. They were slick with blood; he grabbed my hand and shook his head.

"How much can you hear?" I squinted to read his lips while he spoke. His blue eyes were kind, and his smile was comforting as I studied his long hair, which was pulled back in a ponytail.

"A little." It seemed to make him smile, which I assumed was because I was yelling without realising it. He checked my ears and gave me a thumbs up.

"I'll need to take you to the hospital to check you have no internal bleeding. I need to inspect your back." I turned as he looked it over before he faced me again and asked, "Where was the explosion to you?" I pointed behind me. His face scrunched in confusion before he walked to check on my sister. We both had to be checked over at the hospital. They loaded Lucianna onto the stretcher and sat me beside her.

The last of the fire was almost out. She turned to me. "Mum?" I shook my head. It would not be possible for her to have survived that. I knew the explosion alone would have made it quick. Even Mum knew, which is why she mouthed *I love you* before she accepted her end. Lucianna cried as she held her hands over her face. I went to comfort her but was distracted by the golden glow of eyes staring at me. I stood up and my feet moved of their own accord. It was as if those eyes were calling to me.

"Larissa, sit down, please." The male paramedic called out as he closed the door to the back of the ambulance, securing us inside. I walked over to the window and looked out. The glowing eyes stayed on me as the body they belonged to hid behind a tree. Those eyes were familiar. But...this was not one of my dreams. I felt unease spread through me as the ambulance drove us away.

CHAPTER 3
THE AFTERMATH

Lucianna and I were ordered to stay for the night to ensure that our injuries did not deteriorate. We were thankfully given a room to share, but it was pointless. We stayed in the same bed, and I held onto my sister as she slept. I could not stop the images from playing out in my brain on a loop. I could not understand why my mother ran out of the kitchen and just stood at the window. Why did she not try to escape? I played it in my head as I listened to my sister snoring. The fear on her face as she ran but paused in the window long enough to sign that she loved us. She had more than enough time to get out of the house. Sure, she would have been injured, but she did not even try. I sighed. As the ticking clock echoed in the room, I moved out from under my sister to let her sleep, knowing I would not be able to.

I peered out the hospital window. It was still dark. The car park was barely illuminated, the only cars there belonged to the doctors and nurses who were still working. The hospital was tiny, not like a city hospital, but rather like a large doctor's clinic. I went to close the curtain when I noticed movement in the distance. I waited for it to move again, and when it did, it was with a speed that I most likely hallucinated from exhaustion. I closed the curtain before curiosity got the better of me. But I pushed my fingers to make a slight gap as I looked through again. A figure was standing at the edge of the car park. It seemed to lean against a tree. I pulled out my phone to open the camera, zoomed in as far as possible, and took the photo. I noticed the eyes first, the yellow glow that haunted my dreams. I locked the phone and threw it onto the armchair.

You are just tired Larissa, go to bed. I slid in beside my sister and thought of happy memories to avoid thinking of our mother's death.

———

I woke to an empty bed. I rubbed my tired eyes and searched for my sister, but I was alone. I reached over for the glass of water and took a sip; it was warm, but at least it soothed my throat, which was still irritated from the smoke inhalation.

"Lucianna!" I called out with my croaky voice before I cleared it and stood from the bed. The bathroom door opened and Luce came out in a towel and with wet hair. I was confused and she must have noticed.

"Yes, I am aware that I have no clean clothes, but I felt dirty, and I wanted to wash the blood from my hair," she said as she ran her fingers through her curls.

I nodded with a small smile as I walked over and embraced her. "I missed you too," she mumbled as she buried her head into my shoulder. I let her go. "There is a spare towel if you want to freshen up."

"Have we heard from the doctors on when we can be discharged?" I asked over my shoulder.

"Yep, as soon as you woke up." I rushed to the bathroom to wash away the events of last night. Lucianna was right, it was good to clean myself of the dried blood in my hair and on my skin. I looked at the floor, at the bloody water swirling down the drain; it was a reminder of Mum's death. I dreaded going back to the house to see what was left. But if that was where my sister wanted to start, that's where we would go first. I let my head rest on the wall of the shower for a moment before I heard a knock at the door.

"Larissa, all good in there?"

"Sure am. I will be out shortly," I called out to her. I turned the water off and dried myself, then put the same dirty clothes back on. I picked up my phone and saw the multitude of messages from the town, all with their condolences for the loss of our mother. I am not sure what possessed me to open my gallery to look at the photo, but it was gone. I searched the deleted files, but it was not there either.

"I did not truly hallucinate, did I?"

Lucianna knocked on the door again. She had no patience. I rolled my eyes as I looked at myself in the mirror. The dark circles under my eyes showed my lack of sleep and my typically green eyes lacked their usual spark. I brushed my hair with my fingers before I left the bathroom with a smile on my face for my sister. Lucianna was sitting on the bed, twirling her hair in her fingers, sultry eyes gazing at the doctor. She was flirting with him. He must be new in town. I had not seen him yet, but my sister seemed particularly intrigued. I cleared my throat to alert them both to my presence in the room.

"Larissa." It took me a moment to notice who it was before me, the voice saying my name with familiarity.

"Oh my god, Jack, no way." It was Sam's older brother; he had secured a place at an elite university in London to complete his degree.

He walked over, lifted me, and spun us around in a circle. "Little Rissa, all grown up." He had almost ten years on me and would often babysit us when we were younger. Luce never had the chance to sleep with him, so I understand why she was flirting now. She walked over and stood beside me as she continued to twirl her hair, but Jack's eyes never moved from mine.

"I examined both of your scans; you are all clear to leave. Do you need a lift home?"

Lucianna put her hand on his arm. "Yes, we sure do."

I scoffed at her, which prompted her death stare in my direction. "Come on, Luce. Is getting laid right now really that important when our mother just died?"

She forced a smile on her face before glancing back at Jack. "Could you excuse us for a moment, please?" She was as sweet as sugar before she spun back around with her usual spitefulness. "Yes, she is dead, so what? Do I not deserve to get laid? A girl has needs."

I sucked on my lower lip. "You take the lift with Jack. I will call for a taxi. I need to clear my head. Enjoy your fuck." I pushed past her and out of the room.

I smiled at Jack. "I am going to catch a taxi. Luce is waiting for you. Thank you for your help, Jack. It was good to see you again."

"Larissa!" he called after me, but I was not going to bother. Once she set her sights on a guy, she was relentless. I felt sorry for him as I walked out of the hospital and called a taxi to pick me up. I wanted to beat my sister home, at least. I wanted to replay everything in my head despite doing that all night. I needed clarity, and I hoped that returning would help provide some.

The taxi pulled up to what was left of our house, where there was no longer the olive-green door with leadlight surrounding it. There were only broken pieces of wood left. I walked through what would have been the entry and into the dining area and stood exactly where Mum was before the house exploded. I closed my eyes and remembered her calm face. I knew I should not dwell on the moment because I would never have the answers I wanted or needed. Venturing further, through to the kitchen, I saw a black spot on the floor where the stove used to be. That must have caused the explosion.

"Oh Mum, what the hell happened?" I walked to where my bedroom used to be. There was nothing left. I went to Luce's room, and it was the same. Everything had been burnt. There remained nothing salvageable. I found Mum's room and a cold shiver washed through to my bones. I shook it off and crossed my arms over my body for warmth. I did not know what I was searching for, but something told me to look in every room. I reached Mum's special sitting room, as she called it. The floors creaked under my feet. I looked down and noticed that the flooring was different. When I rubbed my foot over it and noticed movement. I bent down and dug my fingers into the side of the piece that was not flush against the floor. My nail snapped before I managed to pull it up to reveal an ornate wooden box. I rubbed my hand over the top, which had a pearl inlay with our last name, Solis, imprinted on it. I picked the box up. It was heavy and engraved with various flowers and leaves. The red mahogany wood had been well preserved, and I could tell it was old from the latches that held it together. The key was placed inside the lock. I decided I would open it when I found a place to stay for the night. I held onto the box as my sister turned up with Jack. He waved at me as Lucianna seductively exited the car. I rolled my eyes and continued to look around for any other possible holes in the floor. Lucianna swayed her hips in hopes that Jack was watching. I chuckled to myself as he drove away.

"His loss," she muttered to herself.

"Yes, his loss on not getting an STI."

She scoffed at me and took the box from under my arms. "What did you find?"

"It was in the special sitting room under the floor. It seems to be the only thing that survived. It looks old."

She started to shake the box.

"*What* the hell are you doing?" I yelled at her and yanked the box away.

"It is just an old box. Nothing special, Rissa."

I observed Lucianna circling the house, verifying the aftermath of the explosion. I sat on the grass outside and watched her. As the sun disappeared, I looked up to see Richard suddenly standing over me, his suit and hat covered him, and he ducked into the nearby shade. Vampires could stand in the sun, but they could not tolerate it for long periods, or it would burn them.

"My condolences for your loss." His face showed sadness at her passing. His brows knit together as his gaze lingered on what was left of the house. If I did not know any better, it almost looked as if his eyes welled with tears.

"Thank you, Richard, it means—"

"Absolutely nothing to us! You can take your fake condolences somewhere else. I will be asking for an investigation into this explosion. You never know how this happened. A person with super speed could have entered and exited before anybody suspected any foul play." Luce crossed her arms and glared at Richard.

"LUCE!" I shouted at her. I did not like vampires any more than she did, but I thought it was better to be polite than rude. Especially when he had come over with kind intentions.

She stared me down. "What, do you like them now?"

"I did not say that. You are being rude. He came over to make sure we were alright. He is the town sheriff, so it is his job to ask for an investigation. Check yourself right now." I glanced back at Richard with a smile to try to ease the tension between the two of them.

"Larissa, you do not need to apologise or justify anything right now. Emotions would be running high for both of you. Let me know if you need anything." Lucianna scoffed and walked towards the house; I ran after Richard as he turned his back to leave.

"Sorry Richard, I hate to bother you, but we have nowhere to stay, and we do not have any money right now. I only have what I was left with, which is not much, and Mum kept all our documents in the house." He put his hand on my shoulder, a coldness seeped through my clothes.

"Say no more. I shall organise it for you. Stay close to your phone." I blinked, and he was gone.

Lucianna stood with her arms crossed as she tapped her foot on the floor. "What the fuck was that about?" I could see her anger, her cheeks matched her hair.

"We do not have anything, Luce, and we need help. It is his job to help us. Where were you planning on staying tonight? Or were you hoping that Jack would fall to your charms, and you could stay with him?"

"Get off your high horse, Larissa. Maybe if you were fucked just once, you wouldn't be such a prude." I could see from the tears in her eyes that this was not about me. She was not sure how to process our mother's death. Anger and grief consumed her, so she projected her frustration onto whoever happened to be nearby. Her words stung but I had to believe that they did not reflect how she truly felt. I rushed over and pulled her into my arms, holding her tightly as she struggled and swore at me before the yells turned into tears and she fell to pieces.

I kissed her head. "I have you, Luce. Let it out." She collapsed to the floor as I held onto her and did the same. Despite my own emotions threatening to spill out, I held them in, knowing she relied on my support. I had always been her rock and I was not about to crumble when she needed me to bash against. It started to cloud over as a cold gust of wind hit my face. A storm was coming.

"Luce, we need to find some shelter. It is going to rain," I whispered to her as she sighed before standing.

Chapter 4

Lord Dankworth

Nik

My steps echoed through the foyer, the marble flooring and glass walls brought a sense of sophistication. It was a personal stamp. As I entered the building, silence followed. I buried my head in my phone to avoid speaking to anyone. There was no point.

"How does one exist to be so handsome?" I heard the young male receptionist whisper to his colleague. I glanced up from my phone and charmed him with a smile. It would make his day and I heard he worked hard at his job.

The elevator smelt of humans who had overdosed on perfume. It tickled my nose. I never understood why females had a desire to cover themselves in strong scents that would burn the hair from people's nostrils. My phone rang, it was a number I did not expect to hear from.

"Richard, it has been a long time since we spoke." He and Valerie were sheriffs of the small town of Shaftesbury. The town was southwest of London and past Winchester, an almost three-hour drive. I despised his wife; she had an air of superiority, which contradicted the life she had before Richard turned her. But when the bond kicked in, there was nothing that could stop mates from being together.

"Lord Dankworth—"

"Richard, we have known one another for long enough that our first names shall suffice."

He chuckled down the end of the phone. "It has been centuries, Nik. I often forget just how old you are."

I snorted at his remark. If only he knew. Not many did, and nobody needed to know the truth.

"What can I help you with, old friend?" I had a meeting in ten minutes and could not afford to waste time on him.

"There has been a strange house fire, which resulted in the death of a mortal. She left behind two daughters. All their papers were inside the house, and they have no money. I wondered if you wished to sponsor them until they find their feet?"

I stroked my chin as my assistant waltzed over holding out a file. "How much is needed?" I queried.

"They have no money, accommodation, clothes, or even food."

I grew restless with his need to draw this conversation out longer than needed.

"Richard, how much?" Though my tone was blunt, I had a pressing meeting to get to.

"Five thousand." This amount would not even make a dent in my wealth.

"Consider it done. Speak with Abigail and she will make the transfer." I pulled the phone away.

"Nik, wait," he called out, and I did as he requested.

"You should know that…" He paused. "Never mind. I hope to see you soon. I am sorry for the loss of Aurora."

"Appreciated." I ended the call and entered my meeting.

"Apologies for my lateness, shall we begin?" I unbuttoned my jacket and took a seat. The young blonde stood; her eyes were trained on mine. Her desire lingered in the air; her attraction was obvious. Her breathing became erratic, and her nipples strained under her white shirt. I bet she regretted that colour choice today. Her legs were clenched together as she stood. A lesser man would bend her over this table and give in to her needs, but I was not that man.

My heart belonged to the only woman I loved. The woman I lost the day the bombs fell. No other compared to her beauty. I sighed as I thought about my love, the woman who made my heart sing, whose eyes could stop a man dead in his tracks. The woman whose heart was so pure that I would do anything to protect it. I remembered the touch of her soft skin and the sound of my name on her lips. I missed her.

CHAPTER 5
SHOPPING TRIP

Larissa

I waited in Mum's café for Luce after Richard told me of the generous donation from a business associate. I was grateful for his help even if Luce was not. The bell chimed as my sister entered and I was glad that she arrived late enough to miss Richard altogether.

"I have organised accommodation for us and some money to buy some clothes."

She brightened a little. "Where?"

"Sally's," I stated, worried how she may react.

She bobbed in her seat with glee. She had always wanted to stay at Sally's, but Mum had a long-standing feud with the bed and breakfast owner. I hoped that Sally would be nice, rather than her usual bitter self. I finished what was left of my hot chocolate before I stood, and Luce joined me.

As we stood at the front of Sally's Bed and Breakfast, I took in the crooked stone path that was shrouded in blue hydrangeas that led to the blue-tinged weatherboard house. It was quaint—the perfect little bed and breakfast for a small town. It had an old Victorian-style look with a porch that wrapped around the front and a swing that creaked even in a soft breeze. Luce opened the gate and started to walk up the path, but my mind suddenly thought about the stranger in the hospital car park and the deleted photo. Also, how the hell did Richard find a person to donate money to us? Or did he lie to make it easier for me to tell Luce? Either way, I was grateful for his help.

I followed Luce in and paused at the swing. I remember I ran to jump on it once, and my mother slapped my face and told me to stay away from Sally because she was nasty and hurt little girls. Luce was already inside, speaking to Sally, as I observed the white wainscoting on the walls with old-looking navy blue wallpaper with little white flowers. The walls were covered with aged photographs that captured the history of Sally. Some were pictures of landscapes and others were people that shared the space with her, every picture told a story of Sally's life.

"Larissa!" Luce shouted, which snapped my attention back towards her with a small smile. Sally peered over her half-moon glasses at us. Her white hair was pulled back into an impossibly tight bun.

"Sorry, what's up?"

"Are we sharing a room?" Her question was open. I knew she needed me, but I needed space to process my own emotions.

"Sally, is there enough space for us to have separate rooms?"

Her stoic face showed no emotion, not a flinch, nothing for anybody to read. I wondered why she hated our mother, but I supposed neither woman was the easiest person to be around.

"Yes, dear. The donor paid enough for either type of room." She slid the old cast iron keys across the counter and said, "Dinner is at six. Do not be late."

Luce and I stood outside our doors, which were beside each other. We glanced at one another before we stepped inside.

My eyes were drawn to the massive fan and light in the centre of the room that covered a beautiful ceiling rose. The dusty pink carpet matched the floral doona on the bed. I walked over and sat on the bed; it smelt musky like the room had not aged or even been cleaned since it first opened. The cream-coloured wallpaper seemed like it was more due to old age than an intentional colour choice. I found it odd when coupled with the colour of the flooring. The cherry wood dresser was antique in its design, along with the smoky look of the glass. I sighed and let myself fall backwards onto the bed. It did not help that it reminded me of old people. I got up and walked into the bathroom. The design of it was not any better; the cream-coloured tiles led to a basin and to the right stood the bath and shower in one. I scoffed as I entered the cold room; the window was open and I tugged on it to pull it closed. It did not work; I now understood why people did not stay more than one or two days. It looked beautiful from the outside, but the inside was as wretched as Sally, sweet but sour. I remembered all the times that Sally would storm into the café and yell at my mother. The screaming matches terrified me as a child, but I got used to them the older I got. I always remembered the one comment that Sally would make, "They deserve better than you!" I wondered why she thought that but as I grew older, I started to understand. My mother was controlling, but she did it out of love.

My phone rang and I answered it.

"Larissa Solis?"

"Yes, this is she. How can I help you?"

"Hello Larissa, my name is Brady Nichols. I am your mother's estate lawyer. I am sure you have heard from the police and fire that her death was considered accidental..." How much time had passed? My head was spinning, it was all happening too quickly for my liking. I was not ready for this conversation, to go over her assets or to deal with who got what. The knock at the door paused my thoughts.

"Sorry Brady, I just cannot do this right now. I will call you back." I hung up the phone before I could listen to anything else. I was not in the right mind frame for that type of conversation.

I answered the door and saw Luce standing there with a smile on her face. It was no less than a couple of hours ago that she was a mess in my arms. Though looking at her, you would think it never happened.

"What is with the smile?" I asked her as I leant my head on the door. She pushed into my room.

"I did not think it could get worse, but your room proves that." She plonked on the bed, and a cloud of dust filled the space around her.

"You are exaggerating." I stood close to the wall; she shook her head and held her key out.

"Please entertain me before we go shopping," she begged.

I pushed myself off the wall and snatched the key from her hand as I walked to her adjoining room and entered. The room was almost the same as mine, except it did not have the same dusty pink colours. Instead, it was a soft blue, with the same smell and the same colours in the bathroom. I returned to my room as Luce started to laugh and I could not help but do the same.

I snickered, "Do you think they were drunk, high or just blind?"

Luce tapped her chin. "Honestly, I think all three." She stood up and rubbed my arms. "How are you holding up?" She tried to keep eye contact, wanting to get a straight answer from me.

I looked away and took a step back. "I will be fine Luce. Come on, we need to get some clothes." I heard her groan behind me, but I knew she would follow. She loved shopping and I would not lie, I did not mind it either. We walked to the main strip arm in arm.

"What is our budget?" Luce asked as she fiddled through the clothing racks. There were only two clothing stores in our small town and one lingerie store. Her fingers drummed lightly on her chin, an indicator that her mind was processing where to start.

"Two thousand. We have one thousand each to spend. Are we staying together or going our separate ways?"

She grabbed my hand and pulled it towards the lingerie store. I guess that was my answer. I followed, dragging my feet a little. While I picked out enough underwear for a week and three bras, I watched Lucianna shop around for things she did not need. I was not going to bother reminding her about our budget. I would just adjust our separate budgets; she needed this more than I did right now. We moved to the next shop, where I bought four pairs of pants in varying colours, four tops, two dresses, two jackets, and three pairs of shoes. I did not bother to look for anything else. I was grateful that Luce was a little smarter in spending the money because we still had about a thousand left over. It was a relief to have enough to cover anything else that we needed.

As we walked back to Sally's, I knew I had to tell her the truth about the phone call with our mother's lawyer. I found it hard to start the conversation; the words eluded me.

"What is it?" Luce asked as if she could sense that I wanted to say something.

"I got a call before from Mum's lawyer," I blurted out.

"Oh? And what did he want?"

I avoided looking at my sister. "I kind of hung up on him, you knocked on the door and I just could not—"

She grabbed my elbow and pulled on it. "Call him back now and put it on speaker." I found my phone and did as she asked.

"Larissa, I am so glad that you called back." His voice was just as peppy as before, which disturbed me on another level. How could he sound so cheerful when he dealt with death so often?

"Yes, you are here with my sister, Lucianna, too."

"Oh, that is perfect. Larissa and Lucianna, we need to discuss your mother's estate and will. I can book a flight for next week to come down and discuss all of this and sort it all out. How does that sound?"

"Sounds perfect. Just text my sister's phone with the details. Looking forward to meeting with you." Luce hung up my phone and continued ahead, leaving me standing there, stunned.

"How the hell can you do that?" My voice was louder than usual.

"Do what?"

"Just pretend that you had a normal conversation and not one that related to our dead mother. What is wrong with you?"

She snorted. "What is wrong with *me*? I know you didn't sleep last night, and you were talking about the man with the yellow eyes again. I saw your phone and you took a photo of a man leaning against a tree. You are delusional, and you need help, yet you criticise me because I want to move on. I am leaving for London next week. I cannot have anything here to hold me back."

Anger coursed through my system. "So, you are just going to leave me to pick up the pieces? You really do not give a fuck about me, do you? I organised our accommodation, the money for us to spend, and you had no issue taking those."

She stomped her feet on the floor, screamed, "I just can't with you!" and then stormed off in anger. I did not bother to chase her. I needed the space from her right now. She only cared about what she could get from our mother and not how she could help with anything.

CHAPTER 6

CHANGE IN RELATIONSHIP

Larissa

It had been a week since our mother died, and we managed to get back on speaking terms after a while, however, there was still a crack between us. It did not matter how hard I tried, I could not find a way to fix it and I doubted that we would be the same again. Today, we were to meet with the lawyer to discuss how our mother's assets were going to be split between us.

I ran up the stairs to my room at Sally's, showered, and managed to get down in time to eat breakfast before I started my shift at the café. The lawyer was coming in at three, which was enough time to finish the lunch rush and clean the café to close early.

It was a quiet day. Not many people came in to eat, and I had noticed that since Mum's death, we had lost customers, but I did not care as much as I should. I found it hard to be motivated in the café in general. My mother's love and spirit kept the café alive but without her, there was a void that could not be filled. I finished cleaning the last table before I snuck out the back and changed into a pair of jeans and a black tank top and let my hair out of its ponytail. My hair was heavy and if it was worn up for too long, it gave me a headache. It probably did not help that it was past midway down my back. I set the table in preparation for the meeting with Brady Nichols. I had notepads for myself and Lucianna, which I knew she would not use, and a bottle of water with three glasses. I had baked fresh cookies during the afternoon to make it seem more inviting. I baked them to help ease my anxieties as my medication did not seem to be helping me today.

I sat down and waited for Luce to arrive when I heard the bell ding at the door. I spun around to see a short, plump-looking man with a blue suit and an obvious toupee on his head that did not match the remnants of his real brown hair.

I smiled as I stood up and walked over. "Mr. Nichols, it is a pleasure to meet you. I am Larissa Solis." He smiled, which was crooked. I wondered whether he'd had a stroke in the past and it had caused some paralysis to his face.

"Hello, Larissa. Again, I am sorry for your loss." His brow creased.

"Luce will not be too much longer." I stood aside and gestured to the table for him to take a seat. I quickly pulled out my phone and texted. Ten minutes passed and I still had not heard from her. I saw Brady's obvious frustration at her lack of punctuality. It was typical of her, but I had stressed to her the importance of being on time. I pulled out my phone once again and dialled her number, it rang out. I did not bother to leave a message as I turned back to Mr. Nichols.

"Is there any way we could do this without her?" He scratched his head, which again made the toupee rather obvious as it shifted across his head. I noted the sweat above his brow line; he was nervous, but I did not quite understand why. Surely, he had done plenty of these before.

"I suppose we could." He lifted his black leather briefcase from the floor, and I watched him put in his code and pull out two document wallets, one labelled with my name and the other with Lucianna's. "Open to page three..." I did as he asked. "As it states, the house was left to the both of you. As it no longer exists, the insurance money will be split between the two of you. The decision is up to you if you decide to sell the land or rebuild the house. All assets within the bank will be split equally between the two of you..." He prattled on about other facts that I nodded along to as I wondered where my sister had been caught up. "Any further questions, Miss Solis?"

"Yes, the café. I cannot see it written within the paperwork and I did not hear you mention it. Unless I missed it because I will admit, this is all a little overwhelming."

He cleared his throat. "The café is not in your mother's name."

"But she owns it, does she not?"

"No." My head was spinning. I knew she owned it. She had always told me that when she passed, it would be handed down.

"Miss Solis, the café is in your name." He pulled out a document and slid it across the table. The café had been in my name since I was three. I read it over before putting it down.

"But...why did she never say anything? I do not understand why it is in mine and not hers?" He shrugged his shoulders, his nerves becoming even more obvious as sweat ran down his face rather than pooling on his brow.

"Mr. Nichols, do you need anything?" He shook his head as his phone rang; he went pale, almost ghostly white before he stood up and muttered, "Excuse me."

I took this moment to try my sister once again, finally managing to get a hold of her and convince her to come to the will reading.

Mr. Nichols left not long before Luce ran into the café, her outfit was thrown together, and her hair was dishevelled. I rolled my eyes.

She strolled over taking a seat in front of me, she muttered, "We are not all saints, Rissa. I needed an outlet."

"I am sure whoever the man is, he is rather appreciative of that. But still, this was important." I added. It was not just about her or our mother. I wanted my sister for support.

"And I forgot, sorry. I forget how you never make mistakes and are always so perfect."

I did not want to entertain another attempt of her starting a fight. I slammed my hand on the table and pushed the folder with her name towards her before I walked away. I was not taking her bait today. She was not worth it when I had to consider that the place that I was standing in was mine and I never knew it.

"Wait…" Luce trailed off as she read through the paperwork.

I closed my eyes as I waited for the question I knew was about to come out of her mouth.

"Where is the café?" My heart sank. This was not going to go down well. I knew my sister, and anything that she was not included in always ended badly. She had to have everything and for once, this was different.

"It is not in Mum's name"

"What? Since when? Who owns it?"

I cleared my throat before I turned around to look at her.

"Me." I handed her the same document that Mr. Nichols had

given me. I watched her eyes read it over as she took in the words before her face showed her rage.

"You were fucking three. You always were the perfect child and her favourite; this just proves it." She flew out of the café and slammed the door behind her. Luce's behaviour did not shock me; it was my norm. Her temper was one for the history books —she flew off the handle at any moment. I always wondered how she managed to snare men when she could easily just flip her shit at them. I sank against the counter to the floor and looked around the café.

"This is all mine...but why, Mum?" I asked out loud, knowing that I would never get the answer that I wanted. She was dead and had never told me the truth. I suppose it made sense, how she paid me a decent wage considering I knew how much profit was coming in. I should have questioned it more, but you never knew when it would be too late to ask those questions. Now, I would quite literally never know the answers. I banged my head against the counter and closed my eyes as tears rolled down my cheek. I took a few moments to compose myself before I stood up and picked up my paperwork and Luce's before heading back to Sally's. The question still bounced around in my head— what was I going to do with myself now? Would I continue to run the café? Or would I be able to finally use the degree that I had worked so hard for? But this would mean leaving the town that I called home. I was not sure if that was something I was ready for.

CHAPTER 7

WHAT THE FUTURE HOLDS

Larissa

I RETURNED TO SALLY'S AND CLIMBED THE STAIRS TO MY ROOM when I ran into Jack with his shirt slightly unbuttoned and his hair all over the place.

"No, please tell me you did not?" He averted his eyes, which told me everything that I needed to know.

"I am sorry, Larissa. I wish that it hadn't happened, but I was drunk…"

"No, do not even start. A dick does not fall into a vagina, you put it there and as a doctor, you would know your threshold to be that intoxicated." I moved up a stair and he grabbed my elbow.

"Please tell me this does not ruin my chances with you." I wanted to cry. I had always liked Jack; I was friends with his brother and his family loved me. His eyes betrayed a flicker of worry as his gaze focused on my face, the whole town knew that there was no point in coming after me if you had been with my sister. I never looked twice at them.

"Sorry Jack, you know my rule. You brought this upon yourself." His face flushed with what I thought could be embarrassment, but I was wrong.

"I missed out on you because of your slut sister. I had sex with her once and it wasn't even that good or satisfying, and now I cannot get a chance with you? That is total bullshit, Larissa. Get off your high horse." Anger rose in my body; it was like tiny pins in my fingers as it climbed to my wrist.

"Go home, Jack." My anger intensified as he shook his head. It was not embarrassment on his part, but pure rage.

"I am sure you would be just as lousy in bed. You have probably never seen a dick," he shouted angrily gesturing wildly with his hands.

"I am looking at one now," I snapped back at him, and he chuckled cruelly.

"I understand why I was warned about staying away from you. Just as fucking nuts as your sister."

Suddenly, the chandelier above his head started to vibrate, before it broke away from the ceiling and fell towards him. He only just managed to jump out of the way. The vibration in my body had dulled now.

"Go home, Jack, and do not bother returning despite her calls." I stormed up the stairs and slammed my fist against Luce's door. She appeared seconds later.

"Did you feel that?" she asked.

"Feel what?" I said as I stormed into her room.

"The whole building shook."

I cocked my head to the side as I thought about the chandelier falling to the floor.

"No, it did not, but the chandelier almost knocked out your

date. You know the one that you ditched the lawyer meeting for?"

She scoffed and walked away.

"Do not walk away from me, Lucianna!" The same anger vibrated through my body as the building shook. Lucianna turned to look at me, her face paled as she took two steps back.

"Larissa, take a breath," her voice quaked as if she was scared of something.

"What is it?" I asked her as I looked behind me and saw nothing. Her expression softened as her body language relaxed.

"Your eyes were red," she whispered.

Suddenly, the room felt small as my temperature rose. The world went dark.

———

I woke with a start, not sure how much time had passed. I glanced around the room, noticing I was in Luce's and that it was dark outside. I flung my legs off the bed and stood up, the door to her room opened.

"Whoa, careful now. You hit your head when you fell." She ran over and grabbed my arm, my eyesight blurred as I dropped back on the bed.

"I do not quite remember what happened." It was all a haze. I came to see her, and I was mad, and then the room disappeared.

"You fainted. Look…" She paused and sat down beside me. "I am sorry. I knew how much you and Jack liked each other, but I needed an outlet, and I made a mistake. I should not have gone after him, but he helped to dull my feelings, which isn't an excuse, trust me I know it. I am not perfect; I don't think of the repercussions of things. I am selfish and I should have thought about you, but I didn't, and I am sorry." I noticed how Luce avoided glancing in my direction, and knew she regretted her actions. I put my arm around her shoulder and pulled her close to me.

"It is only a boy. I mean I am sure there is one in this town that you have not slept with."

She poked my ribs but laughed. "Can I ask you a question?" As she stood back up, I saw her playing with her fingers, she was nervous.

"Yeah sure, what is it?"

"Will you come to London with me?"

CHAPTER 8
THE CHOICE

Larissa

I LAY IN BED, STARING AT THE CEILING FOR A WHILE AS I THOUGHT about Luce's question. Mum wanted me to stay here and take over the café, but now I had the chance to leave and use my degree. I loved marketing; I had fun creating all the flyers for the café and using social media to boost its name. As a result, the café was popular, even in the surrounding small towns. My chocolate chunk brownies also helped.

Before my shift, I went for my morning run to try to clear my head, but it did not work. It only prompted more questions. I dressed and went to the café. I wrapped my apron around the waist and started to put all the chairs down and then remembered what my mother told me one day when she convinced me, or more like guilted me, to stay here with her.

I paused, hearing our conversation in my head.

"Mum, I am bigger than this place. I know it. I was not destined to stay in Shaftesbury. I have a degree; I deserve to use it. If you wanted to keep me here, why did you allow me to study?"

Mum walked over to me and took my face in her hands. "You are bigger than this place, but it does not mean that it is your time now. Your time will come when you least expect it. My only worry is I won't be here for you."

"Typical, just typical Mum. You are still young, do not be pulling this 'I won't be here for you' nonsense. Do not guilt trip me."

"I am not trying to guilt you into anything. You are not ready to move to London—you are too naïve. You don't understand just how imp—"

"Do not start Mother. I am calling in sick today."

"Earth to Larissa." I snapped out of the memory.

I looked at Sam with a smile. "Morning Sam. Sorry, I was just remembering something about Mum." He walked over and wiped my cheek; I had not even noticed that I was crying. I walked over to the sink to wash my face.

"Your mother was difficult, but she was an amazing woman. She always managed to help whoever came to her with their troubles. She was a spiritual woman with a beautiful energy. You are more like her than you realise. Lucianna is the complete opposite." Sam and I both knew that was true.

"Sam, Luce asked me to join her in London. What do you think about that?" He would always give me his honest opinion—that was our friendship.

The door slammed; I had not even noticed the bell, but I looked up to see Richard standing in the doorway. He looked angry; with his brows furrowed and his jaw clenched.

"Good morning, Richard. Is it just you this morning or coffee to go?"

"Coffee for us to go." His tone was curt. He glared at Sam to the point where it even made me feel uncomfortable. Sam left the room to finish doing prep behind the counter.

"Coming right up." It was a blessing that Sam was out the back. He did not like the smell of making coffee with blood. It smelt sweet to me; I did not mind it. I walked behind the counter and turned the machine on to run through its cycle before I prepared the cups.

"Did I hear correctly? You are planning on leaving?"

I avoided his eyes as I cleared my throat and prepared the milk in the jug.

"Luce asked me to come with her to London. I was thinking about it, but I have not made any decisions yet. What do you think?" I finally looked up at him as I pushed the button to strain the coffee into the prepared cups.

His face was flat, it showed no emotion, but his eyes were dark. "I think you are safer here. Remember I told you that you would be rather desirable to my kind? You are heading into a city where there are more than two vampires. You will not be able handle it." The words hit hard.

"So, I do not deserve to expand my life out of this small box of a town? I am to stay here trapped for the rest of my life?"

"At least you would have a life!" I shook my head as I finished making the coffees and put the lids on before sliding them across the counter. "I apologise if the truth hurts Larissa, but your life is here."

"Only because someone made it here. I want to make my own path. I deserve that."

"Larissa, if you move to London, it will be your death." He left the store promptly without turning back. His words echoed in my head.

"That was brutal." Sam rounded the corner.

"Eavesdropping, are we?" I raised an eyebrow at him.

"He did it first."

I laughed as I wiped the counter and then continued to unpack the furniture and fill up the sugar, salt and pepper.

I busied myself and tried not to think about my decision to leave or not. Luce knew better than to pressure me about this decision. She gave me space as she dealt with her own grief. I was so conflicted. I wished I had more friends, but my only friends were my sister and my mother. Now just my sister. Insurance for the house was due to clear in the next couple of days and Luce was leaving as soon as it did.

After work, I went to the local bar to clear my head. All eyes were on me as I walked in. I knew it was because of my mother's death. I sat down and ordered myself a glass of red wine before Jack joined me. I could not stay mad at him. We spoke about his time at university and what he enjoyed most about being a doctor. We weighed the pros and cons of moving to London with Luce, which turned it into a drinking game. It was not the wisest choice.

I did not remember coming home. I barely remembered climbing the stairs, but I knew where I was. Alone, with Jack, who was intoxicated. The room swayed with me and I giggled at all the movements. Then Jack took my head in his hands and kissed me. I pushed him off, and he looked at me strangely as if he were not expecting it.

"I want you, Larissa. I have for years. I pined for you every day that I was away, you were always on my mind." He tried to kiss me, but I pushed him away again.

"No Jack, I do not want this. You need to leave," I demanded but I barely recognised my voice. The room was fuzzy as Jack kissed my neck. I struggled to push him away when I heard banging, but I could not open my eyes.

Suddenly, there was a hand stroking my head. "Sleep well, princess. I will watch over you." The voice was different; it was deep and masculine. I had never heard it before, but it brought comfort to me as I felt a kiss on my forehead. The strong smell of musky cinnamon filled my nostrils as I sighed.

"Thank you," I whispered. I knew the person, but I did not know how, and I was too intoxicated to understand who it was.

As I drifted off to sleep, I thought about this town and all the painful memories. It was time to move on and leave those memories behind.

I made my choice. I was going to London.

CHAPTER 9

SETTLING INTO LONDON

Larissa

I DID NOT TELL LUCE ABOUT THE NIGHT WITH JACK. I WAS JUST grateful that I woke up with all my clothes on and a glass of water on the bedside table. Insurance from the house had cleared in our accounts so we packed what little belongings we had into our car and readied ourselves for our drive to London. I snuck our mother's box into my suitcase without my sister knowing. I still had not opened it, but I would in time.

"Luce! Hurry up!" I shouted as I loaded my suitcase and pulled my hair off my face. I had listed the café for sale, but I did not need to stay behind. It was in Sam's hands for now and I trusted him completely.

"Larissa." I turned to see Richard leaning against a tree in the shade. I walked over to him.

"Have you come to criticise me further?" I asked him as I crossed my arms.

He smiled. "No, you made your decision. I cannot change your mind and I know that. But you need to be careful. It will be more dangerous than you know in London. I can only offer you this." He handed me a card with the name Phoenix and a number on it. "If you are in trouble, call Phoenix. He will protect you."

"Who is he?" I asked as there were no distinguishing marks or a company name on the card, just the name and number.

"An old friend. Someone you can trust; he will protect you," he said as I ran my finger over the number.

"Why?" I asked him. "My family has never been the nicest to you."

He stroked his chin. "You will find out one day. Stay safe, Larissa Solis. The girl who shines as brightly as her name suggests." He stalked away, keeping close to the shade from the trees.

"Thank you!" I yelled out after him as I returned to the car where Luce stood with her arms crossed and a scowl on her face.

"What was that about?" She nodded her head in Richard's direction.

"He told me to be safe and gave me a contact for if I'm ever in trouble."

"Careful, he may be setting you up to be a blood whore." She was referring to people who became addicted to being on-call donors to vampires. The bite gives people a rush that causes addiction.

"You are so funny, but I doubt it. He knows our family has a strong dislike of them. Ready for our adventure?"

We left early in the morning but despite the nearly three-hour drive, we did not arrive until the late afternoon. We made a few unexpected tourist stops and explored other small towns before we arrived in London. I held the map and directed Luce to the address of her new apartment. Her employer had organised an apartment for her to get set up before she found her own space. I would be sleeping on the couch until I found my own apartment because I had no desire to stay with Luce forever. I loved my sister, but growing up as teenagers, we were the complete opposite; she was messy, and I was clean. I picked up after her all the time and I did not want to continue doing that as we both found our independence.

She pulled up at the tiny two-storey apartment; its bland brown façade indicated that the inside would be just as boring and uninspiring. I knew she would be disappointed with this; she had built it up as some magnificent living space for us.

I turned to her with a smile. "It looks amazing. I cannot wait to see the inside."

She put the car into park and sank into her seat, her eyes watered.

"Hey, stop that. You have not seen inside, come on. Let's leave our bags here and check it out first, but you must leave that negative attitude in the car."

Luce rolled her eyes and flung the door open as a car honked at her in response.

"I need to remember that there are more cars here compared to back home." I snorted trying to hold in my laugh. The air did not smell as clean as it did back home; I could smell the fumes from the cars. Luce walked around and reached for my hand; this was her stress and anxiety rearing its ugly head. I squeezed it tightly as we walked towards the front door, and noticed her name was already on the second-floor label. I should not have been surprised, since she was supposed to be here last week but with all the paperwork from our mother, it had been a little delayed. They were more than happy to accommodate her in any way that they could.

Luce fiddled with the keys in her hand before I took them to unlock the door. It was not automated like I thought most things in the city would be by now. I pressed the elevator button to close the door as Luce held on to me tightly. When we reached the door, I turned to her.

"I will not open this door. You need to do it; this is the start of your new life," I told her.

She nodded as she took the keys from me, her breath shook as she turned the key and opened the door. I waited in the doorway to let her inspect her apartment for the first time. I wanted her to have her moment, and absorb the fact that she had achieved this. I watched as she disappeared from view before she ran back to me with a massive smile on her face.

"That seems positive."

"Oh my GOD! It is perfect, Rissa, come and see." She took my hand and dragged me around the apartment. The white walls looked to be freshly painted, the oak timber flooring showed no signs of being worn in. All the furniture was brand new and up to date, but her master suite was the selling point. The king-size bed frame looked tiny in the space. There was a built-in entertainment bookcase with a television mounted in the middle. There was an office space in the corner near the window, to look out at the view, but the spa bath and the make-up mirror really brought it over the top. From the outside, this place looked bland, boring, and old-fashioned, but inside it was a different story. It was the perfect apartment for Luce, and I pulled her into a tight embrace.

"I am so proud of you," I said softly, as I kissed the top of her head. "Mum would be proud." She relaxed in my arms as gentle sobs left her. She needed to hear that, and I knew it.

It took us a few hours to unpack the car, and then I set up the sofa bed for myself, which Luce made sure she asked for when I told her that I would be coming too. I had enough money from the house insurance to get my own place, but I did not want to spend it. I wanted to invest it for my future and find an apartment after I had secured a job for myself. Luce agreed that she was going to do the same. She had the apartment for three months, which was enough time for her to save for her own place. I put my stuff in the corner of the living space and sat on the sofa bed. I looked around. Luce busied herself with unpacking her clothes into her wardrobe as she played her music. I took in the view from the window, it was just rows and rows of apartments down the street, which seemed rather busy with the constant flow of cars.

I sighed. "Luce, I am going to go for a walk. Did you want me to look for anything?" She paused her music and popped her head around the corner.

"Sick of me already?" I laughed as I shook my head at her. "I am just teasing. Coffee, if you find one and take note of any shops. We have no crockery or cutlery to eat on and any takeaway menus for dinner and—" I put my hand up to stop her.

"Essentially any necessities, etcetera, etcetera."

She smiled and went back into her room. I grabbed the keys and my coat and scarf. I was wary of going out without being covered, especially after Richard's warning that I would smell nicer than most humans due to my purity. I quickly popped one of my anti-anxiety tablets before I walked out into the day; it was overcast, which meant that there would be more vampires around than usual. They took advantage of these days to move around in the daylight a little more. I kept the coat and scarf up to cover my neck as I walked down the uneven street. I am not sure how long it took me to reach a store called ASDA. It was massive. I found a box with a crockery set and the same with cutlery. I loaded up the trolley with a coffee machine and some pots and pans and a few items we could eat. I went through the register and paid before I realised that I had no car to bring it home. I waited outside with the trolley as I pulled out my phone to call Luce, but it rang out.

"Bloody hell, Luce."

A throat clearing behind me had me turning around, coming face to face with a stranger. "It is not wise to say a word that is affiliated with blood anymore," he said.

I froze as I took in the stranger's appearance; he was tall with a well-defined jawline, light brown hair swept back into a loose ponytail and soft brown eyes that were brighter due to his olive complexion. He looked almost too perfect to be human. A smile spread over his face, perhaps in an attempt to ease my worry.

"I am sorry for scaring you. I am not a bloodsucker if that was your concern." I breathed out in relief, although it did worry me how attractive he was. "I see that your lift is not here. Would you like one?"

"Ah…no, thank you."

"How about this? I'll help you pack the stuff into my car, give you my keys and you can drive it to your house, unpack and return it." I had not expected such a nice gesture. It was strange; this man did not know me.

"How do you know I will not steal your car?"

"Will you steal it?"

"No." My voice croaked slightly.

"Then I have no need to worry about that." He seemed rather genuine.

"That is incredibly nice, but no, I cannot accept. I will wait for my person to answer their phone." I turned away from him as I dialled Luce's number, but it rang out once again.

"My offer still stands."

I glared back at him. "I told you no. Please go away." I rang once more and was relieved when Luce answered. I told her where to pick me up, then turned back to see the stranger and rub it in his face, but he was already gone.

Luce continued to set up her room the way she wanted it and then started to work on some stuff for her first day of work the next day. I unpacked the kitchen and made us some coffee on our new machine. I had picked up a few other things to make it seem more homely; some candles, photo frames, and other decorative items. It still felt strange, but I knew it would until I got my own space. Luce came out as dinner approached.

"Did you organise something for dinner?" she asked as she slumped onto the sofa bed. She looked exhausted.

"Barely working and already tired, hey?" She snorted and put a pillow under her head. "But yes, I picked up some takeaway menus on my walk, they are on the bench here. I am not bringing them over; you can get up and pick something." She groaned, lifted herself from the sofa bed and walked over.

"Yes, Chinese, please. Did you by any chance happen to get—" Before she finished, I opened the fridge to reveal a bottle of champagne. I knew she would want to celebrate. "This is why we are sisters."

CHAPTER 10
FINDING HER FEET

Larissa

Luce had already left for work. She was grateful that I had most of the champagne so she could avoid being hungover on her first day. My head throbbed from the wine, but a run would reset my body. I dressed in black yoga pants and a crop top and covered myself with a black jacket that zipped up the middle. The street was so busy with cars constantly flying past. I took note of the various businesses, noting that if I did not find a job in marketing, at least I knew I would be able to find one at a café, as there were so many of them. They were open and already full to the brim; it never got that full back home, but I suppose when you lived in a big city it was a little different. I stopped at a local corner store and bought the paper; I did not have a laptop to search for jobs or even a way to connect with a job agency. I lost my laptop in the explosion and had not bothered to buy a new one.

I checked my watch. I had already run over three kilometres and I had not yet reached the city. I was still on the outskirts. I glanced over my shoulder, back towards the direction of home, and pondered whether to push myself further or head home for now. I decided to head home and took a different road that I hoped would lead me back. When I finally noticed my street, I ran to the door and took the stairs to our floor. As I unlocked the door, I checked how far I had run.

"Seven kilometres. Not bad Larissa, not bad at all." I threw the paper onto the bench and showered before I pulled on black jeans and a blue blouse, something simple and comfortable. I warmed my coffee in the microwave before I sat at the kitchen bench and scanned through the paper. There were no marketing jobs, but there was a job agency. I tapped the pen on the bench; I worried about my ego more than anything. I wanted to try to find a job on my own without help. I was aware that it may not work in my favour, but I wanted to try. I called the job agency and booked an appointment for two weeks. That would give me some time to find a job before I would have to ask for help.

I resigned myself to the fact that I would need a laptop and caught a taxi to the local electronics store to buy one. I received a text from Luce.

LUCIANNA

Is it wrong to sleep with someone you work with on the first day?

I snorted at my phone while the driver told me about his move to the big city. I smiled and nodded, but barely paid attention.

ME

Yes, it most definitely is. Do not burn your bridges on the first day. Keep your tiger in her cage for now. You have toys for a reason.

LUCIANNA

Boo, you suck!

She hated it when I was right. When I arrived at the store, I searched until I found all the laptops and tablets that I could possibly want. I felt eyes on me. It was then I noticed that I had not covered myself to the extent that I should have and saw a few glowing red eyes as I scanned the room.

"Don't worry. It is against the law to attack a human. Society may be run by them, but that basic principle hasn't changed." I recognised the voice as I turned to see my stranger from the convenience store standing behind me.

"H-hi," I stuttered before clearing my throat. "I never got to thank you for the kind offer the other day. You disappeared."

He scratched his neck awkwardly. "I was worried that your boyfriend or husband may not have approved."

"It was my sister," I said with a smile, which made him perk up.

"Ah, I see. In the future, I shall make sure I stick around."

"Please do."

Now it was time for him to clear his throat after my subtle flirting with him. "What can I help you with?" he asked, putting on a professional voice.

"I need a laptop. I do not need anything fancy for now, just something standard that will help me look for jobs, reply to emails, all that nonsense."

"Is this the one you're interested in?" He looked at the laptop before me.

"Kind of. I used to have this one. I did love it, but I wondered if there was an upgraded model, as it started to slow down near the end of its life."

"You can bring it in to trade it in for an upgrade."

"Bit hard, it is destroyed." I did not want to go into detail on how badly destroyed it actually was, and thankfully, he did not ask.

"No stress. Follow me." I followed my stranger as he spoke about two different laptops, but I found it hard to concentrate. He was rugged and attractive and my hormones were going crazy. My body seemed to be acting differently lately, I could not explain it. A strange shiver ran down my spine.

"Which do you think is the better one? Please no spiel, just the truth," I added, just wanting his honesty.

"I would take this one. It may be a little more money, but it will do the job better."

"I shall take it," I said cheerfully.

He clapped his hands together. "I will be right back." He left; a cold shiver ran down my spine. My body suddenly felt very alert and on edge.

"Hello darling, who might you be?" I could tell from the sliver of his voice that he was a vampire.

"I am none of your concern. I am being served. Have a good day," I said to the vampire with a smile. I dared not make eye contact with him, but I noted he was only just taller than myself and he smelled of too much cologne.

"I am sure that I could serve you in other ways."

I turned to tell him to bugger off but did not get the chance. "The lady spoke. Leave!" At the raised voice, the vampire slinked away.

"Your beauty makes it difficult to stay away from their eyes." The salesperson had returned.

I looked at his name badge for the first time. "Thank you, James. Shall we pay? I would like to leave sooner rather than later." It would not be getting dark for a few hours, but that did not mean that I wanted to be outside close to that time. James took me to the service desk and asked for all the relevant details, which I wrote down, distancing myself from the prying eyes and ears around me. He handed over the laptop. It seemed like he wanted to ask something but stopped himself.

I decided to put myself out there for once. "James, you are welcome to use my number to check on how my new laptop is going for me."

He smiled and nodded. "Speak to you soon, Larissa."

I left with a smile and called for another taxi to take me home, but I could not shake the feeling I got from the stranger and his words, *"I could serve you in other ways."*

CHAPTER 11
NIGHT OUT

Larissa

I was cooking dinner when Luce came home. She walked in with her hair noticeably messier than it was when she left. I slid a glass of champagne over the counter for her, she took it and finished it in one gulp.

"Rough day?" I asked her as she eyed my laptop on the counter.

"Went shopping, did we?" Luce deflected to avoid speaking about her day, I would allow it for now.

"Yes, I did some grocery shopping and bought myself a laptop to help me apply for jobs."

"Smart." She dropped her bag on the floor. "I am going to shower, please just leave me be for now." I smiled at her and left her alone. She obviously needed to process what happened today, and I was worried about her, but we knew each other well enough to not annoy one another when we needed space. I continued to cook dinner and downloaded the software that I needed before accessing my personal drive and downloading my resume and cover letter. I checked my emails and noticed I had received one from the real estate agent about a possible buyer for the café. I hesitated to open it; my fingers dangled over the keyboard before pressing open. They were looking at offering the price that I had set it at, and the agent was asking if

I wanted to request more. I responded with two words: sell it. I wanted to keep the café running under my name, but I knew that my tie to that place would be a secret calling card telling me to return, and I did not want that to tempt me now or in the future. I slammed the laptop closed; that was enough for the day. I would look for jobs later, in case Luce needed me. She was more important than the need to stare at a computer. Despite this, Luce went to bed early and did not speak of her day.

I woke to a message from Luce telling me she had gone to work early. I worried that reality was hitting her, in that her job was harder than she expected. I needed to keep my focus on myself and the jobs that I would be applying for. I could not focus on Luce and worry about her until she talked to me. It was selfish, but I was an overthinker and I could not continue to worry about a situation that I knew nothing about.

I ran the same route on my run, even stopping at the same local store for a bottle of water before heading home again. Afterwards, feeling like my head was clear enough, I sat down at my laptop and applied for ten jobs before I cleaned the apartment and made dinner. I found a pile of washing in Luce's room and packed it into the basket before heading downstairs to the laundry area. I was alone, so I flipped out my phone and put on some music. I worried about being in a basement with one window and one door; it freaked me out. The music calmed me down as I sang along and out of tune while I loaded the machine. I heard the door slam behind me, and I jumped up to search for the cause of the noise.

"James!" I shouted as he stood in the doorway wearing a stained yellow jersey top and ripped orange football shorts. His face flushed red with embarrassment as he looked me up and down in return. I did not notice that I was still in only my crop top and yoga pants, as all my tops were currently in the wash. He quickly averted his eyes to avoid lingering too long on my tight clothing. He was trying to be a gentleman. I chuckled to myself as I gave him time to compose himself.

He cleared his throat and said, "I did not expect to see you here."

I snorted as I glanced down at myself. "I do not think either of us expected to see each other here."

He started to sort through his clothing and threw it into another machine. An awkward silence fell between us with only the sound of the machines whirring.

"Why did you not tell me that you lived here? I mean, you got my address yesterday, but you never mentioned anything."

"Ah, I thought about it, but I was worried that it may come across as creepy if I was like—hey, we live in the same building." I processed what he said and laughed.

"Yes, would have been super creepy."

"You moved into the business apartment. What do you do?" He was making small talk even if it was incredibly awkward. I explained how I lived with Luce and that the apartment was hers. I spoke about our move and how I was still trying to find a job in marketing.

"Forgive me for being forward, but I am going out with some friends on Friday to the pub around the corner...would you like to join me?"

I froze, wanting to ask why but I fought against it. "Um..." I had no idea how to respond to someone asking me on a date. I sounded like an idiot. I could feel the heat rushing to my cheeks.

"This was silly. Sorry, Larissa. Just forget I said anything."

"No James, I am just taken aback. I do not get asked out all that often. I will think about it and let you know."

James smiled and left as I stayed behind to fold my washing before heading back to the apartment. I checked my laptop to discover that after a couple of hours, I had already been rejected from four jobs with a standard rejection letter. 'Thank you for your application but you are not the ideal candidate for this position.' I was the ideal candidate except for the fact that I had finished my degree a few years ago but instead of working in marketing, I worked at a café.

I sighed and let my head fall back before I snapped out of it, searched for more jobs and applied for them. I was not going to sit at the laptop all day. I needed to get out of the apartment, so I walked the streets, found a few clothing stores and bought myself a few more items of clothing that would not put me over my budget. I had to get a job before I could splurge.

Friday came around and I received a few more rejection emails. It was deflating, but I had to stick to my guns and keep trying. It would happen for me eventually, at least I hoped. Luce came home holding a bouquet.

"Oh, you are a lucky girl, who did you get them from?" I asked as she put a bouquet of lilies on the bench and walked over with a note for me.

'I hope to see you tonight, James.'

Luce crossed her arms and glared at me. "Who is James?"

I knew she would have questions, as I had not mentioned him before.

"I met him when I was buying a laptop and discovered that he lives in this building when I did our washing the other day. He asked me to join him and some friends Friday night for a drink.

I probably will not go, but it was still nice of him to send me flowers." I wanted to change the subject as I dished up dinner for us.

She tapped her foot on the ground. "Is he hot?"

That was always what mattered to her, the looks. I cared more for personality; looks were an added bonus.

"Yes, he is attractive."

A mischievous smile crossed her face as her eyes lit up with glee. "Then we are going! We need to get you laid. You've never dated anyone, and I know that was my fault, but I won't hold you back anymore. Let's get you dressed and go out."

"Luce, I—"

"NO," she shouted at me. "You won't back out of this. Let's go and have fun." She pulled me into her room; she had more clothes than me. Every night she came home from work, she brought more bags, and I worried about how much she was saving. But it was not my job to stress about that, despite *always* worrying about her. She opened her wardrobe and pulled out two black dresses, they were beautiful. I could tell that they would be as tight on my figure as they were on hers, but she always showed skin. The warning from Richard plagued my mind, and I worried about how I might smell to the immortal monsters that came out at night. Luce saw my hesitation.

"I get it, you worry about going out at night and how you would smell to those creatures, but I would protect you and I believe that this James would also not put you in harm's way. You have a way with people, you put out this vibe of needing protection. People get this innate feeling that you must be protected at all costs."

I was not sure how to take that, but could not help but laugh at her. "You are nuts but fine, I will go out. Can we eat dinner first? I will not go out drinking on an empty stomach." She clapped her hands and jumped up and down with excitement. I picked the dress that was more demure than the others. The black dress had a sweetheart neckline that showed off the curves of my breasts. The dress came halfway down my thighs, so I needed to remember to not bend over, otherwise, people would have a clear view of my behind. It clung to my curves and left little to the imagination. Luce did my hair and makeup; she had a way of making my green eyes stand out more than usual. Luce curled her red hair to perfection; it always had the perfect bounce to it. I put on a pair of silver shoes and then we walked to the local pub.

It was exactly what you would expect from a London pub—the place was old, as evident from the interior. The worn-out flooring, the leather booths with stitching coming loose on the edges. The musky smell of wood and stale beer. Luce was in her element as she pulled me inside, and all I felt were eyes on me. Their eyes flared red with desire; I looked away and kept my head down. I squeezed Luce's hand, who returned the favour as we reached the bar. I noticed the pub was understaffed and run off their feet, but the atmosphere was exhilarating. The music was pumping through my body, and I had an overwhelming urge to dance. I had never experienced this before. It was something else, it was like feeling alive. James found his way over to me and I thoroughly enjoyed my time with him, but despite his good looks, there was no spark between us. He was kind and caring and genuine but there was nothing else that I felt towards him. I knew then that he would only be a friend. I watched as Luce went from guy to guy before finding one she liked. She walked over near the end of the night and asked, "Do you care if I bring a person back to the apartment?"

We had not talked about this, but I was not a fan of the idea of listening to my sister having sex when I had no real bed. I could not say no to her, so I asked James if I could stay at his house, but I made it clear that it was just because of my sister. He was more than happy; I am sure because he thought he would be getting some as well. Luce ended up leaving shortly after, so James and I walked back to his apartment.

"You seem to be popular with vampires. A lot of them could not keep their eyes off you. You are beautiful, but I have never seen them quite so taken with a human before," he noted.

I shuddered and looked away. "I am a virgin, which I hear makes me quite desirable to them."

"Ah yes, I have heard that virgin blood is sweeter. Are you saving yourself for marriage?"

I chuckled and knocked his arm. "No, I just never found the right person. My sister made it difficult, as she slept with nearly every eligible person in my age bracket. I had no desire to sleep with the same people she had, so it never eventuated."

"Ah, I get it. She seems quite carefree."

"Oh, you noticed."

He laughed, but when he noticed my shivering, he removed his jacket and handed it to me. He was a gentleman. "Nothing will happen between us, will it?" He sounded rather upset but I had to be honest with him.

"I am sorry, James, you are very attractive, but I just do not feel anything more. We get along so well but—"

He put his hand up. "I get it. I am happy with friendship. Who knows, maybe I will be able to crawl my way out of the friendzone one day?"

I laughed as he pulled me close for warmth. "Thank you, James,"

"No need to thank me. I have a beautiful friend and I will cherish our friendship." I smiled with glee at the thought. I needed more friends, and he seemed like a person that I wanted in my corner. I slept peacefully that night knowing that he would protect me and keep me safe.

———

I woke the next morning with a plan. I was going to ask the manager at the pub if they needed more bartenders at night; they seemed so understaffed. I walked into the bar, which was quiet compared to last night. They were unpacking the chairs from the tables and wiping down surfaces. A plump man came into view. He had a combover and flannel shirt that did not cover his beer gut.

"Who are you?" he spoke with a Cockney accent.

"Sorry, I was wondering if there were any jobs available. I have experience." He took a step back and looked me over as if he was inspecting the goods to ensure they were in good condition.

"Are you comfortable wearing clothing that is a little revealing?" I was disgusted by his voice and the way he spoke—like I was not a person, but rather a thing to be ogled.

"If it aids in more tips, yes," I replied.

He snorted at my response and threw me a black top with the name *Royal* written on it; the name of the pub.

"Be here tonight at seven and we shall see how you go." He grunted and walked away with a limp. A young woman walked over with bleach-blonde hair and makeup that was way too dark for her pale complexion.

"Don't worry about Charlie, he means well despite being a real pig. He is a pretty good boss. I am Olivia. I guess I will see you tonight. Wear your jeans." She bounced away as quickly as she came over. I was excited to have a job even if it was not exactly what I wanted. I would keep working to get into the marketing sector, but in the meantime, I would have an income and a way to save and get my own place away from Luce. Last night was just the beginning of her escapades with men, it seemed. I should not have said yes; I set the precedent.

CHAPTER 12

STRANGER AT THE BAR

Larissa

A COUPLE OF MONTHS HAD PASSED SINCE MOVING TO LONDON. Luce and I had moved apartments as the one supplied by her company only had a three-month lease. We moved across the street into a two-bedroom apartment. The interior did not change and like most of the houses in London, it had a similar floor plan. I was so grateful to have my own room. It did not have much space, but I had enough for a bed and drawers. The one highlight of the apartment that brought so much joy to my life was the fact that the walls were insulated. I did not have to hear my sister having sex as I did before.

After multiple interviews, I still had not found a job in marketing. I kept being told, "You have no experience" and it was incredibly annoying. I had no experience because no one had given me any. How was I meant to get some when no one would give me the opportunity?

Even though I had no luck, the job at the bar continued to bring in good money and the tips were amazing.

It was Saturday night, and we were at capacity. Olivia and I had become fast friends as we would throw what we needed at each other. The more entertaining we were, the more we got in tips, we had essentially boosted sales. We laughed at each other and danced around. We had plenty of creeps hit on us and plenty asked us for our blood. Olivia would allow the attractive ones to drink from her, but I rejected it. I had no desire to be used as a piece of food for those monsters.

The night was long and the rush finally ended, as Olivia signed off for the night and left me alone to finish cleaning up. There was only a handful of people left so I was able to clean and serve at the same time.

We were almost at closing when a man walked in. He almost had to duck to fit through the door. He wore dark pants and a leather jacket that did nothing to hide his huge stature. He flung his head back and I watched his hair fall off his face; it was long and needed to be tamed, but it only added to his dark and mysterious nature. He reached the seat and sat down as I took in his olive complexion and hazel eyes.

"H-hi." I cleared my throat. "What can I get you?" He was not only tall but incredibly muscular; I had never encountered someone like him before.

"You are here."

I tilted my head, confused by his words. The familiar smell of musky cinnamon surrounded me. "Do you mean, I am new here? Should I be serving you any drinks, or have you already had too many?"

He chuckled and moved the hair from his face. "Funny one, are we?"

"I try to be. What can I get you tonight?" He seemed almost confused at my question. "Did I offend you in some way?"

He shook his head and seemed to compose himself. "Roman, and you are?"

"My name is of no importance, only your drink of choice is."

He sighed, more amused than annoyed. "A scotch, thank you."

I turned to grab a more expensive scotch; he seemed like he had good taste from how he held himself. I slyly pointed at the name tag on my shirt for him, which made him chuckle. It was a delightful sound and brought warmth to my heart hearing it. I slid his drink over the counter.

"On the house."

He looked around me at the bottle I had pulled down. "That's an expensive bottle. Your boss won't yell at you?"

I shrugged a shoulder at him. "As long as I flash a winning smile at him, it will be fine."

He leant back on his stool, the movement causing his carved chest to peek through his black shirt. "Do I get to see that winning smile?" He took a sip and licked his lips. I found it hard to look away from him.

"You could see that smile anytime you wanted if you come back regularly." I added a wink to my flirtatious comment, for good measure.

He finished his glass quickly and put money on the bar. "I need to leave."

My heart sank. I put myself out there a little and got rejected. He paused before he left and said, "I need to leave, but not due to your request. I shall return soon for that smile."

I could not help but grin at him as he disappeared as quickly as he had appeared. I finished cleaning the bar and returned home in a happy mood. I knew Luce had her flavour of the month over because I heard her giggle in her room as I slumped onto the bed for the night. Her new flavour was an absolute pig. I disliked him on every level. He had a weird vibe to him that made me feel ill whenever he was near. I knew this meant he was bad news, but Luce seemed besotted with him.

———

I woke the next morning to my bed being kicked. I looked up to see Luce's boyfriend, Peter, standing over me; shirtless and covered in his ridiculous tattoos.

"What do you want, Peter?" I asked, my voice croaky from just waking.

"Time to get up, the day has started."

I turned away from him as I heard Luce say, "She works night shifts, honey bear, let her rest."

"She needs to get her own apartment," he grunted and kicked my bed again; I started to dress myself under the blankets. He was right, but I dared not give him the satisfaction of knowing that I agreed with him. I bit the side of my mouth to stop myself from saying anything. I was close to getting my place, but I just wanted a little more money saved up.

"I pay rent to be here, do you?" I asked him smugly. He snorted and glared at me.

"How do you get that rent? By being a blood whore?" Anger vibrated through me as Luce walked over and stood in front of me protectively.

"My sister is not a blood whore! Check yourself right now." I put my hand on her shoulder to let her know it was fine.

"I am going for a run. Talk to you later," I whispered before turning away.

"Love you!" she shouted after me, as I slammed the door shut. I could not be bothered with him; he saw me as a whore because I did not fall for his charms. His misogynistic charms that he used to treat my sister like a piece of meat. He came around for a fuck and left to go to another girl whenever he wanted, but she seemed to love him.

The fresh morning air seemed to help calm the anger in my system. James joined me halfway through the run. It was nice to run with a person even if you did not talk to them. The simple act of companionship helped to make it more enjoyable.

"Rissa!" he shouted to get my attention.

I looked over at him and stopped. "What is it? Sorry, I was in my head." He pointed towards my phone, which was still ringing. "Thank you," I mouthed as I answered it.

"Hello, Larissa speaking."

"Miss Solis, I have come across your resume, and I wondered if you were free to come in for an interview today." The woman's voice sounded perky and rather optimistic.

"Yes, what time suits you?" I asked eagerly.

"Does eleven work for you?"

"It sure does." I tried to match her perky voice, but it was not in my nature to get my voice that high.

"Excellent, I shall text you the details." She hung up before I could say anything else. James looked at me expectantly as I put the phone away.

"I have a job interview!" I shouted with glee at finally having an opportunity for a job in my field.

James pulled me into his sweaty arms with a smile and said, "Congratulations! Where?".

I paused, realising the woman had not mentioned where it was. "Oh, I do not know. She actually did not say, but she did say that she would text me the details."

"Here, pass me your phone." I handed it over to him and watched curiously as he found the number and tapped a few buttons. I waited nervously. I should have asked and was embarrassed with myself that I had not.

"It is with Refresh Marketing, which is part of Dankworth Industries."

"Who are Dankworth Industries? I have never heard of them."

He laughed. "Sometimes I forget that you come from a small town. Nik Dankworth is the vampire in charge of the city. Everything goes through him. He is the richest person in London; his wealth has no limits, and he buys whatever companies he can manage to bring into his portfolio. I didn't know that he expanded into the marketing industry already. Won't be long till he has his finger in everything, but that is the way of these immortals, especially ones as old as him."

"How old is he?"

"I am not sure, but from the rumours, they say he is as old as Jesus." I laughed at him.

"Race you back!" He handed my phone back and started to run, leaving me laughing and trailing behind. I would never be able to catch him, and I knew that, but it was still fun to try. Plus, he would tire before me. I raced up the stairs to the now empty apartment, thankfully. I could not deal with any more of Peter and his obnoxious energy.

CHAPTER 13
JOB INTERVIEW

Larissa

I DRESSED IN A BLACK PENCIL SKIRT AND A TUCKED-IN WHITE blouse. I fixed my hair and caught the train to the location mentioned in the text. I was nervous, and I was sure it was clear for any person to see as I twiddled my fingers and bit my nails. It was a terrible habit, but it managed to calm my anxiety if only for a little while. I scolded myself for forgetting my tablets this morning.

I walked into the revolving glass doors and noticed the entry was huge, with the roof almost impossible to see unless you wanted to dislocate your neck. The whole entrance was glass with white marble flooring. My heels clacked on the floor. The reception was a black marble desk with two picture-perfect people sitting up impossibly straight. One male and one female, who smiled as I walked over. I could tell they were vampires from their smiles, with one flashing a fang that made my body shiver. I flashed my own smile at the young man.

"Hello. I have an interview with Sarah Blackwood," I said politely when I got to the desk.

He tapped his keyboard before looking back up at me. "Yes, she is expecting you on the third floor." He slid a visitor's pass across the counter and said, "Use this for the elevator and head towards room three hundred and eighty-two. Good luck." He was as perky as the woman sounded on the phone, and it was unnerving. I scanned the pass and entered the cold elevator on my own. The third floor was busy with activity and people on phones. A young female at the desk looked at me as I approached.

"Miss Solis?" she asked, and I nodded, unsure which way to walk. She pointed to my left and I headed in that direction towards the designated room. I had to stop outside the door for a few moments to get my bearings. My nerves were causing me to shake. I closed my eyes and knocked on the door.

"Come in," the same voice from the phone called out and I opened the door with a smile.

"Ah, Miss Solis, it is a pleasure to meet you." Sarah Blackwood stood from the conference table and walked over. She was taller than me with a grey pantsuit and her black hair pulled back into an impossibly tight bun. She was of African descent, and very beautiful. She offered her hand, which I shook, feeling coldness at her touch. She was a vampire; she sensed my change in mood.

"Did I offend you?"

"No, I must apologise. I am from a small town, and I am not used to being around vampires. We had two back home, but they kept to themselves."

She sniggered. "I did notice where you were from, and it is a very small town, but I have heard of the café you worked at. Richard told me about it, and I ventured down one weekend. It has the best cakes and coffee I ever tasted. I must return soon if it's still to the same calibre." She motioned for me to sit.

"I do believe it is. It just changed hands to another local, but they have all my recipes."

"Recipes do not make food; it is the love behind it. I shall see if it is the same." I could not help but laugh at her notion. "Now onto business. You finished your degree, but you did not work in the field, why?" It was the question I dreaded, and my answer never felt right. Sarah asked various questions about my skills and my thoughts on particular marketing campaigns. She leant back into her chair.

"I have a dilemma. I filled the job that you initially applied for, but I have another position available that you may be interested in." I straightened in my chair in anticipation. "I hired internally, as we give many young people the opportunity to see the inside of the business before we promote them to the job that they were initially after. If you are comfortable, the Director of Marketing needs a new assistant, and I would like to put your name forward to him if you are interested."

"How long would that be for?"

"Until you prove that you have skills in the marketing area. Are you up for the challenge?" She smirked as if she thought she was provoking me.

"Absolutely. What would my responsibilities be?" Her smirk turned to a genuine smile at my response, either impressed by my initiative or because she thought I was an idiot.

"You would be responsible for Mr. Baker's day-to-day scheduling, answering all his calls, responding to messages, planning and preparing his day. You will be his shadow, anything he asks, you will do. Are you sure you are up for this?" Her question prompted doubts—did she not think I was capable? Or was it because Mr. Baker was impossible to work for?

"Miss Blackwood, do you believe that I am not capable of this position? Or is the person that I will be working for rather difficult?" Her face flinched only slightly, but enough to give me an answer.

"I get it. I am still up for the challenge; I do not shy away from them. I am sure that Mr. Baker and I can form a positive working relationship." She seemed to relax in her position and stood from her chair.

"Shall I take you to meet Mr. Baker?" She raised her brow, it seemed to be a test that I was about to pass or fail.

I stood to join her. "Yes, I would love to meet him before I start, which would be when exactly?"

"Oh my, I have forgotten to inform you. I will give you a work card to purchase some appropriate attire to wear and you can start at nine tomorrow."

I stopped in my tracks. "Wait, tomorrow?"

"Yes, is that a problem?"

"No, I am just a bit shocked. I thought maybe next week, not tomorrow, but I am excited. Lead the way."

We rode the elevator to the sixth floor. It was quiet, as neither of us spoke. I was not sure what to say. We stopped at the right floor and the doors opened. It was quiet; people were in their cubicles working with their heads down. A few glanced up and watched as we approached an office, the door swung open to reveal a man taller than me. He yelled at the top of his voice, "STACEY!"

His golden hair was styled perfectly, and his striped shirt was tucked into his grey suit pants. He looked towards Sarah and his face changed.

"Sarah, how are you?" He seemed almost sweet, not as angry as he was acting two seconds earlier.

"Andy, I have a new assistant for you. She has a major in marketing." He crossed his arms and scoffed at me. He gave me the creeps as his eyes lingered on various areas of my body.

"Can she answer phones?" The phone rang as he waited for me to answer it. I walked over, picked it up and said, "Refresh Marketing, Andrew Baker's office. How can I help you?" The smug look on his face transformed into a smile as he nodded towards Sarah. It was his way of saying, *"she can stay."*

"No, Mr. Baker is on another call at the moment, may I take a message?" I wrote down the name on the piece of paper and handed it to him. He took the paper and returned to his office. I looked back at Sarah, who smiled.

"You are hired." She handed me her card. "See you tomorrow."

I waited a few moments before I rode the elevator back to the ground floor and slid the visitor's pass back over the desk. The two perfect receptionists gasped and tried to see around me.

"Here is our midday show."

I felt a strange tingling in my body and an unexpected feeling of happiness spread through me. I turned to see what they were staring at in awe. It was a man well over six feet tall with a navy-blue suit that clung to his body perfectly.

"He is perfection" The male receptionist said. I could not lie; I had not seen the man's face, but even seeing the way he strode into the room, the way he held himself, even I was a little besotted with him at that moment. He exuded confidence and power as if he was in control of everything.

"I did not see his face, but I must agree with you. Who is he?" I asked the receptionist as I looked at his name badge. Travis, it said.

"Mr. Dankworth. He is the owner of this whole building and the one next door. He graces us with his presence around this time every day. He makes my knees weak." Travis smiled. "Wait till you see his face."

"Maybe I will one day. See you guys tomorrow."

Chapter 14
It's Time to Work

I SPENT THE AFTERNOON BUYING MYSELF SOME APPROPRIATE clothing before returning home. I researched the company and Andrew Baker, but I could not shake the feeling I had at seeing that man. I could not help my fingers as they typed the name Nik Dankworth into the search bar. It showed his face and his profile. He was the most beautiful man I had ever seen in my life. His crystal blue eyes stared at me through the screen; it felt like they pierced my soul. I could not bear to look away from his face. His jaw was well-defined, and his thin nose made him the definition of drop-dead gorgeous. I understood why Travis and Alina stared at him every day. It was almost impossible to pull my eyes away from him as I heard the door open. I closed the laptop quickly and looked up to see Peter enter.

"What are you doing here?" I asked him as I glanced over his ripped jeans and singlet top that showed off his measly body. He closed the door and leant against it.

"I live here. Luce wants me to move in."

"Right, sure she does." I dismissed him and moved to clean the kitchen. He snorted and grabbed my laptop. "Do you mind? That is mine, you cannot touch it." I walked over as he opened it up.

He spun it around. "I should not be shocked to see his face on here. Is this your new target?"

"He is my boss. I just got a job at Refresh Marketing, and I was looking into the company. Mr. Dankworth owns it," I retorted, not wanting to give him any more ammunition to verbally attack me.

"He is the Lord of this region; I am sure he would appreciate a pretty virginal thing like you to feed off," he snarled as he glanced over my body.

"Fuck off Peter, I am not a blood whore."

He put the laptop down and stormed over to me. "No, but you are a whore. You walk around here in those tight clothes. Trying to steal me from your sister, are you? It is certainly working." He grabbed my face and kissed me. The anger vibrated through me further and I pushed him away. He stumbled but it did not stop him.

"Oh, I like a fighter, it makes it sweeter."

"You fucking pig! Get away from me." The room started to shake, then the door opened, and Luce walked in.

"What is going on here?" she asked as she looked between us, noticing my distress.

"She tried to get me to fuck her, and I told her to go away."

"Are you kidding me? You piece of shit." I clenched my fists barely controlling my rage at this asshole.

"Larissa, seriously? I knew you were jealous of me, but this is another level," she chastised me, even though the situation was the complete opposite.

"Luce, you cannot believe this. Why would I even think about this?" I fumed at her.

"Find somewhere else to stay tonight, Larissa." It was always serious when she used my full name instead of my nickname. I was hurt on another level that she believed him. I did not understand how she was so in love with him that she thought I was lying, and he was telling the truth. I packed all my bags and walked across the road to James's apartment. I knocked on the door. When he answered and saw me, I did not need to say anything. He pulled me into his arms before grabbing my bags.

"You can stay here for as long as you want".

———

I barely slept that night. I did not even get the chance to tell Luce that I finally had a job in marketing. The next morning, I caught the train into the city and walked into work. Mr. Baker called me into his office, which was as cold as he was, with no sentimental attachments. It was just an office with a tiny desk, window, and leather chair.

"Larissa." He handed me a folder. "This is my schedule for today and in the column on the right are the documents that I will need for those meetings. They must be ready before the meeting, at least an hour before, for me to peruse and make sure I'm prepared. All calls will go to message unless it is Mr. Dankworth, Miss Blackwood, or Mr. Salvak."

I wrote down what he said as I waited for more instructions. "I require one more thing." His voice changed as I peered up at him. Something was different in the way he said, "You can wear clothes that are a little more revealing if you understand what I mean. You are the first point of reference and I want people to

—" I put my hand up to stop him, it seemed I could not escape creepy men.

"I get it, please just stop." I would play this game until I secured the job that I wanted.

"I am glad we understand each other. Now get to work."

I left his office and sat down at my new desk. I sorted through his desktop, created a filing system, and organised the desk how I wanted it to be. I was beyond organised in every aspect of my life and it translated into my work. A few people came over and handed me documents that I filed or passed on to Andrew. I walked into his office.

"You can go to lunch; you have one hour."

"Thank you, Mr. Baker. Do you want me to pick up anything for you?" I asked. It could not hurt to suck up to the boss even if he seemed to be an asshole.

"Just a coffee, black, no cream, two sugars," he said not looking up from his desk.

"See you in an hour," I said perkily. I went down the elevator and said hello to Travis and Alina at reception. They were so funny it brightened up my day.

"Wait, where are you going?" Travis called out, his red hair spiked like a nineties boy band and his usual black suit. Alina's caramel-coloured hair was shaped around her face. She wore the same black suit jacket as Travis.

"I am going to lunch, why?" I creased my brow at him.

"The show is about to start."

I chuckled and stood by the desk, waiting as the door swung open. My body tingled, and my heart felt lighter from the sight before me. Mr. Dankworth's face was buried in his phone as it was yesterday, and he did not look up.

"He looks so unhappy. I almost feel sorry for him. I have only seen him twice and he does not look up from his phone," I said to my new friends.

Alina laughed. "He has all the money in the world, I doubt he is unhappy."

"Money never buys happiness. I need to get lunch; do you want anything?" They shook their heads as I made my way out. The happiness in my heart disappeared, I looked back and saw Mr. Dankworth talking to Travis and Alina, but he still did not smile at them. He spoke with stoicism, no emotion. Something deep inside me wanted to hold him and tell him everything would be alright; I did not understand the calling.

After work, I returned to James's apartment; he was cooking dinner in his kitchen. He turned with a cheeky smile and said, "Hello darling, how was your day at work?"

I snorted and bent over in laughter as I put my bag on the aged grey leather couch.

"My boss is a pig, but I managed to get through it. How was your day?"

He wiped his brow. "Today has been horrible. The children were out of control, and I barely got to clean the house."

I swatted his arm as I inspected what he was cooking—pasta! There was nothing better than pasta. I swear in another life, I must have been Italian.

"Did you cook pasta because you knew my love for it?"

"Absolutely, need to look after my girl," he chuckled as he wiggled his eyebrows.

"Thank you, James. How was your video game today?" He turned around to butter some bread, attempting to make homemade garlic bread, which would be interesting. He did not know how to cook other than basic food.

"Funny you ask that, children these days—" He was interrupted by pounding on his door.

I turned to look at it as I checked my phone to see a missed call from Luce. James went to open it, but I stood up and shook my head at him. "If I am not back in five minutes, call the police."

He chuckled. "As long as Peter stays away, that is fine." I raised my eyebrows at him in an *I know* motion. I hovered over the door handle for a few minutes to prepare myself for her attack. I knew my sister, and she would not back down unless Peter decided to dump her, which I doubted he would.

I opened the door with a smile and said, "Hello Luce, how was your day?" She grabbed my wrist and pulled me out of the apartment. I closed the door behind me.

"Do not be fake with me." She looked me over. "What are you wearing?"

"I started my new job today. If you bothered to speak to me yesterday, you would know that."

"You hit on my boyfriend."

I leant against the door; this conversation was not going to go anywhere.

"Luce, I want you to think about something for a moment. Back home, I never wanted to sleep with any of the boys who you slept with, remember? So why in the hell would I want to sleep with Peter when you know how much I despise him?" I pleaded with her to remember and not believe the word of this pig.

"It doesn't change the fact that you hit on him. You did it to prove a point that I deserved better, is that it?" she snarled in response.

"Luce, I did not hit on him at all. Sorry to burst your bubble regarding Peter's 'perfection', but he hit on me. He grabbed my face and kissed me before I pushed him away. I was legit about to kick his scrawny ass when you came home." I shook my head in disbelief that I had to reiterate this because of her inability to believe her own sister.

"That is not what he said happened."

"Luce, we are going around in circles. I will not keep this conversation going, so you need to ask yourself one question. Who do you believe? Me or him?" Her face fell, she was conflicted. I could see it. She had no idea who to believe, and it was breaking her heart. She truly cared for Peter.

I shook my head. I needed to give her peace to stop this inner conflict. I did not like Peter, but I did not want her hurt. I only hoped she would realise how bad he was for her.

"Luce, I will stay with James and keep away from Peter. I only want you to be happy. You can decide who you believe, but either way, you are my sister and I love you."

A tear fell from her eye as she hung her head. "He really did, didn't he?"

I pulled her into my arms and held her tight. I did not respond.

She already knew the answer. I held her for what seemed like forever before we heard a thump, and I saw Peter behind us.

"Luce, you have said your goodbyes. Are you coming?"

The anger started to work its way through my body as it vibrated from my fingers to my toes. He brought out a rage inside me that I never knew I had.

Luce cleared her throat. "Peter, she is my twin and I know when she is lying. You can pack your stuff and leave my apartment. I never want to see you again." She started to shake as I stood behind her for support.

"You believe that blood whore over me, the man you love?"

"My sister is not a blood whore. Leave, Peter."

He stormed towards us before he froze with a look of fear on his face. James had come out of his apartment with a bat in his hands.

"Do we have a problem out here?" James stood taller than usual, a masculine energy radiating off him. His hand rested on my back for support, and it was comforting to know he was here for us. Peter put his hands up in defeat.

"No need for violence, man. I'll leave. But Luce, this is not over." Peter walked away as James pulled on me to follow. I dragged Luce back. He closed the door behind us.

"You are both staying here tonight, got it?" he said as Luce wrapped her arms around me.

"Thank you, James, truly." I peered up, giving him a small smile of appreciation.

He kissed my cheek. "Anything for my best friend."

Luce stayed the night, but I worried our relationship would not be the same after this argument. She figured out Peter was lying, but it did not change the hurt she had suffered; she would question every relationship from now on. I felt the crack appear last night when she stood up for Peter. It was like an invisible string between us that snapped, that would fracture our relationship for the rest of our lives. I knew one thing. I would always love my sister even if she picked a boy over me. I knew it was coming, I felt it.

CHAPTER 15

FIRST MEET

I WOKE IN THE MORNING WITH A HANGOVER. I HAD GONE OUT drinking with Travis, Alina, and Stacey the night before, and even though I always swore that I would not hang around with vampires, they were so normal. Despite being over a hundred years old. It was entertaining to watch them use their strength, speed, and compulsion while we were out. For them, people were so easy to control with compulsion. I questioned whether they used it all the time, but Travis and Alina said they did not like to control people, only using it in circumstances to avoid causing harm to humans.

I dressed myself and went for a run along my usual route, through the city streets to a little coffee store. Well, I could not call it a store. A hole in the wall would be more appropriate and not an exaggeration. It was a window that served coffee; convenient. As my feet pounded against the pavement on the way home, I steadied my breathing, I hoped that this would give me some clarity and ease my anxiety about work. Andrew had invited me to be part of the conference today, taking the minutes. All the big heads from various departments would be there, and I wanted to look professional in every aspect. I needed to impress them, especially if I wanted to be more than just an administrative assistant.

I ran up the stairs and moved through the rest of my morning routine, still struggling with my nerves. I found since my mother's death that my anxiety medication did not have the same effect. Luce caught me checking my hair in the bathroom mirror. "Your nerves are making me nervous; you will be fine." I chuckled as I raked my fingers through my waves.

"It is just a big day; all the big heads will be there. I must take notes and hand out documents and be prepared for—"

She put her hands on my shoulder. "Larissa, if anyone can do this, you can. Stop doubting yourself, go to that meeting, and kick ass." I breathed out and smiled, she was right I tended to overthink every detail long before things began, a habit I'd always been guilty of. "As our mother would say, do not focus on the staircase, think about the first step." I snorted and shook my head at her as I held back a laugh.

"God, I hated when she used to say that," I groaned as I recalled what her voice sounded like. "It was so annoying."

"Hey, it worked for you, didn't it?" Luce beamed at her attempts to ease my anxieties.

"Yes, it always did."

"Now, what is the first step?" she spoke softly.

"Take notes in the meeting." I nodded with the focus clear in my head.

"Good, now just focus on that. Go about your normal routine, get your coffee, have a gossip session with Travis and Alina, and walk into that meeting with your head held high, got it?" I nodded and kissed her cheek. "But first, change that outfit. It is not you."

I looked down at my black pencil skirt and blue blouse, while she pulled me into her closet and pulled out a black and white peplum dress with a plunging neckline.

"Do you think this is a little too low-cut?" I asked. She simply shrugged her shoulders with a sly look on her face.

"You are going to be in a room with some rather rich men, it cannot hurt to come out with a date." She shrugged again as I rolled my eyes.

"You are terrible." I changed into the dress and was shocked to see that the white top did not make my breasts look bigger, as white normally did, but the gathered material managed to hide what I needed it to, while its plunge left little to the imagination.

———

I walked into the foyer holding coffees for Travis and Alina. We had started the practice of taking turns each morning to purchase one for each other. Travis took the coffee greedily and moaned at the first sip. "You need to tell me where your coffee shop is, it is so much better than mine."

"I shall never reveal my secrets, but quick question, do you get hangovers?"

He chuckled as I rubbed my temple for relief. "No, it is a perk of a fast metabolism. A bit under the weather today?" he asked as he batted his eyes at me.

I groaned and let my head fall on the desk. "Yes, and it is the day of the big meeting."

He leant forward and whispered, "I can help you with that."

"I have already taken Panadol. I am just waiting for it to kick in."

He shook his head and rolled up his sleeve. "A little drop in your coffee, and *poof* your hangover will be gone."

I scrunched my nose in disgust as I took a step back, he rolled down his sleeve.

"Sometimes I forget about your prejudice towards my kind," he uttered. I noticed a hint of hurt in the way he said it with his eyes cast down.

Insulting him had made my stomach churn. "Travis, I'm—"

"Larissa, I get it, but heads up. He is here early, probably for your meeting."

I turned to see *him* walking into the building. He wore a blue pinstripe suit and a red tie and looked a little lighter today. It was hard to explain. His entire demeanour had shifted like he had an amazing night's sleep and was ready to conquer the day. My body tingled at the sight of him. I chided myself at the reaction, and turned away quickly, only to spill my coffee on the floor.

"Shit," I hissed as I bent down to pick up what was left of my coffee. Travis and Alina burst into laughter, which echoed through the foyer. "Not funny, do you have any napkins?" I asked as I put the cup on the counter.

"Here, take this." The hairs on my arm stood up in response to the soft and silky voice; there was a hint of a slight accent mixed in with his English one, and I could not figure out what it was. A red napkin appeared before my eyes.

"Thank you," I muttered, as I took it and wiped up the spilt coffee. As I stood, my gaze locked with a dreamy pair of crystal blue eyes. I had seen them only on a screen. I lost my breath at the sight of him, my knees buckled, and I stumbled into him, the remainder of my coffee spilling down his shirt. I cleared my throat; this was so awkward.

"I'm so sorry. I will have this cleaned and get it back to you. Have it sent to Andrew's office, okay?" I spoke fast, then sped away from the sheer embarrassment. The elevator beeped open as I approached it, I ran into it and pressed the button continually for the sixth floor. Mr. Dankworth chased after me. I saw his face as the doors closed; he possessed a devilish handsomeness that the photos alone did not capture. I shook it off as the doors slid open to my floor. I was late, and Andrew leant against his office door frame with his arms crossed. After he looked me up and down, taking note of my outfit, he smiled, and I saw his attitude instantly change.

"I suppose the outfit makes up for your tardiness," Andrew observed as he glanced at the clock.

"Sorry, I spilt my coffee. I will have everything printed right now. Do you need anything else before it starts?" He watched as I sat down and slowly walked over. He leant over the top of me and put his hand on my desk. His cigarette breath reached my nose, causing bile to rise.

"Just my usual coffee, but I must say, this outfit today...I am a little worried about its purpose. If you are aiming to distract those at the meeting today, it will definitely work. I recommend covering up or the vampires will desire more than just a look." I cleared my throat and released the printing that I needed before I stood up and walked towards the break room to get some space from my new boss. I started preparing a coffee for Andrew when Stacey walked in. I noticed her black cardigan, which prompted a thought.

I greeted her with a smile before asking, "Could I borrow your cardigan, Stacey? Andrew told me to cover up before the meeting."

She snorted. "What? Is he worried that others may ogle you? Is only he allowed?"

"Look, I do not care what his intentions are, but I do not want to piss him off, especially since I was already late."

She laughed good-naturedly, as she removed her cardigan and handed it over. She went to pour herself a cup of coffee. "Yes, Alina texted me. Hungover, spilt coffee, and embarrassment, all in front of the big boss. Sounds like a good morning for you, yeah?"

My cheeks flushed. "God, those two. Thank you for the reminder. I cannot be late. I will talk to you later."

"Bye bye." She waved sarcastically as I walked out and readied myself for the meeting.

———

I gathered the paperwork and set up the conference room in preparation for the meeting. I organised bottles of blood for the vampires and poured glasses of water for the humans. It blew my mind that this was my job—to make sure that all parties were satisfied whether it was human or vampire. I took my seat and set up my laptop with a notes page ready and broken down into individual topics.

Andrew walked into inspect and nodded. "Looks good, Larissa, and thank you for covering up. Nice touch with the bottles of blood. Did you warm them?"

"Yes, all ready to go."

"Let's sit down and wait. Do not speak, just take the notes and hand out what is needed, understood?" I nodded and waited, as instructed. A few minutes later, the four other big heads walked into the room and looked me over before each taking a seat. We were all waiting for Mr. Dankworth now. The room was quiet as he walked in.

I noticed the different suit as he adjusted his cuffs and said, "I apologise for my lateness; I had an incident with coffee. Shall we —" His blue eyes landed on me, and he froze, a small smile spread over his lips. "We have a new face, I see. Who does it belong to?" His voice set my body on fire as I crossed my legs tighter.

Andrew stood up and fastened a button on his suit. "Lord Dankworth, this is my new assistant, Larissa Solis. She has proven to be rather exceptional at her job in the last month."

"Month?" He questioned as he took a seat and motioned for Andrew to follow. "Should I be worried that this is your third assistant this year, Andrew?"

Andrew chuckled and looked over at me. "I think she may be a keeper."

"I am sure she is," Lord Dankworth said knowingly before he cleared his throat. "Let us begin." The meeting took off without a hitch; I kept notes on what was being said and any suggestions that each of the department heads made.

Suddenly, Andrew cleared his throat and stood up. "Nik, I had an idea with the TimeShaft app."

I found it odd that he referred to him as Nik when earlier it was *Lord Dankworth*. I did not know the proper etiquette and wondered what to call him. I shook my head to bring my focus back to the app. I knew from reading through the paperwork that this app had potential, but all of Andrew's projections were incorrect. He was focusing on the wrong demographic. I gave him that feedback and even offered some suggestions earlier in the week, but he did not listen.

"I am listening." Lord Dankworth said. His eyes followed me constantly, despite my efforts to avoid meeting his gaze. Every time I stole a glance, he reclined in his chair with legs crossed and head propped on his hand—a posture of authority he flaunted for all to see. I attempted to keep my eyes on the computer screen as Andrew explained his idea on how to market the app.

I could not help but snort. "Is something funny, Miss Solis?" Lord Dankworth asked. I looked up from my laptop to see all the department heads staring in my direction.

"No, sorry. Just allergies. Please continue." He leant forward in his chair, put his elbows on the table and entwined his fingers. His eyes bore into me as if willing me to surrender.

"Miss Solis, I do not appreciate lies. Please speak your truth." I cleared my throat as Andrew gritted his teeth at me.

"I believe Andrew is marketing the TimeShaft app to the wrong demographic. I believe if you sell it to businesses, it will not achieve its full potential. You need to expand the demographic to people like stay-at-home mothers. I do not know if you are aware, but mothers have insane organisational skills, especially those with more than one child. This will help not only women, but men, too. It will stop arguments between couples over who is doing what as they can access it anytime on their phone and coordinate their lives with ease. I would market it beyond only businesses, based on what I have seen outside of this building." I watched Lord Dankworth's gaze, his eyes smiled before it reached his lips. He leant back in his chair and twiddled his thumb and forefinger together as the chair bounced a little.

"I like her, Andrew. Put that into the notes and I will sit down and discuss this further with you tomorrow." Andrew cleared his throat as his eyes darted in my direction. I would be in trouble after this.

"Absolutely. Larissa, can you hand out the Collard Projections?" I stood up and walked around the table, handing them to each person. As I neared Lord Dankworth, my body tingled all over. I handed one to him, and his finger grazed mine, which burned through me. I held in a gasp as I walked back to my seat. I glanced over at him as I continued to take notes. He had an amused look on his face like he seemed to want to laugh at my expense.

———

I was grateful for the end of the meeting. I rushed to the bathroom to take a breath. I needed new underwear; they were that wet from sitting in Dankworth's presence. I was so unsettled by my reaction to him that I rushed down to Travis and Alina and called Stacey to follow me.

"How was it?" Travis asked as he slid a fresh coffee towards me.

"Oh my god, he was late from changing because of what I did and literally froze when he saw me. His eyes are just to die for."

"Yes, they make you melt. I can smell it on you, do you need to change?" I smacked my head on the counter at Travis's question. I forgot vampires could smell arousal.

"Why?" I whined. "I have never had that happen to me before and holy shit." My phone rang and I saw Andrew's name flash on the screen. "Fuck, I need to go and get my ass handed to me. I will see you all later."

"Wait, why? From the coffee incident?" Stacey asked as she grabbed my arm to stop me from walking away without an explanation.

"No, I kind of stood on Andrew's feet, and told him in front of everyone that his idea for the TimeShaft app was wrong and that he should be doing something else instead."

Stacey's face said it all as Alina giggled.

"It was nice knowing you," she said in her sweet purr of a voice. I rolled my eyes and trudged back to my desk with the knowledge that Andrew would be yelling at me at some point. He had only yelled at me once before and that was not my fault, the coffee machine broke.

———

I knocked on Andrew's door.

"Come in," he called from the other side. I opened to door and saw him talking to Lord Dankworth, who turned his head slightly, but not enough to give me his full attention.

"You wanted to see me, Andrew?"

He cleared his throat and Dankworth stood and adjusted his suit. "Actually, I wanted to see you, Miss Solis. Could you give us the room please, Andrew?"

Andrew stood and made sad eyes in my direction as if I should be worried about what was about to happen. I watched Andrew walk out and close the door behind him.

"Miss Solis, please sit." He walked around to the other side of the desk and sat down in Andrew's chair. He opened the folder before him as I sat down. "May I call you Larissa?" I gulped and nodded as I crossed my legs, that unfamiliar tingling and desire erupted throughout my body, to the point where I felt the need to be near him, the need to touch him.

"Yes, Larissa is fine, Lord Dankworth."

He chuckled. "Please call me Nik."

"If it is all the same to you, I would prefer to call you Lord or Mr. Dankworth."

He scratched his chin, his brow furrowing in puzzlement. "Understood. Whatever makes you comfortable." He closed the folder and thrummed his fingers on the desk for a moment.

"Mr. Dankworth if you are going to fire me, can you please just do it? I do not like the suspense." He stood and came around to the front of the desk and leant against it, facing me.

"Larissa, I have no intention of firing you. I find it curious that you took the assistant position when you have a degree in marketing. You are clearly bright and smarter than Andrew realises. He is a dumb brute of a man so it does not surprise me that he would overlook your ideas. So, why did you take this position?"

"Honestly, I've been trying to get a job in marketing for a while now, but I keep getting rejected because I do not have practical experience. Miss Blackwood called and asked me if I wanted this position, and that if I was good at it, an opening in the marketing department may become available. I thought I would try and deal with whatever was thrown my way until a new opportunity arose."

"Interesting, Larissa. Are you related to a Katrina Solis, by any chance?"

"Ah, no sorry I do not know that person." He seemed upset by my response as if disappointed that I was not related to her.

"Anyway, I have told Andrew, and now I am telling you, that the TimeShaft app is now your responsibility. I want you to plan the marketing campaign for it, in addition to your current duties. Are you up for the task?" I was so excited at the opportunity that I stood and threw my arms around him in excitement. His arms wrapped around me in return, and as he pulled me close, my own body melded to his. I inhaled his musky aroma that I could not place. I pulled back suddenly, embarrassed at my body's reaction to him.

"Sorry. I did not mean to do that; it was just a knee-jerk reaction. I have not had much luck lately, and this brightened my day. Can you forgive me?"

"There is nothing to forgive. Truly, Larissa. Would you be able to complete this within a week?" My heart sank. It seemed impossible, especially since I was still working at the bar for extra money. He must have noticed my expression or the lack of excitement from moments ago. "Is this not going to be possible?"

"Could I be given more than a week? I work two jobs and I want to make sure that I do this properly."

"Are you not paid enough by us?" His voice carried irritation, obvious from the short and abrupt question.

"No, it is not that. I need more money to move out of my apartment and they are not cheap out here. I can do this. I do not want you to think that I can't."

He reached for my hand, covered it with his and held it tight. It was comforting and tender. The warmth in my body spread from his touch as he looked at me.

"I think I can swing you an extra week," his voice was soft as his eyes stared into mine. I felt a pull towards him as his eyes dropped to my lips, but I pulled back and took a few steps away.

"Thank you, Mr. Dankworth. I should return to work."

He straightened from the desk and cleared his throat, but a look of displeasure remained on his face. "Absolutely, we shall be in touch."

As I watched him walk away, my chest ached, like I needed to make it better for him, but I wasn't even sure what *it* was. He looked dejected and lonely as he pulled out his phone, put it to his ear, and headed towards the elevator. Andrew came into view, blocking Mr. Dankworth, Nik, from my sight.

"Remember, this is not to interfere with your actual job. You may have flashed your winning smile to the boss, but that doesn't change your responsibilities, understand?"

"Yes Andrew, I will still be your assistant first."

He nodded as he walked into his office. I sat down and continued to do my usual work, which Andrew had decided to pile on top of me. He did not realise that I would be able to handle all of it and more.

CHAPTER 16
AWKWARD INTERACTION
Larissa

I RETURNED HOME LATER THAN USUAL THAT NIGHT AND WAS relieved that Luce had ordered Chinese food for dinner. I had no desire to cook. She slid a glass of wine across the bench for me. I took it and swirled it in the glass before taking a larger-than-normal gulp.

"Rough day? How was the meeting?" she asked, her gaze on my almost empty wine glass. I sat down beside her and started to fill my plate with Singapore noodles.

"It was ah…entertaining, I suppose. It started with me spilling coffee on my boss and I mean, like, the *owner* of the company. I ran to my meeting because I was so embarrassed, he noticed me instantly and kept his eyes on me the entire time. Then I snorted at one of Andrew's suggestions and the boss kind of ordered me to share my thoughts, which embarrassed Andrew. Then the boss came to see me afterwards and offered me an opportunity to work on a marketing campaign, as well as my other job," I rambled on, not stopping to take a breath.

"Wow, that is an intense day. but what a great opportunity! I am proud of you." She put her arm around me for a quick side hug before she continued to eat.

"How was your day?" I asked her before shovelling noodles into my mouth.

"Crap. It's just...the deadlines they expect are ridiculous. It almost makes them impossible, and I suppose I am just a bit lost on what to do at the moment," she groaned as she rubbed her temples, a sign of her stress.

"Have you spoken to anyone about it?"

"No, I haven't, but I am not sure if I should. I think maybe it is just this month, that I just need to get through it, and everything will be fine."

"Hey, I will cancel my shift on Friday, and we can go out for the night. Sound good?" I suggested as a way to cheer her up.

Luce perked up a little. "Yeah, that would be good, some old-fashioned sister time."

I poured her another glass of wine as we continued to talk about the marketing campaign and her issues at work in more detail. We stayed up most of the night talking like we did as children. But the disconnect that happened after everything with Peter was still there, it had not healed. I knew we both felt it, but we did not know how to manage our way around it. I missed my sister even though I lived with her.

The next day at work was just as chaotic as the day before, but I stayed later, once Andrew left for the day, to start on the marketing campaign. The building did not close until ten, which gave me at least four hours to work on it. I printed out everything that I needed and spread everything out in the conference room. I put music on and started to plot ideas on where to start and what would be the best idea for this app. I stood at the whiteboard and wrote down various ideas in between pacing around the room. I had removed my blouse and cardigan, leaving me in only a singlet top. I sat on top of the conference table and stared at the board before I laid back to look at the rough draft.

"Come on Larissa, you are better than these mundane ideas." My body tingled all over.

"I would not say they are all mundane." I squealed as I sprung up off the table and spun around. He was sitting on the chair furthest away.

"Mr. Dankworth, what are you doing here?" His eyes swept over my lack of shoes and rather revealing singlet, where my bra could easily be seen. I grabbed my cardigan to cover myself.

"I heard music on my way out for the night and decided to inspect it." He leant closer in his chair as that familiar pull returned; a need to be closer to him.

"Do you always listen for noises on your way home?" I asked him as I watched his eyes linger on the board.

"I am generally the last one to leave. I listen for noises to make sure that I *am* the last and encourage those who work late to go home." He stood and walked over to the board. "I see you are already thinking about the campaign, but I expected better."

I scoffed at him before packing up. "Wow, here I thought you were a nice person. I was mistaken." I gathered all the papers, threw them into the box and made my way back to my office.

"Larissa, wait." I heard his steps behind me as I kicked the box under my desk and turned to land on his hard chest. The force sent me backwards, but his arm wrapped around my waist and pulled me in to stop the fall. I pushed away from him again, which was against my body's wishes. The need to be near him was just as strong and just as confusing.

"Do not touch me. You said what you said, it is my first day of doing this. It is called a brainstorm for a reason."

He groaned and slammed his hand on the wall, which made me jump and my heart rate pick up speed. "I did not mean that. You are incredibly intelligent. I believed that you were…" His eyes flashed red in anger before they changed to black, with his blue irises breaking through. It was almost beautiful. He shook his head. "I will not say anything again. I apologise. Take my car home, please. A young lady should not walk home alone at night. I insist."

I ran from the floor and ignored his offer. I caught a taxi instead. On the drive home, I could not stop thinking about the man who brought warmth to my body but also terrified me like no one else. Who was this person?

CHAPTER 17
TIME FOR COFFEE
Larissa

Nik walked into the conference room for the second day in a row. I glared at him, and I crossed my arms to show my disapproval of his presence. He removed his burgundy suit jacket and rolled up his sleeves to reveal his thick, muscular forearms. I could not help but stare at them as I thought about rubbing my hands on them.

"What do you want, Mr. Dankworth?" I refused to pay him too much attention, so I busied myself with some documents on the table. I was here to work on the marketing campaign and after yesterday, I would civil only because of him being my boss. He sighed as he stroked his chin, and his eyes leisurely swept over my body, which traitorously tingled with delight. I turned away.

"Larissa, I apologise for my actions last night. They were not the actions of a gentleman, and I am ashamed of myself." I could hear the sincerity in his voice as I glanced over my shoulder at him.

"You are forgiven, but could you leave because I have work to do?" I dismissed him and turned to focus on the board.

"I am unable to leave."

I rolled my eyes, the stubbornness in this man. "Why? Is it past my curfew and time for me to leave?" I turned around once again to face him.

"No." He stalked towards me, and I saw the lust in his eyes like I was the prey and he the predator. I took a few steps back to put some space between us, at which he smirked, obviously enjoying this game. He held out his hand and I felt the need to put my own inside his; I wanted to feel his touch on my skin. I saw my hand reach for his; he gripped it tight and tugged it to pull me closer. He put his arm around my waist to secure me against his body, my breathing grew faster. His eyes never left mine except for one moment when he gazed down at my lips. He wanted permission to kiss me. I involuntarily moved forward, which was all the permission he needed. He grabbed my face roughly and planted his lips against mine. He groaned against me and licked my lips to part them, which they did. I had no control over my body, but the need to have more overpowered me. I put my arms around his neck and ground against him. In a flash, the wall was behind me.

"Naughty girl, Miss Solis." His voice was strained, as if he were holding part of himself back. I watched as his eyes flickered between their crystal blue, red, then black, and back to blue. I chuckled against his lips and nibbled on his lower lip as his hands started to explore every inch of my body. He lifted my legs to wrap around him. His hard cock pressed against me, but I was not ready to lose myself in this moment. I had always romanticised the idea of losing my virginity to someone I loved. I always imagined being surrounded by cliché rose petals, with candles and soft music playing in the room. He paused and lifted his head to look at me, a softness spread against his face.

"I will not sully you, Larissa, you are too precious for that, but from this moment on, no other man shall touch you." He stroked my cheek as he gently kissed my lips.

"No man will own me, Mr. Dankworth," I vowed, relieved that my voice did not tremble or falter. His fangs descended at my words; a small rumbling sound escaped his lips. One hand slid to my hair, pulling it back to reveal my neck.

"You are mine," he growled, as he ran his fangs over the crease in my neck, drawing the slightest amount of blood. He groaned as his tongue licked it up. "You taste divine, Miss Solis. I cannot wait to taste the sweetness between your legs." He got on his knees and pulled my underwear down before—

I shot up suddenly, my eyes frantically taking in my surroundings. I registered that I was at home, in my bed. My body was covered in sweat but also tingled with arousal.

"Holy shit, it was a dream." I shook it off as I looked at my phone and saw it was almost six in the morning. Luce was still asleep, thankfully. I imagined her reaction if she heard me moaning from a sex dream. I could not stop seeing the lust in his eyes and the feeling of his lips on mine. I thought perhaps a run would help with that, so I dressed in my yoga pants and a top and practically sprinted out of the apartment. I could not go to work if all I could think of were his hands on my body and the way he kissed me. It was sweet torture to think about it as I ran harder than I had before, the words echoed in my mind, "You are mine." I did not see the dip in the road until my knee buckled from underneath me and I fell to the ground. I stood as quickly as I could and looked around. It was too early for many people to be out thankfully; many vampires would also not be awake at this time. I inspected the scrapes on my leg and hands, noticing I had cut through my pants as fresh blood stained my knees and dripped down my pant leg.

"That looks like it hurts." I spun to see James behind me, he glanced down at my knee and winced. "I called for you a few times, but I think you were in the zone." My knee buckled when I tried to take a step, but James caught me before I hit the ground again. "I think I'm going to have to carry you home, is that okay?" he asked.

"Okay," I muttered regretfully. I really did not want to be carried through the streets. He lifted me as if I weighed nothing and carried me back.

Luce was about to leave when we approached the apartment door. When she saw us, she gasped. "What happened?" Her face filled with fear and worry as she rushed over to look me over, noticing the blood on my knee.

"I am fine, I just tripped while I was running. I will be alright. Go to work. James will help clean me up." She kissed my cheek before she reluctantly turned to leave for work. Once we were in the apartment, James pulled out the first aid kit so I could clean the small scrapes on my hands, which were tiny in comparison to the wound on my leg. James looked at my pants with pity.

"Just cut them, I do not care. I will buy another pair."

He grabbed the tear in my leg and ripped it wider, before cleaning the wound. As he applied the antiseptic, I held back a scream, a whimper leaving my mouth instead. He continued to clean the wound and carefully bandaged my knee.

"I would recommend taking the day off to rest and possibly get a scan on your knee. You may have torn something; I saw the fall and I wouldn't be surprised if you had a torn ligament from it." I nodded and emailed Andrew to let him know.

———

After waiting an unnecessary amount of time in the clinic's waiting room, the elderly doctor twisted and bent my swollen knee to his pleasure, before telling me to rest. If it wasn't feeling better by Friday, I would have to go back for a scan.

I left and headed to a café close by to wait for Luce to finish work and take me home. The café had a retro vibe, which I loved. It had blue and white booth seats with black and white tiled flooring. If the waitresses had on roller skates, I would have sworn I'd been transported to the fifties. I ordered a coffee and a brownie and sat down on a sparkly red chair that matched the table. I passed the time by mindlessly playing a game on my phone. I watched the crowds come and go while I eavesdropped on various conversations from the tables around me; work troubles, marital issues and even an identity crisis thrown in there. It was like an episode of a crappy daytime television soap opera. A shiver burst through my body, but I did not feel cold. In fact, the café was a comfortable temperature. My confusion intensified when I heard my name.

"Miss Solis." I glanced up from my phone and instantly sat up straighter as I realised it was Mr. Dankworth before me, wearing a navy suit and black trench coat. My body tingled all over.

"Hi, what are you doing here?" I blurted without thinking. I was nowhere near my work so I thought I would be safe not running into anyone. He tilted his head at me, and my cheeks flushed as I realised what I had said. "Sorry, I just did not expect to see anyone from work here."

He pulled out the chair, sat down and flashed a smile as the words "You are mine" played through my head again. I had to push the images away of where his head ended up in my dream last night. I attempted to close my legs tighter, but my knee would not let me.

"I expected to see you at work today but when I heard that you were unwell, I feared that it was my actions that caused you to avoid work."

I snorted. "A bit egotistical, no?" It was the first time that I had seen him laugh, and as he leant forward and adjusted himself into a more relaxed position, I realised it made him even more handsome.

"I suppose it would seem so, but no. My actions last night were not what I would expect from a man such as myself. It was more the monster that made its appearance, and I apologise for that. I am not used to being spoken to in that manner, and that combined with hunger…" He drifted off and looked behind me.

"I accept your apology and I apologise for my own actions. I was tired, and I do not like being questioned, especially when I was still trying to think of some new ideas," I said, offering some vulnerability.

He smiled softly in acknowledgment before he stood to order a coffee at the counter.

When he returned to the table, he said, "I ordered you a coffee. I hope that is alright."

"You assume you know my coffee order?" I bit my lip and saw his eyes follow the action.

"I know many things, Larissa. I have been alive longer than most, and it is easy to read people."

"We shall see if you are correct, I suppose." I raised my eyebrow at him, but as I moved my knee, I winced from the pain.

"What is it?" The amusement on his face was replaced by concern as he reached over the table, as if to touch me. He pulled back before he could make contact, though, which was strange. It was almost like he thought there was more between us, but I could not assume based on what little I knew about him.

"I injured myself while running this morning. My knee buckled and it is a little painful. I have been told to rest it and get a scan if it is not better by Friday." He glanced down at my knee as I spoke, which was covered in bandages, and his brow creased.

"Why are you here then, Larissa? Should you not be home resting rather than out enjoying a coffee?" The drinks arrived and I noted that he ordered me a cappuccino with what looked like extra froth and chocolate on top.

"Wait, how? That is not possible." He smiled and took a sip of his drink, and when the red froth covered his lips, he licked it away. I remembered the feeling of him licking my lips in my dream last night. I shivered at the thought.

He peered at me curiously before speaking, "I know many things, Larissa. You would be surprised. Now answer my question, if you please."

"I am waiting for my sister to pick me up after she finishes work." He scratched his chin, and glanced down at the table.

"May I offer you a ride home?" he asked, but I did not want to share an enclosed space with him.

I smiled at his kind gesture. "No, that is awfully nice, but no thank you. I will wait for Luce."

He took another sip of his drink. This time, the froth lingered on his perfectly manicured beard. I had an overwhelming desire to wipe it away but stopped myself when I noticed him straighten and freeze for a moment, his eyes flicked towards me and paused on mine for only a moment.

"Please do not speak," he said, seconds before a hand slapped his back. It jolted him forward slightly as if he did not expect the strength behind it.

"Nik, what are you doing in my neck of the woods? You never travel down here." I found it interesting that he did not speak with formality, with no reference to Lord or Mr. Dankworth. Due to his earlier reaction, I did not perceive them to be friends.

Nik stood and offered his hand to the man, who was decked out in an array of jewels, and his blond hair was slicked to the side. It was almost like he was overcompensating for something, but I did not know what. He refused to shake Mr. Dankworth's hand, which I found interesting. All the articles I had read suggested he was well respected by many in the human and vampire world.

"I was in the area, forgive me for not alerting you. It was spur of the moment, to retrieve a much-needed drink."

"And you have lingered for what reason?" The blond man questioned as he directed his gaze at me. His eyes were a deep, dark brown that sent shivers down my spine. Mr. Dankworth attempted to take a step to block the man's view of me but seemed to fail.

"Ah, I see. You have found…" The man sniffed the air as his fangs descended and he groaned with satisfaction as he breathed out. "…a rather unique one. She smells delicious."

His eyes scanned my body before landing on my face and offered his hand around Mr. Dankworth, "Daniel Wright, and you are?"

"Larissa," I replied uncertainly, as I shook his hand. Dankworth told me not to speak, but my name would not hurt.

"Larissa who?" I opened my mouth to speak but did not get a chance to answer.

"Larissa Claire." Mr. Dankworth interrupted me and said my name wrong, but something told me not to correct him.

"It is a pleasure to make your acquaintance, Miss. Claire. How do you know Lord Dankworth?" Daniel asked as he glanced between us.

"She is in charge of a new marketing campaign, and we ran into each other and sat down to discuss the next steps of an app that is being produced," Dankworth answered for me and Daniel chuckled in response. He looked over at Dankworth before he spoke to him in another language, which made my boss clench his fists and growl in response. I stayed in my chair, remaining as silent as possible, and waited for the man to leave.

"Goodbye Larissa, I am sure I shall see you again," he demurred, returning to English. I waved as he left, then took a moment to shake off the shivers that man had given me.

"I am hoping I never have to see him again. He gave me the creeps," I said as I watched Nik. He did not speak or even react to my comment. Instead, he ran his fingers through his hair, pulled out his phone, and sent a few messages.

Taking the hint, I stood from my chair and interrupted his texting. "Thank you for the coffee, but I had better go." He looked up from his phone and quickly put it down on the table.

"I apologise for that, but I needed to inform a few individuals of what he said."

"When he spoke in whatever language that was?"

"Yes." His tone was blunt.

"And what did he say?" I prodded for more information about the interaction between the two men.

"He made a few idle threats, nothing that I need worry about."

"Why? He called you Lord. I may need you to explain when it is appropriate to use the different terms. I am not sure that I understand all of that."

"I am to be called Lord Dankworth by vampires as a sign of respect unless they are friends or considered family. They are allowed to call me Mr. Dankworth, Dankworth, or even Nik depending on the individual. I hope that clears it up for you. As I am one of the Lords of this region, I oversee those below me and ensure that they are following all the rules that are in place."

"Yes, the rules that your kind created," I muttered.

"My kind. Miss Solis, I did not realise you were so prejudiced against *my kind*." He emphasised the words.

"You mean the kind that took control of the world and seem intent on keeping us stuck in these little cages to benefit you?" I leant back in the chair, crossing my arms.

"Says the human whose *kind* caused irreparable damage to the earth by dropping bombs they created. Some places are uninhabitable, Larissa, because of *your kind*." Nik did not seem to care about my poor opinion but rather wanted to educate me, which only annoyed me further.

"Truly? Or are you keeping us in specific locations to control us?" He laughed instead of answering me. I took note of his eyes burning brighter.

"What idiocy you speak!" he snarled. I seemed to have annoyed him now.

"Says the man who drinks blood to sustain his life." The words just poured from my mouth.

"Larissa, you do not know the circumstances in which my life began. Do not presume to know. If I could return to that time and tell my past self not to make this decision, I would. I have regrets, as does any person, whether human or vampire." He was fired up, but not enough to provoke any anger within him. I did not bother to ask anything further.

"Why did you lie about my name? Are you trying to protect my identity or protect me from him?"

"Both. Do you remember the day that we first met, and I asked you a question?" I thought back to that day, recalling the coffee incident before the big meeting.

"Katrina Solis?" I questioned, and he smirked in response.

"Yes, she had a reputation amongst our kind. She made a few enemies, and he would have assumed worse than he already did, with seeing us together."

"Glad to know that there is conflict even within your ranks." I chuckled softly at knowing there was some disharmony among the vampires.

"We are still human at heart." He smiled warmly at me, and I could not help but smile back at him.

CHAPTER 18

ACID RAIN

Larissa

WE CONTINUED TO TALK, BOTH OF US SO ENGROSSED IN conversation that I lost track of time. I checked my phone and realised Luce would not pick me up for at least another hour. Mr. Dankworth helped with passing the time as he told me about how he started his company and the hurdles he had to jump through. It was an interesting story, to hear about how hard he worked to develop a reputation and maintain his anonymity before the war started. It was a different time for him, with people having no knowledge of where a young adult man managed to find so much money to invest in his company. I shivered from the change in temperature within the coffee shop and I lifted my jacket over my shoulders.

"Acid rain," he muttered under his breath.

"Sorry, what was that?"

"We are about to be hit with acid rain. Have you witnessed it yet?" I shook my head. I heard about it on the news but had never seen it in person. The warnings always mentioned to shelter in place until it had passed, which could be from an hour to a day. It was the consequence of letting off multiple bombs all over the world.

He cleared his throat. "One of the perks of human mistakes. Acid rain. It is deadly to be in and breathe. Text your sister; I will get you home safely. I promise." A snide remark slipped from his lips, followed by sincerity. The tense expressions on everyone's faces confirmed what words could not: he was not lying. I nodded as he stood and offered his arm, the rain had already started as he pulled out his phone and made a quick call. "The car will be here shortly."

A black SUV pulled up and two men ran inside, holding umbrellas. The two guards glanced at Mr. Dankworth before turning their attention to me.

"We will be escorting Miss Solis home to ensure no harm comes to her." One of the guards' eyes flashed red as they lingered on me.

Mr. Dankworth growled at him in response. "Contain yourself, Mr. Monroe, or step into that rain."

Mr. Monroe stood straighter and handed his boss an umbrella. Mr. Dankworth offered me his arm and leant in closer. In a hushed tone, he said, "Stay close and hold your breath."

I took his arm and pressed myself close to him, taking the opportunity to inhale his scent. The spicy vanilla caused a wave of desire to wash over me. I did not understand how he did this to my body. He peered down at me and smiled as if he knew what thoughts raced through my head. I drew in one big gasp and held my breath. One of his steps was at least three of mine. We rushed towards his car, and he covered my body with his until I was safely inside. I let my breath go and relaxed once the car door closed. My knee ached from walking a little too fast. The driver and guard slid into the front seat as Mr. Dankworth told them my address. It was quiet as I watched the changing scenery and people running for shelter. I heard him sniff the air.

"You are bleeding," he murmured. Feeling vulnerable in a car with blood-sucking monsters, his words made me retreat into my seat, creating a distance between us.

"You can probably smell the cut on my knee," I replied, trying to keep my voice steady. He shook his head.

"No, this is fresh blood." He removed his belt and shuffled closer to me. I wrestled with the urge to either jump from the car or onto him.

He smiled softly. "I would never hurt you, Larissa." His words were so gentle, and his eyes were filled with tenderness, which made me relax.

"Do not move for a moment," he instructed as he brought his nose closer, and inhaled deeply. He closed his eyes before opening them once again. "Remove your jacket."

I did as he ordered. My eyes widened as I noticed the small red dots scattered across my skin, evidence of the rain burning me.

"I barely feel them," I told him as I continued to inspect my arms.

His fangs descended. He pierced his thumb and pressed it to different areas on my skin that had been burnt. They healed instantly and, wordlessly, he settled back into his seat.

I was confused. "Why? How?" My voice faltered, highlighting the turmoil that swirled in my brain.

"Acid rain burns can spread through your system. I apologise for not asking first, but it was in your best interest." He chuckled when he saw the worry on my face. "Your naivety is refreshing. You will not turn into one of us, do not worry. I need to drain you dry for that, and I have not tasted blood from a human in quite a while."

"Why is that?" He sighed and clenched his fists at my question. "Sorry, I did not mean to pry, forget it."

"I believe it is sacred. I only drink from the one I love or those that I am close with."

"That is sweet. Have you been together for long?"

He smiled and turned to look at me. "She is my soul mate." He was speaking in present tense but everything I read stated he was an eligible bachelor.

"Why does the media portray you as a bachelor?" I wondered if I had missed something.

"She died at the turn of the world. A bomb killed her while she was saving human lives." Sadness radiated off him as I reached over and touched his hand. He spun his and held my hand tightly.

"I am sorry for your loss, Mr. Dankworth."

"Do you believe in reincarnation?" He changed the subject so abruptly, that it hurt my heart, but he did not let go of my hand and for some reason, I did not want him to.

"To an extent, I think a soul is reborn, which is why some people are considered old souls, but you would know more about that than I would."

He chuckled softly. "Yes, I suppose I may."

"May I ask how old you are?"

"Older than most," he admitted sadly as he turned to look out the car window. I did not press it further. It was his secret to keep.

"Was she beautiful?"

He turned back to me at my question. "No beauty has ever compared to hers. She is perfection." His face lit up as he spoke about her.

I could not help but smile. "I wish to find a man who will speak of me the way you do of her." He did not respond but rather pulled out his phone to check his messages.

We pulled up outside the apartment building and, sounding displeased, he said, "This is endearing."

"I live with my sister, but I am saving until I can afford my own place."

"We have apartments. I would happily lend you one. It would be closer to work."

"I appreciate the gesture, but I do not accept charity." He snorted and shook his head with a small grin on his face.

"Of course. Shall I escort you inside?" He opened his car door and came round to mine. When he noticed the puddle on the ground, he lifted me and carried me over it, until it was safer for me to walk. I noticed the burn on his face as we reached the entrance.

"I can clean that up." As I reached to touch his face, he grabbed my hand and kissed it. The action made my body flush with excitement. I wanted more of his touch; it brought sensations I had never experienced.

"You forget, Larissa. I heal, so it will be gone in a moment." As soon as he finished the sentence, it had healed.

"Thank you for the lift and the coffee."

He shifted restlessly, his gaze lingering as though anticipating an unspoken desire.

"Your leg will be healed by tomorrow," he said instead.

"Pardon?"

At my confusion, he scratched the back of his head and his eyes drifted towards the car.

"As I healed your burns, my blood healed the wound on your knee, too. You will be able to run again tomorrow if you wish."

"Do I get any side effects from that?" I asked, hoping nothing strange would happen as I wondered what Luce would do if she noticed.

"A few. You will have increased energy, appetite and..."

A surge of warmth flooded me. "Oh, right." I now understood these intense feelings towards him.

"It will pass by the morning." As he went to walk away, I reached for him but pulled back before I made contact. I could not understand the effect he had on me. Was it simply because of who he was? Or was it some dark desire that I had buried inside me, but was now ready to be set free? He turned at the car door and smiled. His lips moved, but I did not hear the words. I waved as he drove away, and I knew I would have to tell Travis about this.

I did just that once I had settled inside the apartment and put my knee up to rest. I snuggled into the couch cushions and opened a bag of crisps. I assumed this was the increased appetite he mentioned. I cleared my throat, dialled Travis's number, and told him all about my afternoon with Mr. Dankworth.

"He skipped his finance meeting for you."

"What?" I sputtered. "He said he was in the area. He never mentioned he missed a meeting. I feel dreadful now."

"Dreadful that you got to spend the afternoon with a beautiful man? Oh, you poor thing." His tone was mocking and I pictured the face he would pull at me.

I snorted. "Shut up, Travis."

"Oh wait, here he is. That is strange."

"What is?" I asked curiously.

"Good afternoon, Mr. Dankworth," Travis said as the phone went dead.

"You shit, you hung up on me!"

I decided to not tell Luce about this. I knew of her hate towards them, and while I shared similar feelings, it was different with him. I used the extra energy to my advantage and worked on the marketing plan, finally nailing down the demographic and the way to approach it. I smiled as I emailed the plan to Mr. Dankworth before sliding into bed.

Chapter 19

COMPULSION

Larissa

I WOKE FROM ANOTHER DIRTY DREAM ABOUT HIM. THIS TIME, HE spread my legs, got on his knees and ate his dessert, as he said. I needed to get laid or at least buy a sex toy to ease the sexual frustration I was constantly feeling. I checked my knee and it had fully healed, but I opted against going for a run. Instead, to shake off the dream, I had the coldest shower imaginable.

As I stood in line to buy coffee for everyone, a tingling sensation coursed through my body, the same one I always had when Nik was nearby. I turned to scan the room but saw nothing. I looked back at the barista, a little deflated.

"Good morning, Larissa." His voice tickled my skin as he appeared beside me.

"We should stop meeting like this." He threw his head back and laughed. "Should I be worried that you are stalking me?" I batted my eyes at him, some subtle flirting. I shocked myself, why did I think to flirt with him?

"You spoke of this place yesterday, and having somewhat tasted the coffee after our first encounter, I thought it best to see if they made a good bloodcino," he commented while his blue eyes stared at me. I wanted to fall into them.

"Travis says it is the best he has ever had. Can't say I agree now, can I?"

He sniggered as my name was called.

As I walked back towards him with the coffees, he smiled and said, "Ah, it appears our time has come to an end. Enjoy your day, Larissa."

"Enjoy your dry clothes." I winked at him and left the store. I turned back to look at him through the large café windows and noticed he was still staring at me even with his phone pressed to his ear. The sense of danger was unmistakable, yet I felt utterly powerless to prevent whatever was unfolding.

———

Andrew was as rude as ever after my day off, and because my knee had healed, he did not believe that I had an injury. I did not tell him the truth—that Mr. Dankworth had healed it. It sounded far-fetched even in my head. I dealt with his attitude, partially because I thought I deserved it, and continued to plough through the extra work he put on top of me. I sorted the paperwork that had been all out of order, my guess on purpose. My body tingled as I pushed it away to concentrate, and it was not until hands landed on my desk that I peered up to see Mr. Dankworth's blue eyes staring down at me.

"A-apologies, Mr. Dankworth, my focus was elsewhere. H-how can I help you?" I stuttered from the sheer intensity of his gaze.

"I need a moment to discuss your proposal. It is rather bold, I must say." I smiled because it *was* bold, but it would work, and I knew it. I heard Andrew yell in his office and prepared myself for the tirade that was about to occur. Mr. Dankworth straightened and listened intently to Andrew's swearing and yelling about my incompetence.

Andrew's office door swung open, but before he could approach my desk, Mr. Dankworth growled through his teeth, "Andrew, I need a word, NOW!" He then stormed into the office, forcing Andrew to backtrack. The door slammed once they were both inside.

Stacey ran over, "I have never seen him so pissed. What was that?"

I shrugged, "I do not know. Andrew was yelling at me, then opened the door and Dankworth stormed in."

"It would be so cute if he's, like, *protecting your honour.*" She said the last part in a mocking, posh accent. I could not help but laugh at her poor attempt at one.

"Right." I rolled my eyes. "*So* not going to happen."

The door opened, and Andrew came out in somewhat of a trance. "Larissa, sorry for my behaviour. I will never treat you in that manner again." His words were robotic, and his eyes were vacant and glassy as if he were a shell of his former shelf. I knew what was happening. I shook my head and glared at Mr. Dankworth.

"A moment," I gritted out, trying to contain my rage. I led the way into a spare conference room with frosted glass for some privacy. He sat on the edge of the table and looked at his hands as if this discussion were beneath him.

"Should I be worried?" he asked rather cockily, as if he knew of the dreams I was having in this very room.

"Are you kidding me? You compelled him and you see no issue?"

He cleared his throat and stood, walking over to me. I backed away until I hit the wall, flashes of my dreams filled my head.

"I compelled him to treat you right and you are insulted by this." He was in front of me, so close that our noses almost touched. My body pulled towards him.

"Yes, people deserve the choice. You took his. He may be an asshole, but he should have apologised in his own way."

One of his hands landed on the wall above me, and the other near my side. "Are you telling me I was wrong in my actions?" He gazed at my lips, as I did at his, before I sunk out of this position.

"Yes, you were." I pretended to stretch my shoulders.

"Come here." I found myself unusually drawn to him, my feet moving on their own before I shook my head to resist the urge.

"No, you do not get to compel me." He paced the room suddenly, creases filled his forehead, and he appeared stressed. Anger surged through my body as it vibrated into my hands. How dare he try and compel me?

"How long have you been able to resist compulsion?" His brow creased as his eyes flared with irritation.

"No idea, I have never lived around vampires, especially ones that would compel me. First time." I crossed my arms in annoyance.

"Fuck, tell no one of this." He stormed from the conference room and the door slammed shut behind him.

Stacey came running in. "What the hell?"

His words played in my head, "Tell no one of this."

I glanced up at her. "It's nothing. Go back to work." I pushed past her and sat back at my desk, flexing my fingers to calm myself down.

CHAPTER 20

A WARNING

Larissa

I COULD NOT SHAKE THE WORRY OF DISCOVERING THAT I COULD not be compelled. I stayed at my desk a little later than usual to catch up on the work that I missed the day before. I put headphones on, old school hip hop helped me focus as my finger drummed to the beat. I came back from the printer to see a white paper bag on my desk. I took my headphones out and looked around.

"Hello?" I called out. I only heard silence as I walked over and smelt the aroma of pasta and garlic. I opened the bag to see a clear container filled with spaghetti in tomato sauce. Pasta was one of my favourite foods. I glanced around once more. The bag had a fork, and a note in there, too. I pulled it out and sat down.

I promise to never compel another person unless it is necessary, Nik. I folded it over and pushed the food to the side. I would not accept this gift, even if I was starving.

"Stubborn as always, I see." He stood before me with a smug look on his face.

"As always because you know me so well," I replied sarcastically, and returned to my work, choosing to ignore him.

"I told you that I can read people and you cannot deny that you are a stubborn woman." I leant back in my chair and looked up at him. He was not wrong, but I refused to answer, which provoked a smile from him. "See, stubborn enough not to answer."

"I am busy, Mr. Dankworth, what can I help you with?"

He sat down in front of my desk. "What can you tell me of your mother?"

"Why is that relevant? You storm out of the room and tell me not to reveal that I cannot be compelled. Maybe you just did not try hard enough, did you consider that?" He snorted at my remark and stood up, spreading his hands on the desk and leaning forward, bringing his face close to mine.

"Larissa, I want you to forget everything that happened today." The fog was settling into my brain as I shook it off. He adjusted himself and got closer. "Tell me what you desire." My mouth opened, but I closed it again and rose from my seat.

"Maybe you are just weak?" It was a low blow to his ego, but I did not care.

"At my age, I can compel any person, even one under the influence of any substance. You will never grasp my power." I rolled my eyes at him, another man in a powerful position flaunting himself. I did not care for it.

"Wow, I'm trembling. Why does it matter?" I do not know where my confidence came from. I needed to remember he was my boss.

He sat back down and fixed his suit. "It should not happen. Nobody can resist compulsion. You cannot tell even those you trust. It is dangerous for you." He played with his checkered blue tie that matched his eyes.

"How is it dangerous?" I leant closer to him wanting to know why something so minor could fill him with so much worry.

"I cannot explain, I need you to trust me." I started to pack up. "Larissa, what are you doing?" Concern creased his brow and tension tightened his features.

"If you cannot give me answers, I will leave. I am not here for cryptic nonsense. Tell me or I am leaving," I demanded. He asked me to keep a secret without explaining why.

"Do not threaten me." His voice echoed in the room and for a moment, I got a glimpse of the monster beneath the surface.

"It is not a threat; it is a promise." Anger started to vibrate through my arms again as he looked down and smiled.

"Then leave." I did not expect that answer from him, but I packed my bag and started for the elevator before I turned back for the container of pasta. I made a show of grabbing it and storming off again.

"Enjoy your dinner," he called out to me as I left. His SUV was out the front and the driver got out to open the door, then gestured me inside. His black hair was pulled back into a ponytail, and he wore an all-black suit. He looked too big to comprehend.

"Miss Solis?"

"What is this?"

"Mr. Dankworth has asked me to drive you home." He sighed; he did not seem to be impressed with this order.

"That's nice. Tell him no."

"Larissa, if you do not get in..." He paused, uncertain. "I have permission to put you in the car."

"You are joking, right?" He shook his head. I looked back and saw Mr. Dankworth in the foyer, watching my interaction with the driver. I did not understand this. What was his fascination with me? Or was it all just in my head?

CHAPTER 21
GROCERY SHOP

Larissa

I WAS GRATEFUL THAT I HAD NOT RUN INTO MR. DANKWORTH. I was frustrated over the secrets I believed he kept. The only correspondence I received from him was emails about my marketing campaign for the TimeShaft app. He gave his suggestions on minor things that I changed only because he was my boss, even though I truly believed that my way was right. Time would tell. Andrew was back to his normal abusive and piggish self. I had come to not even mind the inappropriate comments from him—it was the norm—but I did also write them down, so if he decided to fire me, at least I had evidence of his behaviour.

I signed off for the day and borrowed the car from Luce to do grocery shopping. She was frustrating me more than usual—her mood swings were making it worse. She was stressed about work, and she was taking it out on me. My search for an apartment had not been very successful, as a lot of them were out of my budget unless I continued to work the two jobs to pay for it.

As I walked into the store, non-descript instrumental music was playing, which made the whole experience more mundane than usual. But at least it got me away from Luce. I did not have a list with me, which was never wise. I walked down every single aisle and selected the food that I knew we needed. I stopped in the baking aisle and looked at the instant cake mixes. I missed baking. It used to give me clarity and calm. As I picked up a chocolate packet mix, my body trembled before it shivered. I sighed.

"That is a big sigh over a cake mix," Mr. Dankworth's smooth voice cut into my thoughts. I turned to see him holding a basket and wearing a green velvet suit. I put the chocolate mix back.

"I miss baking. I used to all the time, but I have not had the time recently, between looking for an apartment, working two jobs, and dealing with a grumpy twin."

He stroked his chin and moved closer as he reached past me and selected a brownie mix.

"I will admit, I am partial to chocolate. I missed out on the opportunity to taste it as a human, as I had already turned when it was discovered, so I indulge in it now." He was so close that I felt the magnetic pull between us, I found it hard to focus.

"You have not lived until you have tasted my white chocolate brownies."

He licked his lips, and I was drawn to look at them. I wanted to kiss him right there in the baking aisle.

"The sound of them makes me hungry." His voice was hoarse as he took a step closer. I shook my head and grabbed a cake mix before continuing down the aisle. I knew he would follow me, which he promptly did. We walked and talked through the various aisles. I noticed he had tins of cat food in his basket.

"I am surprised that you have a pet cat. You work so hard; I am shocked you have the time to care for another." He laughed, and the sound of it relaxed my body. I did not understand the affect this man had on me.

"Cats can care for themselves, I simply feed her. I find her presence to be a source of comfort." I smiled at the idea of him sitting on a couch, stroking his cat, but I wondered if he was truly fulfilled with a cat. I noticed that he wanted to say something else.

"You have that face."

He seemed horrified at my remark on his face. "What face?"

"The face you make when you have something to say, but you are not sure how to say it." He cleared his throat and pulled at his black tie to loosen it slightly. He was nervous, it was not a look I had seen on him before.

"You asked the question about Katrina Solis and your inability to be compelled," he said.

I piped up a little. I was hoping I would receive some answers from him. He ran his fingers through his hair. I did not realise my action until I had his hand in my own. I shook my head and let it go before putting a smile on my face.

"Is it something serious that I should not know?"

I continued to shop as he walked beside me. "Katrina Solis was a witch. She was the High Priestess of a coven and incredibly powerful; her magic had no limits, and she knew this. She never abused her power, but she did mishandle it. The elements gave her power, particularly the power of the sun. Through this, she created fear in the vampire community, as the magic that sustains vampires comes from various elements. She was able to channel us and control us for her benefit. She was my friend, and she was the only other person I knew who could not be compelled. When I discovered that you were not able to be compelled, I worried that you were the same as her. Our kind knew of her inability to be compelled and saw this as a threat.

Her death should not have happened. That was why I asked if you were related to her. I feared that others may view you as a threat."

At his explanation, I understood that he was protecting me. "That is why you have been so kind to me, isn't it? You want to make sure that I am not harmed."

He nodded and smiled. "I do not wish for history to repeat itself, I..." He moved closer and held his hand up to touch me, but he pulled himself back and turned. I heard him mutter something, but I could not hear exactly what he said. The invisible pull was back, and I had a strong desire to comfort him.

"I am sorry for your loss, Nik."

He turned and smiled at me; it was strange. It wasn't a smile of thanks; it was filled with love and tenderness. I stared into his crystal blue eyes and felt myself almost falling into something that I would not be able to climb out of.

"Thank you, Larissa."

Time seemed to stop in that moment. We stood and stared at one another, not touching, not talking. Just being near each other provided some form of comfort. My phone ringing broke the trance I was in. I picked it up and discovered Olivia on the other end.

"Are you busy?" She sounded stressed and I heard the music thumping behind her.

"I am grocery shopping, why? What is it?"

"I need you. Can you come in?" I could hear her rushing around while on the phone.

I looked at my trolley and bit my lip. "I can, but it will not be for maybe an hour. Can you wait that long?"

She sighed. "I am desperate right now, so I will wait. Just get here as soon as you can." She hung up and Mr. Dankworth looked at me before he glanced at the trolley.

"You will not get there in an hour with that trolley."

I played with my ponytail. I knew he was right, but I had to buy these items, we needed them.

"She is just going to have to wait until I get there."

He put his hand up to stop me from moving towards the counter. "I have a solution, if I may."

I crossed my arms impatiently at him, I did not have time for this.

"I will have my driver take you to work while I organise for your groceries to be delivered to your home." It was generous, and I almost felt like he expected something in return.

"In return for what?"

He smirked, then put a hand on my shoulder and rubbed it but did not bother to respond. I wanted to help Olivia and did not wish to waste any time. I nodded and quickly raced outside to his driver. I wondered what he would ask for in return, his smile was almost devilish.

CHAPTER 22
ROMAN RETURNS

Larissa

I MADE IT TO OLIVIA IN TIME, AND SHE WAS RIGHT. IT WAS AT capacity tonight. I ran behind the bar to help her, not realising until I heard her whistle, and looking down at myself, that I had accidentally grabbed a pair of Luce's shorts. They were shorter than anything I normally wore. I shrugged my shoulders at her.

"Not much I can do to change that now. Did you want my help or not?" She snorted and threw a bottle of scotch at me. We were smashed for hours, but we loved it. I would be exhausted for work tomorrow, but the tips tonight would more than make up for it. That was all I cared about, the extra money. After three hours, the lull finally started and one of the waitresses went home for the night. I scanned the bar, which was still covered in glasses and bottles, so I grabbed a tray and shouted at Olivia, "I am going to do a glass round."

She nodded and turned back to the paying customers. I started at the furthest end of the bar, which happened to be the darkest. You could barely see anything more than silhouettes. It was where the creeps lingered, so they could hide their erections and disgusting behaviour. I learnt very quickly that if I cleaned it earlier in the night, I would not have to go over multiple times for an extra clean. I would only have to return to clean it after they had left. I snuck along the back wall, hoping that I could hide from any unwanted behaviour. I thought I was clear when red glowing eyes appeared from a dark corner.

"You smell sweet. Are you new here?"

I smiled politely and continued to collect the glasses. "No, I have been here for a few months now. Enjoy your night." As I spun around to return to the bar, he appeared before me.

"How do I get you on the menu?" His voice alone gave me the ick. I got a better look at him and noticed that his large, fat nose did nothing for his plump cheeks and small eyes. His hair looked dirty, and it was slicked back off his face.

"Sorry, I am not on the menu, nor will I ever be." I kept my smile to avoid any negative reactions from him. I tried to get Olivia to look this way, in the hope that she would notice and come to help me. She was preoccupied, so I proceeded to scan for someone else to help when I found a pair of eyes already on me. It was Roman. He looked bemused at my situation.

"Can I do anything to change your mind?" He was going to try to compel me. This was bad. Mr. Dankworth warned me of this. My heart began to race, which seemed to excite him further. I moved to step around him, and his hand landed on my waist before it slid to my ass. A deep growl filled the room.

"Let her go."

It took a moment for me to realise that it was Roman. He stood beside me, and the creep stood taller and pushed out his chest.

It did nothing for Roman but make him laugh. "You vampires think you are the ultimate predator, and it is quite comical. This girl right here is mine and I suggest you back off or we take this outside." I opened my mouth to speak. He would be killed in a second and I did not want that on my conscious. He winked at me with a sly smile, so I let it play out. The creep stalked away as Roman took the tray of empty glasses from me and put them on the bar.

"How can I ever repay you, Roman?"

He tapped his chin as a cheeky smile spread over his face; I could not help but smile in return.

"Have dinner with me." He glanced away, almost as if he was worried I would reject him.

I hesitated before finding the courage to answer. "When?"

"Friday night at seven. I will pick you up."

I clicked my tongue. "Done." I wrote down my address for him and handed him the paper.

"Looking forward to it, Larissa." Roman bowed his head and left. Tonight was worth the extra shift in more ways than one.

CHAPTER 23
THE CRACKS GROW DEEPER
Larissa

I woke the next morning in a good mood and pranced around the unit with a smile on my face. Luce was sitting at the kitchen bench eating her cereal.

"Why are you so cheerful this morning?" She sounded bitter as I made my own bowl of porridge.

"I was asked out on a date last night." I heard a spoon clattering against a ceramic bowl, and I spun back to look at her.

"What? When? Who?" She started with the twenty questions. That was one way we were similar as twins, we had to know every bit of information.

"His name is Roman—"

"Wait, the hottie from the bar?" she interrupted excitedly. I nodded as I took a spoonful of cereal, and she squealed with delight.

"How? Details!" Her voice was sitting at a higher pitch than usual.

"I was trying before you cut me off." She rolled her eyes and motioned for me to hurry up. I giggled.

"I was getting hit on by a creep..." I purposely left out the vampire part. Her hatred was worse than my own. "And Roman came to my rescue and went all caveman on him. I asked how I could repay him, and he said, dinner, Friday night. I said yes." The smile on her face disappeared as she stood from her seat, walked over to the sink, and tossed her bowl in.

"Luce, what the hell?"

"Fuck you, Larissa!"

If I could make my jaw hit the floor, it would have in that moment. "Um, what did I do wrong?" I replayed what I said in my head, trying to figure out what I did to make her so angry.

"Did you forget your promise about being with me on Friday? Or have you just become this selfish since you started mingling with those disgusting blood-sucking creatures?"

"Luce, back off. That is not the case. I simply forgot. I apologise, but it is not such a big deal."

"You are pushing me aside for a boy, you don't call that a big deal?"

"Well, you have done that to me for years, no? This is my first and possibly last time to do it, why does it matter? We can go out another night." She threw her hands in the air.

"That is not the point. You put someone else above me, how could you do that when you know I have been struggling?" I rolled my eyes at the stupidity of her argument.

"All you have spoken about is how you are struggling. I have been picking up the slack and helping you however I can, but have you asked me how I am doing? No, because it is always the Luce show. For once, just one time, I thought about myself. Just once, I have a date with someone who my sister hasn't fucked. I apologise that I was swept up in the moment. We can make it next weekend. Sorry Luce, but I need this."

She stormed from the room, finished with this conversation. I stood there, frozen in disbelief, before collapsing onto the couch. I needed to try to bring my adrenaline levels back down, as I noticed my shaking hands. The tingle in my arms grew, so I closed my eyes to calm myself back down. Luce slammed the apartment door as she left. I grabbed my medication from the drawers in my room, my anxiety was getting worse with all these arguments. I took my time getting ready and messaged Andrew that I would be late. I did not care today. I needed time to process.

CHAPTER 24
DINNER DATE

Larissa

THE WEEK PASSED QUICKLY WITH LUCE STILL NOT SPEAKING TO me. I was so nervous about my date with Roman, though, that I hardly had time to think about Luce and her drama. I had been on dates, but I wasn't the best at them. I was always a nervous wreck. I blabbered, fumbled, and said the wrong things. It was a disaster story, like a bad reality show. I smoothed out my green wrap dress that emphasised my slim waist while enhancing my breasts. The sleeves came down to my elbow, which gave me a little warmth, as the night would be cool. I searched for a pair of shoes in my wardrobe and found a nude pair of sandals. I slid my feet in as the doorbell rang.

"I'll get it," Luce called out, and I ran to stop her. She was still annoyed that I had ditched her for a date. She made that well known when I told her. I got to the door in time to see her glaring at Roman and scoffing. "You picked him over me? Enjoy. He looks super boring."

I wanted to hide already as I watched her walk away,

"Lovely to meet you, Luce," Roman called out politely. I mouthed a quick sorry, but he smiled and waved it off. I had the chance to take him in now. His jeans were baggy, as I believed they should be. Men in skinny jeans were unattractive to me. He paired it with a black shirt that showed off his broad shoulders and his rather large biceps. It looked as if it would rip at the seams. He was so out of my league, but if I got one date, I would be happy. He offered his arm with a smirk, like he knew I was checking him out.

"Are you ready?" he asked. I held my finger up in a quick *one moment* gesture as I ran back to my room and grabbed my nude clutch and gold hoops to put in my ears. I closed the door behind me with a little force to show my annoyance at Luce.

"You were not lying, she is..." He paused to find the right word.

"Unique?" I cut in and he chuckled.

"Yes, that is one word I would use to describe her...although she is not as unique as you." I paused and looked at him curiously, his face flushed with embarrassment. "I was...I mean...you are." He stammered before I started to laugh. We were more alike than I thought.

"You're laughing at me." He was mortified at my reaction, but I put my hand on his arm to reassure him.

"Sorry Roman, I am only laughing because normally I am the one to fumble and cannot talk on dates, but you do as well! I was so nervous all week, I chewed my nail so far down that I made it bleed. But all my anxieties were wrong because you are just as much of a dork as me."

A big smile spread over his face, and he put his arm around my shoulder and pulled me in close. He kissed the top of my head. "It shall make for an interesting night."

"Indeed!" Nobody would be able to wipe the smile from my face. Maybe I had found my match, finally.

He grinned from ear to ear. Roman opened the car door for me. He was driving some fancy BMW with red leather seats; I did not bother to see what model. He closed the door behind me, did a little jog around to his side of the car, and slid in. I could not believe he fit in the car, he was so broad and tall, but it did not look uncomfortable for him. I put my hands in my lap, nerves were creeping into my belly. I was essentially in a car with a stranger. I had no idea who he was or where we were going. He reached over and squeezed my hand.

"We will be at the restaurant shortly. Why don't you tell me about your work?" It was obvious that he was trying to alleviate my worries and it worked, if only slightly. I smiled at him and my shoulders relaxed a little.

"I work for Refresh Marketing. I have only been there for a couple of months. I work as a personal assistant for the head manager, essentially. I applied for another position, but as I have no experience in marketing, I was offered this with a promise that I would have the opportunity to get another position in the future."

"Has that happened?" He sounded curious as he shuffled in his seat.

"The big boss, Mr. Dankworth, has allowed me to create a marketing plan for a new organisation app. I suppose I will let you know how it goes."

"Mr. Nik Dankworth?" he questioned; his voice had a hint of curiosity.

"Yes." I eyed him suspiciously, but he gave nothing away.

He cleared his throat. "Sounds like a wonderful opportunity."

It was almost like he wanted to change the topic, but as I still barely knew Roman, I decided not to press it further. He pulled up at the restaurant, which I found I was a little disappointed at. I thought, not even sure why, that it would have been a little fancier. Not that I had expected to be spoilt in that manner, but I just assumed I would be. I pushed those thoughts aside and got out of the car as Roman offered his hand. I hesitated as I looked at it, his large burly hand had blisters and tiny cuts. I slid mine into it; it was warm to touch. We walked into the restaurant and I peered around to take in the décor. A few female waitresses stared at Roman before glaring in my general direction. There was no denying he was attractive, but their reaction seemed excessive. A skinny man ran over with red hair and freckles galore. His name badge revealed his name, Frank.

"Roman, you made it and I see you brought Larissa."

Roman turned his head and I noticed a touch of pink on his cheeks. He was embarrassed that his little crush had been revealed. He cleared his throat. "Yes, is our table available?"

Frank led us towards the back of the restaurant. He opened a blacked-out glass door, through which Roman let me enter first. I noticed the small table with rose petals and a candle, with an aroma of roses that invaded my senses. I turned to Roman, who leant against the door frame and made it seem almost impossibly small against him.

My hands landed on my cheeks in disbelief. "Wow, this is beyond amazing. I cannot believe you did this for me. You barely know me."

"A lady such as yourself deserves only the best." He sounded so formal and proper, as if he did not belong in this time.

"I assure you; I am no lady, but I will happily accept this for a date."

Roman pulled my chair out and I sat down before he took his seat opposite me. We smiled at each other awkwardly before the waiter emerged with a bottle of red wine. He poured it without saying a word, the silence was painful in the room.

Roman picked up the glass. "To new adventures!" A glimmer of hope danced in his eyes as he spoke.

I raised my own and clinked his glass. "To new adventures!" I tried to match his energy.

We each took a sip. The wine had a strong cherry flavour with hints of something else that I could not place. Roman put his glass down and I noticed that there were not any menus on the table.

"Ah, Roman, how do we order food without any menus?" I turned to glance around the room for them.

He snickered at my remark. "The chef will bring out four courses for us tonight."

"That was a brave choice. How do you know I have no allergies or intolerances to food?"

He leant forward as the candlelight brought out more features in his handsome face. The green in his hazel eyes was brighter than I had realised, it was breathtaking. His olive skin had a softness to it that I had never noticed in the darkness of the bar and there was a small scar above his right eye that cut into his eyebrow.

"I can read people rather well." He winked at me before he leant back. "Tell me about your life growing up."

———

The night flowed smoothly, there was a familiarity, like I had known him my whole life. I had to know if he felt the same.

"Have you ever met someone and felt like you knew them already?"

He smiled and finished his wine. "Yes, like in a past life?"

"Exactly. I feel like I have known you my whole life, but I cannot explain it." He reached over the table and grabbed my hand.

"I feel the same way." The warmth of his touch was comforting as the dessert arrived. It was a selection of sweet cakes.

Roman pushed the plate towards me. "Please, take your pick."

I chose the strawberry cheesecake and scooped some of it into my mouth. "Oh my god, this is heavenly," I moaned. He reached over to try some himself, but I pulled the plate away. "Nope," I said cheekily, which made the room fill with laughter.

"If you do not wish to share, do not moan in that way."

I licked my lips, which seemed to only tempt Roman further. His face darkened with desire as he gripped the table tightly.

"You seem to be struggling a little." I could not stop the grin growing on my face.

"I do not wish to scare you. I am holding myself back."

I stood and began to move slowly in his direction. I ran my hand along the table before turning his chair. He leant back, and I did not know what came over me as I straddled him and put my arms around his neck.

"Now, is this more relaxing?"

His hands ran up my back. "Oh, it certainly could be more

relaxing, if I could taste that strawberry cheesecake." His eyes focused on my lips.

I leant forward and planted my lips on his. He held me tighter as he licked my lips and slid his tongue into my mouth. He groaned before he pulled back. "You are right, it is heavenly," he whispered as he licked his lips. He moved to kiss me again.

"Oh, sorry for the interruption." Frank walked in and I turned my face away to hide my embarrassment over straddling a man in public. Frank collected the plates before leaving with his own red face.

Roman moved his hand to my face to turn it back.

"Why do you hide your beauty?" he asked as he brought me back to meet his eyes.

"I was a little embarrassed that I…" I could not bring myself to finish my sentence as I stood from his lap and sat back down in my seat. I was astounded with my actions. This was not me. I was not this person.

"What is it?" I had not noticed that Roman was kneeling beside me, his voice was so soft and tender.

"Roman, I am not this person. I do not do this, I never have. I am a virgin. I have never been with anyone." He turned my chair as if it weighed nothing and took my hands, placing a gentle kiss on each one. He could melt butter, he was so sweet.

"I do not have any expectations for tonight. I am a patient man, Larissa." His words were so kind as he reached up and kissed my forehead.

"Thank you, Roman."

"I only have one question." I looked at him curiously wondering what he could possibly ask.

"May I have another date? I wish to see you again."

I chuckled and planted a soft kiss on his lips.

"Yes, I would like that."

"Come, I shall take you home." He stood, and I took the hand he offered.

CHAPTER 25
TIME TO MOVE OUT

Larissa

I HAD THE CHEESIEST SMILE ON MY FACE AS I WALKED INTO THE apartment. Luce had waited up and she was sitting on the couch, watching television.

"You are home later than I thought you would be," she commented. I nodded at her as I put my clutch on our entry table.

"What are you watching?" I asked, trying to make conversation as I sat down on the couch beside her. She was watching some ridiculous reality television show.

"So, did you fuck him? I bet you did, you are so desperate for a fuck," she asked with venom in her voice. I turned to stare at her in horror.

"Luce, what the hell is wrong with you?"

She scoffed and pretended to watch television rather than keep her eyes on me. "What is wrong with me? I am not the desperate one who gave our address to a vampire and went on a date with a stranger."

"Wait a minute, so you can go on dates with random men and bring them back to our apartment, but I can't? Can you see the hypocrisy in that?"

"Oh, that's right, pick on Luce because she is a free spirit. She likes to fuck; she likes to see randoms. Real nice, Larissa."

I shook my head as I noticed the empty bottle of wine on the table beside the couch.

"I am not doing this with you while you are drunk. Goodnight Luce." I stood and walked to my room as a glass flew past my head and smashed on the wall next to me.

"Fuck you, Larissa! I hate you! You ruin everything!" she screamed as I turned to look at her. The prickle in my arms started as my anger rose.

"Luce, you are drunk. Go to bed." I struggled to keep my voice level.

"I want you out of here. I want my own apartment without your judgements on who I bring home." Her eyes were crazed, she was beyond intoxicated. I doubt she would remember the conversation in the morning.

"I do not judge who you bring home. I do not care. If this is about Peter, I suggest you stop now."

"Oh, should I be scared of you?" She waved her arms in the air.

"Just stop, Luce." My attempts to keep my cool were slowly vanishing. I wanted to punch her so hard.

"No, it is always about you. Every guy wants you, they never want me, and I am judged all the time for it."

"Oh, shut up. How does every guy want me when I am still a virgin? Listen to yourself and just stop. You are picking a fight over nothing."

"No, I am not. I have never thought more about it. I want you out. Find a new apartment. I am done placating you and living with a perfect fucking princess."

"I was already looking, but fine. Clean your shit up because I am not." I slammed the bedroom door closed. The tingling in my arms was getting worse as I breathed to calm myself down. It was not working. I heard my phone ring, and spun to see who it was and answered it.

"Mr. Dankworth, what can I help you with?" I asked, trying to keep my voice calm and normal.

"What is it, Larissa?" he asked. I heard the concern in his voice.

"Nothing, just…" I wanted to tell him. I knew he would listen. His voice purred down the phone as the tingling sensations died down. "I fought with my sister, it is not important. Just sibling stuff. What can I help you with?" I wanted to keep the conversation professional.

"I would like you to attend the dinner on Tuesday for the TimeShaft app. They would like to hear the proposal in person from the creator of the marketing campaign."

"Oh, sure. Sounds great. Where is it taking place? I will need to buy appropriate clothing for the night."

His throat cleared down the phone. "I will send you something appropriate. Enjoy your weekend, Larissa." I half wished that he would stay on the phone. I wanted to talk more. His voice had a calming effect on my anger.

"Mr. Dankworth, I…thank you." It was quiet on the other end of the line. Neither of us spoke, but he had yet to hang up.

"Larissa, do you want to discuss anything further?"

"I just…" I could not bring myself to say it. I wanted to tell him about Luce. I wanted him to comfort me, but I chickened out. "Enjoy your weekend, Mr. Dankworth."

"Sweet dreams, Larissa." The tingling sensation was gone. I did not understand the effect that man had on me.

155

CHAPTER 26
PANCAKES WITH EXTRA SYRUP

Larissa

I woke the next morning and, before Luce woke up, snuck out of the apartment for my morning run. I went further than I ever had before, and as I rounded a corner, I ran straight into a solid mass. I failed to get my footing and proceeded to fall, but an arm snaked around my waist and pulled me back into a solid chest. My heart raced as I noticed the tingling sensation in my body and the familiar scent.

I looked up to see Mr. Dankworth staring down at me with those hypnotic blue eyes. He let me go as he cupped my face, his brow creased. "Are you hurt?"

The concern was heartwarming, and I nodded, unable to form a sentence. I glanced down at his clothes, his sports singlet was covered in sweat and clung to his body. It showed the outline of his abs. I pushed away the dirty thoughts that started to race through my mind.

"Do you run? Why? You have, like, super speed, do you not?"

He chuckled and stood back as he put his hands on his hips. "Yes, that is correct, but even we can run out of breath. I like to keep myself in shape."

I could not take my eyes off the outline of his body. "Yes, you certainly do," I murmured, as I raised my eyebrows before realising I had said that out loud. My hands covered my mouth. My face flushed as I looked away. "I am just going to keep on running now, bye." I waved awkwardly and proceeded to run away from my embarrassment.

I did not look back to see if he followed, but it did not take long before he appeared in front of me and almost tripped me over again. He laughed as he changed his stance as if he needed to catch me again.

"May I join you?" he asked.

"I am not sure I could keep up with your pace," I quipped back.

"I can run slower, Larissa, if the company is worth it." His smile was sly as he glanced at the ground before peering up at me. His eyes sparkled with hope. I smiled and ran past him with a playful nudge. He chuckled and caught up to me. We ran for a couple of kilometres before I stopped for a bottle of water at a café.

"Do you want anything?" I panted, but he shook his head.

"I had my sustenance before I left." He came inside with me as I bought a bottle and finished it in one gulp. I noticed his hand remained close behind me as we walked. "Larissa, am I correct in my assumption that last night, you wanted to speak further?"

I chucked my bottle in the bin and observed the stern look on his face. "Yes, I did, but I remembered that you are my boss, and it would not be appropriate. We are not friends." He moved closer and extended his hand. I giggled awkwardly. "What are you doing?"

"Take my hand." I paused before sliding my hand into his, the touch of his hand on mine was electrifying.

"I am Nik, just Nik when you need a friend. I will be Nik after the hours of five thirty on weeknights and anytime on the weekend." I rolled my eyes at his clarification on timing.

"Larissa." He bowed his head. "It is my absolute pleasure to be a friend of yours. Now, what seems to be the issue?"

I sighed as we started to walk together, he made everything seem easy. "I had a fight with my sister, and she wants me to move out. Which I was already planning, but I have not had much luck with finding somewhere nice. I mean, I know my standards are a little high and I should not be so picky, but I just want somewhere that looks clean and not like I am going to die once I step inside." He laughed, which filled my body with delight.

"If I may, I know an agent who owes me a favour. If you text me the location and your price range, I can get her to find some places for you." I felt lighter already as I threw my arms around him and pulled him in close.

"Thank you, thank you so much. I really appreciate that." He pulled his arms out and wrapped them around me. Being around him was like settling into a familiar place, where comfort and ease surrounded me effortlessly.

"What was the fight over?" he asked as I heard him subtly sniff my hair.

I groaned. "Stupid, that is what it was. She called me a whore because I went on a date last night. I think she confused me with her. I mean, I am sure you can probably already guess or smell, rather, that I have never been with a man before. It hurt me…" My voice broke off. I did not cry last night, but here with him right now, I was. I wiped my face to hide the emotions that were spilling out of me.

He let me go, taking a step back to look at my face. "Oh Larissa, do not hide your tears. Hiding them does not show strength. Showing them to the world does. Your sister is jealous. It is the oldest story. She wishes she had your beauty and strength to keep yourself for the right person. I assume she has been with a few men."

I nodded and sighed. "I need to keep running, it clears my head."

"Now, you are running from your problems instead of facing them?" He scratched his chin and turned his attention to the café beside us. "Join me for breakfast, so we can continue to discuss solutions to your growing list of problems." His eyes searched mine with an urgent plea. A nagging sense of unease filled my body that this was wrong, but my heart screamed yes.

"Fine."

He opened the door to the café and we took a seat. The café had a modern vibe, its sleek design blended industrial chic with cozy comfort. The polished concrete floors stretched beneath the exposed ductwork, with pendant lights to detract from the sheer size. The lights cast a glow over the wooden tables and chairs. A waitress walked over, and she kept her eyes trained on Nik. "What can I get you, handsome?"

I smiled at the obvious flick of her caramel hair in a flirty manner and the fact that he seemed oblivious to it.

"A large bloodcino and a large cappuccino with extra froth and chocolate powder for my beautiful date."

I smirked over him remembering my coffee order, while disregarding his other comment. It was obviously his way to deter the waitress from hitting on him.

"Do I want to know how you still remember my coffee?"

He leant forward. "I must confess, Larissa, I stalked you and I have an entire folder on you that I study every night."

I burst out laughing at him, as I threw a sugar packet at him. "You are a dork," I said, shaking my head at his ridiculous comment.

He winked and leant back in his chair. As I picked up the menu and flicked through it, I noticed him smiling as he watched me. "If you are so smart, thinking you know what I want, I dare you to order for me."

He took the menu from my hands and read through it before a grin covered his perfect face.

"The pancakes with extra syrup. You have a sweet tooth." The waitress came over with our coffees as she stared at Nik again and ignored me.

"Are you ready to order?" Her husky voice sounded annoyed that I was with this man.

"Yes, we shall take a pancake with extra syrup and the blood pancake." He handed her the menus but kept his blue eyes trained on me.

———

It did not take long for the food to come out as we spoke about everything, or rather, he allowed me to speak about everything that had happened between Luce and me.

"The worst part is the fact that you dropped off the groceries the other day. I told you I was raised to hate your kind. I work with a lot of vampires now and my hate has simmered a little, but it does not change the fact that you still rule our world and take what you wish. She views your kind as pretty much worse than serial killers and rapists. Trust me, I know it does not make sense, but it was what our mother instilled in us."

"Yes, Elizabeth, wasn't it?" He did not show any emotion towards my remarks, he kept his face neutral. I wondered if he did that to show he was listening or to hide how he truly felt.

"Yes, my mother was Elizabeth, why is that relevant?" I tilted my head at his question about my mother.

"I only queried as I wondered if I had had any interactions with her but if I did, it was not memorable."

I smirked at his slight swipe at her. She was dead so it did not matter, and I already knew my mother was not the most reasonable person in the world.

"No, but Luce looks exactly like her." I pulled out my phone and showed him a photo, at which he scratched his chin.

"How are you twins and yet you are not evenly remotely similar in looks? I understand that it can be the case, but it is more like you are cousins than sisters. Did you ever question it?"

"Always. I questioned it for years growing up, but my mother dismissed it. I stopped asking in the end, as Luce and I shared similar traits in other ways. We are both competitive, we are both headstrong, stubborn and plenty more." He laughed as I held up my fork with food on it. "I know why you are laughing and stop it." It only made him laugh more, a light, melodious sound. Other people were drawn to it, as I watched all eyes fall on us.

"Stubborn to the core even with pancake in her mouth," he mused. I stuffed my face and smiled at him with a mouth full of food. "How does one as beautiful as you act so childishly and still be so...amazing?"

"Nik, can we remember that you are my boss? I appreciate the compliments, but this would never work." I avoided meeting his eyes as I cut into another piece of my pancake.

"Why?" He sounded agitated but I only spoke the truth.

"Again, you are my boss. I will not jeopardise my career."

He leant back in his chair. "We shall discuss this at another time, but I do not want you to rule this relationship out." That was the end of the conversation as he changed the subject, which was lucky when his phone rang. While he took the call, I got up and paid for breakfast. I reached the table and sat back down as he finished his phone call.

"You did not pay for breakfast." He was angry, as evident by the lines on his forehead and the intensity in his eyes.

"Yes, I did." I winked at him showing my cheek.

"Larissa, I am old-fashioned. I asked you to breakfast, ergo I must pay."

I put my elbows on the table and held my face in my hands. "Nik, it is the twenty-first century, ergo get over it." A small growl escaped his lips. "Thank you for the company but I had better get home and return to my unsuccessful searching."

He looked at his smart watch as his brow creased. "Hmm, you will not get home for a while. Allow me to organise a driver for you."

"I just ate breakfast; I need to work off the extra syrup you ordered for me."

He laughed as his eyes sparkled further. "Only if you allow me to run with you."

"Oh, so you want to get beaten by a girl?"

"I never mind if a girl ends up on top." My body tingled with excitement as I bit my lip. There was no point arguing as I raced from the table to the street. I heard his laughter as he caught up to me in no time at all.

CHAPTER 27
APARTMENT HUNTING

Larissa

Nik ran all the way home with me before he sped away in a blur. I snuck into the apartment, and stayed in my room, searching for an apartment to call my own. I decided to change my expectations after my discussion with Nik. I should just try to find something within my price range, anything to get me out of here. I searched for hours before I passed out from exhaustion. My ringing phone woke me up. Bleary-eyed, I searched around for it and answered without looking.

"Hello." My voice was croaky. I cleared it and rubbed my eyes.

"Were you sleeping?" His soft voice floated through the phone.

"Mr. Dankworth." I shot up instantly.

"Forgive me for waking you, princess," he said. His voice did not indicate that he was mocking me, but it felt like he was. I waited for him to continue as there was silence down the phone. "I am out the front," he continued.

I got up and raced to my window. He stood leaning against his car in a pair of black slacks and a blue knitted jumper. It was the first time I had seen him so casual; he looked up and saw me. I could not help but smile as he did the same.

"What are you doing here?"

He pushed himself off the car and moved closer. "You asked for help to find an apartment. I have spoken with my agent, and she has found five suitable apartments. She has agreed—"

I interrupted him, expressing my disapproval. "Agreed or was forced?"

"She agreed, Larissa. She will be meeting us in just under half an hour. Get yourself dressed."

"I am dressed, thank you."

He chuckled down the phone. "You are still in your running attire. It is best that you get changed into something more appropriate."

I scoffed at him and backed away from the window. "Using your enhanced eyesight is just cheating. I will be ready in ten minutes. Could you do me one favour?" I hated having to ask this, but I knew if Luce caught sight of him, it would only cause us to fight further. I moved back to the window and saw that Mr. Dankworth and his car had already moved away. I smiled knowing that he knew exactly what I was about to ask of him.

"What is it?" His deep voice asked through the phone.

"Nothing, I will be down soon enough." I hung up the phone and looked in the mirror. My hair was all over the place, my eyes were still puffy from sleep. "Fuck," I swore as I went rummaging through my wardrobe. I found a pair of skinny-leg jeans that I paired with a green blouse. I ran my fingers through my hair, plaited it off my face, and let the rest of it flow down my back. I applied mascara to my lashes and smudged a little on my top eyelid. Excitement thrummed in my body, the idea of shopping for an apartment and spending time with Nik, which was wrong, but I could not help myself. I opened the door to find Luce waiting.

"Where are you going?" she asked as she crossed her arms.

"I am looking at a few apartments, if you do not mind. You asked for me to be gone. Excuse me." I pushed past her and ran down the stairs. I left the apartment complex and saw his car further up the road as I strolled up to it and into the back seat.

"Good afternoon, Mr. Monroe," I said politely as my body erupted with tingles from being near Mr. Dankworth. I dared to glance in his direction as he smirked.

"What is with that look?" I asked as I turned towards him.

"Seatbelt." I rolled my eyes and clasped it around me as his phone rang, and he answered it. I pulled out my own and texted James to see if he wanted a guest tonight on his couch. He was always happy for me to come over. He agreed instantly.

"What are you smiling at?" Mr. Dankworth asked as he put his phone away.

"I am just organising to stay on a friend's couch tonight. I feel the need to be away from Luce right now. She questioned where I was going before I left. She makes me so angry that I scare myself. I just want to—" I cut myself off, feeling my anger grow as my hands burned. I clenched my fists and shook my head as the tingles began. I barely registered him until his arms wrapped around me and he pulled me close, his lips pressed to my forehead.

"Sei al sicuro, amore mio. (You're safe, my love)" His voice was soft and calm as my anger dissipated.

"What did you say?" I asked as I snuggled further into his arms, a calmness settled over my body. He did not answer, but I repeated the phrase in my head, in hopes of remembering for later.

"Mr. Dankworth, how old are you?" I dared not look at him as I held him tighter.

"Is it not rude to ask someone their age?" His voice was muffled as he spoke into my hair.

I chuckled. "It is only rude if you ask a lady her age, which I believe you already know from stalking me, remember?" He snorted but still did not let me go.

"I am older than your saviour, Jesus."

"Whoa, so how old? I am intrigued. Where were you born?" I asked with burning curiosity.

"I suppose what you would call Rome today." He cleared his throat.

"That still does not tell me your age."

"I was alive during the time of the Ancient Romans." I pushed myself away from him. I had to see his face as I asked my next question. I loved learning about ancient history in school.

"Wait, like Romulus and Remus time? Or after that?" My voice came out louder due to my joy at this topic.

"Around that time." I had always loved the stories of the beginning of Rome and how the brothers fought, and how Romulus killed his brother for power. My brain exploded with questions and excitement.

"Wow, did you wear togas?"

He cleared his throat, his face remaining neutral. "Yes, it was the clothing of the time," he added softly. I looked him over in his casual clothing and shook my head.

"I cannot picture it. Wait, vampires are that old? There were always stories in various parts of history but, even back then? Do they date back to the start or—?"

"We are here, sir," Mr. Monroe interrupted. It was almost like he wanted to stop the conversation. Mr. Dankworth moved away and opened the door, exiting the vehicle quickly. I watched as he straightened himself and cracked his neck before he turned back and offered his hand.

———

The real estate agent stared at me as I walked over with Mr. Dankworth, her eyes wandered from my feet to my head and back again. Her black pant suit showed off her tiny figure and her black hair was pulled into a bun.

"Forgive me, Aurora, I did not mean to stare. I did not know—" Mr. Dankworth cut her off with a growl.

"This is Larissa," he said firmly. "Larissa, this is Sophia."

I took her hand and shook it. "What did you not know?" I questioned, wanting her to finish her sentence.

"Pardon?" she asked while raising her brow.

"You said, 'I did not know'. What was that about? I mean you called me another name; you could at least finish the rest of your sentence."

She smiled at me as if she knew something and Mr. Dankworth avoided looking in my direction. I was missing something.

"Shall I show you inside?" Sophia walked backward with eagerness.

"Please," he answered as he walked before me with the agent.

They spoke in hushed tones, and Sophia hung her head as if she was being scolded by him.

"How long have you guys known one another?" I asked, interrupting them.

Mr. Dankworth seemed frustrated and spun towards me. "What is with the questions today?"

"Am I not allowed to be curious, Mr. Dankworth?" If he wanted to be this way, I would be just as cold.

"I thought we discussed that in moments like these," he said, "I would be Nik."

"I would call you Nik if you were not so cryptic and cold," I added while maintaining my anger at the secrets that continued to pile up.

"Fine." He threw his hands up. "I shall wait outside," he grumbled as he stormed out. I reached for him and grabbed his arm. I did not understand my reaction. It made it so difficult to put distance between us.

"Wait." I closed my eyes and let him go again.

He stopped and waited. "What do you want, Larissa?" His voice sounded broken and filled with confusion.

"Stay," I whispered so softly that I was not sure if I even spoke. He crossed his arms and leant against the wall. There was a coldness to him that I had only seen before we met. I had hurt him in a way that I did not understand. Sophia showed me around the apartment, which was nice, but it did not feel like home.

I got in the car, ready to be taken to the next apartment, and turned to him. "What did I do wrong?" I asked him, I had to know why he seemed so upset.

He thumped his hand on the side of the car, his eyes flashed red before turning back to crystal blue.

"Nothing, you did nothing wrong. I expect too much."

"In what way?" I asked gently.

He turned towards me. "Nothing Larissa, just forget it."

"Well, I am sorry for whatever I did wrong," I apologised. I needed him to know that I was sorry.

His rumbles filled the car, but I was not scared of them or him. "Stop the car," he demanded suddenly. Mr. Monroe slammed on the brakes and pulled over. Nik got out of the car.

"Take Miss Solis to the next apartment. I need some air." He slammed the door closed and disappeared as Mr. Monroe did as he was ordered. I sank back into the seat confused about what had just happened.

"Mr. Monroe, may I ask you a question?" I sat up, looking at him in the rearview mirror.

"Yes, Miss Solis," he spoke politely, his face remained stoic as he watched the road ahead.

"What did I do wrong? I am confused…it was all fine until I called him Mr. Dankworth, then he just snapped into a different person. Am I wrong? He *is* older than me…did I insult him?"

He sighed and glanced in the mirror as he pulled over. "I cannot answer that question, I am sorry Miss Solis, but it is best if you speak to him," he answered, but it did not help the situation.

The car door opened as Nik offered his arm. He had obviously run the rest of the way.

"Larissa." He sighed and ran his hands over his face. "I was hopeful that today you would see me as more than just your boss. I organised this as a friend, not your boss, and I hoped we could view these apartments as more than just boss and employee. I want *this* between us. I did from the moment you threw coffee at me. You take my breath away; you challenge me when all others submit. You give me something I have not had in centuries, hope." He grabbed my hand and brought it to his lips.

"Nik, I…" I trailed off, genuinely not knowing what to say to his declaration.

His eyes focused solely on my face and mouth. "Just focus on the apartments for today, but please do not treat me as your boss. I believe I have earned the right to be more than that." He was right, he had. Nik had been nothing but helpful. I had my doubts because of who he was, or rather what he was.

"I will, I promise." The sadness on his face seemed to disappear as he looked hopeful. Sophia drove up behind us and got out of the car. I observed the exterior of the building, noting that it looked old and run down.

"Do not judge it on the exterior, that will be fixed within the month. Wait until you see inside," he assured me, his voice filled with enthusiasm.

"Sophia, do you have a picture of what it will look like for Larissa?" Nik asked as he stayed beside me, but slightly behind, in a way of showing that today was all about me and he was just here to help.

"I shall show you inside." She waved us in as she entered the code, and we walked to the elevator. She pressed the button for the fourth floor. I never liked elevators, much less being in them with others. I closed my eyes to make it go faster. I opened them to find Nik before me. I was pinned against the wall.

"What are you doing?" I asked as I struggled against him.

"Shh," he whispered before pressing his lips against mine. I melted at his touch; his hand ran down my body until he lifted my legs and wrapped them around him.

"Nik," I whispered as he undid his pants, he pushed my underwear aside—

"Larissa!" Nik raised his voice, causing my eyes to snap open. I was still in the elevator. "Are you alright?" he asked as he touched my face. I knew he could smell how wet I was.

"I am fine," I said hastily, as I took my leave from the elevator as quickly as possible. He smirked as I glanced back at him. He knew. I could die from embarrassment. Sophia opened the door and let me enter first; I instantly loved the ceilings with exposed, thick wooden beams that contrasted against the white.

"We are on the top floor, which is why the ceiling is higher than normal. New flooring, new paint and new cabinetry throughout." The oak herringbone flooring was breathtaking, it brought light into the apartment with the one tiny window to look outside. The kitchen was bigger than I could have expected with an island bench and a back bench. There was plenty of room to move around.

I noticed Nik enter the space and my mind raced. I thought about him pushing me onto the bench and fucking me; I shook it off. My body tingled all over. I was craving his touch. As if he read my mind, he appeared beside me. My body relaxed from his proximity as I ventured throughout the apartment.

"It is a two-bedroom?" I asked as I had specifically requested one.

"Yes, but Nik said that you work in marketing, so I thought with the light in this room, you could set this up as a study. Or you could even have a roommate if you wanted help to cover the costs."

I turned to look at Nik and smiled as I mouthed, "Thank you." He bowed his head at me.

I looked at Sophia's pictures of the exterior; it would look heritage, with a touch of modern. It was beautiful and exactly what I wanted.

"What is the price?" I asked hesitantly, as I believed it would be out of my price range.

"I spoke with the vendor, and he was happy to negotiate to pay the higher end of your price range."

I eyed her curiously. "At what cost?"

"Nothing. He is generous. Nik told me about the death of your mother and how you are having difficulty with your current roommate," she said with a tone of understanding.

I lowered my head in thought, before smiling back at her and asking, "He wants the typical bond?" She nodded. I still wanted something a little cheaper to save more and not have to work two jobs.

She must have noticed my hesitancy, because she asked suddenly, "Shall we look at the next?" before moving towards the exit. I stared out the window; this place was perfect. It was *me* and it even felt like home.

"Sophia, wait!" Nik called out, but his eyes were trained on me. Sophia stopped and waited as Nik walked over to me.

"Larissa, if this dinner goes well on Tuesday, you will receive a promotion and oversee their account. Your salary will increase. You deserve this. I saw your face when you entered, you can picture your life here. Take it."

"Nik, if I do, I will not have money to move or buy furniture. The bond amount will wipe me out and I do not want to touch the café money."

"I will loan you the money…" I glared up at him. "As a friend. No interest and we can negotiate a repayment amount that makes it easy for you." Hope welled in my chest as I scanned my surroundings.

"Stop thinking you deserve less than. Take it, Larissa." Sophia listened in on the conversation, waiting for my answer.

"Can I have a few minutes alone to think about it?" He kissed the top of my forehead and moved over to Sophia.

I walked over to the kitchen again and pictured what the living space would look like. I preferred to eat at the counter than to use more space for a kitchen table. I could not help but smile at the idea of coming home to this place every day.

"When would I be able to move in?" I asked Sophia.

"Whenever you have paid the bond."

Nik's hand was suddenly on my lower back, I could almost feel his words in my head telling me to take it.

"I will take it," I said proudly, overjoyed that I had finally found somewhere to live after looking for so long.

Sophia handed me the paperwork and I filled it in. I had never been more excited. I wanted to tell Luce, but at the same time, I wanted to keep it a secret for a little while longer.

"When do you wish to move in?" she asked as she checked it over and signed where she needed to. I leant closer to Nik's body; his touch was comforting as I took this next step in my life.

"Whenever you think you are ready," Nik stated, which made me feel braver.

"Is next weekend too early?" I asked, a smile filling my face.

Nik laughed as he walked to the other side of the bench to see my face before he turned to look out at the space.

"No, but if you desire furniture, we will have to spend a little more time together during the week to order it and get it delivered." He was right, but the idea of going furniture shopping with him did not scare me. I was almost eager for that experience. There was a strange pull to walk over to him, but I wasn't ready for that yet. He had made his intentions known, but I needed to sort out what I wanted first.

Chapter 28

HE IS BACK

Larissa

Nik dropped me around the corner so I could walk in without Luce seeing who I had been with for the last couple of hours. I unlocked the door to find Peter standing in our apartment. I shivered with disgust at seeing him. He had on a tank top and jeans but still looked like a bum. Luce was on the couch in only a top and her underwear. It was obvious she had called him for a booty call.

"Where have you been?" Peter asked, his eyes creeping over my body. I had an intense urge to vomit at the way he seemed to undress me with his gaze.

"I believe it is a place called none of your business." Luce laughed at my remark, which I was a little shocked at. I did not expect that of her.

"How did you go?" she asked. It seemed like she actually cared.

"I found one. I will be moving out next week."

Her face sank like she did not want me to go. I think we needed it; we were in each other's faces all the time. The space would heal our wounds, at least I hoped, and it would stop the never-ending arguments and the unconscious competition between us.

"Who did you fuck to get that?" Peter scowled as he sat down beside Luce putting his hand on her inner thigh and squeezing it.

"Oh, the whole village because I am such a whore. Enjoy your night." I walked into my room. I was glad that Luce and I moved out of our first apartment, and I no longer slept on a sofa bed in the living room. At least I had my own space here, but I could not wait for my own apartment to design and enjoy without any unwanted visitors. My mind drifted, thinking of dinners with Nik. I closed my eyes to focus on packing my bag to head across the street to James's apartment. Luce knocked on my door and walked inside.

"Hey," she said softly as she sat on the bed. "Rissa, I don't want you to go. I said things out of anger, and I didn't mean them. Would you stay?"

I moved to sit beside her and grabbed her hand. "I think it is better for us to have a little more space. We have spent our whole lives attached to one another. I need time to find my feet. We are still sisters, and we shall still see each other, just not every morning and every night."

She leant her head on my shoulder. "I am sorry." Her voice was barely a whisper.

"As am I, but it is behind us." Her eyes searched my face as if she did not expect me to say that.

"Where are you going?" she asked with a soft voice, she sounded sad.

"I am staying with James for the night, especially now with Peter here. I am happy if you are, but do not force a relationship between us. I beg of you."

She laughed. "I just needed a fuck. He will be gone by tomorrow morning."

I rolled my eyes. "Well, I hope he is good in bed because his attitude sucks."

"I know, trust me I know. He is good albeit a little selfish sometimes."

My thoughts wandered to Nik. In all my dreams, he had never been selfish. The sight of him on his knees only excited me. I wondered if he was generous in bed. He had been alive long enough that he would have plenty of experience in the bedroom. He probably helped write the Karma Sutra, he was that old. I needed to stop thinking about him. I hugged Luce and kissed her head.

"Breakfast date tomorrow morning?" I asked, holding her at arm's length.

"Absolutely." She perked up at us spending the morning together. I walked out of the apartment, glaring at Peter. He waved sarcastically. I was grateful to spend the night at James's even though I knew he wanted more. But I had been clear in my lack of interest in a romantic relationship with him. He was trying his best to prove that he could provide all that I needed in a partner, which he absolutely would for any girl, but it was not what I wanted. I needed passion. My thoughts drifted to kissing Roman and the dreams of Nik. I was screwed when it came to those two.

CHAPTER 29
JUST CAN'T RESIST

Larissa

It was good to be back at work on Monday. I was excited for the weekend so I could move into my new apartment. I received an email from Nik about a meeting on Thursday afternoon, noting that the location was a furniture store. I could not help but smile at the idea of going shopping with him. I did not know what was wrong with me. He was a vampire, he was wrong for me, but when we were together, it just felt right. There were no words to describe it. I sent back confirmation and my email pinged again, almost instantly.

NIK

I am looking forward to our next adventure.

ME

Stop distracting me from my work, Mr. Dankworth, it is highly unprofessional.

NIK

And yet, I guarantee you cannot wipe that beautiful smile off your face.

I did not respond, instead closing the messages to focus on my actual work for Andrew. He left for his lunch break without telling me; he was frostier than usual since he discovered my business meeting with Nik regarding the TimeShaft app. I did not care for his jealousy. I breathed out to ease the tension and headed into the breakroom to grab my lunch, and then worked through my break. I was planning on leaving early tomorrow to get ready, so I needed to ensure that everything was prepared for him, otherwise he would throw a fit. I had learnt that there are different men in business. Ones like Andrew, who saw women as a piece of meat and a baby factory. The second were like Nik; they saw potential in every person, but I suppose he had seen a lot of humans in his life to know who was and who was not worth the investment. As I finished the last item on my to-do list for the day, I accidentally dropped my bottle of water on the floor. I reached down under my desk to grab it, and when I sat up, I saw Nik sitting on my desk. His smile was as bright as ever, but it did not compare to his blue irises that anyone could get lost staring into.

"What are you doing here?" I asked softly, not wanting everyone to hear.

"You did not respond." He spoke so seriously, but his face was covered with cheek.

"I did not think that I needed to. I apologise, Mr. Dankworth."

He scanned the room before saying, "They are all listening to music, so we can talk normally."

"I am still at work, so you will be spoken to with the proper title," I continued to speak softly out of paranoia that he was wrong.

"Oh, proper title, Miss Solis. Then you best call me Lord Dankworth." I snorted as he stood up and straightened his tie and purposely flexed his muscles.

"Stop it, please," I laughed as he handed me a coffee. "Thank you."

"Now, do not go spilling this one on any other attractive men. I do not wish for any competition; it will only end in heartache."

"For whom? Them or you?" I asked, staring up at his impossibly handsome face.

"Them of course," he said with a cheeky wink.

"Your ego is atrocious. Do not forget I had a date on Friday and I do plan on seeing him again," I reminded him to keep his ego in check.

He put his hands on my desk and leant in closer. "As long as he does not touch what is mine, we have no issue." He spoke so smoothly that my body shivered.

"Do not forget we kissed," I said with a smirk. A small growl escaped his lips. "Jealousy suits you, Lord Dankworth." I winked at him, but it was true. I did kiss Roman, but he did not need to know all the details.

"Do not provoke the monster, Larissa." He looked up and around the room. "Respond to my emails in the future." Then he walked away.

Andrew returned not long after. "It is not time to slack off, Larissa. Get to work," he grumbled as he walked into his office and slammed the door shut.

Nik and I flirted through email for the rest of the day. I worried more than anything about someone seeing them and using them against me or even him, but who would dare go up against the Lord of the region? Then again, you never truly knew anymore.

———

I left work early on Tuesday and raced home to get ready for the business dinner. When I arrived in the office that morning, there was a dress box on my desk. I did not dare open it while at work. I finished doing my hair and makeup, then paced the room. I was worried, especially after the last few days, about what this dress would be like. Before I could talk myself out of it, I pulled off the white lid and pushed back the black tissue paper to reveal a deep green dress with glittered detail. I picked it up, the sleeves were long, and the cut was low enough for everyone to easily see all of my breasts. It was stunning with the glitter throughout. I slid it over my skin as I noted the thigh-high split. I pulled out my phone and texted Nik.

ME

How is this appropriate for a business meeting? It is like a buffet of flesh.

NIK

Maybe that is the point. It shall make my night more memorable, to have something beautiful to look at.

ME

Perve!

NIK

Do not deny that you shall be perving on me.

I did not respond. Instead, I pulled out a pair of silver strapped heels and a sparkle clutch. I stared at myself in the mirror, shocked at how different I looked. My hair was perfectly waved to frame my face, with my eyes smoky, but not excessively, and my olive complexion made the dress sparkle on me. I checked the time; Nik would be here shortly; I stocked my clutch with basic items including my anxiety medication and grabbed the door. Luce was nowhere to be seen, so I quickly darted from my room to the hallway. I breathed out in relief. I would not be able to handle another little spar with her. I checked my phone; I was ready earlier than expected, so I waited outside for Nik's limo. It was not long until it drove up. As he opened the door, I lifted my dress and slid into the car. His eyes took in every inch of me, and his fangs descended before he looked away.

"Did you not eat?" I questioned. He shook his head and glanced back. I found I was not afraid of seeing him in this manner, he remained the same caring and handsome Nik in my eyes.

"I apologise, but it is only because of how incredibly beautiful you look. I want nothing more than to touch every inch of you." His words sent my body into overdrive. I dared myself to look away from him as I took in how sexy he looked tonight. This was bad. I clenched my fists so tightly that my nails pierced my skin.

"Tell me, Larissa, why do you fight this?" He reached over and grabbed my hand. He carefully uncurled it and cut his finger to heal my scratches.

"You are my boss." The same sentence I had repeated to him on multiple occasions. It sounded stupid, but it was true. He was my boss; I could not cross that line.

"But you desire me, as I you." He moved closer as he placed his hand on my thigh, his thumb circled my flesh, my body burned for him.

"You are mistaken," I whispered.

He nuzzled into my neck. "I can smell it. You want this." He peppered small kisses along my jaw. It reminded me of the dream the other night. How good it felt, how much I wanted it. Nik pulled back and waited; he was expecting me to make the first move. He was holding himself back until then, waiting for me to give in to my desires. He stroked my face and ran his thumb over my lips, which intensified the blue in his eyes

"If you want this, stop using your vampy powers on me," I begged.

His brow creased. "What vampy powers?" he questioned as if he had no idea what I spoke about.

"Stop giving me those sex dreams. Stop pulling at me." His laugh echoed through the car.

"Oh, Larissa, I wish I had that power. I have plenty, but that is not one. Your dreams are your own. That pull, however, is the mate bond calling."

"Mate bond?" I asked him, praying it did not mean what I thought.

His eyes smiled. "Shall I call it another name? Soulmates."

"Oh bullshit, now you are making stuff up." I scoffed at him; it could not be true.

"I wish it were. Let me guess, your body is tingling right now, you feel an invisible pull to be near, you feel warmth and safety at my touch, and you crave more." I hung my head in embarrassment.

"We are destined to be together. I can wait for you to come to this realisation, Larissa. I am a patient man. I have lived long enough to be." His words thrilled and terrified me.

"Do you feel the same?" I needed to know if he was all jumbled up, too.

"Yes, very much so. If I had the choice, I would be on my knees worshipping your body at this very moment. I want nothing more than to hear you moan my name."

"Maybe you should." The words slipped out and I covered my mouth in horror. He chuckled as he slid off the seat and kneeled before me, he sniffed the air and smiled. He ran his hands up my legs and played with my underwear. He pulled on it as I watched his eyes never leave mine. He took them off and tucked them into his jacket pocket before sitting back beside me.

"What are you doing?" I asked breathlessly, barely containing my desire to jump on him.

"I want every vampire to smell your desire for me as we walk in. I want them to know that..." He turned and slid his hand up my thighs, dragging a finger over my clit before sliding it inside of me. I moaned as my body erupted. Too soon, he pulled his finger out and brought it to his mouth and sucked on it.

"You taste better than blood," his voice rasped. I moved to be closer to him and touched his face. He stared at me as if I was the most precious thing in the world. The car stopped.

"We are here," the driver spoke through the intercom. Nik looked at me expectantly.

"Well," I groaned and moved away. "I hate you."

He smiled wickedly as he ran his finger along my leg. "Hold onto that, it will make you taste even better."

This dinner was going to be torture.

"I am not getting out until you hand me back my underwear." I crossed my arms over my chest. He grumbled and handed them over before I slid them on again.

CHAPTER 30
PITCH MEETING

Larissa

THE RESTAURANT WAS STUNNING. IT WAS OBVIOUS THAT IT WAS A five-star, especially when I compared it to my café back home. The tables were all set to perfection, everything was in line, and polished. Even the clientele looked like they belonged. I understood now why Nik bought me the dress. None of my clothes would have been appropriate for this place. The chandelier in the middle of the room was the statement piece with its levels of crystals, all various sizes and shapes. It reminded me of those chandeliers in an old-fashioned ballroom.

Nik pulled at my elbow gently to keep me following him. He put his arm around my shoulders and pulled me in close. His eyes scanned the room as I noticed the near perfect appearances of every person here.

I whispered in his ear, "Are they all Vampires?"

"Mhmm," he muttered softly. I snuggled into his body further. I understood this was a way of showing everyone that I was his property, and I found I did not mind it one bit.

"Can you put into normal terms what I am to you guys? I get that I am desirable, but how?"

"I am not sure I know the correct words, but it would be like crack to an addict. It would be all they could think about until they had just one little taste," he elaborated as I worried about being someone's meal.

"And you can resist it, how?" I asked him, curiosity getting the better of me while I kept my eyes trained on those around the room.

"You are not the first virgin I have come across. In the beginning, I had no restraint. I learnt to control my animal instincts, to push aside the calling of the blood. Here we are, game face on, Larissa."

He let go of me and walked over to embrace the two men. One was the same height as Nik with brown hair and pale skin, his brown eyes were trained on me while he spoke to Nik. His black suit was missing a tie, but he still had an air of superiority to him. The second had long golden hair plaited down his back. He seemed slightly more casual with his black jeans and red shirt. It was strange to see almost two polar opposites as business partners. Their eyes were focused on my every move as I plastered on a smile and walked over holding out my hand to introduce myself.

"Nik, you did not lie, she is the same..." Nik shot him a glare. What was with his glares at people and some of their comments? It was like they knew me, but I did not know them.

"She is a beauty beyond belief. A pleasure to meet you, Larissa. I am Julian and this is my partner, Stuart. Nik has told us so much about you, and the proposal you put together blew our minds," he said as he held out his hand.

Nik pulled out my chair and helped me to sit, ensuring he was as close to me as possible.

"She is a rare gem," Stuart agreed as his eyes flashed from hazel to red.

"She is mine," Nik growled as he leant forward. I could feel the power radiating from his body.

"Um, am I now? I do not believe we have had this discussion. I am under your protection, I would say, but I am not yours." Nik's head snapped in my direction but did not correct me.

"Oh, I have missed this." Julian laughed at the interaction between us.

"Shall we discuss business?" I had never seen Nik flustered. I enjoyed how uncomfortable he appeared.

"Pardon, but miss what?" I asked watching as Julian smiled. He looked at Nik, who seemed to lean forward in a warning manner.

"I miss people who challenge our Lord, but he is right. Let us get down to business." I noticed the hint of his accent was like Nik's.

"Are you as old as Nik?" I asked with curiosity at the similarity in their accents.

He shook his head. "No one is as old as Nik." He cleared his throat as the waiter came over. I noticed the bite marks on his wrist and the grey colour of his skin. If I did not know any better, I swear he would pass out at any moment. Stuart leant in with eagerness and Nik growled in warning.

"This is why some still fear us. Look and listen to him, Stuart, he has given enough," he scolded his friend for even considering it. I looked at him with admiration, he had no fear in telling anyone what to do.

Nik turned towards the waiter. "Tell your boss you are going home," he said, and slipped him some money. I moved close to Nik.

"Did you compel him?" I whispered, but he only smiled in response as a round of drinks were brought to the table.

Julian put his elbows on the table. "So, in your proposal, you decided to change the demographic. Why?"

Nik waited for me to respond as nerves crept through my system, clearly my medication was not helping. Nausea rolled in my stomach. Nik put his hand on my leg and squeezed gently. My nerves disappeared and were replaced with confidence, warmth, and safety.

"Honestly, this opens up your app to more clientele because if a wife likes it, she will tell her husband, who may tell his boss and it will have a flow on effect."

Stuart crossed his arms and leant back. "Nik, she needs a promotion," he said, nodding at my idea.

"What is the first step?" Julian asked as I relaxed into my seat. I enjoyed a glass of wine as we talked about the steps and process. I discussed the need to make a few changes to their app to make it more beneficial to the new market. The two courses came and went as they listened. Julian sat back in his booth seat.

"Larissa, you are something else. Where have you been hiding? Nik, this girl is going places. You should remove that pig, Andrew, and put her in his position."

Nik smiled proudly and put his arm around me. "Oh, I know it." He took another sip of his whiskey.

I wiped my mouth. "If you gentlemen will excuse me for a

moment," I said as I started to stand. Nik straightened and grabbed my wrist.

"Where are you going?" His voice was not of anger, but more worry.

"I am human, and I still need to use the bathroom even if you do not."

He let go and stood. When I glared at him, he sat back down. I walked into the bathroom and noticed it was made of marble, so white it was almost blinding. As I looked in the mirror, I noticed the glassy look in my eyes; the alcohol was hitting me. I took a breath to centre myself before I left and ran into a person. He knocked me on my ass in a second.

"Ow," I muttered as I stood and dusted myself off.

"Watch where you are going, human," he sneered. I bowed my head submissively, an action I did not even mean to make.

"Sorry, I did not see you," I whispered my apology. I did not want to provoke him any further.

He tilted my head up and I noticed his blood-stained mouth and red eyes.

"You smell sweet." He licked his lips, the tingle in my body started. It grew from the prickle in my fingers to my forearm. It grew in strength; I had never felt something like this before. He moved closer as I took a step back.

"I belong to another," my voice croaked. It did not sound believable. His eyes were solely focused on me as he reached and moved hair from my face.

"You have not been marked. You belong to no one. Such a pity for someone as precious as you." He sniffed the air and breathed out with euphoria. "I cannot wait to taste." He shoved me into the wall behind me.

"I belong to Nik Dankworth, please," I begged.

He laughed maliciously at my comment.

"Nik? I doubt that. Good try." His hand ran along my neck and grabbed my hair in a fist. "Just stay still, this will not hurt." He was trying to compel me, but I shook the power of the compulsion off.

"NO!" I brought my knee up to his groin and he doubled over in pain. I took those few seconds to try to escape, but it did not work. He grabbed my hair, pulled me back and threw me against the wall. "NIK!" I screamed seconds before he covered my mouth.

"I told you to stay still!" The red in his eyes grew brighter; he was trying to compel me again. I wasn't going to submit, even if it meant revealing my inability to be compelled. I fought against his hold before Nik leant on the wall beside me with a devilish smile.

"Hector, why are you touching what is mine?" His voice was laced with warning, but his face remained calm.

Hector froze and let me go. I scurried over beside Nik. He grabbed my hand as a form of comfort.

"Lord Dankworth, I apologise. She had not been marked." He fumbled with his words; I wondered if it was because he did not believe me.

"Did she vocalise?" he asked. I had never heard him use this tone. It sounded almost monstrous.

"Yes." Hector hung his head.

"And yet you decided to touch what is mine, why?" I wanted to run but was too scared to move.

"Humans lie, but she resisted my compulsion," Nik growled as his fangs descended and his eyes glowed. He turned to me.

"Larissa, please return to the table." I nodded and rounded the corner to see Julian, who held me close and took me to the table. I wanted more than anything to leave. Bile rose in my throat and the sensation in my arms was burning. I could not stop fiddling with my fingers.

I stood from the table, almost dramatically. "I need to leave. Tell Mr. Dankworth that I am sorry."

Julian reached for me, but I pulled away and stared down at him. He pulled back as Stuart gasped.

"Get home safely, Larissa Solis." Stuart bowed his head as I rushed from the restaurant. I saw a taxi outside, so I flung open the door and told him to drive. I could not stop the burning in my arms as I told the driver my address.

CHAPTER 31

GIVING INTO DESIRE

Larissa

THE WHOLE DRIVE, MY SKIN ITCHED AND BURNED WITH A NEED that I could not understand. I did not know how to stop it. I barely registered how long it took to get home before we had arrived. I gave the driver my fare and went to rush inside.

"Larissa." Nik appeared from the shadows, but I pointed at him to put distance between us.

"No, I've made my decision. Stay away from me. I do not want to be part of that world. He tried to compel me to take something that wasn't his. He made my skin crawl, and I can't stop it. I still feel him touching me, I feel sick. Sorry, Nik, whatever this was or is, it's done."

His jaw clenched as I turned to head inside. "I never picked you as a chicken," he shouted after me.

His words made me freeze. "Excuse me?" I spun back around and glared at him.

He smirked and leant against the gate with an air of superiority. "You heard me, I did not stutter. My world is the same as yours. Men try to take what does not belong to them; the only difference is the power we use to take it. This was why I fought for the laws to protect humans against the abuse of our power."

"Your words mean nothing. It does not change that you are monsters," I spat back, my voice filled with hate that I barely recognised.

He stood straight and focused solely on me. "Do not affiliate me with men like Hector," Nik said firmly, his eyes ablaze with anger. "I respect choice. I have given you a choice from the start. I never lied. I told you what I was and what I wanted. Now that we are growing close, you want to run. I do not know why I am shocked."

"I do not run from things!" He snorted as I walked over to him and poked his chest. "You do not know me. You do not get to make those comments when you have no idea about the person I am," I snapped at him with frustration. He did not know me.

"I know you better than you know yourself!" he exclaimed with an air of confidence.

"Oh please, you guessed my favourite coffee. Woah, hold the news. Mr. Dankworth knows a coffee order," I shouted sarcastically.

"You run to clear your head, but it is more than that. You find it hard to focus and running provides you with clarity. You cannot stand up for yourself and you allow people to use and abuse you. Your kind heart tries to see the best in everyone. You hide behind your sister with why you never allowed yourself to give in to your carnal desires. You want more than anything to have a man fuck you. It has never been about saving yourself, it is about the fear of committing," he retorted, spewing facts that he thought I wanted to hear.

"I can commit. Again, you are full of shit," I criticised while clenching my fists.

"And yet here we are, and you are running from this. You will not commit to this despite wanting to spread those sweet legs for me. If we did not arrive at the restaurant earlier, you would have given yourself over."

I remembered his touch on my skin, and my desire grew before I pushed it away once more.

He groaned. "That is exactly my point, you felt the need for more and pushed it away, why? I told you we are bonded," he begged, his voice pleading for me to see reason. Reason I refused to admit to myself.

"Can you just stop?" I urged him. I could not take the thoughts running through my head.

"Stop denying what we have. Stop denying what you feel. You want this, you crave the darkness, you desire the unknown. Give in to those desires," he spoke with conviction. I wanted to listen but I worried what would happen if I did.

"I can't. You are a monster," I argued, using words that I knew would hurt him. But it was too late to take them back.

"Tell me, how I am a monster? I have never harmed you. I have been nothing but a gentleman to you," he insisted. "Tell the truth, you fear wanting this because of what I am, say it, Larissa."

He was right, I knew it, but I could not give him what he wanted. I rubbed my face, my head swayed between logic and desire.

"You need to leave." I could not continue this conversation. Luce had exhausted me, and now this. I moved to walk away but he grabbed my wrist and spun me into his arms.

"Not until I kiss you." His eyes brightened as they focused on my lips.

"Do not Nik, please." I was not fighting him as he stroked my face. His lips pressed against mine as the burn in my arms disappeared. It was soft and gentle, and before he could pull away, I wrapped my arms around his neck and kissed him harder. I bit his lower lip before his tongue invaded my mouth and massaged my tongue in ways I never knew were possible. He pulled me tighter against his body as his hands roamed mine. I wanted more. I craved his touch, grinding into him.

"If you keep doing that, I will become your monster," he whispered against my lips. I bit on his lip again. "Larissa," he warned as I saw the desire in his face, he was holding himself back.

"Show me," I said with confidence I did not know I had.

"Pardon?" he asked, searching my face to confirm that he heard correctly.

"Show me."

"I will be a monster for you tonight because you need it." He lifted me from the ground as I wrapped my legs around him. He growled not in anger, but in raw desire. I could feel his longing pulsating through him, his passion enveloping me like a warm embrace. The sensation was intoxicating, leaving me wanting more. He paused and stopped to look at me.

"Larissa, stay the night with me." His words were loving and tender. "I promise that I will not pressure you for anything more than your lips on my own. But if you want more, I shall be more than happy to indulge."

I looked up to see Luce standing at the window watching me. He turned my face to focus on him.

"Do not think of her. What do you want?" His blue eyes pleaded with me to go with him. I wanted him in a way I could not explain. I nodded and a smile crossed his face.

"Hold on tight," he ordered as I wrapped my arms around his neck.

"What for?" He gripped me tighter as he rose from the ground and floated. I laughed with excitement.

"Hold on tighter," he warned after my initial movement.

I did as he asked and buried my head into his chest.

"I have you, Larissa. I always will."

We floated through the air until we landed gently on a penthouse balcony.

CHAPTER 32

SPENDING THE NIGHT

Larissa

THE VIEW WAS BREATHTAKING, OVERLOOKING THE CITYSCAPE where bright, twinkling lights illuminated the night. London was sprawled before us, its undeniable beauty

"Wow, this is amazing." Nik put his arms around my waist as I leant my head on his shoulder. He kissed the top of my head.

"Any regrets yet?" he asked. I could hear the worry in his tone.

I smirked while I turned to wrap my arms around his waist. "Yes, many. I am terrified. My brain is going into overdrive."

"Did you want me to take you home?" His voice was barely a whisper, I tilted my head to meet his eyes.

"No, just do not push anything and we shall be fine."

He pecked my lips. "Oh, I will not. Come inside, it is cold."

He unlocked his door, slipping his hand into mine and walking us inside. Holding his hand was a strange and wonderful sensation. It gave me a sense of belonging as well allowing me to almost feel his affection for me. In the darkness, he released my hand to clap both of his; the room lit up and the fireplace roared to life. The soft grey and blue tones were not what I was expecting, but I noticed that the space was devoid of pictures. It felt warm but cold. I ran my hand along the grey leather couch as my shoes clacked on his soft grey marble flooring. I turned back to see him watching me.

"Did you design and decorate this place?" I asked, wanting to know more about him. Sadness crossed his face as he shook his head and pushed himself off the wall, almost like I did not give him the reaction he wanted.

"No." His voice was curt and direct.

"Oh, your partner did before she died." He did not respond, instead, he removed his jacket and opened the fridge.

"Would you like a drink?" he asked without glancing in my direction.

"Sure." I continued to walk around the living space, noticing that he used his table as a desk. I could almost imagine him working all night with his hair mangled and his shirt unbuttoned while twirling a glass of whiskey in his hands.

"What is that face for?" he asked while he strode over holding a glass of wine.

"I was picturing you working at your table and looking very different to your usual self."

"My usual self?" he questioned as he took a sip of whiskey.

"The shirt, the hair, nothing out of place." He laughed as he walked over to the couch and sat down.

"Nik, I need to ask you something." I feared asking him questions, not from his reaction but what they would mean.

"Only if you permit me to ask you a question as well."

"Fine, twenty questions it is."

I sat down beside him, and he grabbed my legs and draped them over his lap, the slit in my dress made it difficult cover my legs in this position.

"What will happen to Hector?" I asked as I took another sip of wine to calm my nerves at being in a man's apartment, alone. A man that had my underwear in his pocket a few hours ago.

He rubbed the bridge of his nose and sighed as he removed my shoes to allow me to relax. "He touched what does not belong to him. He tried to compel the mate of another, and before you object to our law, we *are* seen as mates. It is forbidden to touch a human who belongs to another vampire. He will be executed, which is for the best." He exhaled, sounding both relieved and annoyed.

My mouth dropped open with shock. "How can you be so cold about it?"

He shook his head and moved closer. "Larissa, you misunderstand. It is for the best because he discovered you were not able to be compelled. I told you, that needs to stay a secret. You should have pretended to give in to his compulsion," he responded with frustration in his voice, like the situation was my fault.

"Why? To become someone's meal?" I snapped at him, abhorring his reaction.

"I sensed you were in danger. I was already on my way over before you called my name."

"Sensed? Oh right, I forgot. Your blood in my system, fucking hell. You really have claimed me as your own." I was frustrated as I stood from the couch and paced the room. "You told me I had a choice; this seems like you have already made it for me."

"Larissa, everything I have done has been to protect you, including compelling Stuart and Julian tonight."

I snapped my head in his direction. "Wait, what? You can compel other vampires? What the hell did you need to do that for?" My head threatened to explode at this revelation.

"I told you; my powers are vast. I am very old, Larissa. I did it to protect you," he stated nonchalantly.

"Protect me from what? Are they planning to come after me as well?" I asked while crossing my arms. Why was all this important?

"Surely, you know." He sighed shaking his head.

I threw my arms up in defeat. "Clearly I do not, Nik, please enlighten me." My anger threatened to explode.

"Your eyes," he said suddenly. Worry worked its way through my body.

"What of my eyes?" I pretended I did not know.

He smiled and moved closer to me. "I know when you lie. How long have you known?"

I refused to answer. I did not want to admit this. I began to chew my nail and slumped back down onto the couch. Nik joined me, pulling my legs onto him once more.

"Since the first time it happened. I was fighting with Luce, and they turned red. Did it happen again? Do you know what it is?"

He exhaled, his face softening in relief.

"Why do you look relieved?" I asked while leaning back into the comfortable couch.

"I worried I had started the transition process, but this started before me. I do not know, but a human who cannot be compelled and has eyes that glow red needs to be kept in the dark."

"Will you not get in trouble for this?" I probed, hoping he would not.

He laughed almost demonically. "Larissa, I am the Lord of the region. I control most things; I cannot be *in trouble*. There are no other vampires like me. They wouldn't dare try anything." He sounded so confident in himself; I wondered what power he had within his vampire realm.

"What does it mean when my eyes flash red?" I feared knowing this answer.

He shrugged his shoulders as he massaged my aching feet. It felt nice, relaxing. I had never had this before. For once, I had a sense of safety and security with him.

"It can mean any number of things; it does not make you a vampire. May I say something that may cause you some distress?"

"I suppose, I mean you know nearly all my secrets, but I do not know any of yours. Go for it." I leant my head on the edge of the couch as the sensations from Nik's hands ran through my body.

"I do not believe that Elizabeth is your mother. Twins who share the womb have a similar smell, but you and Luce do not. You smell like flowers and sunshine; she smells like trees. I never met your mother, so I am not sure, but you spoke of her red hair, which you do not share. You have the same eyes, but she is pale, and you are olive. There are too many conflicting factors."

"Wait, are you saying that Luce and I are not related?" I sat up and crossed my legs.

"No, I am saying you are not sisters. I could be wrong but…"

"You are thousands of years old, so I doubt you are wrong." I covered my face with my hands.

Nik touched my leg. "Larissa, I did not mean to upset you, but I think there are secrets you need to uncover. Whoever your parents were, they were not human."

"Y-you said I was human," I stuttered, my heart racing at the idea of being a supernatural creature.

"No, I said you were not a vampire. I do not know what you are. There are many creatures in the world, Larissa. Vampires, werewolves, ghosts, witches, demons, angels, and Gods," he explained.

My face lit up. "Wait, angels are real? I sometimes forget how old you are, you have probably seen so much in your lifetime. I am so frustrated!"

"I can tell." He snorted at the change in my tone.

I rolled my eyes at him as he moved closer. "Using your abilities on me is not fair. Let me guess, you can smell my emotions?" I speculated.

He grabbed my hand and squeezed it. "I told you of our connection and how we are mated. I do not smell it; I can feel and sense it. Whenever your emotions are so extreme, I feel them as if they are my own." He projected a softer, tender voice to explain this bizarre connection.

"That is a little creepy," I added but I figured I would discover more as time went by.

He chuckled as he stood and filled his glass with some blood. "You do not need to tell me, I live it."

"Have you always felt them? If we are mated, have you felt my them since I was born?" I wondered, because it would only increase the creepiness level. Especially if he felt my sadness at wanting a bottle as a baby.

He scratched his chin. "Good question, but no. I felt something when you started to work in my building. The day you spilled the coffee, I knew it was you. I felt the embarrassment and I knew. It was why I chased you, it was why I have been a little persistent since then." He held up his fingers to show a small amount while he winked.

"So, you admit you have been a little forceful?" I teased as I poked his chest.

"I call it persistence. I have never forced you. I told you that you have a choice." It suddenly clicked in my head, the day after the fight with Luce. He was near my apartment while I was going for a run. He sensed that I was upset and distraught by it.

"Holy shit, that was why you joined me on the run." He smiled and bit his lip. "Wow, you sensed how upset I was and purposely ran into me, yes?"

He avoided eye contact with me, as I poked him playfully in the chest again. He grabbed my hand and pulled me onto his lap in a flash. "If you wish to play fight, you had better be prepared."

I giggled as he kissed my hand. "This does not seem like play fighting; this is more like foreplay." I winked before he helped me sit back on the couch.

I was confused. He seemed like he wanted more, but he put a stop to it. He stood and put his hands on his hips with his back to me. He would pull me towards him, but in moments like these, he pushed me away. I was getting whiplash from his constant change in attitude.

"Sorry, Larissa. I know you are confused. I am holding myself back. I do not want to force you," he said while he hung his head.

"When you do that, it feels like you do not want it, though. I cannot read those cues; I have never seen them or experienced them. I do not get it."

He sighed and turned around as he rubbed his face.

"Stand-up." He motioned by pointing to a spot on the floor in front of him. I walked over. He wrapped his arms around my waist and pulled me against his body. "If I acted how I felt, I would scare you away."

I put my hands on his shoulders and stared into his beautiful blue eyes as I said, "Nik, if I feared you, I would not have agreed to come here. I literally do not know where you live, and we entered through the balcony. I could not run away if I wished to."

He leant his forehead against my own. "Larissa." His voice was strained.

"Just promise me one thing," I said, and he lifted my chin to search my face.

"Anything for you," he whispered as he stared into my eyes.

"Do not bite me." His chuckle filled the room, and my heart, as he kissed my forehead.

"I would not dream of it. That is a rather personal thing between partners." I nodded as I looked away. I was worried about it hurting, and about what it would mean after. My brain was going into overdrive. He grabbed my face in his hands and pressed a soft kiss to my lips.

"Does that ease your worries?" he whispered, and I smiled as I tried to keep my legs stable when they wanted to melt into a puddle.

"I do not know, I may need more." I provoked him, definitely wanting more.

He chuckled and happily obliged as he kissed me again. The tension in my body relaxed.

"Again," I demanded, and he was so much gentler than earlier, it was like he wanted to take his time and savour every moment.

"Nik," I whispered. "I am not ready to take this further. My body is telling me yes, but I cannot, at least not yet."

He smiled and almost seemed relieved by my comment. He kissed my hand and clasped his own around it. "Come, let us go to bed and rest."

He led me up the stairs and into his room where I saw a pile of women's sleepwear laid out on the edge of his king-size bed.

"Do I want to know?" I asked as I picked them up to view the sizes.

"I wanted to be prepared for anything. I have several outfits, but I was not sure what you would prefer to sleep in." Nik dug his hands into his pockets; he was shy and embarrassed as he turned his head away from me.

I sorted through them and selected a silky white nightie to wear. I had never worn anything this beautiful before; Mother never allowed it. I ran the material through my hands as I held it up against my body and stood before the mirror. Nik wrapped his arms around my waist and perched his head on my shoulder. "It suits you," he breathed into my ear. I could not help but smile.

"Nik, is this real or am I dreaming?"

He rubbed his nose against mine before kissing it. "This is real, Larissa. I will leave you to get changed."

Nik left the room as I walked into the bathroom, the lights turned on automatically as I entered. The black tiled floors contrasted well with the white cabinetry and benchtop. I noticed the towel and shower behind me.

I popped my head out and raised my voice to say, "I am going to quickly shower if that is alright?"

I heard his voice in the distance and assumed that was a yes. I slid the gown over my shoulders and pulled my hair up into a bun to keep it from getting wet. The water warmed my skin, and as I washed off my makeup, my thoughts were of Nik and what life would be like if we were together. I could not stop the dirty thoughts of him, they were consuming. I put my hands on the wall and braced myself as I tried to shake them off. I heard the bathroom door open.

"Just checking that you are alright," he said with a slight chuckle.

I chuckled along with him, knowing the real reason he came in. He was a gentleman.

"Yes, sorry. I assume you can sense that," I answered him as I tried to keep my embarrassment levels down.

"Yes, but it is fine, Larissa. I shall meet you in bed when you are ready."

I turned off the water and dried myself before slipping into the silky nightie. I hung up my towel and crept out nervously as I held my arms across my body. Nik threw the blankets back and tapped the bed beside him.

"Do not be shy. Come and sleep."

As I lay beside him, he slid an arm around my waist. I wished it would travel south.

"Larissa, it is time to sleep."

I rolled over to face him as I stroked his face in the dark. His skin was soft, and his beard tickled my hand.

"Just because I do not wish to have sex, does not mean we cannot play." I could not understand the intensity of my desire for him.

His head moved away from my hand. I was not this brave normally. I was shy when it came to intimacy, but having Nik so close, the desire to be touched was overwhelming.

"Is this part of the bond? I crave to be touched."

His hand travelled from my face, down my neck, where it grabbed the strap of the nightie and slid it down to reveal my breast. Hoarse breaths filled the silence as his lips found mine. I groaned at his fingers flicking my nipple, then his lips travelled down my neck and sucked hard. His other hand played with my other breast.

"Fucking hell, Nik," I moaned as he ground into me. I wanted him badly. My body needed to feel him inside me. This was a bad idea. He stopped, sensing my hesitation.

"Larissa, I know this is strange and you cannot form a coherent thought, but I want to try something with your permission." I wished to see his face, but I would have to settle for the outline in the dark.

"What is it?" I asked him, my voice barely a whisper.

His hands landed beside my head as he kissed the sensitive spot between my neck and shoulder.

"I want to put my head between your legs and eat your pretty pussy." His words, although crude, set off emotions and feelings I did not know I had. His hand slid down my body in an *S* pattern. Nik's fingers toyed with my underwear as he said, "I will not until you consent."

"What do I do?"

"Lay back and enjoy." I proceeded to get comfortable as Nik disappeared under the covers. His hands slid under my bottom as his breath warmed my legs. He licked down my thigh before moving to the other and dragging his fang along it.

"You are so fucking wet for me."

His tongue just touched the surface of my clit a few times to allow me time to adjust, before his strokes intensified. I had intense feelings that I had never felt before, this had never happened and my brain could not comprehend the sensations from his tongue. He held me in place, moving his tongue in different ways to increase my satisfaction. His fangs grazed that one sensitive spot and my body rose from the bed slightly. I heard him chuckle before his tongue continued to lick its way up and down. My moans filled the room as I panted, trying to catch my breath.

"Nik...Nik...Nik," I moaned.

The orgasm grew and grew, and when he took a little bite, I fell apart.

"HOLY FUCKING SHIT, NIK!" I screamed. It was an out-of-body experience, the sensations coursing through me were intense.

He laid back beside me. "I do not need to see you to tell you to wipe that smug look off your face." I laughed as I finally caught my breath. "What about you?"

"Please Larissa, it is fine. Time to sleep."

"That does not seem fair. What if I…" My hands moved down to his hard cock, and I stroked him a few times. He groaned as I cupped his balls. I had no idea what I was doing. He grabbed my hands and brought them to his lips.

"I do not need anything other than giving you my everything. It is time to sleep." I snuggled into his chest, love and adoration enveloped my body, cocooning me in a bubble of warmth.

"Nik?"

"Yes," he answered, his voice gentle, a stark contrast to what he had just done to me.

"Will I feel what you feel as well?" He stroked my hair tenderly.

"Not yet. If you transition, you will feel it, but not in your human form. I shall never force this upon you, and I will also never expect you to transition. It is your life. Your love is all I need." He continued to stroke my hair as he hummed softly. I knew the tune, but I could not place it. It brought me comfort as my eyes slowly closed, welcoming the darkness of sleep.

CHAPTER 33
TIME FOR LASAGNA

Larissa

I FELT SOMEONE WATCHING ME AS I OPENED MY EYES; THERE WAS a figure before me. It was hidden in the shadows, and I moved, but Nik's arm tightened its grip on me.

"Larissa," the voice whispered as the ethereal figure moved closer. I was paralysed. The figure came into view as it grabbed my arm, the touch burned my skin. It was my mother, her hair was fire, and her skin was charred and peeling off. I tried to pull away, but it was no use. She held on as if she had super strength, and then spat on me. "You disgust me. How dare you lay with that filth? You are no daughter of mine."

I screamed as I thrashed my body, trying to free myself from her iron grip. It wasn't until I hit the floor, and my arms were pinned down, that I woke. Nik was on top of me, he held my arms above my head as he stared into my eyes.

"You are safe it; was only a dream," he said in a voice that settled me easily. As he released me from his hold, I moved and touched my arm. A red handprint where my mother had grabbed me remained. I pushed Nik off me and grabbed my clothes. I could not be here; she was giving me a warning. I did not understand it, but I needed to be away from him.

"Larissa, where are you going?" he called out, panicked, as he chased after me. I reached the door to the apartment, but Nik forced it shut before I could leave. "What the fuck is happening?" His eyes were red, not from rage, but rather concern. I held my arm up to show him the angry mark.

"That was no ordinary dream. I need to go; I need to be out of here. Let me go," I choked out the words, I had never been more frightened in my life.

He shook his head, his hand remaining on the door. "No, you need to compose yourself. I will not let you go until I know that you will be safe when you leave here." I pulled the door with all the strength that I had in me. Nik's face was filled with shock, he took a step back as I saw my reflection in the hall mirror. Bright red eyes flashed in the mirror, the colour around my eyes was darker than usual. I looked almost demonic. Before Nik could stop me, I ran from his apartment and found my way home.

I slammed the door shut and hid in my room; I did not dare to look in the mirror again. I feared what may be looking back at me. It wasn't human, and it wasn't a vampire. I was something else entirely, something that scared me. I texted Andrew that I was unwell and that I would not be in, before covering myself with blankets and curling into the foetal position. The images of my mother's burnt body played through my mind on a loop and the burn on my arm tingled with every replay. I could feel her hatred in those words, and she was not wrong. I was in bed with a monster, and I let him touch me and put his hands on me. I was disgusting.

———

It was a few more hours before I dragged myself out of bed. I grabbed my phone and saw that there were several missed calls from Nik, a few emails from Andrew, and a text from Roman. I opened the latter as I had not heard from him since our date on the weekend.

ROMAN

How is the woman of my dreams?

I could not help but smile at his text.

ME

Are you sure you are texting the right person?

ROMAN

Brunette, stunning green eyes, legs for days, charming personality, lips so alluring that I could kiss them forever?

ME

Oh, that girl? Yeah, she is here somewhere...

ROMAN

Is it too late for a dinner date tonight?

ME

Pick me up at 6

ROMAN

Would you care if I cooked dinner for you?

ME

Absolutely not

It was risky, but if I could spend the night with a vampire, I was sure that I would be fine with a human. I showered before I sorted through my clothes. If it was at his house, I wanted something sexy but not too revealing. I picked a pair of jeans and a low-cut red blouse. It was still another hour before

Roman was due to pick me up, so I passed the time by cooking dinner for Luce before she got home. I dished it up and left it in the microwave with a note for her saying that I would not be home and to not wait up for me. She did not need to know the details, especially since I suspected that her one night with Peter had lasted a little longer than she expected.

The doorbell rang and I ran down the stairs to meet Roman. He had his back turned as I opened the door, but when he turned to face me, I took a moment to take him all in. He was wearing his statement black leather jacket with a blue shirt and a pair of jeans. He looked every inch the bad boy, but that was not the person that he was on the inside. His hooded eyes draped over my body with eagerness as he licked his lips.

"You look even more beautiful than the last time that I laid my eyes on you."

My face flushed with embarrassment, which caused a laugh to spring from his mouth. He offered his hand and led the way to his car. He opened the door and waited until I was inside before he closed it behind me. I settled in as he drove for a while until we reached the outskirts of London. He parked the car and pointed up ahead as he said, "This is me."

I looked before me at a house that seemed the same as the others beside it. He got out of the car and walked over to open the door for me.

"I am glad chivalry is not dead," I said with a wink.

"You could say I am old-fashioned." He offered his arm, and I slid my own into his as he unlocked the front door and let me enter first. I assumed it was his way of making me comfortable. I took slow steps, examining my surroundings, noticing that his polished concrete floor and modern interior did not match the look from the outside. It was cold; the place had no warmth to it and not just because of the lack of heating. The apartment displayed a consistent grey hue in various shades. He clapped his hands and the fireplace roared to life. It was hard being here; I felt guilty like this was some form of betrayal towards Nik. I knew he would be able to feel this, but I needed to not think of him. After seeing my mother this morning, I wanted it to be over. I wanted whatever was between Nik and me to be done. I would bury every emotion I felt towards him, I needed that to move on. Roman removed his jacket and hung it on the back of a chair.

"Would you like a drink?" he asked as he strode into his industrial-style kitchen. It had sleek, grey tones that dominated the aesthetic, from the walls to the stainless-steel appliances. The focal point was a sturdy concrete bench, its smooth surface contrasted with a rough texture. The lighting overhead created a warm glow that enhanced the romantic mood.

"Yes please." I walked over to the bench and took a seat on the wooden stool. He poured me a glass of red wine, then washed his hands and threw a towel over his shoulder. As he pulled out a pot from the oven, I sniffed the air.

"Ah, Bolognese?" I queried from the delicious smell that filled the kitchen.

He tapped his nose. "Close, but not quite. Lasagne."

"Wow, I cannot wait. I love pasta. I would often make the joke growing up that I was Italian in a previous life." I chuckled, remembering how I would often try to speak the language. My mother would tell me I was foolish.

He raised an eyebrow and chuckled, "You may be if you believe in reincarnation." His comment reminded me of the conversation I had with Nik in the car. I pushed the thought of him aside to focus solely on Roman.

"You seem distracted." He sounded concerned. "Are you alright?"

I forced a smile onto my face. "I'm just having some issues at work and other stuff." I shrugged my shoulders to show it meant nothing.

"Do you wish to discuss it further?" I shook my head as I took a big gulp of wine.

"No, I wish to enjoy my evening with you." I got up from the stool to get closer to Roman and watched him as I pulled myself onto the bench beside him. I noted his precise movements as he layered the lasagne and sprinkled it with the perfect amount of meat, cheese, and sauce before he added another layer.

"How many women have you made this for?" I asked as I quickly stole the spoon and tasted the bechamel sauce. The flavours danced on my tongue. "Wow, that is to die for."

Roman laughed as he took the spoon back. "To answer your question, none. No women have made it past the first date."

"Oh, careful now. A lady may get used to this," I said, licking my lips to savour the amazing taste.

"Oh, I pray that you do." He flashed a cheeky grin as he sprinkled the top with the final layer of cheese and put it into the oven. Roman set the timer and turned to lean against the oven. His eyes were that of a predator stalking his prey. He stalked over, took my glass of wine and placed it on the bench. "I need to do one thing that I have been craving since the moment I laid my eyes on you tonight."

"And what is that?" My thoughts wandered back to Nik—the memory of his touch, gentle yet electric. It sent a wave of longing through me. The guilt rose in my throat, along with an overpowering need to vomit. I grabbed Roman and kissed him, wanting to erase Nik's touch from my body. I wanted to replace it with another, I needed to do this, or I would never have any sanity again. Roman groaned as I put my arms around his neck and brought him closer.

"Larissa, if you continue with this, I may not be able to hold myself back." His voice was hoarse as his hands ran up my sides.

I bit his lower lip. "That may be the point."

He groaned and pushed himself back, holding me a safe distance from him.

"I won't. I can't do that. I want you to be sure of who you give your virginity to. It is not something to be rushed." His words did not seem to match the longing in his eyes.

I shook my head; I hoped that I could. All my body wanted was Nik and I hated myself for it. Roman picked up his wine and took a sip before putting it down again, then offered his hand. "Come."

I slid my hand into his warm grip and slid off the bench as he walked us over to the tan leather couch and sat. The fireplace warmed the area and gave some comfort to the cold building. Roman wrapped his arm around me and held me close to his body. "How did your big meeting go?" he asked, taking another sip of wine.

I did not want to answer, as it reminded me of the night with Nik but how could I avoid it?

"It went very well; I might be receiving a promotion."

"Might be?" he questioned as I snuggled closer to his warmth.

"I did not attend work today. I felt unwell and stayed home. It was probably not wise, but I just needed…"

"The break. There is nothing wrong with that." He stroked my hair before kissing the top of my head. It was relaxing to be in his arms. I had no internal conflict like I did with Nik. Roman gave me a different kind of security.

Conversation flowed effortlessly with him. Every word he spoke carried an earnestness that made me trust him completely. He seemed so genuine and honest.

We fell asleep talking, and when I woke early the next morning, Roman was nowhere to be seen. I rolled over in the bed. I could hear a clatter in the kitchen as I rubbed my eyes and walked out to investigate the noise. Roman had several pans on the stove and he shifted between all of them. He was shirtless, only wearing a pair of black shorts. I snuck onto the bar stool and admired his flexing back muscles. I noticed him put his finger into a sauce and licked it. When he spun around, he froze as he saw me.

"Good morning," I said with a smile on my face. He put down the pan and jogged around to my side.

"It is a good morning to wake to your beautiful face." He kissed my lips. "Coffee?"

"I think the smell of the food woke me up more than coffee ever would. What have you cooked?" I asked trying to glance over his shoulder.

"Poached eggs with smoked honey bacon on sourdough and hollandaise sauce." He beamed with pride at his culinary skills.

"Mmm, I am one spoilt girl." My eyes drifted over his unclothed body; his abs on full display with hair slightly covering his pectoral muscles. "Very spoilt," I murmured as I bit my lip.

"Hey, no objectifying, unless I am allowed to objectify the sexy thing in front of me," he exclaimed as he glared at me.

I put my arms around his neck and pulled him closer. "Oh, absolutely." He ran his stubble along my neck, and I laughed as it tickled before my phone rang. I glanced over my shoulder to see it was Andrew. I groaned as I reached over to grab it.

"Good morning, Andrew, how can I help you this morning?" I spoke with a cheerful voice I knew he hated.

"Are you planning on coming in today or are you still hungover?" He grumbled into the phone as Roman kissed down my neck and up again. I was struggling to focus.

"I will be in today. I shall see you shortly." I hung up the phone quickly as Roman giggled. I pushed him off, noticing the time.

"I must eat and leave. Is it wrong to ask to see you this weekend?" I pouted at him, I had more fun than I imagined I would. Roman made everything seem easy.

"You took the words from my mouth." He pulled the stool out and let me sit to eat as he cleaned up.

Roman drove me back to my apartment, and then I quickly dressed and rushed to work.

CHAPTER 34

YOU DESERVE BETTER

Larissa

I got to work just before Andrew and started to sort through the multitude of emails. The tingle in my system caused me to glance around the room before it promptly disappeared. Nik was obviously in the elevator and not on my floor, a thought that was interrupted as Andrew slammed a whole pile of paperwork onto my desk.

"I need this done before the end of the day." It was a daunting amount. "If it is not, do not bother to come back tomorrow." His voice filled with warning.

Looking at the amount of work I had to do, I wished Nik was here. I had not heard about the promotion, but when you almost sleep with your boss before you run out with demonic eyes, it did not seem likely. I would prove Andrew wrong and get all this work done and more to shut him up. I worked through lunch as the office floor was quiet, which made it easier to smash out more work. I heard the elevator ding, alerting me that someone had arrived on my floor. I took that as the opportunity for a coffee break, so I grabbed my cup and headed into the breakroom. I put my hands on my shoulders and kneaded to ease the soreness in the muscles.

"A bit tense?" Nik's sultry voice asked behind me.

I had felt the tingle all day, but it had disappeared quickly. I did not even register just now that it did not even appear. I refused to turn around and simply decided to ignore him.

"It would be polite for you to tell me what I did to upset you." His voice almost sounded broken, and my heart ached as I closed my eyes and remembered my mother's warning.

"Good afternoon, Mr. Dankworth, would you like a coffee?" I put on a fake smile and faced him; the sight almost broke me. His hair was all over the place, his eyes were dull, and his clothes were not as picture-perfect as usual. His misery was obvious as I looked him over, and I wanted to run into his arms and hold him tight.

"Will you explain your actions the other night? Or shall I continue trying to guess why you ran out? And how you were harmed?" He crossed his arms as his nostrils flared in anger.

My mother's voice rang through my head, "Traitor, traitor!" I heard it over and over again. I closed my eyes. "Mr. Dankworth..."

He growled; he wanted me to say his name. He wanted to hear the words directed at him and not hidden behind any formalities. I was overcome with nausea as I raised my head to meet his gaze.

"Nik..." I held back the tears as my mother's voice continued to shout at me. "This cannot happen. I will never be able to accept you for the person that you are. You deserve better than this. I am sorry. I thank you for all the opportunities you have given me but—" He pushed me against the wall and kissed me harshly. I wanted to push him off, but I could not; my body betrayed me as it rubbed against him. My mother's voice shouted at me to stop but I could not. Every fibre of my being wanted him and craved his touch. It was nothing like with Roman. The passion I felt electrified my body, it was euphoric. He groaned and pushed his body against mine.

"I know you want this. I can feel it. Tell me the truth, what is stopping you?" he rasped against my lips.

I shook my head. "I cannot be with you. Can you not just accept that?"

He slammed his hand on the wall beside me, his eyes flashed from red to blue. "Tell me the truth," he ordered, his rigid body hinting at his struggle to remain in control.

The door to the breakroom opened and he moved back instantly as Andrew entered.

"Ah Nik, how was the meeting for the TimeShaft app?" he addressed Nik, completely ignoring my presence.

I moved to exit the room, but Nik grabbed my hand. He pushed for me to stay. I knew he would beg if it were possible for him right now.

I stopped as he answered, "It went perfectly. Larissa showed her knowledge and impressed the owners. She will be given a promotion to assistant marketing director. She will work underneath and not for you from next week. You will need to hire a new secretary."

Andrew choked on his coffee, and said, "I thought I was to be brought into these types of discussions, this is *my* company."

Nik smiled slyly as he winked in my direction. "Andrew, it was your company but due to your failure to manage its finances, it is now my company, which I respectfully allow you to continue to run. If you are not happy with this, I will happily have security escort you from the building. Now, will this be an issue going forward?"

Andrew gritted his teeth. "No." As he turned to leave the room, he spat my way, "I suppose it helps when you fuck the boss."

In a flash, Nik had Andrew around the throat and against the wall.

"What did you say?" His rage filled the room, squeezing the air until it felt thin and suffocating. A coldness descended that seemed to make my own throat constrict.

"I have seen the way you look at her. She is hot. I would fuck her as well," he muttered hoarsely.

Nik brought him closer to his face and growled, "Pack your junk and leave. You are fired." He dropped him to the floor and stroked his chin.

Andrew stood and opened his mouth as Nik turned to glare at him. "Do you have something else to add?" His tone was menacing and monstrous.

Andrew took a step back, understanding the warning. "No, I will be out by the end of the day," he whimpered.

He ran back to his office, and I heard the door slam closed behind him.

Nik turned and replaced his glare with a smile. "Where were we?" He stalked towards me like I was his prey.

"No, you cannot be serious. You just fired that man because he questioned if I was ready for the promotion, which even I will admit, I do not think I am."

"Firstly, you are, and you will accept the position. Secondly, tell me what happened the other morning." His voice was unlike I had ever heard it. He was pleading for the truth like he needed it to survive, but I could not give it to him. I knew I would sound insane, so instead, I shook my head.

"I told you we are finished. You deserve better." My eyes fell to the floor, I found it easier to avoid staring into those beautiful blue eyes that would beg for me for the truth.

"This discussion is not over, Larissa." He left the break room in search of Andrew. I heard him speaking to my former boss in his office. I quickly collected my work and headed into the conference room. The doors locked from the inside, and I doubt Nik had a key. He rang my phone several times, but I ignored him.

CHAPTER 35

CREEPS IN THE SHADOWS

Larissa

LUCE AND I DECIDED TO SPEND ONE FINAL NIGHT TOGETHER before I moved out the next morning. We planned our night out at my bar so at least we would get cheaper drinks. I texted Roman to let him know that I was going out with my sister and that I would see him tomorrow night. He planned to help me unpack my boxes after I moved.

I borrowed Luce's clothing for the night as all my own were packed. I pulled on a pair of jeans and a black halter-neck top. I was covered more than my sister; she was doing it for attention, which I should be used to from her, but she still shocked me with the clothes that she wore. Her tight black skirt almost looked like she could not move in it and her crop top showed off her midriff. Her confidence astounded me. I never had any, but I also feared to show any skin knowing that vampires would love to have a taste of me.

Luce offered her hand. "Are you ready for a night on the town together?"

I nodded as I walked over and slid my hand into hers. "Let's do this!" We spent the night dancing and drinking together, we laughed like we had not in years. It was what we both needed, and I felt the rift between us beginning to heal. There were no boys around to get between us, no thoughts or discussion around Nik or Peter. The thumping music beat within my system, and it brought a sense of joy. I could not remember the last time I had been so happy and carefree.

It was nearing the end of the night when I could feel a familiar disdain, that I had sensed only once before. I scanned the bar before my eyes found another set that was already trained on me. It was the creep from the night at the bar when Roman had to step in and save me from him. I made my way over to Luce and whispered in her ear, "We should leave."

She was incredibly drunk. "Why? The night is just getting started."

I shook my head and grabbed her hand. "No, please Luce. We can keep going at home. We need to go."

Her eyes searched my face before it registered that I was being serious. "Let's go, but I want an explanation." Her voice slurred as she stumbled a little.

We snuck out the back and into the night air. Luce started to walk, but I paused and pulled on her arm. "We should catch a taxi home."

"We are not far, we can walk. There are two of us, we will be fine." She was confident but worry coursed through me as I observed the surrounding area. I did not see the creep, but he was near, I knew it.

We stayed close to one another as we walked into the darkness. It was a warm night; we giggled and spoke of our mother and her silly superstitions. It was like nothing had happened between us, like we were once again the silly girls who would race through the streets without a care in the world.

"So, tell me about your promotion, what is the new job title?" she asked. I was grateful for the distraction.

"I am Assistant Marketing Director for Refresh."

"Bugger, you still have to answer to that pig, Andrew?" She snorted as she tripped but remained on her feet.

I breathed out through my teeth. "Well, actually, Mr. Dankworth fired Andrew earlier in the week because he implied that my promotion only happened because I slept with him. It's not true. Mr. Dankworth became rather angry and confronted Andrew about it, to which Andrew said, 'I get it, she is hot'. I think that was the last straw." My eyes continually watched our surrounding area.

"Does that make you the head of marketing or still an assistant?" I stopped; I had not thought about it. Nik had not mentioned anything. After I told him it would never happen between us, he had been professional in all instances. By professional, I do mean, cold. He was trying to keep his distance, which I understood. We were both trying to heal. The ache I had for him never relented, I found that to be the hardest part. Roman filled the void, but I longed for Nik and his touch.

"Larissa, what is it?" Luce's voice cut into my thoughts. I shook my head slightly, clearing my head.

"Sorry, I was thinking about what you said. Mr. Dankworth has not said anything, so I would assume not." We rounded the corner; it was normally lit up by streetlights, but tonight, they were off.

Fear spread through me. "Luce, let's find another way. Something isn't right."

"Oh, you are being silly, come on," she urged me on.

"Luce, please, something isn't right. I feel it. Every part of me is screaming to not walk down there."

She shook her head and walked down the street. "Don't be a baby."

I could not leave her, so I followed her cautiously. I knew Nik would be able to sense my fear right now. I flipped out my phone to text him:

ME

I am fine, just walking down a dark street.

He would come and I did not need to explain that to my sister. I saw the dots appear, telling me he was going to respond, but they stopped. My heart sank, despite expecting it. I caught up to Luce and held onto her hand. My body was on edge. There was a loud bang behind us, and I spun to see a figure dart across the road.

"Luce, walk faster," I whisper-yelled at her.

"Why?" She laughed and flicked her hair. "It is a nice night, can't we just enjoy it?"

"Luce, I think we are being followed," I uttered into her ear as I pulled her close.

She let go of my hand and skipped ahead. "Come and get me!" she taunted them.

The tingles in my fingers started and trickled their way up my hand and arms. I searched for the figure and turned in circles before I saw them standing behind Luce. The same creepy smile I recognised.

"Luce!" I shouted. She froze as he disappeared again. "The creep is here. The one from the bar."

She ran back towards me, and I held her close as we walked cautiously towards the lights.

"They won't protect you," his shrill voice echoed through the street. "Where is your big strong Alpha? Pity he isn't here to protect you tonight." He circled us from the shadows. I could barely see him as he moved with his super speed.

"Forgive me, Luce." She would hate me for what I was about to say. "I recommend you leave. I am under the protection of Lord Dankworth." I hoped this would cause the creep to run away in fear. I hoped that hearing Nik's name would cause him to doubt his actions tonight. The creep came out of the shadows.

"Ah, is that so?" He sniffed the air loudly. "That is a lie. He has not marked you as his. How dare you name drop a man that you have no affiliation with!" he spat with disgust.

"A mark is not needed if one can verbalise that they are under the protection of another." I was quoting from their laws, and the creep growled. His eyes were glowing red in the dark, but he suddenly composed himself.

"Why don't you come with me into the shadows?" The compelling nature of his words ate at me, but I fought it off. However, this was not the case for Luce. I pulled at her arm as she walked closer to him.

"Luce, stop! Resist it, Luce." Tears were falling down my cheeks as I struggled to keep her from him.

The hands of another landed on my shoulder. I barely had time to register what he looked like. "Come now, pretty girl. It will only hurt for a moment. A virgin such as you is simply too much to resist." His lips were on my neck and the tingling sensation in my body threatened to explode. I threw my head back to hit the man behind me, and the pain seared into my skull. I ran for Luce and threw an arm around her; it was all happening so fast.

I held my hand up to the creep. "No!" I shouted, as a sudden warmth escaped my fingers, a bright light shot out at him. It was like the sun as it lit up the area around us. I suddenly grew weak, like I put everything into whatever was happening, and now I had nothing. A haze surrounded me, the attackers moved closer again. The creep grabbed me by the throat and lifted me from the ground.

"You will taste even better, little witch. I have not had one of you for centuries." I raised my hand to attack again, but he tossed me aside. I landed on my ass before my head fell back and smacked the ground. I heard Luce scream and I turned to see her attack the creeps. She pulled a knife from her pocket and lunged.

"Nik, help me, please," I whispered, before the world drifted away.

CHAPTER 36
BRIGHT LIGHTS AND HEAVY HEARTS
Larissa

I woke to the sound of dulled sirens. The lights were incredibly bright. We were in a hospital, but I could not remember the ride in the ambulance. I knew I had a concussion, but I did not care. I only worried about Luce, who was still unconscious from the attack. She put herself in front of me to stop the vampire's attack. I was the target.

When we arrived at the hospital, Luce was about to be rolled away on a stretcher, but I rolled off my own and went over to grab her hand and refused to leave her side. The nurses and doctors ran over, but I would not let go of her. I would not lose my sister as I had lost my mother.

"Miss Solis, step away. We need to look her over." The pretty young nurse said as she tried to pull my hand away, but I held on tighter. I rubbed my head; the noises and the happenings of the world around me were all getting to be too much. I felt faint. Hands grabbed me before my legs collapsed and could no longer hold me up.

"She has a concussion. She will need a scan to ensure there is no brain bleed!" the paramedic yelled out. I reached for Luce again. I had to be sure my sister was okay.

"We have her, Larissa. We need to get you looked at." The male voice helped me to my feet and pulled a chair for me to sit down. I covered my eyes; the lights were killing me. A warm hand landed on my knee. I tried to focus on its owner's outline, but it was too fuzzy to focus.

"I need to send you for a scan to make sure you do not have a bleed, but first, I need to know what hurts. What is going on?" I peeked between my fingers to see a bald doctor in his late thirties, his hazel eyes looking me over, trying to find clues about my condition.

"The lights are burning my eyes, and I feel heavy almost." He removed the bandage on my head and looked at it again.

"Alright, stay here. I will find you a wheelchair and get your head looked at. Just keep your eyes covered if it helps." As I sat there waiting, the tingle in my body alerted me that Nik was close. The sensation grew stronger until I knew he was in front of me.

"I should have known you would be here," he sniggered. I could feel him sitting beside me. "I heard you call for me. Now give me a look."

I had not seen him since Wednesday morning, and I had ignored all his calls since our last discussion. I moved my hand away and saw his blue eyes. My body melted at the sight of him. He removed the bandage and pricked his finger. I moved to grab his hand, but he glared at me.

"You do not get to ignore me or disobey me right now. Hold still." He rubbed his finger over the cut on my head and licked it as the doctor arrived with the wheelchair.

"Lord Dankworth." He bowed his head as the light started to dull, and my eyes began to feel normal.

"Doctor Cauca, how are you?" The doctor's eyes flashed red, and it was as if silent words were spoken between them.

"I shall care for her with everything I have, sir." His voice almost sounded robotic

"As long as you understand that I shall not leave her side." He stood, nodding his head at the Doctor.

"Absolutely."

Nik took my hands and helped me into the wheelchair. The doctor wheeled me deeper into the hospital, but I could only think of Luce.

"I healed the wound on her head, she will no longer need stitches. Do you know what occurred?"

"No, I was not told, but I could smell vampire blood on the other girl."

Emotion coursed through my body; it was like I could feel Nik's worry.

"Luce and I were attacked. She protected me and I saw her get sliced, she has a massive wound on her leg." I tried to look up at Nik to let him know, my mind compelled me to tell him about what happened during the attack.

"She will need a blood transfusion," Doctor Cauca muttered.

"I am her twin. I can donate the blood." Nik put his hand on my shoulder to quieten me.

"You need to focus on yourself." His words were filled with a combination of love and worry.

"She risked her life for me. Do not tell me what to do. She can have my blood," I demanded as I snapped my head around at Nik, he bowed his head and looked at the doctor.

"Twin blood *is* better. We shall test your blood to be sure that you are compatible." The doctor rolled me up to the CT room. He spoke to reception before turning back to Nik and said, "You have two people in front, you will have to wait for a moment. I shall retrieve the kit to take Larissa's blood before I return."

I noticed that he focused solely on Nik and did not even glance in my direction. I waved my hands in the air to get his attention. "I am sitting right here, please do not ignore me. Nik is not my care person nor are we in a relationship. He does not need to know anything."

Nik cleared his throat and took a step back.

"My apologies, Miss Solis, I will ensure it does not happen again." The doctor bowed his head at Nik and left quickly.

I crossed my arms as Nik took a seat beside me and unbuttoned his navy suit jacket.

"Now, shall we discuss this immature behaviour?" I did not bother to look at him. I played with my hands instead, at which he scoffed. "Typical. I do not know why I expect better of you."

I glared at him. "Nobody asked you to be here. I certainly do not want you here. The door is right behind you, you can kindly walk back through it."

A smile played over his face. He baited me, and I fell straight into it. I rolled my eyes and searched the corridor for something else to stare at other than his hypnotising eyes.

"What happened? We had a wonderful night together and then you woke and ran out with no explanation. I would certainly like one. I do not believe the whole, 'I deserve better' and 'You cannot accept me.'"

"I believe I told you enough, we are finished, and I am dating someone else." My voice was clear despite the raging emotions underneath.

"Yes, I am aware." His nose crinkled in disgust. "I will not stop trying to be with you, no matter how much you fight this. What happened tonight?" He leant forward in the chair with his hands clasped between his legs. I ignored him.

He stood up and smacked the wall. "Fucking hell, Larissa, you were attacked by one of my own. I am the Lord of this region, and I must ensure that he or they are punished for this. What happened?" His voice boomed down the hallway as a crack formed in the wall, proof of his strength. He was holding his monster back, I knew, because he would have easily been able to punch straight through that wall.

"I went out with Luce. We went to a bar. A vampire hounded us. He had already been told last time that I was not interested. We eventually left, but they followed us. I wanted to call for a taxi, but Luce wanted to walk. They attacked; we tried our best to push them away, but it was no use. I was thrown backwards, and I hit my head on the floor. Luce protected me and was cut on the leg and now here we are." I conveniently left out the part about shooting blinding light from my hands.

Nik eyed me suspiciously. I was hoping he could not read my thoughts through this stupid mate bond.

"I can tell you are leaving something out, what is it?" he asked as he lifted my chin to scan my face.

Doctor Cauca returned and bent down to draw my blood. Nik and I continued to stare at one another. I could feel his anger and frustration because he knew I was hiding something.

Doctor Cauca looked uncomfortably between the two of us. "Would you like a moment alone?"

I shook my head. "No, I have given Nik all the important details." I gritted my teeth at him.

"What *you* think is important. I need all the details to ensure the attackers are punished properly." He ran his fingers through his hair, worry etched on his face.

Doctor Cauca drew my blood before I was called in for the CT scan. Nik stood in the doorway eager to get more information from me.

"Forgive me, sir, but you cannot enter during the scan. You can wait outside until it is over. It is hospital protocol, and it trumps your position," the doctor nervously informed Nik with a shaky voice.

Nik crossed his arms and waited on the wall outside as I poked my tongue out.

"Doctor Cauca, could you ask him to leave? I do not wish for him to be here," I pleaded as Nik continued to stir emotions that I had been trying to bury.

"I am unable to, Miss Solis. I would if it were possible, but with his position, I am unable to do that." I nodded as I lay on the table and waited for the scan to be over. It did not take long before he escorted me from the room.

Nik was on the phone. "I *do not care*. Find them. They do not get to attack my mate. This is a breach of one of our most sacred laws." The word mate stuck out to me. He would always protect me, even if we were never to be together. He smiled as he laid his eyes on me. He put his phone away to put all his energy and attention on me.

"What happens now, Doctor?" I asked as I peered up at him.

"Luce has been given a semi-private room. I will leave you to rest until she is in recovery. I doubt you will need one after Nik healed the wound on your head. Nik will take you up to the room to wait." He smiled and walked away.

Nik beamed as he grabbed the handles of the wheelchair, but I moved to stand.

"I can walk," I muttered, but he put his hands on my shoulders, forcing me down.

"Sit down!" he ordered. I could tell he was frustrated and angry, so I stayed in the seat as he wheeled it towards the room. Once inside, he closed the door. I knew what was coming.

"Now tell me *everything* that happened." I stood from the wheelchair and walked over to the lounge, to get comfortable.

"Nothing else to tell." I tried to hide my face from his view.

"Larissa, I know when you lie. I cannot protect you unless I know the whole truth. What happened?" He was not going to stop asking.

I yawned. It was early in the morning, and I was tired. I had no energy for this fight.

"Nik, please, let me rest."

He removed his coat and laid it over the chair before he pulled the blanket from the cupboard and laid it over me. He lifted my head and laid it on his lap.

"Rest, but you will tell me once you wake." He stroked my hair and my body relaxed at his touch. I sighed as tiredness enveloped me.

"I wish you knew the truth, my love," he whispered as I fell asleep.

"I wish you knew the truth, my love," he whispered as I fell asleep.

CHAPTER 37

WAIT, WHAT?

I was shaken awake. When I opened my eyes, I saw it was Nik who had a hold of me. I could barely focus as Doctor Cauca came into view.

"I apologise for the awakening, Miss Solis, but your results are back. You have no brain bleed. If you did, I believe Nik may have healed it for you incidentally. There is no evidence of any injury in the scans." He paused before scratching the back of his neck. It was obvious he was dreading saying whatever was to come next.

"What is it, Doctor?" I asked as I rubbed my eyes to observe the awkward look on his face.

He sighed as he exchanged glances with Nik. "I cannot use your blood for the transfusion. You do not share the same blood type as Lucianna."

"I do not understand. I know it is normal, as we are not identical twins, but if we are sisters, do we still not have the same blood type?" He shifted in his stance as I moved closer. I feared what was about to come out of his mouth.

"Miss Solis, you…ah…you do not share the same parents." I wanted to vomit.

"So we are half-siblings?" He shook his head. Nik put his hand on my lower back for comfort, which took effect instantly.

"No, you do not share the same mother or father. From the blood, I can determine that you are cousins, and *your* blood type is rather unique. You are not an appropriate donor for your sister."

My legs fell from under me. Nik's arms were around me quickly as he pulled me against him and held me tight.

"I have you Larissa, take a moment. Thank you, Doctor."

The words slowly sunk in. "She isn't my sister and Elizabeth is not my mother. But how? When? Why? I do not understand. Luce is not my sister. Why was I never told? Who is my mother?" My head was going a million miles an hour and I could not focus. Nik released me from his grasp as I paced the room. It felt like everything in my life was a lie. The tingling sensation in my arms grew and I started to scratch at them. Nik walked over and grabbed my face in his hands. He kissed me, knowing it was what I needed. I relaxed and closed my eyes at his touch. I could not understand how he managed to calm me down so easily.

He rested his forehead on mine. "It will be fine. We shall find the answers. You need to rest. Come and lie down. I fear that my stay will be rather unwelcome once your sister arrives. I would prefer to be here for you, for as long as I can." Nik walked me over to the couch and I lay on him again. Despite his legs being muscular they were soft enough to be the perfect pillow.

"You were right," I whispered as I gazed at his face.

"I did not wish to be." The softly spoken words showed just how much he meant that.

"Do you think Katrina is my mother?" I knew the answer, but I needed to hear it from him.

He stroked my hair, as his eyes remained on the door. "I have thought it for a while. The dark hair and stubbornness make it difficult not to draw the comparisons."

"You said she was evil," I stated as I picked at my fingers.

"Rest, Larissa. You do not even know if Katrina and your mother are related. Elizabeth raised you and will always be your mother, even though she did not birth you."

I sat up, the need to be touched by him was overpowering. I needed the comfort he brought me, I flung my leg over his lap, straddling him.

"Just for a moment," I whispered. "I need the clarity that you give me."

He smiled as I ground on his lap. "I have a better idea. Do you trust me?"

I looked into his beautiful blue eyes and saw the desire and need within them. I did trust him, but I did not trust the monster inside. I nodded and bit my lip; he pressed a kiss to either side of my face, one on each cheek before he kissed my lips.

I closed my eyes as images flashed in my mind.

I was standing in Nik's apartment. I glanced around the room. Nik was in the kitchen. He was cooking while wearing a silly apron that had a fat man's body on it. I laughed as I saw it. He turned towards me.

"When did you get home?" A smile beamed over his face as he put down the pan and scooped me into his arms, lifting me from the floor.

"Just now. I like your apron, but I like what is underneath better."

Nik kissed my lips and put me down. "I missed you too," he whispered.

I put down my bag and settled onto the bar stool.

"It smells delicious, what is it?"

He winked at me playfully. "It is a secret, but I know you will enjoy it. How was work?"

I noticed a wedding ring on my finger. It was not as massive as I would have expected from him, but it was simple, delicate, and about a carat or possibly two. I played with the ring as he walked over with a plate and set the table. He snapped his fingers and the candles ignited to reveal a romantic dinner set up.

"I needed this," I let out as I walked over. I buried my face in his chest. He kissed the top of my head.

"I know. I love you."

"I love you, too."

I blinked as the hospital room around me returned. Nik's gaze flickered with caution as he silently observed my impending reaction. During that entire dream, I felt happy and loved. There was no inner conflict that I struggled with around him.

"Is that what our future could be?" I watched as his face fell, but he quickly replaced it with a smile. I had hurt him, but he tried to hide it. I wondered what I said that brought on that sadness.

"Yes, it could be. Did you enjoy it?" he asked with eagerness, raising his brow in the hope that it would change my mind.

I could not help it as I wrapped my arms around his neck and kissed him. "I did. I felt incredibly happy. I was at peace with you. It just felt perfect."

"Then let it happen, Larissa. Let *us* happen," he requested as my mind raced with what could be.

The door to the room opened and I stood instantly for the visitor. Luce was rolled into the room; she was still unconscious. Doctor Cauca entered behind her.

"She will be fine," he assured me. "She needs to rest. I have organised for a bed to be brought in for you to rest, too."

Nik stood and joined me. He rubbed my shoulders and kissed my cheek. "I shall leave you to be with your sister."

My heart ached. I did not want him to leave. I wished that he could stay. He paused at the door and glanced back. "Larissa, I will not be leaving this hospital. I shall be closer than you think, but you both need rest." He paused as he held onto the door handle, it was like he wanted to say something else.

"Say it, Nik." The words were barely audible as they left my mouth, but I needed him to be honest.

His blue eyes stared into mine, as he gently confessed, "I love you, Larissa."

The words were too soon, but they provided the comfort I needed. He closed the door and left as I held onto Luce's hand.

CHAPTER 38
WITCH WAY NOW!

Larissa

THE BED WAS BROUGHT IN, AND I PUSHED IT BESIDE LUCE'S. THE guilt was unbearable. It was the early hours of the morning before I woke, and Luce was still soundly asleep. I needed to find answers about who my parents were. I flicked open my phone and called the doctor back home, who, supposedly, personally delivered us both. I knew that to be a lie now, as we were not even sisters. I left the room and I saw Nik sitting outside, asleep on the chair. He looked peaceful as I sat beside him and dialled.

"Larissa Solis! How is London treating you and your sister?" The doctor answered the phone cheerfully and I wanted to yell and scream; he was still lying to me.

"Doctor O'Leary, I just discovered the truth that Lucianna is not my sister. We do not share the same parents, so please do not lie to me." The phone went quiet as I pulled it away to ensure he had not hung up on me. "Doctor O'Leary? Hello?"

He cleared his throat. "You need to speak with Annie. She can answer your questions. I only hope you forgive me for the dishonesty." Annie was supposedly a family friend who had moved away when we were younger.

"How do I get in contact with Annie?" My phone beeped and I pulled it away to see a new notification on the screen. He had sent me her phone number.

"Did you get it?"

"Yes, thank you, Doctor O'Leary," I said, not giving him a chance to respond before I disconnected the call.

I tapped the phone against my chin. Our mother had always told us that Annie moved away because she hated how naughty we were. I leant my head back against the wall. How many lies had I fallen for? I tapped the number on my screen and took a deep breath. I had no idea what to expect. The last time I spoke to Annie, I was just beginning puberty. The phone clicked to alert me that it had been answered.

"Annie speaking." Her voice was soft and almost like she was singing.

"Hello, Annie, this is Larissa Solis. I am not sure if you remember me, but I am the daughter of Elizabeth Solis." Even saying *daughter* sounded strange. It burned my tongue knowing it was no longer true.

"Yes, I remember you." Her tone was blunt like she had better people to speak with.

"I am sorry for calling you, but I was told you would be able to give me some answers on a few things. Elizabeth died a few months ago and I just...I have since discovered that I am not her daughter. Doctor O'Leary gave me your number." There was a tapping down the phone, before a deep sigh.

"Where do you live now?" she asked.

"I moved to London with Luce after Elizabeth died. Do you

know who my mother is?" I asked impatiently, wanting to know the answer.

"I told Elizabeth that you should know the truth. Has it happened yet?"

"Has what happened?" I questioned what she was referring to, but deep down, I had a sinking feeling about what she was going to say.

"You are a witch, Larissa. Your mother, Elizabeth, blocked Luce's and your magic to protect you both. She used it for her own gain, which is why I told her that I wanted nothing to do with her anymore."

The words echoed in my mind. Witch. Witches were real. Nik had mentioned this to me but hearing that I was one of them made sense. It explained what happened earlier and why my eyes often changed to a different colour.

"You thought as much, I am guessing from your silence. You need to find your mother's grimoire. Elizabeth had it hidden under the floor in her room. She refused to speak about her sister. She believed her to be a traitor, but she was wrong. Katrina was no traitor." My mind raced, thinking of the antique wooden box that I found after the fire. I had not told Luce and I still had not opened it. The box sat in my wardrobe. Is that why I kept it? Did I subconsciously know what was inside? Katrina's name kept bouncing around in my head. Nik had spoken about her. He was right. I was her daughter. The woman who used her magic against vampires. I hung up the phone, needing to process.

Nik stirred beside me, and then he opened his eyes and observed his surroundings.

"You do realise you look dead when you sleep," I teased as I nudged him in the seat.

"It would do you well to remember that I *am* the living dead." He chuckled as he stood and stretched out his impossibly long legs before straightening his suit and sitting back down. "I do not require much rest, but I see that you did not manage any." I leant my head on his shoulder, and he kissed the top of it.

"What is it?" he asked, knowing something plagued my mind.

I sighed before tears fell down my cheeks. "I know that Luce is going to need to be cared for. I will not be able to move out this weekend as I had planned. I will have to let that apartment go; I will still pay you the bond that you generously paid for me. It is just not possible right now. I was so close to being my own independent person, and now it has been taken away from me. *Again.* It is like living with my mother. Oh wait, sorry, the woman I *thought* was my mother. Do not worry, I just discovered that you were right. My mother is Katrina, and wait, there is more. I am a witch, what even is that? How did this all go from me being a boring human, to now having ma—" I was interrupted by Nik grabbing me and whisking me with his super speed to another room. He slammed the door shut. I failed to get my bearings before I grabbed the wall to help stabilise myself.

"What the fuck was that?" I swore as he ran his fingers through his hair. I noticed his eyes flashed red to blue and back again.

"You CANNOT say that!" he yelled at me. I took a step back. "By the Gods, Larissa, witches are not accepted within society. We are told to eradicate them. That was why your mother, Elizabeth, wanted you to hate us. It was a form of protection. Katrina fought for more rights for witches. You cannot tell this to anyone, do you understand?" I nodded and kept my distance from him.

"Fuck, now you are scared of me." I could feel his fear and worry.

"No, I am not!" I lied.

"I can feel your fear, Larissa. This is not supposed to happen. You are supposed to..." his voice trailed off.

"I am supposed to what?" He ignored me as I walked over and grabbed his arm to pull him around, he yanked his arm away. "Answer me, Nik. I am done with this cryptic behaviour; this is why I do not want to be with you. I can feel that you are not being honest with me."

"Feel?" he questioned as his head turned to look at me.

"Yes, you said you could feel my emotions. I did not understand it at first, but today I can feel or sense your emotions."

"I have to go." He moved to walk out the door.

"If you leave now, do not expect to talk to me later. I deserve answers, Nik."

He ignored me and slammed the door on the way out. I collapsed against the wall. He was exhausting. It was like he had two personalities: the lover and the monster.

———

I sat with Luce until she woke, her pale complexion alerted me to just how long her recovery was going to be.

"Hey, you," she croaked as she moved to sit up.

I rushed over to stop her. "No, do not move, stay there." She winced in pain. "I will call for the doctor," I said to her as I popped my head out the door to see her surgeon already waiting.

"Miss Solis, I was just about to check on your sister. Is she awake?" Doctor Tankos was one of the youngest doctors I had ever seen, but it was obvious that she was a vampire. Her perfect complexion, hair, and eyes were all further proof. Her blonde hair was pulled back into a bun and her brown eyes were gentle. She floated into the room and smiled at Luce.

"Lucianna, how are you feeling this morning?"

Luce glared at the doctor and did not answer.

"Luce, please do not be rude, she is only here to help." I urged her, hoping she would see reason.

"I want a new doctor. I refuse to be looked after by a bloodsucker." Her hatred was getting worse. She had never been this rude towards them.

Doctor Tankos smiled politely. "I will happily retrieve one for you. I apologise for your lack of empathy towards my kind, I wish you all the best in your recovery."

She spun around to leave, but I stopped her. "Wait! Doctor Tankos, could I ask about her recovery?"

"Rissa, don't you dare." Luce shot daggers in my direction as I left the room with Doctor Tankos.

"Larissa, Lucianna will be on bed rest for at least the next month. She will be able to work from home, but she must keep her leg elevated until it is fully healed. Once she has the stitches out, she will be able to move more freely. She will need some form of physical therapy to repair the muscles and the general function of the leg. She will need to stay in the hospital for the next few days to ensure there is no infection before she can return home. Do you have any questions?"

"No, thank you Doctor Tankos, and I apologise for my sister."

"There is no need to apologise, Mrs. Dankworth." She disappeared from my sight before I could correct her. I was not with Nik, but I knew he would have informed those of importance that I was to be taken care of while I was here. I sighed as I realised that there was no point in even correcting her. I shook my head and waited outside in the corridor as another doctor entered the room to give Luce the news.

I checked my phone to see a message from Nik:

NIK

I promise, I will give you all the answers in time. Please trust me, Larissa. If you need anything, simply ask.

I did not respond. I did trust him, but I doubted that I would get the answers I wanted. I remembered that I had not spoken to Roman in all of my phone calls. I thought it best to alert him to what had happened over the last two days. I dialled Roman, but it went to voicemail.

"Hey Roman, I just wanted to let you know that I am in hospital with Luce right now. We had a run-in with some people, and she was injured. Um, I do not even know what to say, but thought you would want to know. Talk to you later."

It was no less than five minutes before his name flashed across my screen.

"Where are you? I am coming now," he demanded.

"Roman, you are at work. At least I am assuming. You do not have to. I am fine and it will all be okay."

"Larissa, which one?" His voice was tense.

"The Royal London Hospital."

"I will be there in a few minutes." He hung up. I stayed outside Luce's room. It was almost like I could feel her hate through the wall. The recovery between us was going to be long, if not impossible, and knowing that she was no longer my sister brought on even more grief. I heard shouting and my eyes followed the sound. Roman came racing around the corner.

"You cannot tell me that I cannot see my fucking girlfriend. Call security, I don't care." I could not help but smile at his use of the word *girlfriend*. His eyes found mine as he raced over, security on his tail. I wrapped my arms around him as he lifted me from the ground and held me tightly against his hard body. Security caught up and bent over to catch their breath, presumably from their lack of physical fitness.

"Sir, we explained—"

I interrupted them and put my hand up. "I appreciate the need for security, but Roman is my boyfriend and I need his emotional support right now." They looked between the two of us and nodded. They were probably confused after Nik had told them I was his mate.

"Fine, but he is to listen to reception before barging into a hospital."

Roman ignored them as they walked away and looked me over for any injuries.

"I am fine." I hesitated to tell him the truth, but I could not lie. I wanted us to be honest with one another. "My wounds were healed."

"Healed? How so?"

I cleared my throat and fiddled with my fingers. "My boss, Mr. Dankworth, healed a wound for me once and as such, he can sense when I am in danger. He rushed to find me and pricked his finger to heal the cut on my forehead. The doctor believes it also would have healed anything more serious." I waited as Roman scrutinised my every word, concentration etched across his face.

"As long as you are better," he finally said. "How is Luce?"

I explained to Roman what happened with the creep he saved me from that first time. I spoke about Luce's injuries and how long her recovery would be. Roman just listened until I finished, and then he touched my face gently.

"I am so sorry. I know how upset you must be. You were looking forward to moving out on the weekend. Are you able to keep the apartment?"

A tear ran down my cheek, it gave Roman the answer to the question he asked. He wiped it away.

"I am so sorry, Larissa. Did you want me to pay for a couple of months for you?" The gesture was amazing, but I could never accept it. I only shook my head in response. Roman stayed with me until it was night and visiting hours were over. Luce was still angry with me. It was going to be a long recovery for the both of us.

CHAPTER 39

FAST FORWARD

Larissa

IT HAS BEEN SIX MONTHS SINCE OUR MOTHER DIED AND THREE months had passed since the attack. The vampires involved were hunted down and killed for their transgressions against Luce and me.

Nik kept his distance, but he gave me Andrew's job, which meant we were going to be around one another, whether I liked it or not.

Luce had healed. I still took her to her physical therapy once a week to make sure I could keep track of recovery. We barely spoke to each other than texting appointment times.

Roman and I had moved into together. I was disappointed that I never got to move into that perfect apartment, but I had turned Roman's apartment into more of a home. I decorated it with colours and textures. He gave me the freedom to do as I liked with the space. I cared for him deeply, but I struggled with the notion of loving him. I was devoted, caring, and tender. I was the perfect girlfriend, but whenever he told me he was in love with me, I could never bring myself to say it back. He told me there was never any pressure for me to say it, but I doubted that was true.

———

I stared at my wardrobe for clothes to wear for our mystery date tonight. Roman promised we would celebrate our three-month anniversary, and our one month since moving in together.

"Roman!" I yelled out to him. He popped his head around the corner, looking as suave as ever. His hair was slicked back, his grey polo shirt was snug against his frame, and his jeans hugged that amazing ass.

"Yeah, what is it?" He leant casually on the doorframe as I stood in my underwear, staring at the wardrobe. I noticed his eyes dart up and down.

"No, do not dare to use those eyes on me. You are taking me on this mystery celebration date, but you have not given me any clues on what to wear. Just give me a smidge of detail, please." I batted my eyes at him.

"You do not need to bat your eyes at me. Wear something cute but comfortable."

I stamped my foot on the ground in frustration. "That does not help, that could mean a summery dress or a pair of jeans and a nice top. Both of those are cute but comfortable."

"Jeans and a nice top with comfortable shoes that you can walk in."

I grabbed my jeans and threw them onto the bed before I sorted through my drawers for a top. While I was bent over, Roman wrapped his arms around my waist and kissed along my spine. "We have some time to spare." His voice was laced with desire.

"Either we stay in and have sex, or we are going out, one or other, mister." I stood as his kisses made their way to my neck.

"That is not fair," he grumbled as he slumped onto the bed.

Sex with Roman was amazing, but it always felt like something was missing. It did not matter how many times we would have it in one night, I never found myself satisfied. I did not have the heart to tell him that, though. We were happy, and he was the perfect boyfriend.

"It is not fair when you do not tell me where we are going on dates." I poked my tongue out playfully.

He chuckled. "Fine, fine." He sat up on the bed and groaned as I dressed myself and climbed on top of him.

"The surprise is nice, though." I kissed him on the lips and then slapped his cheek gently. "Time to get going. Do I have to wear a blindfold?"

He leant up and kissed along my jawline. "Maybe when we get home."

I moaned and regretfully pushed myself away. "Come on, you horny bugger. Otherwise, I will have to use my magic on you."

"I'm only this way because you are amazing on the inside and the outside," he called out as he wandered into the bathroom.

"Alright, suck up. Let's get going. I cannot wait," I said impatiently as I fluffed my hair one more time.

Roman took my hand and opened the car door for me. He rested his hand on my leg as he drove to our mystery location. He had a habit of always keeping his hands on me, even when we were on the couch. He always had to be touching me.

Roman broke the silence in the car. "How are your magic lessons with Sofia going?"

I ended up confessing to Roman about the revelation that I was a witch. We spoke at length, and he believed me. He did not even contemplate that I could be losing my mind. He understood and had been supportive ever since. I was dumbfounded. I half expected to be tied up and burned at the stake, or even stoned in the middle of the street.

I had not told Luce about us not being biological sisters. I thought it better not to, despite my frustration at her poor attitude. She may not be my sister, but I considered her one all the same. We spoke once a week now and it was never personal. Annie gave me Sofia's number, who taught me the significance of my magic and how to access it without losing control.

"Yeah, it is going well, she said the upcoming blood moon may cause my magic to become a little scattered. Not sure what she means exactly, but we shall see," I said happily as I watched the scenery change from cityscape to landscape.

Roman shifted in his seat and looked out the window searching the sky for the moon, at least I presumed.

"Is there a blood moon coming?" His voice sounded almost strained.

"Yes, in two days." He raised his fingers on the wheel and stared at them. "You are acting a little weird. Is everything alright?"

He snapped his fingers around the wheel again, "Yes, just fine. We are almost there. Do you have any guesses?"

It was obvious he was trying to change the subject; it almost reminded me of the way that Nik avoided answering questions. I looked ahead and saw bright lights flashing in the distance.

A grin spread over my face as I beheld the sight before me. "This is incredible!" I exclaimed.

"Say it, Larissa." Roman's smile reached his eyes as he saw my delight.

"It is a carnival!" I pushed the button to lower the window, and I heard the distant noises that you would typically associate with a carnival; the music, shrieks of fear and excitement from those on the rides, and the general merriment of all the visitors. I could not help but laugh with glee.

"Good idea for a date?" he asked as if seeking my approval.

"Yes, I hope you brought enough change. Our mother never let us go to one, but I always dreamed of going on the Ferris Wheel and riding it to the top and kissing the person that I was with." He squeezed my leg. He had spoken about his dislike of my mother and how she kept me contained, as he would call it.

"We shall save that for the end." His eyes had a cheeky gleam to them. Roman parked and then ran around to open the car door, but paused and glanced around like he was waiting for something. I opened the door, but he pushed it closed again.

"Roman, what the hell?" I shrieked as the door almost hit me.

He snapped out of his somewhat trance and opened the door. "The floor is muddy. I was looking around to see if you would be able to walk. I am going to carry you for a little while. I do not want you falling over."

I rolled my eyes at his attempt to be chivalrous. "Fine." I was not entirely sold on his chivalry; his actions were strange.

He lifted me from the car and carried me till the ground was harder, then he gently set me down.

"Happy now?" I questioned as he kissed my cheek.

"Absolutely. Where to first?" He slipped his hand into my own, and warmth spread through my body. I could not help but smile.

———

We spent the first couple of hours trying our luck at the different games that were typically rigged to make sure that people never win. Even though we did not win, it was simply fun to be there. Roman seemed to be acting a little more protective than usual. If someone was close to bumping into me, he would bring me closer to him. He had never acted this way before.

"Roman, is everything okay?" I asked.

"It could not be more perfect. I think it is time for the infamous Ferris Wheel ride." Something in his voice was off, I could feel it deep inside. I knew the answer, but it seemed to be locked away in the darkest parts of my subconscious.

"Are you sure? You are acting different tonight," I questioned. I had to know what was going on.

"How so?" he mumbled while avoiding eye contact.

"Well for starters, you are acting a little more masculine than usual and secondly, you are being insanely protective. If anyone comes close, you are super sensitive and bring me in as if you are my bodyguard." He rubbed the back of his neck as we walked slowly to the Ferris Wheel line.

"Yes, I suppose we have never been on a date like this before. I love you, Larissa, and knowing that your boss said you smell different to bloodsuckers, well, I want to make sure you are safe from them. It is dark and more of them are out at night," he added. I remained suspicious.

I touched his cheek, turning him to face me as I stared into his puppy dog eyes.

"Roman, I do not think I smell as nice since the night you took my virginity." I laughed with him as I remembered the romantic night we spent together. He took me away for the weekend. It was rather cliché; he put rose petals all over the bed and scented candles on the bedside tables. He was soft and gentle and made sure that he did not hurt me. It was the best night I could have ever expected for my first time.

"Yes, but I bet they would be able to smell your magic. Supernatural creatures have a sense of each other. Since you are a witch, you fit into that category. I don't trust them."

I glanced around. He was right. I suddenly felt vulnerable out in the open. It was strange. I was paranoid that all eyes were on me. Roman squeezed my hand as a form of comfort. His protection now made sense. He was trying to be the alpha male and keep me safe. We had wandered around the whole carnival before finally arriving at the Ferris Wheel. We lined up as he held his arm around my waist and kept me close to him.

I shivered as the cool breeze hit me. "Are you cold?" Roman asked noticing my teeth chatter slightly.

"I am a little, but it is fine." He removed his large leather jacket and helped me into it. "I said I was fine."

"You don't need to catch a cold," he commented.

"But now *you* will," I argued as he stood in his polo shirt.

"Please, you know I am a sauna." He fobbed off my concern.

"Yes, I never need the heater on when in bed with you," I teased. We reached the Ferris Wheel and Roman helped me into the pod. I was grateful for the jacket now. Slowly, it went upwards as the pods were filled one by one. I was nervous once we reached the top and I grabbed Roman's leg out of fear. He slid his hand over the top of mine, giving me a sense of security as it spread through my body.

"Thank you," I said softly as I leant my head on his shoulder. The lights below were minuscule in the distance, but the stars were beautiful.

"The sky right now has no comparison to how you look tonight." I looked up at Roman, whose eyes met my own. They flickered with his love and affection for me. I pressed my lips to his and felt all his love hit me hard. I gasped and moved back.

"What's wrong?" He touched my face, his own filled with concern. I could feel my eyes changing. It was the start of the blood moon; it was already starting to affect my magic. Roman was never scared of my eyes.

"My magic, I can feel it bubbling inside. When you kissed me, I felt your love. It was overwhelming and powerful," I explained as my body buzzed.

"Alright, we shall head home when we get down. Close your eyes for me. I want you to block out all noise and just focus on my voice. Just whatever you feel, trust me." I did as Roman asked and closed my eyes. He kissed my cheeks and made his way down my neck as he nuzzled into it. His kisses were calming, and the excess magic dissipated with every press of his lips.

It did not take long until we were on the ground. My eyes flew open as Roman took my hand and led me from the Ferris Wheel. He carried me back to the car; we were quiet after. Roman dropped me at our apartment but did not move to go inside.

"What's wrong?" I queried as he stood in the doorway.

"I forgot; I have to go out of town for business. I will head in and collect a bag before I leave again."

"Did I do something wrong?" My heart sank. I did not understand why he was doing this. I thought he accepted me.

"No, no, no, you did not." A small, almost growl sound escaped his mouth. "I simply forgot, that is all." He smiled, and my anxiety lifted a little.

We walked inside in silence, and I watched Roman pack his bag. He kissed me before he left.

I changed into my nightdress and slipped into bed to read through my emails, but the shift in Roman seemed to plague my thoughts.

Chapter 40
The Secrets of Nik

Roman entered the den in his signature leather jacket and jeans. It was late. He slumped onto my couch. His wolf smell irritated my senses, but he was my brother, and I loved him unconditionally. Even if we were considered mortal enemies.

"What is it, brother?" He looked exhausted, more so than usual.

"The Blood Moon. I had not sensed it till tonight," he noted as he stared at his fingertips darkening.

I straightened in my chair. I had noticed that my bloodlust was stronger than usual. "Neither was I. Now it makes sense."

I had noticed a shift in Larissa's energy and my own. I also noticed the dark rings around Roman's eyes. "Anything else?" I probed him for answers.

"No. I forgot about Larissa's sexual appetite. She can never get enough." He exhaled with frustration as he threw his hands in the air.

I fought the need to rip his throat out. It was not unlike her to pick him over me. She had in the past, but he was never able to satisfy her. I never cared in the past about her sexual partners, but she had never been a virgin, which made my need to claim her stronger than usual. Even her rejection hurt my heart.

"Are you alright, brother?" he asked as I looked up at him.

"Yes, just the usual paperwork for the area." I cleared my throat and rolled my shoulders. "Why?"

"Your pen."

As I glanced down, I noticed it had exploded from the pressure of my frustration. I cleared my throat and chucked it away to grab another.

"You said you did not care if I pursued her. Has that changed? Or did she shatter your ego?" Roman attempted to bait me. He enjoyed a wrestle on days when our powers were amplified.

"My ego is never shattered with her, as you recall in the past, she always comes back to me. Remember brother, you are never able to truly satisfy her." He growled as I smiled at him.

"This fucking curse. You just had to go after her and go against her wishes, didn't you?" He slammed his fists down in anger.

"I did not think she would reject me in the way that she did, nor give up her gift…" I snarled at him, my anger flaring, an effect of the Blood Moon.

"I did not expect to take it and I apologise." I saw the sincerity in Roman's eyes. She was mine, but I could never hate Roman. We both loved her.

"No need. She makes her choices, and we accept them." I sighed, knowing she would return to me in her own time.

"This is not like you. Something has changed…Nik, we must tell her the truth." He had been begging since he first laid eyes on her in the bar.

I put the pen down and eyed him suspiciously. We had always decided to let it happen naturally, but this was taking longer than usual. I was unaware of when the opportune moment would arise.

I scratched my chin. "She has made me feel something I thought I had lost long ago, Roman. I do not know what it is. I also do not know what to do about her memories. Not once has she not remembered. When I ran into her that day, I could not believe it. She had barely been gone and she had already returned, but she smelt different."

"What did the witch do? You asked for help to break the curse." Roman never liked Katrina and always made it known that my affiliation with her was disgusting.

"Katrina refused to help me, but I have since discovered that she is Larissa's mother. Larissa does not know of anything of the past, and I cannot make sense of it. If only I were able to have a séance, but I have no witch contacts since I had to run them from town. What would you have me do?"

He shrugged. We had never been in this situation before; she had always remembered us. The day of meeting her brought about a new heartache; her body knew me from its obvious desires, but her mind did not.

"If we wait, she may never remember, but if we tell her, she may never forgive you." The pain registered from one of her past lives, when she hated the choice I made on her behalf. She would often not remember, but a kiss or a touch would bring it all back.

"Do you think a bite would help her remember?" I asked, curious if what started the curse would trigger the return of her memory.

"She hates your kind, she would never allow it. She ran from you after she dreamed of her mother, who called her a traitor."

"She does not hate, she does not *understand,* which brings a different fear. She was raised to hate. Elizabeth made sure of that. Katrina would have raised her differently."

"Elizabeth would have made that choice because you killed Katrina," he retorted, blaming me for this situation.

I opened my mouth to rebut his remark, but it was pointless. The circumstances surrounding Katrina's death were not my fault, but I wore them anyway. I could have stopped it, and I would have had I known she was the mother of my true love. One question plagued my mind. She had no memories, but fate had still brought her to me. Elizabeth kept us apart, but circumstance made it so that we were not kept that way. I was hopeful, despite her current relationship with my brother.

I stood and poured two glasses of whiskey for us before I sat beside him. I ran my fingers through my hair.

"How is her magic coming along?" I questioned, feeling it bubble in the bond between us.

He took the glass and had a sip. "She has yet to specialise. She is not sure if she is a Spellcaster or an Elementalist."

"What do you believe she would be?" Katrina was a High Priestess, but even I was unsure of which specialty she was. As I considered her use of magic, I guessed she was an Elementalist. She was able to control anything. Katrina had more power than I had seen any one person possess in my entire life.

"I think she may be a Spellcaster," he mumbled as he yawned. The Blood Moon affected him more than I.

"If her mother was an Elementalist, it will be interesting to see what she specialises in. Do we know why she had no access to her magic before now?" Roman had the insights that I wanted.

He gave me comfort knowing that I could still know about her life even while she shut me out.

"Yes Elizabeth, cast a spell to keep her magic at bay." He snorted. Katrina often spoke of her dislike of Elizabeth; she stated she was always jealous of her power.

"That is a lot of magic, more than she ever had." I raised my eyebrow.

Roman nodded as he finished his glass. "She found her mother's grimoire. Elizabeth used magic she had no right to use, but witches are not as easily kept in check as vampires or werewolves."

"Hmm, that is true. That may be about to change." My enemies were about to make Larissa and my life more difficult.

"How so?" Roman questioned as I heard the change in his tone. He was worried, rightfully so.

"The incident with Hector, he spoke about Larissa and her inability to be compelled. He has put forth an appeal stating that due to the use of magic, he should not be executed."

Roman snorted. "That would not work. No one would dare go up against you, especially those who know your true identity."

"Duzi," I said by way of explanation. The one man who had plagued us for centuries.

"That motherfucker. I knew he would come back to haunt us one day. How does he still live?" I shrugged. We had encountered Duzi on several occasions. He was a rather short man and had the belief that he was given this gift from the Gods. He was mistaken. God did not turn us into monsters, the Devil did.

"He hid in the shadows most of his life until the uprising was on the horizon. He is using this as a platform to push me out." I pinched the bridge of my nose in frustration before I threw my glass across the room. It smashed into tiny pieces.

Roman chuckled. "I still love to see your temper flare."

"If he wins, Larissa will be questioned on her magic use." I shot him a glare, he needed to understand how serious the situation was.

"But—" Roman stopped short.

"Yes, exactly. Her inability to be compelled does not stem from her magic. I do not know how she is able to resist. She will become a pawn for the highest bidder. We cannot allow that to happen."

"When is the appeal?"

"Tomorrow." I groaned at the amount of work that I still needed to complete.

He slammed his hand down on my shoulder, as he stood. "It is all on you to protect her then. I shall be dealing with the consequences of the Blood Moon. I will take my leave now. Good luck, brother. I will see you on the other side." He raised his glass and handed me his phone before he took his leave.

I closed my eyes to feel for Larissa, she was asleep for the night. I heard her whisper my name and I smiled. She still dreamed of me despite the nights she spent with my brother.

"One day, my love." I stood and pressed the button on my intercom.

"Maria, I need a clean-up in the den when you are available." Not only did she need to clean the glass but also the stench left behind by my brother. I opened the window to help for now.

"Yes, Mr. Dankworth, I shall be up shortly." I collapsed in my chair

"Maria, bring some spray. It smells of wet dog in here." I asked before I continued to sign the documents well into the morning.

Larissa woke for her morning run. She was on edge about Roman's absence, so I unlocked his phone and sent her a text to ease her worry.

CHAPTER 41
SOMETHING IS NOT RIGHT

Larissa

IT WAS SUNDAY NIGHT, AND I WAS GLAD TO BE WORKING AT THE bar. I needed the break. My mind was still going crazy over Roman's sudden absence, but his messages had been a little dirtier than usual, which I appreciated. He would be back tomorrow night and I was hoping to surprise him wearing something sexy. As long as I beat him home, because he did not tell me what time he would get back.

A sense of unease ate away at me, I could not understand why. It was the last night of the Blood Moon and the strength in my magic was returning. I had avoided using it over the last few days, especially after Sophia's warning. I sat out the back on my quick ten-minute break before I started to clean the floor.

Luce called me twice before I rang her back. "Hey, I am at work. Is everything alright?"

"Yeah, sorry. I forgot, no stress. I will order an Uber to bring me some food."

"Did I not drop off enough the other day?" I made her lasagna, a chicken pie, and a stir-fry dish. The phone went quiet. Of course, she had given some to Peter. I did not understand the hold he had on her. She was smart but with him, she lost all her brain cells. "I can bring some after work if you can wait?"

"Nah, I will call an Uber. Bye." The call was short and that was on purpose. She had him over. I would do anything to make him disappear, but even the thought of casting a spell would have dire consequences. Magic cannot be cast for personal gain, but I questioned where that line was. Sophia could never give me an accurate answer. There was a bang in the alley, and I scanned my surroundings but saw no movement. I brushed it off and took it as a sign to head back inside.

I could not shake the feeling deep inside that something was wrong. My finger hovered over Roman's number. He told me not to disturb him while he was away, but I wanted protection tonight. I flicked through my phone and came across Nik's number. It only rang once before he answered.

"Miss Solis." His soft accent sent a rush of desire through me.

"I apologise for the late call, Mr. Dankworth. Are you free tonight?" I asked, feeling incredibly stupid.

"I have a prior engagement, but depending on your needs, I could reschedule."

I felt guilty about disturbing him.

"No, it is fine. Do not worry, enjoy your night." I heard him calling my name as I ended the call.

I ran back inside and pocketed my phone to clean up, rushing through the closing duty. I wanted to get home where I felt safe. Right now, it was like I was being watched or hunted. I cast a simple protection spell, but it was weak against the constraints of the Blood Moon. I would risk it and catch a taxi home instead of walking.

I set the alarm on the door and waited on the street for the taxi to arrive. According to my app, it would arrive in around ten minutes. It was cold and unusually quiet, not even a cricket. It was eerie and did not feel right. I kept checking my phone for the estimated arrival time. My foot started to tap involuntarily. I grew increasingly anxious when suddenly, I felt a breath on my neck. The hairs on my arms stood up. I took a step forward and turned. I knew this man's face. I had encountered him before, and this was not good.

"Hello, Hector," my voice cracked. Not the best timing for it, especially when he smiled and flashed his fangs.

"The girl responsible for my possible death."

I put my hands up in defence. "Those were your actions, not mine."

I was hoping Nik could feel my sudden change in mood. I buried my fear, not wanting Hector to see it. He chuckled and started to circle me like the prey I was.

"I suppose, but you are still not marked. Interesting...why is that?" He tapped his chin as he continued to circle.

"Nik does not feel the need to, our bond is more than enough." I kept my gaze trained ahead and my ears listened for any change in his pace.

"A mark carries a heavy weight in our law. It binds you together, and yet, he has not done it. Why? Could it be because you belong to another? Roman perhaps?" My heart skipped a beat. He had been watching me.

"What do you want, Hector? An apology?" I crossed my arms to show my annoyance at him being here.

His smile was evil, it made the hairs on my arms rise. "I want to destroy Nik and you are my ticket to do that. His influence has lasted too long. It is time for a new leader."

"You do not need me for that." I felt another presence appear; my magic prickled at my fingertips in anticipation.

"Destroying the woman he loves would help. Now, tell me, what magic do you possess to resist compulsion?" I swallowed hard. What was taking him so long to get here?

It was as if Hector knew and snickered. "You are not the only witch around. We are covered in a bubble, he won't sense you until she allows it."

"She is weak to turn against a fellow sister," I snarled as I used my magic to find her. She was close. If I could reach her, I would be able to break her spell. I hit a block and shook my head, there were two choices. Number one, attack her mentally, or number two, use as much magic as possible to weaken her powers. As I did not know the witch, my only choice was to use my magic to overwhelm her. Hector bared his teeth, as did his companion who stayed in the distance.

"This is going to be fun." I blasted both with a spell that threw them off their feet. It wasn't long until they stood and attacked once more. I kept pushing an attack on the other witch, her magic waning against my own. Hector grabbed my throat and lifted me from the ground, so I touched him and lit his hand on fire.

"Bitch!" He dropped me, but not before his companion wrapped his arms around my waist and held me tight. His breath was on my neck.

I used what was left of my energy on the other witch, and as her spell crumbled, teeth sank into the back of my neck. I screamed at the pain and heard him gulping down my blood. I fought against him as hard as I could. I threw my head back and hit him, which caused his arms to loosen slightly. It was all I needed to squirm away. As I did, his teeth ripped my skin and warm liquid rushed down my back, this was not good.

"LARISSA!" I heard Nik scream before the world turned dark.

273

CHAPTER 42

FAMILIAL CONNECTIONS

Larissa

I woke suddenly the next morning. I was lying in just my underwear in a room that I did not recognise. The sun entered the room from small windows above the curtains. Despite being almost naked, I was warm. I wriggled my fingers and toes to make sure I was not paralysed. I reached back to touch my neck where I had been bitten. It was completely healed but it was tacky from my dried blood. How was I alive? Surely, with my skin being ripped apart, it wasn't possible. I swung my legs off the bed and onto the plush, light grey carpet below. I noticed clothes sitting in the armchair near the bed with a note.

Towels are in the bathroom. Shower and dress. Nik

I rolled my eyes; I could hear his voice in my head as I read the note. I walked over to the curtain and looked out; we were at his apartment. The city appeared so small beneath us. I did not remember Nik's room being as soft-toned as this, I thought as I noticed the soft, cream-coloured doona. Nik's room, from memory, had a masculine energy.

I opened the door to the bathroom. It had the same soft, grey tones, and the taps were matte black. I removed what was left of my clothing and turned the taps on. The water pressure was perfect, and it did not take long for the water to warm up. The shower door closed behind me as I stepped in and let the water wash over my body. I noticed the amount of blood that coloured the water at my feet. It took a while for the water to finally run clear before I washed my hair and finished up.

I searched the cupboards for a hairdryer. If I knew Nik, he would have whatever I needed. The top drawer had a hairdryer that was already connected to the power point, with a hairbrush and comb. I could not help but smile at his ability to think of everything. I dried my hair before putting on the clothes he had left for me, a pair of denim shorts that were shorter than I expected them to be and a black tank top. I opened the door to the room and walked out. The last time I saw this place, it was at night, and during the day, it did not seem as masculine as I had initially believed. I walked down the staircase.

"Nik," I called out. "Are you here?"

All I heard was silence, but my sense of smell was better than usual. Nik had fed me his blood; it was obvious from my heightened senses. I decided to follow the smell of coffee, hoping that it would lead me to Nik.

"Brother, are you here?" I turned back towards the voice to see Roman standing behind me. I ran towards him.

"Roman!" I jumped into his arms, and he took a few steps back to catch my full weight. I was so happy to see him after the attack last night. "Wait, why are you here?"

My mind started to race as I remembered the word he used as he walked into the apartment. "Hang on..." The familiar tingle in my body told me that Nik was close.

"Good morning, Larissa." Nik's voice was as sensual, as always. It made me horny instantly, damn effect of the blood.

"Not right now," I dismissed him before I locked eyes with Roman. "You said 'brother'."

I stood to the side and glanced between Nik and Roman. They had the same dark hair, the same strong jawline, and the same perfect nose. "Holy fucking shit." I clasped my hands over my mouth.

Nik laughed as he took a sip of his coffee before turning away. How did I miss this?

"Seriously, Nik?" Roman called after him. I turned and slapped Roman's chest.

"You did not think to mention that you were related to my boss?" He rubbed the back of his neck but did not speak. "You were not even here for me, were you? Is this your business trip?" Anger surged through my body.

"Larissa, sit down," Nik's voice echoed through the apartment. My body was compelled to follow his instructions as I walked away and sat down at the kitchen counter. Nik slid a coffee over to me. "Yes, we are brothers. Twins, to be perfectly clear. Roman was helping me with some business over the last few days. He has no knowledge of the events from last night. He has only returned this morning; I was hopeful that I could have informed him before you woke, but it seems I was mistaken."

"What happened?" Roman glared at his brother before turning back towards me. Nik beamed, he seemed to enjoy this a little too much.

"Hector." Nik broke the silence, and a deep growl escaped from Roman's throat. I noticed his eyes glow yellow. I jumped off my stool and took steps to get away from him. My head pounded against my skull. I closed my eyes, and the memory came rushing back.

"Stay here, you will be safe. We just want to talk to your mummy." Roman's face was in full view, he closed the cupboard door as I heard screams on the other side. I banged against it trying to get to my mother before one final blood-curdling scream rang out.

My eyes sprung open, and I saw Nik and Roman standing above me with concern on their face. When had I fallen to the floor? I jumped to my feet and ran behind the couch to put space between us.

"Get away from me both of you!" I yelled at them. The man who plagued my dreams, the man with the yellow eyes, was Roman.

"Larissa, what the hell happened?" Roman asked as Nik leant against the wall, taking small sips of coffee. He was too casual about this, it was unnerving. I did not know where to begin.

"How can you—why did you—how the fuck can you look at me and think it is alright to date me when you were there the night my mother died? I saw you the night of the explosion and you were waiting outside the hospital. How could you not tell me that you were a supernatural creature?"

"Wait, you knew she was alive again?" Nik had pushed himself off the wall and stalked over to his brother. Roman clenched his fists.

"Do not start, Nik." I stood in front of him and held my hand up to block him from his brother. "I need answers."

Roman huffed out in a rage, "I am a werewolf and if you want answers, ask the man who killed your mother." He pointed at Nik, and those words ripped my heart from my chest. The man who invaded my every thought had killed my biological mother?

"What?" Tears filled my eyes, and Nik avoided meeting them.

"It was an accident," his voice broke as he spoke. I could feel the guilt as he said the words.

"But you knew that, and you decided to try and pursue a relationship with me. That goes for both of you. That is just fucking sick. You, Roman, saw me as a child, you…you tried to protect me. You listened as I told you about the dreams I had of the man with the yellow eyes, and you never thought to say anything. While you, Nik, kept secrets about everything related to my mother." My heart raced as my magic flared.

"In my defence, I did not know you were there. I was already in a conversation with Katrina." Both brothers glared at each other before dragging their attention back to me.

I clenched my fists. "That makes no difference at all. I was a child, and you took my mother from me. There is no defence to that." I threw my hands up in defeat. I needed to be anywhere but here. The fact that they knew me when I was a little girl and decided to hide the fact that they were part of my mother's death was incomprehensible. I moved towards the apartment door.

"I am leaving. I cannot be here right now. I cannot deal with the fact that you stalked me," I pointed at Roman, before turning to Nik, "and you killed my mother!" I stormed towards the door but slammed into Nik's hard body.

"I cannot allow you to leave." His voice was stern and filled with warning.

"Nik," I issued my own warning, "do not piss me off right now." My magic sparked from the tips of my fingers.

"Larissa, you broke the law last night. You killed a vampire; you are to be detained until the circumstances of the night can be verified."

I scoffed. "I was attacked, and I am the bad guy? You cannot make me stay." I pushed past him and reached the door, but as I turned the handle to open the door, it slammed closed.

"Larissa, I am serious. You will be staying here until the trial. I have secured a lawyer for you. She will be coming to see you tomorrow to decide what type of defence you will need."

"I do not care. Put me up in a hotel room. I will not be staying here with the man who killed my mother."

"Nik, she has a point," Roman spoke up in my defence.

"Stay out of this, wolf!" I shouted over my shoulder at Roman.

"No, she does not. I am the Lord of this region. It is my duty to ensure the accused is kept in a safe and secure location. There is no safer place than mine."

"I am not staying here." Nik noticed the glow from my hands.

"Your magic does not scare me, Larissa. You will stay or else." He moved closer, his eyes flaring as his monster made an appearance.

"Or else what? Are you going to tie me up and keep me locked away until then?" His eyebrow rose as if I had just given him an idea and a smile spread across his face.

"Nik, I will fight you if you harm her," Roman warned as he moved closer.

"Roman, she killed a vampire. She must plead her case; you know the laws. Stand aside this one time, I beg of you." Without another word, Roman bowed his head and left the apartment. I turned to try to follow him, but Nik grabbed my arm and spun me around before throwing me over his shoulder.

"ROMAN!" I screamed in the hope that he would help me, but he never came back through the door. He had abandoned me.

"Nik, I swear to God, if you do not put me down." I put my hands on his back and sent a blast of magic through my hands. He did not even flinch. I tried again but nothing. "Why does my magic not work on you?"

"I am possibly older than your magic, Larissa." He opened the door to my room and dropped me onto the bed. He turned to leave.

"Nik, please!" I got on my knees and held my hands together in front of me. "Do not do this."

"Do you swear to stay within the confines of this apartment?"

"Yes, I swear," I lied through my teeth, and he chuckled.

"Do not forget I can sense your emotions, especially after the amount of my blood you took last night. Good try, Larissa. I will bring up food and you have the television. I shall bring you a laptop to do some work." He closed the door as I ran over to it, but he locked it behind him. I pounded against the door, but I was alone.

Roman was a wolf, Nik had killed my mother, and I was trapped.

CHAPTER 43
WHAT HAPPENS NEXT?

It was a couple of hours before Nik entered the room. I resigned myself to sit on the bed and wait. Pounding the door did nothing but bruise my hands. Nik sauntered in with a tray of food and a smug grin on his face. He was enjoying my captivity.

"I'm not hungry," I said defiantly, knowing full well it was a lie.

"The noises your stomach is making disagree." He glanced at my stomach as it grumbled.

I blasted him with a ball of energy and watched as it bounced off him.

"Why are you not affected by my magic?" I crossed my arms, but it only increased my anger and the magic that I wanted to throw at him.

"I told you I am older than your magic." He chuckled at my attempt to harm him.

"You are lying. I can feel it."

I did not know why, but he *was* lying. Even though we had not been together or interacted every day that passed, the strength of the bond deepened between us.

"Is this all necessary?" I asked, motioning around the room. He placed the tray on the bed before me and sat in the armchair opposite. It looked tiny with him sitting in it.

"I told you that it was." He was not giving away any more than he needed to.

"I do not understand it. I was attacked and almost died, but I am the bad guy?"

"You used your magic to kill a vampire, Larissa. It is against the law." The words echoed in my head.

"But I wasn't using it on them!" I shouted at him. "There was another witch, and she was shielding your ability to sense me. I used it all on her when I was attacked from behind. His fangs ripped into my skin. I tried to run but I could not because he was holding me in position. I did not use magic to kill him. I do not know how he could have died." I stood from the bed and paced the room, rubbing the back of my neck where the vampire had bitten me. There was no mark left behind, or anything to prove that I was attacked. "What did you see when you arrived?"

Nik's hands turned white as he grasped the armchair tighter. "I felt unease before I heard you call for me. It was the fastest I had ever flown in my life and when I got there, I saw you on the floor, bleeding out. I ran over and pushed my wrist into your mouth as Hector ran from the scene. I watched as his accomplice started to choke. He held his throat and proceeded to cough up all the blood he had taken from you before he dropped dead. In my entire life, I have never seen a vampire die in that manner from the blood of a human." He leant forward in the chair as his brow creased.

"So, have you seen a vampire die similarly, but by drinking a different type of blood?"

He stroked his chin before he relaxed. "Yes. Vampires can take from each other, but…how do I say this?" He clicked his tongue, trying to formulate the words in his head. "If a young vampire were to drink my blood, they would have the same reaction, just without the death."

I stood dumbfounded. "Why?" I asked him, wanting to know how this piece of information fit into the big picture.

"The purity. I am one of the oldest and therefore, my blood has not been tainted by the evolutionary changes that have occurred, including the diet of ever-growing preservatives. As you are not a vampire, it does not make sense."

I leant against the wall and lightly banged my head in frustration. "Would it be so impossible that it was my blood? What if you tried a little? I mean, that guy drank a lot, surely a drop would not have the same result."

He launched himself from the chair, and before I knew it, he was before me. He put his hand above my head as he leant in. Nik caressed my face, and an explosion of love and desire filled my body.

"If I were to ever drink your blood, it would be because you beg me for it. Not to test a ridiculous theory," he spoke softly, every word dripping with sex. My heart started to pound in my chest, his eyes drifted to my lips. The pull towards him was stronger than ever.

"I will never beg for you to drink my blood," I whispered as I tried to keep my body from launching at him.

He chuckled deeply as his chest vibrated with the sound. "Larissa, I can sense how badly you want this right now. You are craving to know what it feels like, you are craving to feel my fangs pierce your soft skin and suck your precious blood. You want to hear me moan as I feast on the delicious taste, while you come from the sensation of pleasing me."

I was throbbing with need. He was right, my body was desperate to know what it would feel like. He kissed my cheek, which set my body on fire. He pulled back as I stared into his crystal blue eyes. I could tell he was holding himself back. I could see it and I could feel it. He was provoking me, wanting me to make the first move. I glanced at his lips, which were calling to me. I closed my eyes and pushed his chest.

He sighed and crossed his arms. "I love your denial. It will make it that much sweeter when I finally get to taste all of you."

"GET OUT!" I screamed, but he sat on the bed with a mischievous smile.

"No, but I will let you out of your room if you promise to not run away." He would be able to sense my emotions. I would have to hide them from him if I was to escape. I walked over and stood before him as I leant down to allow him a good look at my cleavage.

"I promise I will not run away." I batted my eyes and spoke with a seductive voice.

His eyes drifted as he licked his lips and a soft grumble echoed through the room.

"Do not tempt me unless you want this." His eyes brightened. He wanted me. I could feel it.

"Maybe I do," I said as I mounted him and wrapped my legs around him. My arms rested on his neck as his hands drifted up and down my back. He was holding himself back. Sophia told me that once vampires were distracted, they were not able to fully sense everything.

"Larissa," he whispered as he sniffed the crook of my neck.

"Nik, may I leave to get some coffee?" He let his head fall back and I could feel how much he wanted to bury himself inside me. It made my body ache for more, but I needed to stay focused.

"Absolutely." He inhaled one more time before I stood.

I swayed my ass as I left the room and kept up the ruse of wanting him as I walked down the stairs. I needed to overwhelm his senses in other ways to avoid him sensing my true intentions. I made it to the bottom of the staircase and the door came into view. I smiled to myself as moved towards it.

"Nice try, Larissa."

I reached the door handle, only to discover that it was locked. I groaned and banged my head on the solid wood.

"How? Sophia said I can overwhelm senses."

"You can, but with a true mate, you cannot. I feel all your desires as they are my own. I will let you walk around the apartment, but the door will remain locked, and I have had it enchanted as well. Two days, Larissa, that is all." Nik walked down the stairs with an air of confidence.

"Sophia told me that witches cannot be mated to vampires and that everything I feel towards you is from your manipulation." I crossed my arms and clicked my tongue, displaying my own confidence.

"Sophia is an idiot," he said as he floated by me and flicked on the kettle. He moved around the kitchen to make me a coffee, so I sat on the bar stool and watched him. "Yes, it is strange for a witch and vampire to be mated, but it is not unheard of. There have been tales in the past. Sophia said this because when you turn, you will lose your magic."

"When I turn?" I asked, wondering why he thought I would ever agree to become a monster.

He spun and flashed a brilliant smile at me. "I do love your ignorance. Yes, when you turn, Larissa, you will no longer have access to magic. It comes from the Earth and as you will be dead, there will be no more connection to the Earth."

I scoffed at him. "Your arrogance has no limits, does it?"

He winked at me as he finished making the coffee and pushed it across the bench. He sped upstairs and came back again with the plate of food. "Now eat," he ordered.

I salivated over the French toast. My stomach grumbled once again as I picked up the knife and fork to eat. I knew I would be famished for a few days while the blood in my system started to work its way out. I was grateful that Nik saved my life, but he was also the reason that it was in danger.

"Are you going to tell me why Hector attacked me?"

Nik stiffened briefly before he relaxed and pulled out a cup. He filled it with blood before putting it in the microwave. As it warmed, he remained silent, avoiding my question.

"I have never seen you drink so much blood before," I noted as he pulled the cup out and sculled it.

"You took a lot from me last night. If I was even five seconds later, you would either be dead, or you would be a vampire."

The thought made me shiver. I had no desire to become an immortal bloodsucker. I wondered if I would be thankful if he saved my life at that cost.

"Thank you, Nik." He nodded in response, but I kept going. "You ignored my first question."

"Hector is not happy that I embarrassed him. You are my mate, and it was the easiest way to attack me. His trial was due to take place this week." He opened another bag of blood to fill another cup. I must have taken more than I thought.

"Wait, how is my trial Tuesday and his was months after the attack?" The justice system seemed a little out of touch.

"Murder is a serious crime." He reached over the counter and grabbed my hand. "Larissa, I will do whatever it takes to keep you safe. Do not allow yourself to worry."

I smiled at his touch before I pulled back. "Is Roman allowed to visit?"

He shook his head. It made sense why he left so quickly, instead of staying to help me.

"Am I allowed to talk to him?" Nik nodded but said nothing else. "I am scared, Nik. What is the worst-case scenario here?"

"I will not answer that." His shoulders stiffened as he finished his cup.

"Why not? I want to know, to be prepared," I demanded.

"Because it will not happen." Nik remained tight-lipped, but I had a feeling about what it could be.

"You do not know that! I apparently killed a vampire and have no evidence that I had no intention of doing so." My voice level was slowly increasing.

"I said it will not happen." Nik's voice rose in unison with mine.

"Just tell me, Nik." I put my hands together in a prayer-like manner.

"Larissa, leave it alone. It will not happen." He turned away from me as if he was done with this conversation.

"Nik, bloody hell. I deserve the truth."

"Fuck, Larissa, I will not lose you! I will not let it happen. I would die before I let it happen." He hung his head and rubbed his forehead. I got up and walked over to him, before touching his chin and lifting it to make him look at me.

"I trust you. I just want to know. I need to know."

He held my face in his hands as he murmured words I did not understand.

"What did you say?" I asked, gazing into his eyes for an answer.

"Nothing of importance. I need to head to work. The apartment is yours. There is plenty of food in the fridge, so please help yourself."

I followed him to the door, where he turned and paused with a smile. "I love you, Larissa Solis, more than life itself. I will bring home dinner for you tonight, so make sure to text me your order." With that, he closed the door and locked it from the other side. I heard his footsteps depart before silence enveloped me. I walked back upstairs and collapsed on the bed.

CHAPTER 44
HOW MUCH LONGER WOULD THIS LAST?

Larissa

THE SOUND OF MY PHONE VIBRATING WOKE ME UP FROM MY slumber. It was Roman. I rushed to answer the phone. I missed him, and the fact he left when his brother pulled rank was understandable, but I wished that he had fought a little harder for me.

"Hey!"

"How mad are you?" he asked instantly, and I heard the anxiety in his voice.

"A little, but I'm more confused. Nik explained why you left—because he is the Lord of the region—but it does not explain why you stalked me my entire life. You were there the days that both my mothers died." There was silence down the other end of the phone.

"I won't be able to give you the answers that you want. I have watched over you since that day under the stairs. You were only a child. I had Richard keep me updated through email, and I would come down to see you in person every couple of months. I should have told you, and I apologise." Roman never lied to me, I could always rely on him for this, but his voice sounded different.

"I feel like there is something else you need to tell me."

"In time, I promise I will, but for now I cannot," he explained.

I sighed and shook my head, which was screaming to end the relationship, but my heart was saying no.

"Larissa, I love you, but if you wish to take a break for a while, I will understand. You want something I cannot give you." I wondered what he meant but I was too afraid to ask.

"I love you too, but... I am so confused by all of this. I do not know what is going to happen. Nik is promising that I will be okay, but I feel so much anxiety, like something big is going to happen."

"If I know my brother, he will do whatever he can to protect you."

It brought a little comfort to the ever-growing anxiety in my belly. Roman and I spoke for longer about nonsense. He was trying to get me to think about anything else, rather than the possibility of dying in a few days. Part of me wished I had listened to Richard and had never come to London, but then I would not have met Nik, Roman, Travis, James, Alina, or even Stacey. I sighed as I realised my relationship with my sister would still be normal and not fractured if not for her dalliance with disgusting Peter.

Nik had sent several messages throughout the day telling me to eat, drink, or do something else. I ignored all of them. I still did not agree with being trapped here, even if it was luxurious and for my own safety. I had another message from Nik asking what I wanted for dinner, but I honestly did not care, so I ignored him.

I ventured around the apartment aimlessly, bored. I noticed cameras on the ceiling and waved at them. Nik would be watching my every move, but I did not care about that either. I sat down and thought about the events of last night, wanting to remember in more detail what had happened. I found my way back to that moment as if I were a spectator and watched as not long after the bite, the unnamed accomplice started to choke on my blood. His face showed confusion, as did Hector's, as he ran from the scene when Nik arrived. His death did not happen because of my magic; it was my blood, but I had no way to prove this. I knew one thing though; I would be stir-crazy by the end of the week.

CHAPTER 45
JUDGEMENT DAY

Larissa

JUDGEMENT DAY HAD ARRIVED. I LOOKED AT THE TWO OUTFITS ON my bed. One was what I had selected, a simple black pencil skirt and a white blouse. The other was Nik's selection, a pink skirt and white blouse. His idea behind it was to show my femininity and purity. He wanted me to portray myself as innocent and believed this would show that. I rolled my eyes and dressed in the clothes he had selected. He was the expert, after all. I pulled my hair back and pinned it off my face as I walked down the stairs. Nik was wearing a navy pinstripe suit with a matching pink handkerchief.

"You thought it appropriate to match?" I snorted at him.

"I am sure you will understand why during the trial. It should be relatively brief, but as I explained yesterday, you will be sitting alone at the docks. Amy, your lawyer, will be at the benches, and I will be up the front with the other five judges."

"Yes, three humans and three vampires."

Nik explained that I simply had to sit and listen to the evidence and answer any questions that were asked, but he was almost one hundred per cent confident that I would be fine. He mentioned he had secured video footage to show that my blood had caused his death. Roman was not allowed to attend, but he rode in the car with us and held my hand. When the car stopped, Nik exited the car and he waited outside, giving us a moment of privacy.

"Don't worry, Nik is confident that it will be fine. I shall see you after." He kissed my lips and pulled me into his arms, but it did nothing to ease my anxiety, which seemed to have skyrocketed with my rapidly beating heart. I had not taken any medication to help with my anxiety today. My stomach rolled with nausea and my hands sweated profusely.

Nik knocked on the window. "Being late is not a good look."

I rolled my eyes and kissed Roman again before sliding out of the car. Nik offered his arm and I clung to him as we entered the courthouse. It was a century-old building that had kept its original features, aiming to remain as heritage as possible. We stepped into the elevator, and it soon began to move. The upward motion did not help my whirling stomach.

Suddenly, Nik pressed the emergency stop button and stood over me. "Whatever happens, I did this for you. I want you to remember that, understand?" When I gave a confused nod, he leant back and straightened himself before pressing the button to continue. I decided against prodding for more information from him. I knew I was going to get nothing from him, and honestly, I had much more important things to think about.

It did not take long for us to reach the third floor. Nik walked us down the corridor and stopped in front of Amy. She smiled. Her blonde hair was pulled back into a tight bun and her black clothing seemed tighter than the previous day. I also noticed how she flirted with Nik, who simply rolled his eyes and kissed my cheek before leaving us.

Amy spoke a million miles an hour. I was too overwhelmed to even understand what she was saying, and it got worse once the courtroom doors opened. Amy led me to the dock, where I stood waiting to be told to sit down. The six judges entered soon after. It was obvious who the humans were, with the dark rings under their eyes. Nik was in the last seat, I noticed, and he smiled at me, then mouthed for me to sit down. I took my seat and sat with my hands together on my lap. Amy spoke clearly and consistently about the events of the night in question. She showed the footage before the prosecution stood and Hector walked in. Nik's rage at seeing him filled the space, and it was worse when Hector smiled in my direction and blew a kiss.

"Hector, can you tell us the events of the night as you remember them?" the prosecutor asked. He was bald, short, and fat, with a perpetual frown and the bushiest eyebrows I had ever seen. It was strange that I was getting trialled by a human. You'd think that he would be wanting to keep me alive.

"Yes, I wanted to see Miss Solis to apologise for my behaviour on the first night we met," Hector spoke clearly but I could see the evil glint in his eyes.

"What happened instead?" The prosecutor asked as he glanced in my direction. I noticed his double chin wobble.

"She used her magic on me. She said that she did not forgive me for my actions and hoped that I would burn in hell."

I moved to open my mouth and protest the lie, but Amy shot her head round to stop me. I listened as Hector prattled off lie after lie about the events of that night. Amy then stood to ask him questions.

"As the video shows, there is the use of magic, but it was never directed at you. It was directed at the witch that you hired to help aid your attack. She was trying to contact her mate, Lord Dankworth, to let him know that she was being harmed by you again."

"Is there a question?" he asked smugly. Amy shook her head.

"No, just a statement about the obvious holes in your story."

"Objection, badgering my client," Bushy Eyebrows barked from the other side of the courtroom.

"Sustained," Amy said as she sat back down. The judges spoke to one another quietly as I waited patiently to find out if I was to live or die. Nik growled at one stage and slammed his fist down; it wasn't going the way that he wanted it to.

Amy stood and walked over to me. "That does not mean anything," she reassured me, "he could be frustrated at the fact that Hector is receiving no consequence for his actions. Don't worry, it will be fine." Her words did nothing to ease my worry as I waited for what seemed like an eternity before they sat back in their seats. Nik no longer appeared angry; I could feel his joy at the verdict that was about to be reached. One of the human judges stood. His grey, balding hair stuck out at odd angles. Like he had slept on it wrong.

"Miss Solis, please stand." I did as instructed and stood slowly from my seat. "We find you not guilty of the murder of Adrian Ridgeway. You cannot control the purity within your blood, even if we do not understand how or why it is this way. We do, however, find you guilty of practising witchcraft and using it in an unsafe manner. Witchcraft, if not practised correctly, can lead to serious mistakes. Witches are a plague on society and must be dealt with immediately. In normal circumstances, you would be put to your death, but as you are mated to the Lord of the region, you will be placed under his control. If you continue to practice magic, you will have sanctions placed upon you. Lord Dankworth has negotiated the conditions upon your magic, and within a suitable time frame, you shall marry. Do you accept this sentence?" I glared at Nik; it made sense why he looked so happy, that the joy I was feeling was almost overwhelming. He was getting exactly what he wanted.

I refused to answer, so Amy rushed over and whisper-yelled, "Say yes!"

"What if I do not want to? I will not have someone tell me that I must marry him." Nik stared me down, and I made sure to enunciate each word clearly enough for him to hear.

"Larissa, say yes or you will be put to death," she implored, obviously not understanding why I would consider death over marrying Nik.

I crossed my arms and glared at Nik, who was clutching the table and staring back at me, a furious expression on his unfairly handsome face.

I turned to the dishevelled grey-haired judge and said, "Fine," before I plonked back onto my seat. I was truly trapped now.

"It is done. Court is now adjourned." As the judges left, I stormed outside to Roman. I wondered what he would think about this. I was being forced to marry his brother when we were still in a relationship and living together. I hoped that he would punch Nik in the face.

CHAPTER 46

I OWN YOU

Larissa

THE TINGLE DISAPPEARED BEFORE IT GREW STRONGER, AND THEN *he* appeared beside me. Nik's face was stern and serious, very different from the smug, satisfied look he wore in the courtroom.

"Do not tell Roman, it will not end well," he ordered.

"Watch me," I said through gritted teeth.

When I stepped outside, I saw Roman waiting for me, leaning against his car. I reached it quickly and I fell into his arms. He held onto me tightly and spoke softly into my ear, "I'm guessing it went well. You are free." He sounded so happy. What I said next would shatter him.

"Yeah, I suppose, if you count being forced to marry someone for your freedom." My voice was muffled, as I pressed my face into his neck, but it was clear enough for him to understand.

"What? Marry who?" Roman stiffened and held me away from him by the shoulders, looking between Nik and me.

"Who do you think?" I turned to glare at Nik.

"I did what I had to, Roman. They wanted to kill her for

practising magic, and they heard that she could not be compelled," Nik attempted to explain his actions.

"Of course, it is always what is best for you, isn't it Nik? How many times will it take for me to learn? She deserves better than both of us." Roman pushed himself off of the car and away from me.

"Roman," I called as I ran after him. "Wait, please!"

He stopped and spun around. "Larissa, we are done."

My heart was in my throat, he said the words so coldly, as if the past couple of months between us meant nothing.

"Just like that? We can fight this." I pleaded with him.

He refused to meet my eyes; he had given up. My heart broke a little more. I had given this man so much and he wasn't even trying.

"Vampires rule. There is nothing I can do. I am just a werewolf and seen as an even lesser creature than a witch. I am powerless against him. He knew this. He got what he wanted…he always gets the girl." He left me standing in the street alone.

Nik was waiting patiently behind me. I shook my head and walked away from him. I would not do this. I refused.

Nik appeared before me. "Larissa, be smart about this. Get in the car." His cool manner had disappeared, and an asshole stood before me.

"Why? You tricked me. You manipulated me. I deserved the choice, but you took it away, *again*!" Nik winced at my words.

"I have always given you a choice." He opened the car door, his way of saying we could discuss this further inside.

I refused. I wanted everyone to hear about their precious Lord of the region. "No, you have not. I will do as I agreed but do not expect me to be an actual wife. It will be on paper only."

He smiled like he knew that I would give in to my temptation eventually.

"Larissa, I own you. You do not tell me how it is; I tell you. I warned you not to practise and you ignored me. This is the consequence. Now get in the car." He grabbed my arm and pulled, but I planted my feet. So instead, he picked me up, threw me over his shoulder and dropped me into the car. He slid in beside me and then slammed the door.

"Drive," he barked. When I tried to get out the other side, he pulled me back again.

"I HATE YOU!" I screamed, and in that moment, I meant it with every fibre of my being. I did hate him; he had taken so much from me. My words stopped him in his tracks; he moved back to his seat and did nothing but put space between us. Guilt and anger radiated from him.

My tears continued to fall. London was the worst choice I had ever made. I wished I had never come here.

———

I took in my surroundings. I was no longer in the car and no longer in Nik's apartment. The room was bigger than the first apartment I had with Luce. The bed was enormous. The pale pink bedhead had cute little golden buttons pressed into it. I traced my finger around one of them when I registered the tingle. Nik was here. I got up and ran over to the door and locked it before I took a few steps back.

My legs were cold. I glanced down to see I was wearing pyjama shorts and a white top. It was not the same pink skirt I wore when I entered the car. I noticed a robe hanging over the end of the bed, so I picked it up and pulled it on. I searched around the room, trying to figure out where I was. There were two armchairs with a table in between; it seemed like a retreat space. I noticed two doors, and I grabbed the golden handle and opened the first one. I was met with darkness. I ran my fingers along the wall, looking for the light switch. I took a step inside, and the lights turned on automatically. It was a wardrobe full of clothes that were not mine. I stepped back out and tried the other door, which ended up being a bathroom stocked with towels. I opened the cupboards and found my makeup and every accessory I could ever need. I tried to slam the door, but it had soft-closing features. I groaned and stared at the ceiling, hating how he had to think of everything.

"Not to your standards?" I spun to see Nik perched on the end of the bed. I pulled the robe around me tighter.

"I locked the door." In response, he held up a key before he flashed a smile. "I locked the door for a reason," I clarified.

"I know and I unlocked it. We need to talk." What Nik wanted, he got, and again, I had no choice in the matter.

"There is nothing to talk about. I wish I had never met you. Please get out. I do not wish to see you." I pointed towards the door as I waited for him to leave.

He tapped his legs and did not move. "I will not deal with a petulant child."

"I am not a child! In two days, I went from living happily with my boyfriend to being attacked and almost charged with murder, to ending up having to marry someone that I do not want to marry! I can act however I wish." I pulled the robe tighter, feeling vulnerable at my lack of clothing.

"Firstly, you are a fool to think you were happy. You did not even know my brother was a wolf. You did not know that he stalked you. Secondly, I saved your life, and thirdly, I did what I had to do to protect you. Get over yourself, Larissa. Get yourself dressed and we shall discuss more over breakfast." He stood in triumph like he had won this argument.

"Like hell will I be having breakfast with you," I spat at him, my anger flaring at his ridiculous demands and the belief that I should be thankful for him.

"You will do what I say when I say it." I flinched slightly at the sternness of his voice.

"I do not have to listen to you." I glared at him, wishing he could feel just how much I hated him right now.

"In the eyes of the law, I own you."

"You will never own me. Even when we eventually wed, I will never be yours. Now GET OUT!" I screamed at him, but instead of leaving, he stormed over to me. I took a step back before I hit the wall, allowing him to not only tower over me and trap me, but to lean down and sniff my neck.

"You cannot deny this or what you feel." He breathed in before he stood back and exhaled. "I will ask one more time before I make you. Get dressed and meet me downstairs."

My body betrayed me every time with Nik. My brain was screaming no, but my body just wanted to scream his name.

CHAPTER 47

THE CONTRACT

Larissa

I DRESSED MYSELF IN A CASUAL BLACK DRESS WITH SHORT SLEEVES. It did nothing to show off my curves or breasts, which was how I wanted it. I did not want to give Nik any opportunity to perve at me. He deserved to suffer. I slipped on a pair of black ballet shoes and opened the door. The hallway was impossibly long with multiple doors up and down. The white walls contrasted with the dark wooden floors, and the roof was so tall that the space echoed with every step. There were pictures on the wall, some were of landscapes and others were of Nik and people that I assumed were important to him. I reached a mini foyer, where the floor changed to marble white tiles and there was a staircase with a black railing. The dome ceiling was glass and brought light into the room. The sun reflected off the massive crystal chandelier in the centre of the room, creating little rainbows that reflected onto the walls. It was magnificent and impossibly beautiful. I smiled and put my hand up to catch a rainbow reflection, my fingers danced amongst the colours. In the middle of the foyer was a large, bronze statue of a wolf with two children underneath.

"It is the story of Romulus and Remus." Nik appeared from the shadows, leaning against the wall. He could not quite look me in the eyes.

"The founders of Rome, correct?" He smiled at my question, so I continued. "The story I heard in school was that the boys were sent upriver after birth and a wolf nursed them and raised them before someone else took them in. The brothers fought and Romulus killed Remus for control or power." His laughter filled the space and sent shivers down my spine.

"That is the human fable, but I assure you it was vastly different." He straightened as a smile spread over his face.

I registered the words he had spoken. "Wait, were you alive then?" I asked, intrigued. I had always loved ancient mythology.

"Yes, a piece of me was…" He drifted off as his face filled with sadness.

"What is the true story, then? And why has it never been changed?" I subconsciously took a step closer to him, eager to hear what he had to say.

He half smiled before he cleared his throat. "Why change the stories of the past? You humans can barely handle when the power goes out, much less a change in your history."

"Fair point." I nodded and flashed him a smile. "I'm intrigued, though. Will you tell me?"

"The twin brothers were raised by the she-wolf, Rhea, who was a God in her own right. She loved them and made them into the first werewolves. They were immortal. They built different areas of Rome and yes, they fought as any brothers do, but they did not kill each other. As they were immortal, they created the story that they fought so that they could disappear. They watched the city rise before them and helped it along the way. Romulus fell in love with a human girl. She was the epitome of beauty and perfection. He worshipped her beauty, but she was married to another…" I gasped at the realisation, and a smirk crossed his face. "Yes, his brother. She loved Remus, but they knew they would never be together. The brothers confided in her, told her about their abilities, and she kept them safe from persecution. The fall of the Roman Empire was due to the discovery of the *demon brothers*, as they called them. The beauty was taken and tortured for their location, but she never gave it. The ruler, Romulus Augustus, burnt the city to find them. Romulus fled for his life, but Remus searched for his love and found her. Werewolves do not possess the ability to heal others, so he bartered a deal to save her life at the cost of his." Nik finished and straightened himself to brush off the emotion within his voice.

"Did you know the brothers?" I asked him as I stared at the statute before me. The boys standing under their wolf mother.

"Yes, rather intimately," he whispered.

"Is Romulus still alive? I assume Remus is dead."

"That is an answer for another time. Come and eat, we have much to discuss." He clapped his hands and walked away as I listened to the sound of his shoes clacking on the floor. I looked back at the statue. "What a sad story. A girl ruins a brotherhood."

I could not help but admire Nik's behind as he walked away.

———

The kitchen was as grand as the foyer and the bedroom. The kitchen was bigger than my bedroom, with floor-to-wall shaker-style white cabinets and a black marble benchtop. There was a plate of food and a cup of coffee waiting for me. I picked them up and followed Nik into the dining room, where the table was big enough to seat twenty people. I sat at the head of the table, opposite Nik on the other end. He cleared his throat and tapped the space beside him that had cutlery waiting for me.

"Is this going to be what it is like?" I said softly.

"You do remember that I can hear even the smallest of sounds, yes?"

"You do realise that I do not care, yes?" I mocked him, as I grabbed my plate and sat down, trying to be extra loud.

Nik slid some papers across the table towards me. "You will need to sign this."

I picked them up and read them over. It was the court document stating that I would, in the future, become his wife. I put it down and picked up the second piece, a mate contract. I inspected the document and saw rule after rule of what I was allowed and not allowed to do. I had to ask permission to do various things.

I threw it at him. "Do you honestly think that I am going to sign this? I am not your pet."

He straightened the paper and put it before me. "It is the law, Larissa, and you will sign it."

"I will not sign it, I would prefer to amend certain areas," I demanded, refusing to have my choices taken from me.

"This agreement would not be necessary if you agreed to be turned."

I slammed my fork down on the table. "Seriously, Nik? Please tell me you are joking." When he said nothing, I pushed my plate away. "I will not sign this unless you agree to make changes." I fled from the room in anger.

"We are not finished, Larissa," he growled from behind me, following me. I walked faster, knowing full well that it was pointless. He would easily catch me.

"I will not be your pet!" I shouted at him over my shoulder.

"I am not asking you to be my pet. You will be my wife," he said, making it sound like the perfect dream.

"Yes, a wife who has her husband pick her outfits, a wife who must remain silent at social events, and a wife who must be dressed appropriately at all times even in the comfort of my own home," I retorted, shaking my head.

"That is for your protection," he tried to reason with me.

I scoffed and threw my arms up in the air. Did he not think this was ridiculous?

"How the hell is that for my protection?" I fumed at him, ready to explode.

He grabbed my hand and spun me around as I landed against his chest.

"Everything I do is for your protection. We are mates and you will be by my side at all functions. I do not wish to have others desire you as I do. I do not wish others to see you as a way to harm me. I do not wish for you to be taken advantage of, I do not—" I put my hand to his mouth. I had to make him stop, his words sounded angry, but they were filled with love.

"Nik, I understand, but you cannot control everything, and that includes me." I pulled away from him, but he held me tight.

"You cannot possibly understand. I need you safe. Sign it, I beg of you." I shook my head and his desperation morphed into anger. "Fine. You are forbidden from leaving this house. You will remain here at all times."

He walked through the closest door and slammed it closed behind him. I heard roars and crashing coming from the room. I felt his rage and helplessness, too, but I would not entertain his tantrum. Instead, I walked away. I refused to play by his rules.

————

I sat in my room for a while. I heard Nik's shoes clacking on the floor and snuck out to see. He shook a man's hand and led him into another room, which I presumed was his office. I wanted to prove a point to Nik, even though I knew I would pay a price afterwards.

I changed into a pair of tight yoga pants and a crop top. I snuck downstairs, turned on the television, and found some music. I searched through the selections to find songs that had the loudest bass possible. I smiled to myself as I clicked and turned the volume up as high as it could go. I started to do a workout in the middle of the room, stretching my arms and legs. I found the best position to be able to see when Nik came out of his office. It was perfect timing. As he entered the open space, I lowered myself into a deep squat.

The door slammed open, and Nik's eyes were flashing bright red. He was filled with rage; I could feel it in my bones. I stood up and turned to him. I watched as his eyes travelled over my clothing before his associate walked over to inspect the scene. I had seen this man talking with Nik on a few other occasions around the Refresh office.

"What is the meaning of this?" Nik asked through gritted teeth, his fangs slowly descending.

"You said I was not allowed to leave the house. You know I like to run in the morning, so this is my alternative to running." I flashed a smile, knowing it would only infuriate him further.

"Go upstairs and use the gym," he ordered as his fists clenched.

"Oh, I did not know we had a gym," I shared with a smile. "I have not been given the grand tour yet. Who is your friend?"

Nik turned his head to look at his associate, who was smirking. He seemed to be in his thirties. His bronze-coloured hair was cut short, and his suit looked as expensive as Nik's. He smiled while taking a step towards us but was stopped by a soft growl echoing through the room. It was Nik's gentle warning to back off before he stormed over, threw me over his shoulder, and raced upstairs.

"It was nice to meet you," I called out and waved as Nik sped away at inhuman speed. He raced into my room and threw me onto the bed as I bounced upward and giggled.

"I am glad that you find this entertaining. You are to stay in here until my meeting is finished."

I pushed myself off the bed. "Not happening." I stood my ground, I refused to be walked over anymore.

He pushed me back down. "I told you that you will stay here."

"I am telling you that I am not. I was controlled for my entire life; I had a mother who lied to me, kept secrets from me, and manipulated me to stay near her. I *will not* be told what to do anymore!" I shouted, before schooling my voice into a tone more sinister. "Change the attitude, Nik, or I will make your life hell."

He opened his mouth to speak but stopped. His attitude shifted and changed in a heartbeat. He bowed his head and said, "I understand, Larissa. We can discuss this later at dinner after I have finished my meetings. You have my word. But may I have one request in return?"

I crossed my arms. He had no right to request anything right now.

"What could you possibly ask for?" I snarled at him, ready for another round of shouting.

"Could you read over the contract once again? And please put on some more clothing?" he asked so gently, so kindly, I was instantly suspicious, but I could play nice.

Instead of biting back, I shrugged. "I suppose I could do that."

"I shall see you for dinner." He turned on his heel and left. I did not put any extra clothes on as he requested, my way of saying screw you.

CHAPTER 48

KATRINA'S DEATH

I CHANGED INTO A NICER DRESS FOR DINNER. NIK WOULD TAKE IT as a sign of respect. He always wore a suit to dinner, so I flicked through the multitude of designer clothes he had bought before landing on a red dress. Not too formal and not too casual. The halter neck covered my chest and showed enough skin to still distract him. The back was lower than usual. I grabbed a pair of strappy heels and pinned my hair off my face. I walked out of my room to see Nik standing at the bottom of the stairs on a phone call.

"Yes, I will leave tonight to fix your mistake." I worried Nik may cancel our negotiations. He winked and smiled as he got off the phone. "I assure you, Larissa, I will not be going anywhere until we have our discussion."

His eyes swept up and down my body. I tingled with delight but pushed it aside. He chuckled. "You are perfection."

I noticed that Nik was not wearing his usual suit. He was dressed a little more casual in a dark knitted jumper and a pair of jeans.

"I seem to have missed the casual memo," I quipped as I glanced down at my formal gown.

"After your attire earlier today, I decided to follow your lead." I laughed and made my dress twirl. "I can change if you would feel more comfortable," he suggested, being his charming self again instead of the monster I had seen over the last couple of days.

"No, it is fine. Let's get started. You have to leave to fix something." I walked past him and into the dining room, which was lit by golden candlesticks that had been carefully placed around the space. Dinner was already on the table and two wine glasses were filled. He pulled the chair out for me.

"When did you have time to do this?" I asked as I took a seat, and he pushed me closer to the table.

He smirked. "Larissa, you should come to expect this. You will be my wife and I will ensure your every need is taken care of."

I grabbed the glass of wine and took a big gulp. I was nervous, he put his hand on my remaining free hand.

"Why are you nervous?" he questioned as his touch seemed to calm the nerves slightly.

"We barely know each other. I am not this person who dresses up and looks perfect all the time."

He moved to take his seat beside me, picking up his glass of wine and taking a sip.

"As long as you are happy," he murmured, keeping his eyes on me.

"Where was this attitude earlier?" I grumbled.

"I had some time to reflect, and I think, especially after your incident earlier, and came to the conclusion that you were right. I should not try to control you. Elizabeth did that and I refuse to do the same. Now, tell me what you would like changed." He put a copy in front of me and another before him. He pulled out a pen, ready to take notes. Sometimes he was adorable and other times, I wanted to rip his head off. But it would not change the fact that he killed my mother.

Over the next three courses of food, we spoke in length about what we both expected from our inevitable union. In the end, he still had a say in what I wore to events. And even though it was a hard one to change, I negotiated so that I was allowed to speak at events. Once it was completed, we both signed the documents. The vampire world was complex especially while I remained human.

"To our future nuptials." He raised his glass as I did, and we toasted. I lowered my glass without taking a sip and looked at him.

"Nik, I need to confess something." He had listened to me and negotiated, I felt it only fair that I give him some honesty.

"Yes, what is it?" He put his glass down on the table and gave me his full attention.

"I am not sure if I will be able to reciprocate in this relationship." I took a breath before I continued. "Nik, you killed my mother and that is a hard thing to overcome."

He sighed and raked his fingers through his hair. I watched as his bicep flexed beneath his jumper, hating the effect he had on my body, the way I needed him against all logic.

"I could show you what happened that night," he finally said. "It was an accident, Larissa, I swear it. Katrina was a friend who was trying to help me."

I raised my eyebrow at him. "How would you show me?"

"You have to let me into your mind to project my memories of that night."

It sounded insane, and the thought of letting Nik inside my head made me anxious. But I needed to know the truth, and he was finally offering it to me.

"It makes sense. So, I just close my eyes and, what?" My voice trembled.

Nik smiled seductively. "Think of me."

I rolled my eyes and leant back in the chair, then closed my eyes and thought about Nik. It was like a switch went off in my brain, and suddenly, I felt him there.

"Do not freak out. Just relax," his soothing voice echoed in my head. I took a deep breath in and exhaled slowly.

The darkness shimmered and transformed into a house. His hand squeezed mine and I looked over at Nik as he said, "Just do not let go"

I knew this room. It was Mum's house, with the cathedral ceiling and the old-style kitchen. I moved to see it more but was reminded that it was not real. This was only a memory.

"Come out, come out wherever you are." Katrina's voice rang through the air. I almost wanted to cry.

I heard the little girl version of me giggle, and then Mum came into view. We were so alike. We had the same dark hair and green eyes.

The doorbell rang, and her face went cold.

"Larissa, stay hidden," she whispered.

It was like she sensed who was behind it. She uttered a spell before walking over and answering the door.

Nik pushed himself into the house. He appeared the same as he did now. Roman skulked in after him, not seeming at all pleased to be there.

"Nik, Roman, to what do I owe the pleasure?" She was trying to be calm, but it was obvious she was worried.

Nik sat down on the couch and crossed a leg over his knee. "Katrina, we have been friends for a long time," he began, rather blasé in his attitude, which was unlike him.

She glanced over at the cupboard where little me was hiding. "Yes, we have been."

"Tell me, why did you run? And why are you hiding? We both work for the same person, and he does not take kindly to these acts," he asked as he moved forward to intimidate her. I had seen this act before.

Katrina was terrified of this person, but who was it?

"I refuse to work for him. I will not go back because of his demonic acts, but I assume he already knows this, or he would not have sent you." Her words quivered slightly as she maintained her posture.

Nik smiled and stood. "Yes, and you know he does not take kindly to this."

The little version of me bumped something in the cupboard. Nik glared at Roman, who moved to check it out.

"What is it?" Nik asked as Roman turned to look at him. Katrina glared at Roman.

"It is nothing to worry about," he said before turning back and putting his finger to his lips.

Nik spun his attention back on Katrina. "He wants me to bring you back immediately."

"Nik, I beg of you. Tell him you could not find me. Tell him I am dead. Tell him whatever is the most believable," she begged as she backed away from him.

"You know I cannot, Katrina. Do not make this difficult." His words were stern, but his eyes were soft. He had no control over the situation.

I could see Katrina searching for a way to get Nik to stop. "I found a way to break the curse."

Nik froze. "Do not try to save yourself with unfounded lies. You searched for a way and told me it was impossible. I remember your exact words, 'You will never be together.'"

Nik squared his shoulders as his eyes flared red. His anger radiated from him, but it wasn't directed at Katrina, it was more towards this curse that they spoke of.

"I swear, Nik, on my life, that I have found a way."

"Your life means nothing, you soulless witch." Nik's eyes were flaming red as his fangs descended.

Katrina took a step back. "I can prove it to you."

Nik raised his hand. "Enough of this. Come with me now or I shall throw you over my shoulder and deliver you to him."

She refused and walked backwards. Her hands were moving in a strange motion as she uttered words, her eyes glowed green.

"Katrina, stop!" Nik warned as he braced himself for her attack. It almost seemed like he wanted her to hit him, as if he did not wish to live anymore. A glowing white orb appeared before her and she moved her hands around it to make it grow. She glanced up at Nik. "I am sorry," she cried but her eyes met mine. Could she see me?

She forced it towards him, but Nik did not move or dive to get away. His shoulders slumped and he waited for what could have been his ultimate end. The orb flew towards him but bounced off his chest and flew back towards Katrina. She screamed as the orb hit her and she burst into flames.

Nik ran over, but it was too late. She was a pile of dust on the floor. He dropped to his knees and roared.

The dining room suddenly came back into view, but I could not see Nik. I searched the room, finding him standing over by the fireplace. He was not lying. The death truly was an accident. The orb bounced off him and back at Katrina. His face showed sadness from having to relive that moment.

"You truly cared for her," I whispered, amazed at the revelation.

He nodded as he took a drink of his whiskey. "Yes, very much and one wrong spell ended her life. She was the first witch I had ever encountered who befriended me rather than ran away. That night plagues my dreams. I wish I could go back and tell her no. I wish I knew..." His voice trailed off, and my body pushed to comfort him, but I refused. I had to fight this bond.

"Who was he?" I asked, referring to the man they both once worked for.

He looked up at me, his face covered in sadness. "Someone you never need to know about."

"I disagree. She ran from him, hid from him. She was either scared or trying to protect me." Surely, he would understand and give me the answer.

"It is not open for discussion, Larissa." He finished his whiskey and turned away to stare at the fire.

"Well, I want to open it back up for discussion," I demanded. He was not getting out of this.

"No, he is not worth your time." His dismissal only annoyed me further.

"Seriously Nik, think about this. She said a spell before she answered the door. You could not sense me, and neither could Roman. But, when Roman heard me, he did not tell you. Why?" He needed to understand that she had a reason for her actions.

Nik scratched his chin, as he processed my words. "Do you think?"

"Yes, I do. It is why Roman stalked me my whole life." I sighed as I paced in a circle, "I believe he was bound by magic to protect me. It was all part of the spell. She was protecting my existence from him. Now, who is he?"

Nik's phone rang, and he pulled it out to answer.

"Don't you dare!" I warned as I walked over to him.

He ignored me and answered the phone. I reached and tried to grab it from his hands, but he wrapped his arm around me and held me close to his body with his super strength as he spoke on the phone.

"Yes, Cody, I told you I would leave after my meeting tonight. It can wait an hour. I have more pressing issues to deal with." He paused as he listened to this Cody on the phone. "The issues are concerning my mate. She is in distress over Hector's actions. I wanted to ensure she was settled before I left. Cody, you were hired to fix these situations. *Handle. It.* Until I arrive." He spun me out of his arms and put his phone away.

"What's going on?" I questioned as Nik paced the room, anger radiating from him.

"Hector has asked for my businesses to be audited. He knows he cannot attack you now and will attack my fortune, instead," he barked, not impressed with Hector's strikes against him.

"Would it not be easier to just kill him?" I suggested as I shrugged my shoulders.

Nik looked at me and laughed.

"Yes. Before we took over the human world, it would have been, but now there are consequences. I have too much to live for now." He stroked my face, his eyes dropped to my lips as he licked his own.

The magnetic pull for him made my body ache. I wanted his hands on me, to feel every part of him. Nik's chest rumbled as he brought his body closer to mine. I dropped my head and took a step back.

"One day, you will not resist me, and it will be the best night of your life," he whispered as he brought my hand to his lips.

I chuckled and took his hand to kiss it in return. "Careful now, you do not want to talk it up and not deliver," I baited him with a mischievous smile.

He laughed. "You will find out I always deliver. May I have one final request before I go?"

"You have had plenty of those tonight." I rolled my eyes.

"Would you drink some of my blood?" he asked as he moved a stray hair from my face.

"What?!" I screeched. I had no desire to drink his blood, and on the few occasions that I had, it was only due to being injured. He put his hand up to indicate that he wanted me to listen. I huffed in frustration but stopped.

"Just listen to me. I will be able to feel if you are in any danger because our connection will be stronger." I screwed up my face at the thought of tasting blood. "I will mask the taste in another drink. You will barely notice." He made sense, even if I wanted to vomit at this moment.

"Fine," I sighed, gesturing with my hand for him to go ahead. He poured a glass of red wine and cut his wrist into it before handing it over to me. "Bottoms up," I said as I sculled the entire glass. When I drank the last drop, he kissed my forehead.

"I will be back before you know it. If you need anything, call or text me. There are several butlers and maids that will help you with anything you need." I nodded as he took my hand and led me to the door. "You will be safe here." I could feel his regret in leaving. He wanted to stay and continue to sort out our future together.

In a flash, my back was against the wall and his hands were on my face. He kissed me. It was raw and passionate and filled with lust. I ground against him with need, not able to stop myself. He nibbled on my lip. "Careful, Larissa, someone may see and believe you truly want this."

He rushed from the room. I stayed still for a moment to catch my breath. This man was going to be the death of me.

CHAPTER 49

WHO IS THE ONE THEY ALL FEAR?

Larissa

Roman had stopped talking to me and refused to respond to any of my messages. Nik said it would only be a few days, but it had been a week, and he could not give me an accurate answer on how much longer he would be gone.

He had organised for an escort to take me out for a run every morning. I did not have to ask for anything, it was already done for me. I asked Nik if I could continue practising my magic with Sophia, and he allowed it. Practising magic brightened my day and seemed to cure my loneliness.

The conditions of the court forbid it, but he found a way around that. His exact words were, "There is always a loophole."

Sophia arrived promptly at nine, as she always did. I flung the heavy glass and iron door open to welcome her.

"Morning Sophia!" I beamed at seeing her face.

"Hello, Larissa." Sophia smiled as she walked in with her air of mystical energy. I had been extra friendly to her all week. I wanted to find out who this person was that Nik had worked for. I offered her a coffee as per usual and we sat down. She took a sniff and put the cup down.

"Marjoram? Really, Larissa?" I bit my lip as her eyes noticed the rosebuds in the centre of the bench.

"Why not just ask me? Have I ever lied to you?" She reached out to touch my hand.

I sighed and put my cup down. "No, you have not, but I wanted to make sure that you did not this time." I foolishly thought she would not notice.

"What is it?" she asked, her voice seeming to understand.

"You knew my mother, Katrina; you knew she had relationships with vampires and made side deals. Did you ever hear of one so powerful that she ran away and hid me?" The energy in the room shifted. Sophia knew. "Who is he?"

She put her cup down and covered her face. "He has many names, but none that I dare speak. There are many tales of his beginning, but it is hard to decipher the truth from fiction. He makes wishes come true at a price; his powers are limitless. Any who see his face never lives to tell the tale. Why do you ask?" The story did not make me scared or worried, it had the opposite effect. I had to know more.

"I am trying to understand why she ran from him and why she hid my existence from him," I prodded her.

Sophia shook with fear.

"Larissa." The growl came from behind Sophia as Nik stormed into the kitchen, his fists were clenched, and his anger radiated through the whole room. Sophia bowed her head in submission, which made me consider why I had never feared him in this way.

"Lord Dankworth, please excuse me. Larissa, I shall see you

tomorrow." She ran from the room, the door slammed behind her.

I smiled at Nik and sauntered over to him. I put my arms around his waist and embraced him.

"You did not tell me you were returning. I was beginning to miss you." I batted my eyes at him to distract his monster.

"Do not try and flirt your way out of this one. I told you this discussion was over," he hissed as he pulled me closer.

I hated the way he did this. "I reopened it. I found more answers in those two minutes than I did talking with you."

He stroked his face and sighed. He knew I was right. "I understand your need to find answers. Can I make you a promise?" he requested, taking a step back.

I rolled my eyes and threw my hands up in the air. I wanted to slap him. "What?" I snapped at him.

"I will give you answers in time, stop looking for him." Worry lines appeared on his face.

"Fine," I muttered as he strolled over to the fridge for some blood. I pushed him out of the way and grabbed a bag before putting it in the microwave to warm it for him. He smiled and sat down.

"How did everything go with Cody and Hector? Is it all sorted?" He groaned, pulled his tie off, and unbuttoned the first few buttons on his shirt. I could not stop my eyes from dropping to his chest, or thoughts of wanting to run my hands through his chest hair and feel the warmth of his skin under my own. I was feeling a little hornier than usual. I pulled out my phone to check my menstruation app. I was ovulating. Nik sniffed the air and laughed as he removed his suit jacket and rolled up his sleeves.

"Do you think I could not resist you?" I crossed my arms at him and glared.

"With how elevated your hormones are right now, it would be difficult," he cockily added.

I took the cup from the microwave and slid it across to him before I left the room. Unfortunately, he followed.

"I walked away for a reason. Go away, Nik!" I shouted over my shoulder at him.

"I needed to discuss an upcoming function with you." I heard him take a sip of the blood in his cup as I stopped and turned to meet his gaze.

"I am guessing that I have to attend due to officially being your mate in the eyes of the law," I grumbled remembering the ridiculous contract between us.

He leant against the wall and took another sip of his blood. I watched the muscles on his forearm flex. He made drinking look sexy, and it was annoying.

"Yes, and it is important that we make it believable. Hector will use any opportunity to find a way to appeal your sentence," he explained the importance of this function. It only annoyed me further to pretend to be a person I no longer was.

"Very well. When is it?" I resigned myself to the fact that this was my life, engaged to a successful, ridiculously rich, handsome vampire Lord.

"Thursday." He took another sip of his blood as his eyes flared briefly. He was enjoying the taste and annoyed with the situation surrounding Hector.

I sighed. "What is this function on Thursday?" I asked him as I tried not to let my eyes linger on him for too long.

Nik smirked. "It is a ball where all the rich and famous give money towards charities and offer their support for those in need. It is pomp and pageantry, but it will cement your place in society as my mate. It is the only reason why we need to be believable, as all eyes will be watching the human mated to the Lord of the region." He exhaled with eagerness in his eyes.

"How do you suggest we make our relationship believable?" My feet moved closer without thinking.

He stroked his chin with a cheeky look on his face.

"Other than that, Nik. I will not sleep with you until I feel that I am ready to do so." Did I just say that? I could not believe the words had left my mouth.

"I understand, but it is the fastest way to grow our bond." His eyes drifted over my tight jeans and low-cut black tank top.

I sighed, putting my hands on my hips. I still had to figure out a few things between us.

"I have another suggestion that may help," he said.

I tapped my foot on the floor as I waited for his suggestion. I worried it may be another comment about a sex act. My mind drifted to the time I spent the night. I cleared my throat and focused on his face.

Nik smiled as he took a step closer, putting his cup down. "We need to be more comfortable together. We have not had the opportunity to spend time together outside of work or you being held captive in my home." He made a joke to make light of our ever-evolving situation.

"So? Do not leave me in suspense." I cocked an eyebrow at him.

"Why do we not go shopping together? You would be able to pick a gown for the ball that we could both agree would not be too revealing." He slowly circled me with his hands behind his back.

"Does that include shoes?" I questioned; I loved shoes.

"If you wish," He answered nonchalantly.

"Jewellery?" I prodded further to see how far I could push him.

"Yes, absolutely. I have money and would love to spoil you." He stopped before me.

"What about…" He put his finger over my lips, and I fought the desire to kiss it.

"I want you to think of this as a date. We shall do whatever you wish." I could not help but smile. The thought of spending a day with him made my stomach bubble with excitement. "I feel that you like the idea. Go get dressed." I looked him over in his suit. "Yes, I will change also."

I ran upstairs to change. I had a date to get to.

CHAPTER 50
DRESSING TO KILL

Larissa

IT TOOK A WHILE TO SORT THROUGH MY WARDROBE BEFORE THERE was a knock on the door. I was trying to pick a pair of shoes to wear.

"Come in, I am just in the wardrobe," I called out. I heard the door open as I sat observing the multitude of shoes that Nik had filled this room with. The tingle alerted me to him being behind me.

"Wear something comfortable, I said." He sat on the ottoman in the middle of the robe, his leg dangerously close to touching my own.

"Yes, that is my problem. A pair of boots would be comfortable as would a pair of sneakers," I explained my conundrum to him.

He chuckled as he walked to the shelves and grabbed a pair of black boots off a row. I took the chance to take in his outfit. He was wearing black pants and a blue sweater top that brought out the brightness of his eyes. Why did he have to be so handsome? He bent down and picked up my foot, then slid it into the boot and zipped it up, then repeated the process on my other foot. He straightened his knees and put his hands on either side of my body on the ottoman.

"Try not to get too hot and bothered over how handsome I look today," he whispered.

I smirked and moved closer to him. "Same to you. Wait until you see just how good my ass looks in these jeans." My heart started to thump in my chest, and my body filled with excitement at his closeness.

"Everything you wear looks good, as it does on me." He moved closer as he sniffed the crook of my neck before straightening to gaze at my face.

"A little full of yourself, aren't you?" I clicked my tongue as his eyes drifted to my lips.

"Muscular arms, thick hair, blue eyes, sexy voice, never." Every one of his words dripped with sex, and I wanted him badly. "But that does not compare to the green of your eyes and the luscious lips before me. I would love nothing more than to sink my teeth into them and suck them raw." He playfully snapped his teeth together before he stood, offering his hand. I took it and he twirled me around. "Yep, looks as good as I pictured."

I chuckled and walked off ahead of him. I grabbed my bag and phone and headed down the stairs towards the front door. He took my hand and dragged me in another direction. "The car is down here."

"But is it not normally out the front door?" I asked as I pointed towards the door.

"No driver today," he informed me as I followed him down a darker corridor.

"Why?" Confusion and unease settled in. Nik always had a driver.

"It is our day. I am strong enough to look after us both." He pressed a button, and an elevator came into view. My eyes grew wide in surprise. I had searched the entire mansion during the week alone and I had completely missed this.

"What? You have a hidden elevator?" I gasped as it opened. It was just big enough for two people.

"Yes, it goes down to the garage and the panic room."

I peered at him curiously. "Why does a vampire have a panic room? Why do you need one? You are immortal." I laughed at the image of a vampire hiding in a panic room.

"The panic room is for you." We stepped into the elevator as he pressed the buttons on the keypad, *476.*

"Interesting selection of numbers. The date for the fall of the Roman Empire. I would love to hear the stories from that time." I thought about just how long he had been alive and everything he would have seen.

"In due time, you shall." The elevator sped down before the door opened again to a typical-looking garage. Although, I was a little shocked. He only had three cars. I stood still as I glanced around the room.

Nik squeezed my hand. "What is it?"

"You only have three cars. I am a little shocked you do not have one for every day of the week and an extra for public holidays."

He snorted. "I flaunt my wealth, but not to that extent. Which do you like?" He pointed towards the cars. I shrugged, not caring which car we drove in.

He picked up a set of keys for the Audi, walked over to the car, and held the door open for me. Nik pulled out his phone and put it on vibrate before he started the ignition. The car ride was silent; not awkward, just quiet. Even with the closeness we shared, I found it hard to speak with him.

We arrived at the shopping complex, and he was a typical gentleman, opening the car door. I slid my hand into his and it warmed my whole body.

"Where shall we start?" Nik asked as I read all the store names.

"I do not know, I must admit. I do not know much about fashion. Where would you recommend would be the best for the future wife of the Lord Vampire?" I goaded him as I nudged him playfully.

He tapped his chin before his face lit with excitement. "Come." He led the way to a rather large store called Dresstacula, and I burst into a fit of giggles.

"Wow, that is unbelievable. They named a gown store after Dracula." I snorted as I struggled to stop laughing.

"I thought you would enjoy the laugh. Come, I shall take you to Chanel." He walked off when I noticed a beautiful gown. It was strapless with a black bodice that had ruffles, which slightly changed the colour to green. Nik tried to pull my hand again, but I refused to move.

"What is it?" he asked. I pointed at the gown in the window.

"What about that?" I hoped he would say yes. I could not take my eyes off it.

"You should try it on," he suggested.

"Is it acceptable?" I dared not look at him as I asked.

He creased his brows. "Larissa, I promised in the new contract that I would not control what you wear." Then added, "Too much."

"Yes, I know, but I also do not want you to be uncomfortable with me wearing something that may attract attention. I cannot have a jealous Nik ripping people's heads off." I wiggled my eyebrows at him.

He sniggered at my remark. "During our time apart, I realised that I did not care. I want you happy, and if that dress makes you happy, then I am happy too."

I giddily entered the store and requested my size. I slid into the gown with ease, but the changing booth was almost too small for how big the skirt was. I felt like a princess as I twirled and watched myself in the mirror.

"Larissa." I heard Nik call for me as I pushed the curtain aside for him to see. His eyes glowed brighter than I had ever seen them.

"You are a vision, you are angelic, you are perfection. May I kiss you?" His question caught me off guard, and I froze. "Forget I asked," said quickly as he rubbed the back of his head, a flash of embarrassment passed through our bond. He ventured to the clerk, and I saw him pull out his card and pay for the dress. I walked out of the store and found Nik checking his phone.

"I thought you promised not to use it today?" I groaned at him. We had barely been shopping for an hour.

He smiled and pocketed it. "It is away, as promised."

"Nik, did I do something wrong?" I asked him after feeling embarrassment in the store.

"You did nothing wrong. Sometimes, it is simply hard to

contain myself around you. I feel a constant pull to be closer to you. I want to feel your skin on mine. It is hard to resist."

His words were smooth and sensuous, and they lit my own senses up. He growled and turned to look behind him, before taking my hand in his and dragging me to another store. My arm was almost dislocated from his strength.

"What is it?" I asked as I shook out the pain in my arm.

"Paparazzi. They would have seen the court documents," he said while glancing over my shoulder to keep an eye on them.

"So why is a photo of you important?"

He put on a fake shocked face. "I *am* the most eligible bachelor, and you are the lucky woman who has snatched me off the market. They want to see who this beautiful woman is," he stated with a smile that reached his eyes.

I planted my feet as he tried to pull me along. When he turned to me, I pointed out, "Are we not supposed to sell the idea that we are in love? Why not start now?"

He scratched his chin as he contemplated what I said. Hector was trying to find a reason to appeal my sentence and get me taken away from Nik. I saw this as an opportunity to sell the idea further. "You know that means we would have to be a little more affectionate towards one another," he reminded me.

"Nik, do I need to prove it to you? You may get that kiss after all."

"I am not sure you could pull this off," he said, a challenge in his voice.

I took a step towards him, trailed my finger up his chest and bit my lip. I stared up at him seductively. "Is this selling it enough?" I asked, my voice barely a whisper.

He took in a deep breath; he stroked my face as desire and affection seeped from his body.

"I am not sure if I can handle this," he whispered, struggling to hold back his desires.

"Kiss me and find o—" I was interrupted by his lips crashing against mine. His hand snaked around my waist and pulled me closer. I grabbed onto his sweater, and his tongue invaded my mouth and massaged my own. I moaned with pleasure before he stopped the kiss abruptly.

"We need to keep shopping," he groaned as he readjusted himself in his pants.

I giggled. "Cannot handle the heat, can you?" I shot him a wink, then took his hand to lead him to a few more stores. I consciously kept touching him, putting my arm around his waist and holding his hand with an occasional cute peck on his lips or cheek. It felt natural, like this had always been our relationship.

"Let us take a break," he suggested as he squeezed my hand gently.

"What, are you tired?" I winked at him playfully.

"No, but I am hungry. The next fake kiss, I may just bite you to get my fill." His eyes flared for a moment.

"Hey, who says it is fake?" He was taken aback by my remark.

"*Is* it real?" I could see the hope on his face. The hope that I was no longer acting. But I would not admit to him that I was not even sure if I *was* anymore.

"Does it seem real?" I teased him as I stood before him again. He put his arms around my waist and pulled me close.

"Oh, it does, but I am not sure. I feel and smell your lust, but I am not convinced that it is not purely a game to you anymore. I cannot read your whole mind." I kissed him on the lips, no longer able to hold myself back.

"Well, well, well, the great Lord Dankworth is struggling to read a woman. This is an interesting turn of events. Come on, I will tell you over food because I am starving." I took his hand, leading him towards the food court.

He groaned as we entered the restaurant. We were seated instantly because everybody knew who Nik was and we were given a booth to enjoy our privacy. I sat down and Nik slid in beside me. He put his arm around my shoulders and held me close. I picked up the menu, but he took it from my hands and put it down on the table.

"No need, the chef is a friend. He will bring out a selection of food," he assured me. I snuggled into the warmth of his body as the paparazzi continued to take photos of us together.

"Is it always like this for you?" I quizzed him, the constant flash in my periphery.

He seemed completely unfazed by the constant invasion of privacy. I saw a flicker of sadness cross his face before he looked in my direction.

"Yes, but I have become accustomed to it. Do you wish for me to send them away?"

I shook my head; we needed this proof to stop Hector from having any grounds to appeal my sentence. I turned and put my leg up on the booth.

"What are you doing?" he queried as he glanced at the photographers.

"It is hard to have a conversation with you beside me. I thought I would turn to see those beautiful blue eyes." I batted my eyelids at him, really playing up the flirtation.

"Well, it is better to see your face. May I ask you a question?"

"Yes, you may."

"When did it stop being a game for you?" I knew he was referring to the kisses. I enjoyed them, as well as the feel of his hand in my own. He would be able to sense a slight change in my emotions, so there was no point in lying to him.

"I think maybe after the fifth or sixth kiss. When did you feel it?" Two glasses of wine were brought over to the table. I picked one up and took a drink.

"After the second. Your need increased, but I did not pressure anything further." He smiled with a knowing look in his eye.

I chuckled at him. "That would have been hard."

"Oh, exceptionally but like I said, I do not want to push you. Our situation has been forced and I was hopeful that it would evolve in time between us." He put the glass down and sighed in frustration.

"In other words, you were secretly praying that I would break up with Roman and start dating you?" He winked and smiled. That was a yes. "Is it weird that I was dating your brother like a week ago?"

"It would be if we were human, but when you are as old as Roman and I, time makes no difference. I desired you and I would have waited decades to have you."

I snorted. "Even if I were old and grey?"

"I see the attraction beyond the beauty, Larissa. Your kind and gentle soul, the soft and caring nature. I understand the struggle between what you were raised to believe and what you feel, but ultimately, I believe it was a spell to keep you safe. I think Elizabeth planted the seed with a spell and it grew as time went on," he acknowledged, and I knew deep down he was right.

"I do not understand how you knew Katrina, but you never knew Elizabeth," I pondered, as he seemed to know Katrina so intimately.

"Katrina had spoken of her in passing, but I never had the pleasure. Katrina and Elizabeth had a fractured relationship. She would often make the joke that one was blessed with light while the other was blessed with darkness." He laughed at the fondness of the memory.

"Which was she?" I probed further wanting to know more about her.

"She never said but I like to believe she was the angel." He took another sip of his wine.

I asked more questions about my mother, wanting to know the person that she was, and Nik was more than eager to talk about her. I finally had an insight into the woman who died to protect me. We were very similar, so it made sense why I never had a strong relationship with Elizabeth.

The food was delivered. Nik refused to eat human food today, so instead had a large glass of blood. I devoured the steak and vegetables before laying back in the seat, rather bloated, and rubbed the little food tummy. He laughed, but his emotions indicated a wanting.

"Tell your chef friend that he is an amazing cook," I added while I tried not to burp from the fullness of my stomach.

"I shall. Larissa…" He paused, but I could tell he wanted to say more.

"What is it, Nik?" I sighed knowing what it would be about.

"I may have to break a promise to you."

I rolled my eyes. "Let me guess your phone."

"Yes, I received eight phone calls while you were eating. May I check it?" He was always so polite.

"Fine, you may." I waved my hand at him.

He bowed his head in thanks. "Please excuse me for a moment." Nik stood and walked away to check his phone, while I pulled my own out and flicked through my emails. I was so behind on work, but I suppose it did not matter when I was due to marry the boss.

"Larissa?" I glanced up from my phone to see James standing next to my table.

"Oh my god!" I stood and embraced him.

"How have you been?" he asked. We hadn't seen each other since I moved into Roman's house.

"I have been good! What about yourself?" I wasn't about to go into detail on what had happened recently.

"Not bad, not bad at all. How is work?" He asked with a sunny smile on his face. James had always been so kind.

I wasn't sure how to answer. I hadn't worked in over a week.

"Good," my voice croaked from the lie.

He put his hand on my arm. "Is everything al—"

It happened in a flash, his head was slammed onto the table.

"Do not touch her," Nik hissed, appearing out of nowhere and holding James down.

"Nik!" I screeched. He glared at me with red eyes. "Let him go," I ordered, but he ignored me, pushed down on James, and whispered in his ear before letting him go.

"I'll speak to you later, Larissa," James blurted. I waved awkwardly as he ran from the restaurant.

"What the fuck was that?" I turned my anger towards Nik.

"He had no right to touch you," Nik growled. "He is a pig."

I rolled my eyes, storming away from him.

"Larissa," he called across the restaurant, but I ignored him and continued my path to the exit. He soon caught up to me and practically scolded me. "Larissa, stop or we shall leave."

"Then we are leaving, I am so upset by what you did! Maybe upset isn't the right word, embarrassed is more accurate."

"You do not understand..."

"I do not need to. He is a friend. He helped me out so much," I chided, remembering just how much he had done for me.

"Trust me, he is not a friend," he snarled as he glanced over my shoulder in search of him.

"Where do you get off? I met him the day I moved to London. He has been nothing but friendly and now he probably will not speak to me again."

"That is not a bad thing," he replied calmly. I wanted to scream; he was infuriating. He had been so kind all day and now the monster was coming out again.

"I want to leave now." I crossed my arms.

"Very well," he sighed, probably thinking the same. That the day had been going so well, and this had ruined it.

He attempted multiple times to hold my hand, but I brushed it away. I refused to hold his hand even for the cameras. "We will speak of this in the car."

"Oh, I look forward to it," I said with a snarky tone. I was going to let him have it when we were out of the public eye. He held the car door open for me like usual, and I slid into the car. I pulled the car door and slammed it on purpose. He hopped in and started the car, but we did not speak until we were well out of the city.

"You are forbidden to speak to James ever again," he stated, keeping his eyes focused on the intersection before him.

"You do not get to tell me who I can and cannot speak with. You do not own me," I reminded him. He growled and elbowed the window. It smashed from his strength. The car had stopped, so I got out.

"Get back in the car, Larissa," he snarled.

"No, you just smashed a window. I am not going anywhere with you!" I yelled at him.

"I will not ask you again, Larissa. Please get in the car." The sound of a wolf howling broke my glare at Nik. He appeared beside me in a moment. "Now, it is time to get in. We do not want a quarrel with wolves."

"What? Are you scared of a little old wolf?" I snorted and took a step away from him.

"Wolves are more dangerous than you know." He swallowed as he scanned the surrounding area.

"I lived with one. Roman was never dangerous," I retorted, remembering how he never smashed a window near me.

"Roman is thousands of years old. He has controlled his wolf. The younger wolves are the ones to fear. I beg of you, get in the car."

I stormed back towards the car and got in, slamming the door again. He drove off faster than before. "Do you have to fight me on everything?"

"Sorry that I will not be a complacent housewife. I told you, I was complacent for years and I will not be for you. Accept me or let me die."

He slammed on the brakes as my head jerked forward. "That will never happen. I will not lose you again," he fumed. My ears pricked at his choice of words.

"Again? What do you mean again?" I asked. He had done this a few times.

He shook his head and shut down.

"Answer me, Nik." He stayed silent for the remainder of the car ride until we reached the garage.

"Dinner will be served at six. I will see you then." He dismissed me, but I would not accept it.

"No, not until you tell me what you meant by *again*. Give me an answer or I will starve myself."

He spun with his fists clenched and his eyes glowing red.

"I have lost too much in my life. I will not lose my mate!" He did not elaborate, and he left swiftly. That did not feel like the whole truth.

I went down for dinner as he requested, but I refused to speak to him. I ate and went up to sleep for the night. I heard Nik pacing outside the room. He wanted to come in, but I sensed when he walked away. It would only end in a fight between us. It was always the same story with us, but I refused to change for him. I had buried myself for years for the sake of the woman I thought was my mother, only to discover the lies that she had spun.

CHAPTER 51

DATE DAY

I WOKE FROM A RESTLESS SLEEP. I ROLLED FROM MY BED AND grabbed my running attire for my morning routine. Nik's guard was already waiting outside my door.

"A little later than usual, Miss Solis," Andreas said by way of greeting. He had always been incredibly kind.

"Yes. I did not sleep well, Andreas." He bowed his head out of respect.

His hair was pulled back into a bun atop his head and his singlet top and shorts were matching black. I wondered if Nik implemented a dress code on purpose. It was obvious from Andreas's name and looks that he was of Greek heritage. I had many questions but kept them to myself.

"Are you sure you want to run this morning?" he asked politely. I nodded.

I needed to work through my frustration towards Nik, and I knew running would help. We ran along our typical route, up the hill and around before coming back down again.

"Let's take a break." Andreas stopped and sat down.

"Why, we still have to get down the hill?" He had never done this before.

"You are not your usual self today, and I will not push you to the point where you hurt yourself. Sit down, if only for five minutes." I slumped down beside him as he pulled out a bottle of water and handed it to me. I took a drink.

"Is he always this infuriating?" I asked, knowing that he would not be able to answer my question honestly.

"I assume you mean Lord Dankworth. I will admit that I don't find him infuriating. He is fair in all his decisions." His answer did not help me. "He is different with you, though. The Lord that I know can be cutthroat in all his decisions. He sees a solution and decides without hesitation, but with you, it is different. He thinks before he acts. He is letting emotion control him. He loves you, Larissa. If I may speak plainly..." He looked up to gauge my reaction. I nodded, encouraging him to continue. "...You need to understand that he is from a different time. He is making allowances for you, but I have seen you give very little in return."

I sighed; he was not wrong. But it was complicated.

"Why should I, Andreas? Since he appeared in my life, it has been nothing but trouble."

"If you stop fighting, you would be the most powerful couple in the whole world. Your magic with his vampiric power, nobody would dare question you." Andreas's phone rang and he answered it quickly.

"Yes, my Lord." He hung up. "We had better get back. Nik is waiting for you." I stood and dusted myself off before we headed back to the mansion. Andreas was not lying. Nik stood in the foyer, tapping his foot on the marble flooring. He smiled once he saw me and nodded towards Andreas in thanks. I could not help but wonder if he had planted Andreas to say that information to me.

"Good morning, Nik." I greeted him with a fake smile as I was still angry at him.

"Larissa, I very much enjoyed the day yesterday, and I would like for us to spend another day together. I will allow you to pick the location." He smiled and placed a hand on his chest, over his heart, conveying his apology for yesterday's events in his own way.

I could see that he was trying. He wanted us to build a relationship. We had sexual chemistry, but no friendship.

"How about we compromise?" I answered after considering what Andreas had said.

"Oh, how so?" Nik sounded cheerful at my attempt to work together.

"I would like to go out to a bar tonight. Get some drinks and dance to the music. What would you like to do during the day?" I could tell he did not agree, but I had left it open for him.

"Laser tag." He raised his eyebrows with glee.

I laughed and smiled. "You wish to shoot me now? Am I that annoying?"

"No, I want to build trust with you. We shall work on a team together."

"You are brave," I added. "I like your thinking, but first I need food."

He stood aside and walked with me to the kitchen, where there was a plate of pancakes and a coffee already waiting. I sat down and ate as Nik stood at the bench and drank his morning bloodcino.

I ran upstairs to change, and as I came out of the wardrobe, Nik was sitting on the bed wearing black tracksuit pants and a black singlet top. It showed more of him than I had ever seen. Desire spread through me, and Nik smiled.

"Like what you see?" he drawled.

"A little concerned about you showing so much skin. Do you feel alright today?" I touched his forehead with the back of my hand to check for a non-existent temperature.

"You seem to wear revealing clothing, which leaves little to the imagination, so I thought I would follow your lead and do the same. Can you handle it?" He stood and flexed his muscles. I tried not to give in to temptation, but he was too perfect to not stare.

I decided to make it more interesting, so I re-entered the robe, changed my black top to a crop top and came out again. His eyes flared with desire for a split second before he stalked over to me. I leant against the wall as he put his hand above my head, and his fangs descended. I could feel how badly he wanted me.

"Am I a bad girl?" I asked seductively as I bit my lip.

He growled, "If you wish to show off, I will as well." He straightened and said, "Let the games begin," before he slipped his hand into mine.

I beamed with happiness, but I could not understand why this brought me joy. I was also confused about why he decided not to fight me on my clothing.

———

Laser tag was exhilarating. We worked together to win the first round. During the second, Nik found me standing against a wall, panting, with sweat dripping off me.

"I suppose the mate bond helps with finding me in the dark," I joked.

He laughed as he leant on the wall beside me. I saw his chest rise and fall and the muscles contract before me. Nik turned his head to look at me, his eyes glowed bright blue. He dropped his gun, took my face in his hands, and kissed me. I could not fight it and I found I did not want to. It was a burning desire deep within my soul, a carnal need for him. I had never felt it before.

"Bella Mia," he whispered as he lifted me and pressed me against the wall. I needed to feel him deep inside. Every atom of my being wanted more. His passion intensified as he nibbled my neck. His fangs grazing that curve sent my body into overdrive.

"Nik." Voices grew louder as our opponents approached. I touched the wall and cast an invisibility spell. They stared directly at us but saw nothing before continuing. Nik put me down.

"Your eyes are glowing," he said while staring into them.

"They do that when I use certain magic. Sorry." I bowed my head in shame.

"They are beautiful, do not say you are sorry." I moved away from Nik. It was a reminder of the answers that I so desperately wanted but would never know. Nik reached for me. "What happened?"

I refused to look at him. "You still have not given me any answers. Why do my eyes glow? It is only when I use certain magic, but why? You told me months ago that you would give me answers, but when will I get them Nik?"

He ran his fingers through his hair. I noticed the sweat on him and became envious of it getting to be on his skin.

"You are not ready," he added while stroking his chin.

"Who are you to decide when I am ready?" My voice rose.

"You will not be able to handle it."

He was doing it again and these were the moments that annoyed me.

"You are a controlling dick." I stormed away from him and purposely made myself invisible to him to avoid him chasing after me. I knew he would be able to sense me eventually, but it would annoy him as much as he annoyed me. I leant against the car and watched the worry on his face as he scanned the area for me. I smiled at the worry written on his face.

"Larissa!" he called out.

I walked over to him, and said, "It is not funny when people hide things from you, is it?" before returning to the car. He was still not able to see me.

"Larissa, you have made your point. Show yourself!" His tone became serious.

"I will in time." I slid inside the car, and Nik saw and raced over. I snapped my fingers to reveal myself.

"That was not funny. I will not play your games like a child."

"Then do not treat me as one. Give me answers."

"I HAVE NONE TO GIVE!" he shouted in frustration, slamming himself back into the seat and running his hands through his hair.

"What do you mean you have none?" I asked in disbelief.

"I do not know who your father is. I searched through Katrina's past and found nothing. I do not know who he is, and I can find no trace of him. I do not know why your blood is so pure, nor do I know why your eyes are red. I have not given you answers because I cannot give you any." The air was still between us.

"Why lie?" I was confused about why he said he would when he had none to give. What was the purpose of his lying? What did he gain from it?

"I wanted to give you comfort that you would eventually know something worthwhile. I felt like it would be better for you to be lied to than to have nothing, to help give you comfort, and in the meantime, I could search for the answers you needed. It was foolish of me. I want to give you everything your heart desires, but I cannot even give you the one answer you seek on whom your father is." He appeared defeated as we sat in the car. I reached over and touched his hand.

"Thank you for being honest." He lifted his hand with mine attached and kissed it. We drove in silence.

CHAPTER 52
GROWING CLOSER

W E WERE ESCORTED TO N IK'S PENTHOUSE. I T WAS FUNNY BEING here now. I thought it was large the first time I came here, but compared to his mansion, it did not seem as big. Nik did about an hour of work while I watched television to busy myself. There was a knock at the door, and I stood to check it. I answered the door to find Andreas holding a suitcase.

"Miss Solis." He handed the suitcase to me, but I was barely able to hold it.

"What is this?" I asked as I dropped it on the floor. It was heavier than Andreas had made it out to be, but I guess vampire strength did that.

"Nik requested that I pack a few items of clothing, your makeup, jewels, and hair accessories for tonight." I peered over my shoulder at Nik, who was still deep into work. He scratched his forehead and wrote down a few things, muttering to himself.

"Not sure if we will make it out tonight."

"He has booked the VIP lounge at the most exclusive club. I don't doubt that he will make sure he holds up his end of the bargain. Enjoy your night." Andreas winked as he left.

It was a challenge, but I took the suitcase upstairs before returning to the couch. There was a weird sensation in my body like I needed to thank Nik for this. I glanced over my shoulder at him again. He was ridiculously attractive even when stressed. The creases in his forehead deepened and his eyes intensified as they flicked between red and blue. The bond called to comfort him, and before I knew it, I found myself massaging his shoulders and down his arms. His skin was soft and silky. I pictured touching his entire body.

"What are you doing, Larissa?" His voice croaked.

"You know, I am not entirely sure. The bond called to comfort you and I thought I should after receiving that suitcase."

"Oh, Andreas was here? I barely noticed." He put his pen down and stretched his neck out. I watched his hands rub a sore spot. I swatted them away to rub it for him.

"You have been working rather diligently over here," I murmured. "Is there anything I can help you with?" He flicked through the work to show me all he had been doing.

"I am tempted to offer you the role of secretary until I am sure that you will be safe, but I feel as if it is a demotion with your skills." He groaned as my hands worked his sore spot.

"If it keeps me busy while being stuck in a mansion, I will do it." I shrugged my shoulders; I had been rather bored watching television all day.

"You make being waited on seem like a job." He chuckled as he signed another document.

"I am not a fan of it. I do not feel worthy of it," I confessed. He grabbed my hand and kissed it.

"You are a princess. You are more than worthy." He nipped at my hand.

"I am only a princess in your eyes, so it does not count." I stopped touching him.

He turned in his seat to see my face. "Is my word worth nothing?" His eyes sparkled, teasing me.

I rolled my eyes in response. "Sometimes it can be."

His hand slid up the back of my leg and paused at the bottom of my ass.

"Now, do not be cheeky," I pretended to scold him.

"I fear I am always a little cheeky, Miss Solis." He bit his lip as his hand remained at my bottom.

It was weird when he said my name like that. It was almost like we were strangers, but we were more than friends at this stage.

I tapped his shoulders. "I had best get ready for tonight. Do I dare ask which dresses you asked Andreas to select?"

"Actually, I allowed him free reign. I said, 'Allow her to be sultry without any stipulations'."

"I will enjoy tonight more than I thought." I winked at him.

His head fell back with laughter before he sobered and asked, "I will need about another hour, is that alright?"

"Considering it will take you five minutes to get ready compared to my hour, I think that is fine." I purposely walked off, shaking my ass a little to tease him. His laugh filled the room as I spun and poked my tongue out at him.

The barrier around my heart shifted, as his laugh brought life to my soul.

CHAPTER 53

THE BIG BANG

ANDREAS HAD CHOSEN QUITE A SELECTION OF SULTRY CLOTHING, as Nik called it. I had never in my life shown this much skin. I bit my fingernails as I decided which I would be more comfortable in. I grabbed my medication as I prepared to take one before heading out. I stopped myself. With Nik, I did not feel as if I needed them, his touch could ease my worries in seconds.

Tonight felt different. The air between Nik and I had changed earlier in the day, and I worried about what it meant. My body wanted to explore more as excitement thrummed through me.

I fixed the waves of my hair and kept my makeup rather simple and understated, as it often was. I picked up a dress, which was black, had one sleeve, and a big cut out of fabric from just under my boob to my hips. The dress went to just above my knees, and as I looked at myself in the mirror, I knew would set Nik on fire to see me like this. I walked down the stairs to check and see if he was ready. The table had been cleared and it was empty,

"Nik!" I called out as I searched the lower floor. I spun around when my body tingled. He came out of the shadows wearing black jeans, a white shirt that was buttoned halfway, and a leather jacket. It reminded me of Roman, but it suited him better than his brother. He had the biker boy look—dangerous with an air of preppy to him. His eyes glowed brighter than usual, which was a sign he was enjoying the view. "Is this sultry enough for you?"

He nodded as he bit his lip. I could sense that he was holding himself back. "There is no doubt that you are the sexiest, most beautiful, angelic woman on the planet, Larissa."

"You are not going to ask me to cover up?"

"I would love to, but then I would miss out on the view, and I don't believe in torturing myself." His eyes roamed over my body.

I laughed and walked over to him. "I do not think I have ever seen you show as much skin as you have today."

He raised a brow at me suggestively. "Do you like what you see?" He flexed his arms.

"Do I have to answer that?" I chuckled at his actions.

"It would not hurt to hear the words rather than feel them."

"Yes Nik, you look incredibly sexy," I acknowledged. I had rarely told him that.

He straightened the collar on his leather jacket and beamed. He relaxed the more time we spent together. He did not seem as uptight and put together. I enjoyed the freer Nik, he appeared surer of himself. He held out his hand to me and I slid mine inside.

"I hope you are ready for tonight."

"Are you?" I poked and teased him.

"In more ways than one."

We arrived at the club and the music was pumping. It set my body on fire. Nik took my hand and led the way to our VIP section, which was filled with the who's who of celebrities. There were actresses and supermodels, but Nik's eyes stayed on me and never once strayed towards the beauties that surrounded him. He led me over to a purple booth, sat down and tapped the seat beside him. I sat next to him and got close to his chest. He took a sip of his drink and laid his arm on the back of the booth behind me. His eyes constantly scanned the area.

"Would you relax?" His constant worrying put a damper on the night. He shook his shoulders in an attempt to relax.

"Nik? Is that you?" a voice purred. As I followed the sound, he stood and kissed a woman's cheek. They spoke in what I believe was Italian. Her dark features were overwhelming. She was incredibly beautiful, and I noticed the small touches she placed on him. I grew increasingly jealous and stood to slide my arm into Nik's. She glared at me but remained focused on him. Nik smirked. He would be able to sense my annoyance at this girl, but I was not impressed with her attitude towards him. I cleared my throat as Nik spoke over her.

"May I introduce my mate, Larissa?" he said while he raised my hand to kiss it.

"Please, she is nothing more than a blood bag. Don't call her your mate, it is an insult." I pushed her aside, grabbed Nik by the jacket, and pulled him in for a kiss. It was carnal. I wanted all of him as he groaned and put his arms around my waist to pull me flush against his body. I let go and glared at the girl.

"Is this a typical response from a blood bag?" I snarled at her as she stormed away.

Nik wiped his lips. "Jealousy looks good on you."

I pushed his shoulder playfully as I sat back down. He put his arm around my shoulders again and pulled me closer. "You do not need to worry about those types of girls. I only have eyes for you and have since the moment you spilt coffee on me."

My cheeks flushed red as I recalled that eventful day. "Will I ever be able to go back to work?"

He smiled. "Yes, but I must ensure your safety first. Once I am confident that Hector has stopped his nonsense, you will be able to return to work," he assured me, but I doubted that would happen. He seemed relentless.

"Do I dare ask what is being said around the office?" I tore my eyes away from him. I worried about the rumours.

"I will tell them the truth. Did you expect me to lie?"

"No, but I worry what I will go back to. We are due to marry and—" The song changed, and it made my heart beat a little faster. Nik put his hand to my mouth.

"Enough talking. You came here to enjoy yourself, let us do that." He led me to the dance floor. The music ignited my senses as I swayed. Nik's hands rested on my hips as he swayed behind me. I let my head fall back onto his chest and let the music take control. His hands travelled up and down my sides, and I heard his breath hitch, which made me giggle.

"What is it?" I shouted for him to hear over the music.

"Just do not move." I spun around quickly and felt a solid object poking me.

"Oh, *hello*." I put my hand on his chest and kept my eyes trained on his as I dragged it down before stroking his erection. He groaned with need.

"Larissa," he muttered breathlessly.

"Yes?" I wanted him to say it. I was waiting to hear the words that would make me come undone. I feared what would happen, but I wanted it. I craved it within my soul. A burning desire to have him and be closer to him.

"I want more." His lips crashed onto mine, and I let all my reservations go. He was all I needed, and I could not explain it. I never had this deep yearning with Roman.

"Take me, Nik," I whispered in his ear. He paused to look at me and moved the hair from my face. He was checking that I truly wanted this. I smiled at him and nodded, and he lifted me into his arms.

"Hold on," Nik commanded, before he sped through the club. I heard a door slam behind him. We were in an office.

"Nik, you cannot break into the club's office. Even *you* can get in trouble for that." He licked his lips and held up his arms.

"So much to learn. I own the club," he announced as he spun around with his arms out.

"Wait, what? What do you not own?" I scoffed at his obscene wealth.

"Now *that* is a more appropriate question." He stalked over like a predator and lifted me onto the desk. "Where were we?"

As his hands gripped my thighs, I motioned towards the club. "They cannot see in," he reassured me, sensing my fear.

"It is not just that…it is also…what if the manager comes in?"

"I shall lock the door."

"He will have a key," I retorted quickly.

"Larissa, if you are not ready, simply say it. I shall have no untoward feelings." I was nervous, but not for the reasons he thought. He had been alive for centuries and been with countless women and yet, I had only been with one. He lifted my chin to look at him. "What is it?" he queried, stroking my face with tenderness.

"I am worried I may not be good enough. I have only been with one person, and you have been with who knows how many. I am not overly experienced."

His lips landed on my cheek. "I do not care about that. Every touch of yours makes me feel alive. Every kiss burns a mark on my soul, and yet, all I crave is more of it. I just want you." His words were my undoing. I pushed his jacket from his shoulders and onto the floor. He lifted me from the desk and carried me into the bathroom, not the most elegant place for our first time.

"Ah, um, explain," I said as he placed me on the sink.

"You were right, the manager has the key and the only eyes that should see your beauty are mine. I will not share you with the world, you are M.I.N.E." He said the letters of *mine* slowly and seductively, each one sending tingles through my body. I wrapped my legs tighter around him and brought him closer.

"Then you are mine as well."

His eyes glowed a brighter blue, it was magnificent. "Till the day I die."

He nuzzled into my neck and peppered it with kisses. His hands grabbed my thighs as I pulled at his pants and unbuttoned them. "Eager, are we?"

I smiled before I nibbled his lip. "Is that an issue?"

"No, I quite like it." He removed his shirt and I stared at the perfection of his muscles. In my perusal, I noticed a small scar on the left of his chest and ran my finger over it.

"An arrow?" I questioned at the odd shape.

"Yes, how did you know?" He took my hand and kissed it.

"The shape, I think?" Even I questioned how I knew.

"I was shot trying to save someone," he added. I pressed my lips to the scar before kissing him directly on the lips. His hands touched every part of me as he pulled on my underwear and tore them. I could not help but giggle at who was more eager now.

He lifted my dress over my head and kissed my neck while his other hand fondled my breast. I moaned at his touch; my skin was on fire. I pulled at Nik's shirt as he tore the buttons to remove it. His fingers grazed my thigh, running circles on my skin. He grabbed my hair at the back, tilting my head up to look at him.

He was panting, "You are so fucking beautiful, principessa." His accent was a little stronger. He kissed me hard as I ran my hands down his back, feeling the muscles move and contract under my touch. He plunged his finger inside as I closed my eyes. "No, look at me. I want to see your eyes as I make you come." My body clenched around him as he pushed another finger inside. I kept my eyes trained on him as his thumb toyed with my clit. "That's a good girl."

"Nik." I panted as he increased pressure, and my toes curled as the orgasm tore through me. His eyes flared with lust at the sight before him.

"Fucking perfection." He licked his fingers before kissing me and I could taste myself on his lips. He dropped his pants and kissed me as he lifted me to the end of the bench and thrust inside me. I moaned in ecstasy, and Nik stopped.

"What is it?" I asked, concerned over his lack of movement.

"You are so tight," he moaned as he moved at a slow pace. It was strange, everything seemed brighter, everything seemed stronger, and I could feel emotions that were not my own. I could feel everything he could, every thrust, every kiss, every breath. We were connected in a cosmic way. It was like we would not be able to survive without one another. I needed more as I pushed him in deeper and kissed him harder.

"Larissa," he groaned and increased his speed. His mouth found my breast and he bit my nipple. His touch sent electricity through me. I screamed in pleasure from another orgasm, but Nik was not even close to finishing. He plunged himself deeper as I wrapped my legs around him tighter, needing to feel every single inch of him inside me. "Look at me." He grabbed my face, kissing me as his eyes grew impossibly bright before he grunted, leaning his forehead against mine. He wrapped his arms around me, holding me against his warm body.

"Are you alright?" he panted.

My legs were jelly and my body ached like it had run a marathon, but I did not care. I had never felt more satisfied in my life. I beamed at him before I untangled myself and kissed him.

"That was something else," I said against his lips.

He laughed and dressed himself before lifting me from the bench and helping me to my feet. I wobbled at first before managing to stand. I saw my dress in the corner.

"Did you feel it?" I asked as Nik smiled.

"Yes, that is the mate bond. We are bound to one another. There are no words to describe it, yes?" I nodded.

"It was almost heavenly!"

He laughed. "Heaven had nothing to do with it, but yes. Come, let us go home."

"But we have not been here long, can we say?" I pouted, for added effect.

"We can, but I am not sure how I feel about my mate having no underwear in that dress. It is too tempting for me to consider." His eyes sparkled with lust.

"You want more?" I was giddy with excitement, over the possibility of more.

"It will be all night if I have my way, Larissa. Are you coming?" He extended his hand towards me, I ran over and took it.

"We shall see if you can keep up. I have a high sexual appetite," I teased.

"That is only to match my own." He winked as we walked with haste from the club and towards the car.

CHAPTER 54

WILL YOU EVER HAVE ENOUGH?

Larissa

NIK OPENED THE CAR DOOR FOR ME, AND I SLID IN WITH excitement. He put up the blinder between the driver and us, then turned in his seat towards me.

"Shall we christen the car?" he suggested. I undid my seatbelt and climbed onto his lap.

"Are you sure you can get it up again?" I kissed him and nibbled on his lip playfully.

"One of the perks of being immortal is that there is no recovery period or maximum on how many times I can get it up."

I tingled with excitement as he slid his hand between my aching thighs and ran his finger up and down my sweet spot. I moaned.

"I could get you to scream just by doing this," he rasped into my ear.

"I knew you were arrogant, but this is on another level," I whispered while focusing on his fingers touching me.

He stroked again as I throbbed against him. I let my head fall back, enjoying the sensation. He reached up and bit my neck. I froze and pushed myself away.

"What are you doing?" I rubbed my neck fearing that he had bitten me. He laughed and took my hands away and held them.

"I would not dream of biting you. Besides, it is against our laws to do so even when you are mates. I will never take anything from you without you agreeing to it first. Now, come back over here." He licked his fingers, the ones that he used to stroke me. I grew wetter by the second.

He sniffed the air. "You are a naughty girl," he cooed.

He kissed me harder than before. The car pulled to a stop, and he slid his arm under my legs and got out of the car, holding me before he flew to his penthouse. He put me down and murmured, "Bedroom. Now." He smacked my ass.

I ran up the stairs to his room but noticed he was not following,

"Nik?" I called after him as I peered down the stairs. There was silence. I walked back down slowly and saw Nik in the kitchen, warming a glass of blood. I crossed my arms and waited as he turned and smiled.

"Did you need that right now? I mean I was literally running upstairs to have sex and you disappeared." He gulped it down and sped over as he stood on the stair below me. He was still taller than me.

"I did it for your protection."

"My protection?" I asked as I raised my brow at him.

His eyes grew dark. "Do not forget that I am a monster and the desire..." he ran a finger along my neck, "to taste you is overwhelming. I wish nothing more than to sink my fangs into your precious skin and enjoy the pleasure of your blood." I gulped, but I tingled at the thought. He smiled devilishly, "Careful Larissa, your desires are seeping through."

"Not happening and besides, I am deadly to drink from, remember?" He snorted as I turned back to the stairs. He scooped me into his arms and sped to the bed where my clothes were gone in a second and thrown onto the floor.

I stood before him, naked. As I went to cover myself, he took my arms, and lovingly said, "Never cover your beauty. You are perfect and exactly as you are meant to be." He ran his fingers along my shoulder, down my torso, and came across my birthmark.

"What is this?" His fingers traced the peculiar shape.

"My birthmark."

His face turned white, which was unusual for his usual olive complexion. "A strange place for it," he said as he moved to examine it closer.

"Nik, I am standing in front of you, naked, and you are staring at a birthmark rather than any of my womanly assets."

"Yes, I apologise." He seemed distracted but snapped out of it quickly as he pushed me onto the bed. He removed his clothing before climbing on top of me. He kissed every inch of my body; it was on fire with need. I could only think of him touching me. He bit my nipple, and I screamed in delight as he thrust his fingers inside.

"Nik," I moaned breathlessly.

"Tell me," he demanded.

"Tell you what?"

"Tell me what you want." His voice was strained like he was holding himself back. My climax was building, and his thumb started to circle my clit as my body arched for more. He increased the pressure, hitting that special spot before my body shuttered with delight. Nik sniffed the air and growled, his eyes bright red as he thrust inside at the same moment. He held my leg against his body, there was no gentle love. It was animalistic and primal. I wrapped my arms around his neck and rolled on top. He laughed as I lowered myself onto him. He threw his head back into the pillows.

"Tell me what you want, Nik," I moaned as he reached up, grabbing my breasts.

"Every single inch of you." His voice croaked as he lifted me off, rolling back on top.

"Nik!" I screamed as another orgasm took me to heights that I did not know existed. He groaned, hitting his release, before collapsing beside me. I laughed and rolled onto his chest. I never wanted this to end.

———

I woke the next morning in Nik's arms. He was warm and comfortable. It was almost like my body had melded to his—we fit like two pieces of a puzzle. He groaned and muttered in his sleep, and I tilted my head to listen. He was speaking in another language, so it was impossible to know what he was trying to say. I moved out of his arms slowly to allow him to sleep a little longer, and made my way down the stairs to turn on the coffee machine. I pulled out some of Nik's blood and put it in the frothing machine while I set up the coffee shots. I had become pretty good at making his coffee and was proud of myself as I snuck upstairs and back into the room. Nik sniffed the air and sat up. I could tell he was craving his morning cup of blood. I handed it to him and sat back on the bed beside him.

"Careful Larissa, I could get used to this morning treat."

I chuckled. "As long as you get used to this and not your desire to drink from me."

"I told you last night, I would not do that unless you asked for it," he said, taking a sip from his cup.

"Do you really think that I would ask for that to happen?" He winked and ran his fingers through his hair.

"I have known many people in my long lifetime, Larissa, many who have hated and feared my kind. I discovered that beneath the fear and hatred in every human being, there is a hidden, dark desire." Nik moved closer and pressed his lips to my own before trailing down my neck, his coffee forgotten. "A desire so dark that humans come to crave what it feels like to reach out and touch that darkness."

My heart started to pound, and my thighs clenched together as his warm breath skated across my neck. He dragged his fangs along my skin, not hard enough to pierce it, but enough for me to feel every sensation they sent through my body. He was not lying, it was like a hidden desire I did not even know I had. I was conflicted. I wanted to tell him to take a bite, while another part wanted to push him away. Nik must have sensed my internal conflict and pulled back with his signature smirk.

"You have proved your point." I rubbed my neck and got up to get myself dressed. He sat back and watched me intently as I moved into the bathroom to wash away the night's antics. I stopped to question something.

"Nik," I called out from the bathroom as I turned the water on. I spun around to see him standing there, naked. I laughed at the sight of him leaning with his arm on the wall. "What are you doing?"

He glanced down at himself. "I thought it was rather obvious."

I shook my head. "I was not calling you in here for more sexy time. I wanted to ask you a question and I feel like it is going to sound very stupid once I ask it."

"Nothing that comes from your mouth is stupid. What is it?"

"You cannot get me, like, pregnant, can you?"

He threw his head back and laughed while walking over to where I stood by the running shower. "No, it is not possible. If you felt more comfortable, I would be happy to wear a condom."

I shook my head. "It is fine, I was just worried and thought it was better for me to check." I slid my nightie off my shoulders and stepped into the shower. The water was perfect, as usual, and I relaxed instantly as I heard the shower door open again. Nik's arms surrounded me and pulled me close to him.

"More already?" I turned and raised my eyebrows at him.

"It will never be enough," he moaned, sounding almost desperate. "I will always need more."

He kissed me so hard that my lips swelled, and I knew to expect a bruise later.

I stared into his eyes as I got on my knees. "I have never done this before. Be gentle." His fangs descended as I wrapped my mouth around him.

CHAPTER 55

A TRUCE WITH LUCE

Larissa

NIK AND I HAD GROWN CLOSER SINCE THE NIGHT AT THE BAR, after what we did in the office bathroom. It was not my finest moment, but I found it difficult to say no and I had no regrets. He allowed Luce to join us at the ball—he wanted me to have someone I knew there. He bought her a dress and shoes, and I waited eagerly on the driveway for her to arrive. When the iron gates parted and I saw her, I ran. She jumped from the car into my arms awkwardly, as her leg was still healing.

"Luce!" I screamed as I held her tightly in my arms.

"I have missed you," she said while squeezing a little too hard. She let go and reached back for her bag, which one of Nik's many servants had already collected for her. "Is it always like this?" she asked as she glanced around at the number of people around us. I nodded.

"Unfortunately, but when you are held captive by the Lord of the region, it is normal." I had not told her the truth—that we were mates and had a contract to marry. I knew she would overreact, especially with her hatred towards vampires. I wanted to be sure that she would accept Nik as a person before attempting to tell her. Nik had agreed to limit our physical contact to avoid Luce getting suspicious that something more was happening. I would tell her in time, but I worried that she would stop talking to me if she knew the truth.

"Yeah, how much longer is your probation?"

"Until they can decide that I am no longer a threat to them, so forever sounds good." I laughed it off as we headed inside.

"At least you can be spoilt in the meantime," she spoke in hushed tones as a flurry of people moved about.

"Exactly, now we must hurry. Nik has organised a hair and makeup person to make us even more beautiful for tonight." Shit, I slipped up.

"Nik?" The hairs on the back of my neck stood up. I was going to avoid using his name to make our relationship seem, more distant, but saying his first name had already made that come, a little undone.

"Yes, he requested that I call him by his first name in his home," I lied, hoping she did not suspect anything.

"Ah, do I have to?" she groaned as she crossed her arms with her signature scowl.

I shook my head. "Only if you are comfortable."

I could feel Nik getting closer as we climbed the stairs to my room. He waited at the top with a big smile on his face.

"Miss Solis." He bowed his head at Luce. "It is a pleasure to meet you. Larissa has told me so much about you." Luce gave me a sideward glance that showed how unimpressed she was that I had been speaking about her.

"She has not spoken of you, Lord Dankworth," Luce replied bluntly. He raised a brow at her, Nik understood that I had spoken to Travis and Alina about him, but not to Luce.

"Oh." He was being cheeky, and I filled my body with anger to alert him to stop. His eyes fell on me, and he instantly stopped with his playfulness. "Everything you need is within the room, if you require anything else, you need only ask."

"Yes, I would like some champagne glasses, as I bought a bottle from our small town to enjoy while we get ready." Luce smiled at the small amount of power she had, ordering a vampire to do her bidding.

"It shall be done." He walked backwards a few steps before spinning around and walking away. I enjoyed the view of his backside for a moment before I showed Luce to my room.

"Holy shit, this is massive. It is bigger than our first apartment." I chuckled as I remembered that was my first thought, too.

"Nik was not sure about which dress you would like. Your choices are hung up in the robe."

"What happens to the others that I do not like?" she asked. I shrugged my shoulders; I knew the answer, but I feared what she would say.

"I think he said he would return them. Come on, do not worry about that. Time to get ready, pick a dress and decide how you want your hair." I motioned for her to move on.

She picked a burgundy dress that suited her skin tone and hair colour. Nik had organised for two women to do our hair and makeup.

We giggled, drank champagne and spoke about our life growing up with Mum. It was peaceful and relaxing until Nik called upon me through our bond. Since we had slept together, he now projected when he needed to see me, as I could with him. He said he had never heard of it being this strong before. We were linked through an invisible string that

I did not understand. I pushed back against him to let him know that I was not able to leave Luce right now. I could block it out, but only for a while before my body would become ill. Nik persisted and pressed for it again, so I stood and excused myself as Luce was getting her nails and hair done.

I walked out of my room and saw Nik leaning on the balustrades just outside the room that looked down at the foyer. I could see the tension in his shoulders.

"What is it?" I asked as I put my hand on his back to comfort him. He spun and took my hand in his.

"Hector." One name that I was tired of hearing.

"What is it?" I worried about what he could have possibly done now.

"I have heard from my spies within the court that if we do not sell our relationship tonight, the appeal will be granted. I have tried my hardest to stop this, but I am rather disliked by a few, and it is coming back to harm us." Nik was disliked by a few. I never would have guessed with his mood swings.

"We already agreed to do that, and we are together, so what is the issue?" He glanced towards my bedroom door. I had asked to not show any affection for the sake of Luce.

This made it a little more difficult. "I will speak to her and explain that my life is on the line and tonight is just an act." I leant forward, and whispered, "When we both know it is not anymore." I said it to reassure him and could tell it worked by the way his eyes glowed brighter and he licked his lips.

"If it were possible right now, I would bend you over the balustrade and fuck you so hard that your moans would fill the room, and everyone would know you are *mine*."

"Do not make promises you cannot keep," I giggled and strolled back to my room. I closed the door as Luce eyed me suspiciously.

"So tonight, when you see me touching and kissing Nik, just ignore it. I have to do it otherwise there will be an appeal of my sentence and I could possibly die."

Her face fell as tears welled in her eyes. "What?"

"Hector, who was the one behind the attack, is very much against me living. Nik is trying to stop the appeal, but it will be granted unless Nik and I look like an actual couple tonight," I elaborated.

"What do you need me to do?"

"Just, if anyone asks, we are a couple, that's all." She seemed fine with it as I helped her into her gown. I checked my phone and pretended that Nik had messaged me when he had already let me know through the bond that he was waiting downstairs.

"He is ready for us whenever we are done."

Luce twirled her dress and looked in the mirror at her red hair that was placed neatly in a fancy updo.

"We need a selfie." She flicked out her phone and we took a variety of nice and silly photos together. We laughed and giggled as Nik pulled a little harder for me to come downstairs.

"Come on, we need to get going." I grabbed the silver clutch and put on the two-carat diamond ring from Nik to symbolise our mate bond. He picked the princess-cut platinum ring, which I was in love with. I was not a person who was over the top, but I wanted something bigger to show everyone that our relationship was serious.

I walked down the stairs before Luce and saw Nik drinking a glass of whiskey as he leant on the wall. He wore a black tuxedo with a jade pocket square to match my gown. His hair was perfectly tended to, and the scruff on his face was perfect. He oozed sex appeal. I wanted nothing more than to push him into a room and fuck him. He smirked as he sensed my rush of desire and put out his hand.

I slid mine into his as he bowed and kissed my hand. As his gaze locked with mine, he murmured, "Pulchra mate mea."

I turned my head at him curiously. "What does that mean?"

"My beautiful mate in Latin." I smiled and I could feel my cheeks blushing.

"You can quit the act. Only do it when you need to," Luce snapped as she pushed past me. It would be a long night with her.

"It does not hurt to start early," Nik bit at her. I could feel his frustration towards her. He was not impressed with her attitude, but I could not do anything about it. Luce stormed outside to the car, and Nik turned back to me. "I shall meet you outside shortly." He finished his whiskey.

"Nik, I apologise for her behaviour in advance." He did not want to hear it. He grabbed my face in his hands.

"It is not her; it is just this night. I am going to top myself up on blood to ensure that I can contain myself around you and around anyone who would cause us harm." His eyes ran down my neck as he licked his lips, and a thrill rushed through my body. Against all reason, I wanted him to drink from me. This bond caused so much internal conflict.

"No, we do not know what would happen if you did. Could we

not just tip some of my blood into Hector's glass and be done with it?"

He snorted into a laugh. "We would be prime suspects, but I did think of it." He kissed my hand again and left to get some blood.

I walked outside to join Luce in the car. She was on the phone and I heard her say, "Yeah, we are leaving soon, I will. Love you, too. Bye."

"Who do you love? What did I miss?" I beamed with excitement at discovering she had a new love interest in her life. It may make it easier for her to accept my relationship with Nik.

All she said was, "You don't know him, it is still early," and did not elaborate any further.

I decided not to press the issue as Nik slid into the car beside me. He slid his hand into mine out of sight of Luce. His touch was a constant source of comfort, and I needed it to get through tonight.

CHAPTER 56
THE BALL WAS A BLAST

Larissa

THE CAR RIDE WAS QUIET WITH MINIMAL TALKING. I HELD NIK'S hand under my gown. He stroked my knuckles as a way of offering comfort as we drove into the city. Night had arrived by the time we reached the venue, which was massive. My eyes were drawn to the magnificent dome roof. The chandelier was illuminated with fire from the hundreds of candles that surrounded it.

Nik bent down to whisper, "It does not compare to how beautiful you are."

I nudged him playfully as I took his arm so he could escort me inside. He offered his arm to Luce, but she refused to take it or to even take my hand. Flashes of light alerted me to the number of paparazzi. I smiled as I remembered that the more affectionate we were, the better it would be for us. I snuggled into him as Nik looked down lovingly and kissed the top of my head.

He led us to the bar, where Luce ordered glasses of champagne for both of us. Nik eyed me pointedly, his warning to keep my head clear for the night, as we had no idea what was in store for us.

Nik showed me off to various business associates and important Lords of other regions. He suddenly tensed, and I spun to see what made his sudden attitude change. Roman stalked towards us.

"Nik, how are you?" He bowed his head as a sign of respect.

"Well, Roman, and yourself?" Instead of answering, Roman's eyes flicked in my direction, and he sniffed the air and scoffed.

Nik growled, "Do not start, not tonight" His warning did nothing to deter Roman.

"That didn't take you long," he sneered at me.

"Pardon?"

"You moved between brothers rather quickly. You break up with me and fuck my brother no less than a week later."

Nik flared with anger, and I put my hand on his arm to settle him down.

"Roman, you broke up with me. You have no right to be mad about the choices that I made once you ended our relationship." I glowered at him while keeping a smile on my face for those around us.

He crossed his arms and scowled at me. "I should not be surprised; it is just history repeating itself. You always return to him."

"What?" Roman went to walk away but I grabbed his arm.

"Wait, you are sleeping with him?" Luce's voice cut through it all, and I turned to see the disappointment and anger on her face.

Nik fired up. "Yes, can you not accept that your sister is happy?

That she put herself first?" His hand held tightly onto his glass as it cracked. He was trying to remain in control.

"Nik," I said in warning tone, before turning to my sister. "Luce, it is not what you think."

"Pardon, Larissa?" Hurt travelled through the bond.

"Nik, just stop please." I was arguing with three different people at once, as I searched for Roman, who had already left.

"No, I will not. We have made love on several occasions; we sleep together at night and cannot bear the thought of being apart and you are telling *her* that it is not what she thinks? Do I mean nothing to you?" His eyes flared.

"Nik, I am not saying that," I pleaded with him to stop. I needed everyone to just stop bickering.

"What are you saying then, Larissa?" Luce snapped, her face matching the colour of her red hair. "Forget about it, I expected better of you, and so did Mum." She stormed off, but when I moved to go after her, Nik held onto my arm tightly.

"It is not the right time, Larissa." His voice took on an authority I did not like. I pulled my arm out of his grasp.

"She is my sister," I hissed at him.

"She is not your sister, remember? Leave her to her childish ways," he appealed to me as he searched the room of all the eyes on us.

"She is the only family I have left, and I will not lose her, Nik." I kissed his cheek.

I ran after Luce. It would not look good for the courts, but at that moment, I did not care. I wanted to know that Luce was okay. She had jumped back into Nik's car; I grabbed the door in time and pulled it open.

"Luce, please let me explain. Come back inside," I pleaded with her. I cared for Nik, but I could not tell her the truth. It was breaking my heart that I had to choose between them.

"If you want to explain, you can do so in the car. Which is it, Rissa? Me? Or him?" I glanced back and saw Nik watching us. His eyes were begging me not to go as he pulled on the invisible thread between us. I mouthed, "I'm sorry," as I slid into the car with Luce. His rage exploded and it made my body shiver. I watched him as we drove away. He pulled out his phone and barked out orders to whoever was on the other end as Roman appeared beside him.

"Wow," Luce said as she appeared to be watching out the window for something.

"What Luce?" I was full of anger, half of it from me and the other half was what I was feeling from Nik.

"I am shocked you came with me; I thought his compulsion would have forbidden you. At least I know I can save you." The words hurt as they hit.

"Save me? I do not need saving, Luce. I am not in trouble, and I am not sick." I yelled at her; her assumption was so wrong.

"You are *fucking* a vampire!" she screeched, motioning back towards Nik.

"What are you more upset about? The fact that I have someone who adores me or the fact that I made my own decision?" I shook my head at her.

"Adores you? Don't make me laugh! He has bought your love.

They do that." I had never seen her like this. Her words had more venom than usual.

"He has not bought anything, he has not compelled me. You do not know him to even understand." I wondered if I should tell her the truth.

"How do you know he hasn't compelled you?" She raised her brow at me curiously.

"I cannot be compelled. I do not know why and neither does Nik, but I just cannot. I can resist compulsion."

"Is that why you have to stay with them?" She moved closer to inspect me further.

"No, it is because I killed a vampire with my blood. He drank from me and died. They must investigate if I am dangerous to them or not. Are you happy?" She went quiet, I would regret telling her that.

"So, Nik hasn't drunk from you?" Her question set off alarm bells in my head.

"Not that it is any of your business, but no. He is not allowed to, and I do not want him to." Her face twisted as she processed the facts.

"It doesn't change the fact that you fucked him," she spat.

I groaned and let my head fall into my hands. "How is it any different to me having sex with Roman? He is a bloody werewolf."

"They don't exist," she snorted

"I assure you, they do." I stood my ground.

"Well, they wouldn't be as harmful as vampires," she argued. I wanted to strangle her.

"You are so jaded, you cannot see reason. What are you more upset about? The fact that I am sleeping with one or the fact that I made a decision that you or Mum did not approve? I am happy. Why can you not accept that? Mum controlled everything I did. I finished my degree, and she manipulated me to stay."

"That was to keep you safe!" she yelled, but there was something more behind her words. She knew! My mouth fell open.

"Holy shit! You knew?" She did not answer or look at me. "How long?" I gritted my teeth at her, my magic was aching to be released.

"Since we were little," she finally admitted.

It was like I had been punched in the stomach. She lied to me her entire life.

"You did not think to tell me?" I shouted at her. I had to stop myself from flying into a rage.

"Mum told me not to. Everything she did was for you. *We must keep Larissa safe.* It was all I ever heard." She mocked our mother.

Tears fell down my cheeks. Everything was a lie.

"You should have told me after she died. The night you were attacked, I found out the truth and lied to protect you."

"Pfft! Protect me? That's a laugh."

"What happened to you?" I shook my head in disbelief.

"You did. I had a great life, then your mother stupidly killed herself, and we were stuck picking up the pieces. Mum stopped you from accessing your magic. It was supposed to come to me when she died, but no, it returned to you. I deserve that power, not you!" Her words were filled with hatred. I could not handle it.

"Stop the car," I called to the driver, but he did not listen. I slid forward and put the blinder down, but it was not Nik's driver.

"If you think I am letting you out of here, you are mistaken. I want Nik dead," Luce sneered. My heart pounded. I knew he was coming after me, I could feel it. I reached for my bag to call him, but she yanked it away.

"Give me my bag, Luce."

"No, Nik is dying tonight. It is the start of the revolution." I lunged for it, but she pushed me away and I tumbled to the floor. Nik was close, he roared at my pain. I tried to contact him, but it was no use. The car pulled to a stop as Luce got out and locked the door. She took my bag with her. The car had a phone, so I raced to grab it and dialled Nik's number. It barely rang before he answered.

"Larissa?" His voice was frantic.

"Do not come. Please. She wants to kill you; it is a revolution, she said. Do not come, I beg of you." I searched outside the windows for the sight of him.

"It is not that simple. I will not lose you."

"Nik!" I screamed; the line went dead. Luce leant against the car. I could sense her fury.

"Out, now." I followed her instructions. She did not know how much power I had, and I would use that to my advantage. There was another car before us, and as my eyes adjusted, I saw who was waiting. Luce walked over and embraced Peter.

I rolled my eyes at their affection towards one another. "You judge me and yet you are with that pig of a man?"

Peter laughed. "At least she is with a real man."

"Sorry, I do not see one here," I snapped at him. He sauntered over before lunging at me and holding a knife to my throat.

"Careful now," he taunted.

"I am not scared of you, I never have been. You disgust me," I spat at him, and he slapped my face hard. I heard a roar in the distance.

"Good, he will be here soon."

I glanced behind me. That was not Nik's roar, it was Roman's. I smiled at his ignorance.

"What is that for?" He eyed me suspiciously.

"You're dead and I will enjoy, seeing you being ripped apart." My arrogance reminded me of Nik's.

He held up his hand to strike me again, as I prepared myself for what was about to come.

"DO NOT LAY A FINGER ON HER!" Nik bellowed from behind.

Roman and Nik appeared from the darkness. Their eyes glowed with power, and Roman stood wearing no shirt. Nik had removed his suit jacket, and his eyes were trained on Peter, but he pushed through our bond to make sure I was alright. I proceeded to move slowly towards them.

"Ah, the Lord of the region," Peter crowed. "It took me a while to find you. Always so protected, always so hidden. I suppose when you are one of the oldest in the world it is expected."

"What do you want?" Nik glared, his fists clenched.

"I want the end of your species. I want the world back under human control," he demanded as he spat at the ground.

Nik sniggered as he glanced at Roman. "That will never happen."

"It will once those who started it are dead." Peter seemed to believe he could win this.

"We started it to stop your extinction, you fool. We do not intend to rule forever and never have," Nik growled.

"Lies!" Peter shouted.

I neared Nik, only a few more steps.

"I am not lying. It is people like you who are ruining it for those who have changed. The world cannot be sustained by the old ways," Nik explained calmly, even though he was consumed by rage on the inside.

Peter held up a shotgun at Nik. I cast a small protection spell over both Nik and Roman. My magic was waning. It was strange. It felt harder to touch. I moved to stand in front of Nik.

"Larissa move!" Luce shouted at me; her voice filled with worry.

"She deserves to die, as do all of them," Peter declared.

Roman growled as his started to shift. His body erupted in fur and his fingers turned to claws. Peter flicked off the safety and aimed. I kept shielding Nik as I spun my hands to access my magic.

"Larissa, what's wrong?" he asked, sensing my worry over my magic.

"I am struggling to access the full strength of my magic," I said over my shoulder at him.

"Move, I shall heal you." I refused, and that was when I heard the blast. Luce screamed as I looked over Nik and Roman, who were untouched. Roman roared and ran towards Peter as Nik caught me. I did not even know I was falling. The pain hit me suddenly as I noticed blood seeping through my gown.

"If you were ever in doubt about my feelings for you, I suppose this would have cleared it up." I reached up for his face as he bit into his wrist. I barely made it to him as my eyes grew heavy and the world seemed lighter.

"No, no, not again!" he shouted as he forced his wrist into my mouth. I could barely drink, I was so tired, and instead spat it out.

I saw a figure with dark wavy hair walking towards me, she was angelic, but pained. Sounds disappeared, as did the angelic figure.

CHAPTER 57
DON'T LET ME GO

I HEARD THE SOUND OF CAR HORNS AND BUSY STREETS BEFORE I shot up. The world was bright again, the penthouse bedroom came into view.

"Careful now." Roman's voice echoed in my head. I scanned the room before seeing him sitting on the edge of the bed. His face was etched with worry, but his eyes softened as he watched my chest rise and fall with every breath.

"What happened?" I croaked. My throat ached as did my entire body.

"Peter shot you. Nik was able to save you." He sighed as he ran his fingers through his thick mane of hair.

"Luce?" I dreaded the answer. I hated her, but she did not deserve to die. She was my sister.

"Peter and Luce escaped. We would have never harmed your sister. Peter on the—"

"He has been on the most wanted list for a few years." Nik came into view and sat on the other side of the bed. Love radiated from both of them. I reached for their hands and squeezed them tight.

"Thank you, both for you. I do not know why I could not access my magic." I had never been so happy to see them. I held back tears.

"I tested the champagne that Luce brought. It was not wine, it was a potion. She had it all planned. I am sorry, Larissa. I know this will hurt you." Nik lifted my hand to his mouth.

"She knew about all of it. Elizabeth told her the truth from the start. I do not understand." I shook my head in disbelief. Everything had been a lie.

Roman tapped my hand. "There is no point in trying. You will never understand why."

"What happens now?" I asked as I smiled at Roman before meeting Nik's intense gaze.

"I will double the guards and search for Peter and..." He paused, and I knew the words before he said them. She broke the law. "...Luce. In happy news, your sacrifice put enough doubt in the appeal. You can return to work if you so desire." I saw on Roman's face that he did not support this.

"Do you not agree?" I asked Roman. He shook his head.

"No, I think you should stay here under guard until the perpetrators are captured," he muttered with a scowl on his face.

"We discussed this. She is better off continuing her life rather than being locked up. She is not designed to be stuck." Nik seemed rather persistent with his brother, but Roman refused to budge.

"Better safe than dead," he argued, and the words stung as Nik sighed and rubbed his temple.

"Larissa, you be the judge. What would you prefer?" I glanced between the two of them. They both had valid points, but ultimately, I could no longer be caged. I think that was why Nik made the suggestion.

"I would prefer to return to work." I lifted my shoulders and held them for a moment before breathing out.

Roman shook his head, slapped his knee and sighed as he stood. "I should have known better. She always picks your side." He walked out of the room.

"Why does he always say stuff like that?" I watched him walk away as I pondered what he said.

"Like what?" Nik asked as he moved closer.

"I *always pick your side*. I mean, I picked him over you at the start and I do not think I pick sides." He bent down and kissed my head.

"He is an alpha who does not like to lose. It is not personal. Now rest." He turned to leave but I had to know the answer.

"Did I… almost die?" I barely got the words out.

Nik scratched the back of his head. "Yes." He shook his head at the memory. "The bullets scattered through your chest and abdomen. They hit an artery and your heart."

"Would you have turned me?" I wondered if he would, knowing I had no desire to lose my magic and become a blood-sucking monster.

"Yes. To save you, yes. Without question, yes." He knew I did not want that, but he would prefer me to be angry than dead.

"What happens to Luce?" I feared asking this question. Despite everything, I could not bring myself to hate her.

"She is an enemy of the state, she will be hunted down. What happens after that, I cannot be certain. I know you want to protect her, but I fear it is too late. Peter has committed atrocious crimes in the past; he burnt down a school filled with vampires and humans. He opened fire in a shopping centre. He does not care for anyone or anything but himself. I am sorry."

"Nik, I need you to understand that I will try to save her." Love radiated through our bond and he touched my face.

"I know, as will I. Now please, rest." I grabbed his hand; I was not ready for him to be gone. I needed comfort, and as I pulled on the string between us, he groaned. "Let me make a call and I shall return in a moment, I promise."

I laid back down and waited. I despised Luce for what she did, but I loved her unconditionally. I would forgive her, but what would it cost me?

———

I woke with Nik sitting up in the bed, typing away on his laptop. I rolled my eyes.

"I thought, for once, you would just lay with me." My voice was husky from waking, so I cleared my throat.

"I have not left your side, as you requested." He did not look away from his laptop.

"Oh wow, a whole what, hour?" I chimed in as I moved to sit up.

He laughed. "Try two days."

"What?"

"Your body has needed time to heal. It has been three days since you were shot." He finally looked at me and kissed the top of my head.

The realisation that I almost died set in again.

"I think I saw Katrina. She was there before I passed out," I said, remembering the angelic figure with wavy hair that moved towards me. I did not hear the words she tried to speak.

He put the laptop away. "Possibly."

"She was in pain, surrounded by light, but in pain."

He sighed and raked his fingers through his hair. I noticed the muscles in his bicep flex. He slid the laptop onto the table beside him.

"Katrina was an angel, but I doubt she would have made her way into heaven. She cursed the wrong people, but she did it for the right reasons. The Gods do not view the reasons, only the actions."

Nik lay down as I snuggled into him and breathed in his scent. I missed him despite being next to him.

"I missed you, too. Three days was too long to be without you." His arms tightened around me, cocooning me in love.

CHAPTER 58
RETURN TO WORK

Larissa

I returned to work the following week. Roman still voiced his concern, but I disregarded it. I wanted my life to feel normal again.

I searched through my wardrobe for clothes that would make me feel more confident at work. I stood in my bra and underwear as I scanned the various items of clothing that Nik had bought for me. My body tingled as he appeared behind me.

"Do you always have to sneak?" I asked without turning back to look at him.

"Is it sneaking when you feel my presence?"

I clicked my tongue and spun to see him leaning against the door, drinking his morning bloodcino.

"Yes, I still consider that sneaking," I said playfully and poked my tongue out at him.

His eyes draped over my near-naked body as his desire hit me hard.

"No, keep it in your pants. I do not want to be late for work." I wiggled my finger at him.

He winked. "You are right. I can spend all day with you in a conference room." He pushed himself off the wall.

"Boundaries, Mr. Dankworth. Do I need to remind you of the ones we put into place while we are at work?" I said while he wrapped his arms around my waist, his arms warming my naked skin.

He groaned. I knew he would be unable to contain himself around me. I was the same around him. We promised to not partake in any sexual acts while at work and avoid using our relationship for any type of gain or advantage. It would be difficult, but I feared the way people would view me now. I was sleeping with and due to marry him. The reminder of that was constantly in the back of my head.

He looked around the wardrobe. "I think it is about time that we move all of this into our room, do you not think?" He pulled me against his chest and kissed my forehead.

"Why?" I asked. I was enjoying my own room filled with clothes.

"So I may enjoy this view every morning for the rest of my life." He kissed me deeply.

I blushed. "Well, get your multitude of servants to move it all across, then. Although, I do not think there will be enough room."

He smiled and reached to grab my hand. "Come with me."

I looked down at my lack of clothing and he removed his jacket and put it on me before we left the room. He led me down the hall to another room and pushed the double doors open. He walked in and opened the curtains. It was the largest bedroom in the house.

"What is this?" I asked, dumbfounded at the size of this room. The bed, although a king, looked tiny against the sheer size of the space.

"This is the master suite. Come and look at the robe." He took my hand and whisked me into the robe. It was bigger than my bedroom.

"Do you not think it is a little too big?" As I gazed upon the rows and rows of space for clothes, shoes, and jewels.

"For you, never." He looked at his watch. "We are going to be late. I will organise the renovations for this room to be done by the weekend. Get dressed."

I rolled my eyes. "We are late because of you. No more distracting me!"

He put his hands up in defeat as I rushed out of the room and down the hall. I pulled on a blue skirt and white blouse, fluffed my hair, and put on minimal makeup. All the vampire blood in my system had made my skin glow.

I could not wait to see Travis, Alina, and Stacey.

Nik and I checked our emails in the car as it pulled up. I paused as I saw Travis, Alina, and Stacey, all standing in their usual spot for the morning gossip. Nik put his hand on my own.

"They will be fine, do not worry." He could sense my anxiety at all the questions they would have. I realised he was still buckled in.

"You're not coming in?"

"No, I need to check in on another one of my holdings. I will be back here to spend lunch with you. I promise." He lifted my hand and kissed it softly.

I sighed and summoned the courage to get out of the car. I straightened my skirt and walked into the foyer. Travis saw me first before Alina looked in my direction and Stacey turned to see. I walked over slowly and waved awkwardly.

"Hey," I dragged the word out with a grimace.

They were quiet before Stacey threw her arms around me. "We need all the details," she squeaked with joy. Travis answered the phone and rolled his eyes.

"Drinks later." He did not ask; it was merely a statement that it would happen.

I nodded as I walked to the elevator with Stacey. I flicked out my phone and texted Nik to let him know that I would be going out for drinks with my work friends. I knew he would not be happy, but I needed this. I wanted human contact again. Despite our intimacy, he still had an occasional coldness to him, and I lived off the warmth of others.

"How has work been without me?" I smirked at Stacey as she shook her head.

"Horrible. After Andrew got fired and you were gone, it fell to pieces. No one was here to run the place, and everybody tried to take over the role. Once Nik sent out the email that you would be taking over and explained what everyone needed to do in the meantime, that settled it. But that raised more questions about how the receptionist became director of marketing and now co-owner because of her impending nuptials."

The elevator doors sprung open, and I smelt the tension in the air. There was no respect for me, the vibes they were throwing in my direction were overwhelming. Stacey smiled and walked to her office as I made my way to mine.

It was weird sitting in Andrew's office. I could almost hear his remarks even without him there. I scanned through the paperwork; it was going to take me all week to get through this. I pulled out the most important documents to work on first. The business had been working to its usual capacity, but it was barely turning a profit.

Stacey brought a coffee in for me. "How is it looking?"

"Do you want my honest opinion?" I glanced up at her as I took the coffee from her hands. It was refreshing and did the job, but it did not compare to coffee at Nik's house—now my house. I needed to remember to say that to myself. It was all going to be mine once we married but it did not feel like home.

Stacey nodded, so I continued. "We are still making money, but barely enough. All of these are offers that we have possibly missed out on. There are so many bills to pay and a lot of grovelling phone calls to make. I am also dreading speaking to Nik about possibly extending us a line of credit."

"I suppose sleeping with him would help with that?" she said with her usual amount of perkiness.

I rolled my eyes. "Not when I purposely put in boundaries for us to keep our personal life separate from our business life."

Stacey laughed. "That was silly, wasn't it?"

"I did not foresee this issue before I came to work this morning. I thought it would be fine, but I was wrong. I have lunch with him today, so I will talk about it then." I chastised myself for putting in boundaries but hopefully, I could appeal to his business sense.

Stacey smiled and walked out of the office. I focused solely on the budgets and future marketing campaigns. We had four solid offers that would bring in good money. I started typing in the details when I heard the door open. I felt Nik before I saw him. He looked puzzled as he walked in and sat down.

"Did you not feel my presence before I entered?" I shook my head.

"I spelled the room," I explained. "All I can feel is hatred from the staff because they think I got Andrew fired."

He growled in frustration. "Would you like me to say something?"

I stood suddenly. "No. Please do not. It will only fuel the hatred. I will just have to work harder." I wanted to earn their respect not have it brought on with fear and intimidation.

He grew angrier as he went for the door. I locked it with my magic, and he turned with a slight smirk.

"My magic may not affect you, but I *can* manipulate other objects." I smirked as I looked up from my computer.

"Smart girl," he said seductively, as he turned and leant against the wall. His desire hit me hard and my knees buckled.

"No!" I said a little loudly, and he put his hands up in surrender.

"Fine, but I was promised lunch." He exhaled in defeat. "Where we shall discuss your evening plans?"

"Before lunch, can we talk business?" I requested hoping he would say yes.

"We can talk about it at lunch. I am starved." His eyes glowed brighter. He was starved, but not for food. He was starved for me.

I grabbed my bag and a few documents to refer to and followed Nik through the door. As I exited, the hatred hit me hard. He could feel it through our bond and growled, then clenched his fists. All eyes were on us. I grabbed his hand and silently begged him to not do anything. He looked at me apologetically, and I closed my eyes in preparation.

"For anyone who thinks that Larissa was given the position because she is my mate, I kindly ask you to leave the premises. You are not welcome here. She earned the position by securing an account with a successful business that pledged a partnership for all future business. Andrew was not capable of forming these relationships. He was only capable of sexual harassment against any and all employees. Does anyone wish to leave?"

Fear spread through the office as I stood in front of Nik.

"I understand your distrust. I truly do, but I earned this role before Nik and I discovered we were mates. There was no favouritism and there never will be. At work, we are colleagues and will remain so. We have a fantastic team at Refresh Marketing. I do not wish to make any changes; I simply want what is best for the company. If you feel the need to leave, please place your resignation letter on my desk. It will be left open while I am in the meeting. That is something Andrew never did; I promise to be honest and open about all decisions made within the company." I did my best to sound professional and like I knew exactly what I was doing while filled with nausea.

I took Nik's hand and led him towards the elevator as I spelled it to open for us. We entered and the doors closed. I was shaking. He pushed me against the wall and his arms snaked around my waist.

"I know we said no naughty business at work," he said as he leant over and pushed the emergency stop button, "but I fear after that speech, I need to break that rule."

He kissed me hard, and I wound my arms around his neck as he lifted me and pressed me against the elevator. I craved his touch. I wanted it more than anything, but I tapped his shoulders.

"That's enough, Mr. Dankworth." He groaned and put me back down. He fixed his hair and grey suit before he pressed the button again.

CHAPTER 59
FIGHTING AT WORK

Larissa

WE ARRIVED AT THE FANCY RESTAURANT, AND THE BLACK AND gold interior showed a reflection of the clientele inside. All wore expensive clothes and jewels. I peered down at my clothes, instantly feeling underdressed. The tiny stars on the floor glowed with the dark mood lighting. The restaurant had class but did not feel warm. We were seated instantly. Nik being the Lord of the region certainly had its perks. He ordered our drinks and food without asking. He knew I hated this and did it anyway. It was something that I would have to work on.

He put his elbows on the table and clasped his hands together. "Now, what business did you need to discuss?" His eyes focused on what little cleavage was peeking through my blouse.

I breathed deeply and let it out again. "Honestly, how could you let the business get this bad? You should have let me work while being held against my will. I do not even know where to start. We need money just to cover the basic expenses for this month, or I will have to lay some people off. I thought you were a smart businessman, but you have left me with a mess."

He smirked and reached across the table to squeeze my hand. "You can handle this."

This irritated me further. "How? We have no money. Could you give us any more?" I was trying to contain my anger at his blasé attitude.

"How much would you need?" he asked, sensing my annoyance through the bond.

"Maybe ten. Here look at the numbers." Nik took the paperwork from me and flicked through it making multiple worrying facial expressions.

"I will give you five." He handed the paperwork back to me.

"That is not enough." I scrunched it in my hand before letting it fall to the table.

The food was delivered, and he started to eat, but I pushed mine away. My stomach grumbled from the amazing smell. I hated how he ordered for me, but always knew what I would like.

"Eat Larissa," he ordered. I crossed my arms and leant back in the chair.

"I do not care that we are mates, but right now you are wrong on so many levels."

I stood from the chair and headed towards the exit. Nik did not follow me as I took the car back to work. I was relieved to see that I did not have any resignations on my desk. I locked myself away and poured over the paperwork again. Nik tried to call me several times before I turned off my mobile. I refused to speak to him until he saw some reason, or rather, my reason. My office phone rang.

"Larissa Solis."

"Larissa Dankworth is the correct term." His voice was as clear as ever.

"We are not married and even *if* we wed, I would prefer to keep my name."

He growled. "We are mates and are recognised as such through the courts. You are Larissa Dankworth and that is final."

I slammed the phone down, but it did not take long for it to ring once more.

"Larissa Solis," I said defiantly with a smug smile on my face.

"Larissa, I do not have time for childish games." Irritation was obvious in his tone.

"That's good, neither do I. I have a mess to fix."

I hung up on him again and disconnected the phone. I knew this would drag him down to the office. I planned on it. I wanted people to see me standing up to him. It was not long before my office door flung open, his eyes glowed red as rage radiated from his body.

"You dare ignore my calls and treat me in such a manner!" he roared as he slammed the door behind him.

I leant back in my chair and crossed my arms. "Anything else?"

He was stumped. He did not know what to say. "You dare to speak to me like that?"

I stood up and put my hands on the desk. I needed to stay in control of my magic.

"Could you please show me the document that states you own me? That states you control all my decisions? That states you control what I eat and drink? I told you that I am my own person, and I will not have you treat me as a lesser being."

He scoffed and walked over to my desk. I watched him drag his finger along the edge as he pushed lust through our bond.

"You forget that you *are* a lesser being. You are also my mate."

I glanced at the ring of my finger and pulled it off. "Well, I refuse to be your mate despite what fate dictates. I am done. I asked you to help me save this company and instead, you took it as an opportunity to manipulate what food I would eat and what I would drink before dismissing the business needs in general. You had no right to do any of that." I put the ring on the desk and sat back down. He picked it up and glared at me.

"You say that I give you no choice and you manipulate my emotions for your gain. How are you better than me?"

I smiled at him, but nothing about it was friendly. "I can admit my faults, can you?"

He stroked his chin and threw the ring at me. I caught it. "Put it on and I shall give you fifteen thousand." I dangled it over my finger. This was pure manipulation, but I needed him to see that I would not be pushed around.

"Is that it?" I baited him for more.

He growled. "Yes."

I moved to put the ring back down, and I could feel his monster banging against the invisible cage.

"Fine, I will stop trying to control your decisions. You can enjoy your night with your friends. I will not dictate a time for you to be home. I will not dictate the amount of alcohol you should consume. Is that better?" I slid the ring on and relaxed. I had won for now.

"I suppose. Now please get out of my office. I will discuss more with you later." I waved at him dismissively.

"Larissa." His voice was filled with warning.

"I am still mad, Nik. This discussion is not finished." I glanced up at him as I pretended to busy myself.

He winked at me. "Oh, I am more than aware." He turned and left the office. I knew the fight when I got home would be worse, but I was right. He needed to stop controlling me.

CHAPTER 60
THE BOND EFFECT

Nik

I agreed against my better judgement to allow Larissa to be with friends tonight. It wasn't safe for her to be out in the open. I did not know where Peter and Lucianna were located. It worried me to every extent what their next move would be.

I played with my glass of chilled blood and whiskey as I sat in my study. I had every intention of working, but I found myself distracted by Larissa's changing moods. She had thankfully agreed to drink some of my blood before she left for drinks. It was easier to sense her when it was fresh blood. I felt her every emotion as they flicked between happiness, anger, frustration, and being horny. Larissa was not aware that I had placed undercover guards to watch her all night. She would not approve, but I would deal with the consequences of her tantrum later. I pulled out my phone and texted her.

ME

> Are you enjoying your evening?

LARISSA

> It would be better if you joined me. I have a thing about being fucked in club bathrooms.

ME

> That can be arranged. I can arrive in ten minutes.

LARISSA

> No, I am still mad at you. I will see you tonight. Late, once you are already asleep.

This was Larissa's way of saying she would not be responding anymore. I sighed and ran my fingers through my hair. My worry was presenting in the need for more blood, so I filled my glass again and finished it in one gulp.

I walked down to the gym to work off the excess energy that coursed through the bond. She was drinking more than she should and the use of energy drinks did nothing for my own nerves. I removed my shirt, wrapped my hands, and approached the bag. I let out all my frustration.

She had not remembered her past lives, even after we had been intimate. We had declared each other mates and this still had not shifted her memories to the surface.

Every punch brought about more frustration than relief. I growled as I felt the overwhelming desire to rip into a throat and drain the body dry. I hated the monster within me, the creature that plagued my life, the darkness that never left.

One night changed everything and despite my anguish, I would make the same decision in a hundred lifetimes. I knew the anger would not stop until I let the inner monster out, so I called down Maria, my maid. In the past, she had allowed me to drink from her. She entered the room; her racing heart made my fangs ache. I itched for the taste of real blood from a vein. Her dark hair was pulled into a bun and her deep brown doe eyes stared at me. She wanted to feel the rush as much as I wanted to taste her.

"Do you consent?" I asked her, as it was stated within our law to gain consent before we drew blood.

"Yes," her voice wavered, but it was a resounding yes. I rushed over and took her head and body in my arms before I sank my teeth into her neck. She moaned from the pleasure of the bite, and I groaned from the warmth of the blood sliding down my throat. I growled as I bit a little harder. I heard Maria's heart start to slow, and so I stopped. I healed her wound and carried her to her quarters to rest for the evening.

———

Larissa was close, and she was highly inebriated. It would not make for an enjoyable evening for her. It did not take long for her to return home. As she stumbled up the stairs, I opened the doors for her to enter and was greeted with a slap on the face.

"You pig!" she shrieked at me.

Confusion and anger coursed through me. I was unsure about what I had done to deserve this from her. I smelled the air and noticed that it was not just alcohol, she had also been drugged. The distinct smell of GHB. I held her head in my hands.

"What happened?" I asked her as I scanned her eyes. She was unharmed physically.

"You drank from another!" I took a step back. How did she know? She could not possibly know.

"How?" I asked her as she wobbled on her feet. I reached out to steady her, but she swatted my hand away.

"I felt it. The pleasure you gained from touching another and drinking from them. You cheated!"

I smiled at her, her ignorance of our laws was laughable. "Larissa, drinking is not considered cheating."

"It is to me, you touched another girl, and you drank from her. That is personal."

I scratched my chin. "How did you know it was a girl?" How did she know this? It had never occurred in the past.

"I felt it and I saw it. You enjoyed it and it disgusted me. You have not drunk from me and yet you let the lips that kiss me touch another woman?" Her dizziness overpowered my senses; the drug had taken its full effect on her. Her heart was beating faster than it should have and her temperature was rising fast. I grabbed her and rushed her up the stairs. She fought me every step of the way.

"We can argue later. For now, we need to calm your body down. You have been drugged." I removed her clothes and my own as I pulled her into a cold shower. She slammed her hands against my chest as she repeated herself.

"Drink from me." It was not like her, this was different. I leant down to smell the crook of her neck. She had been spelled. Peter and Lucianna. She drugged her own sister? For what? I could not understand.

Larissa continued to beg, "Please drink, I want to give you that pleasure. Drink...I want to feel it, Nik. Please."

I fought against my inner monster, who was dying to give in to her pleas. Her body began to relax as her pleas died down and she slumped against my chest. I stroked her head as she cried. I would rip Peter to pieces once I faced him again. I could not tell her about this. The knowledge that her sister had spelled her again would devastate her. She was barely coping after losing

Lucianna to a man like Peter. She would never admit it, but I felt it through our bond. She wished it never happened. She wished London had never happened.

405

CHAPTER 61

THE TRUTH IS REVEALED

Larissa

I woke the next morning with a throbbing headache. I wanted to blame Nik, but I could not. It was my own fault and my own jealousy. The idea that Nik drank from another person, let alone another girl, did not sit well with me. It was a feeling that I could not explain. A wanting for more, a need to be closer to him.

He was right and I hated him for it. Inside me, there was a hidden, dark desire that I wanted him to bite me. I shook my head as I got up out of bed. I washed my face to remove the leftover makeup from the day before. I would have to show my face at work today, but I would go in later. I was the boss, so technically it was allowed. Nik had not left yet; the bond told me he was downstairs.

I ventured down the hallway to our future bedroom. The door creaked. I ran my hand along the wall to find the light. There was a massive chandelier in the middle of the room and several small wall sconces all around. There were boxes packed from old materials that were already in the room. I smiled at the idea of Nik's old life and what he had been through before me. I could barely imagine him as a little boy. It was more likely he was born as the adult he is today.

The room would no doubt be as beautiful and elegant as the rest of the house, with its timeless features made modern. I found a diary and I flicked through it. Various items fell out.

"Shoot." I bent down to pick them up quickly as one flipped over, and it was like looking in a mirror. The photo was in black and white, of a woman who had the exact same features as me. We were almost identical, other than a small beauty spot on her chin. Nik and Roman's words flooded back to me: 'She always picks you', 'I cannot lose you again'. My knees buckled as I fell to the floor.

The door creaked. "Larissa?" Nik's soft voice carried through the room, and he ran over and helped me up when he saw me on the floor. I pushed him away. I wanted to be sick.

"What is the meaning of this?" he demanded. "Are you still upset from last night?"

I shook my head and held up the photo. I did not need to look at him to know he dreaded this conversation.

"Explain this," I said shakily. My body trembled with adrenaline. I wanted to scream and cry at the same time. My magic wanted to explode, but I pushed it deep down to keep it contained.

He cleared his throat. "It would be better if you sat down."

"Do not tell me what to do right now, just give me answers. Who is she? Is this her, your ex? Is this why you wanted me? "

He sighed and ran his fingers through his hair. "She is you. Or at least a version of you."

"How?" My voice trembled. I feared the answer as Nik spoke under his breath.

"I am cursed, and you are part of that curse," he mumbled. I could feel his fear of admitting this.

"WHAT?" I wanted to hurt him, and I could not explain why.

"My real name is Remus and Roman is, only naturally, Romulus." He paused as he sat on the bed. "The stories are true, to an extent. We were raised by a wolf after we were cast out by the Gods. We were the first werewolves to roam the earth. We were bitten once she considered us to be men. We were twelve. We stopped aging just after turning thirty, but we never understood why. The transformation was horrible at such a young age, but Roman and I got through it together. We founded Rome. The stories of us fighting to the death still make me laugh. We fought, but as I was the second born, it was Roman's by birthright, and I gave it up willingly. The Ancient Romans did not understand why, but I decided to step back from society and allow Roman to rule. History has told the story that he murdered his own brother, which, as you see, is not true. I helped Roman from behind the curtain before it was discovered that he did not age, and he was forced to disappear after a storm swept through the city." He sighed as his foot tapped on the floor.

"We stayed in the darkness and watched from the sidelines as the humans fought over nonsense. Rulers were overthrown or murdered for another's gain. We planned to leave and explore the world when Roman saw you walking through the town. You were known as Liyana, and you were married to the Emperor at the time. He was a barbarian. You were his prize due to your beauty; you were purity and grace. Roman would watch you walk through the town; you always had a sad look on your face. Roman spoke to you first and befriended you, and I had to know who this human was that my brother spoke of. The moment I laid my eyes on you, I had a desire deep inside, and I knew that you were born to be mine. Roman brought you home to meet me, and it felt like everything made sense when you were close. I kissed your hand and sparks ignited between us;

you were mine from that moment on. Roman was powerless to stop it, but he accepted that our love was stronger than what he felt for you. We kept our relationship secret and hidden from your husband." He paused again. "James is the image of your husband, which was the reason behind my attack on him. All my rage from centuries ago rose to the surface as I remembered that day when it all changed."

I sighed and took a seat on the armchair in the corner as I kept the photo in my hand. "What happened?"

"The fall of the Roman Empire, the day it all changed. Your sister told your husband about your infidelity. He tore Rome apart to find Roman and me. It was not until he held you up in the city centre and stabbed you before everyone, and left you there to die, that I rushed over and held you in my arms. You were bleeding to death, and I could not lose you. I refused. There were stories of a man who could grant wishes at a cost. I was shot with arrows as I rushed you to him. You pleaded with me to stop and begged for me to let you die. You did not believe you were worth the cost of my soul. I held you in my arms as we walked into his temple. I heard your heart stop as I laid you before him, and I begged him to bring you back. His condition was becoming this," he gestured at himself, "one of the first blood-sucking monsters. A plague. A darkness on the Earth. I agreed. I became his puppet, and I had to do whatever he asked. I did not care, as long as I had you."

A tear fell down his cheek. I had never seen him show so much emotion. The scars I had seen, they made sense. They were thousands of years old before he became the immortal he was now.

"I do not understand the curse. You called me your curse?" I questioned.

"Once I agreed, he brought you back to life. I still remember his smile; it sent shivers down my spine. I pushed away my fear that he had done something untoward. We lived together; we were happy together. It was not until you died that I regretted my decision, but it was around a hundred years later when we found each other again. You were the same, but a little different. We lived together until you died again. It happened over and over; your soul was reincarnated. Each time, you would remember the past. You would remember from a look, a touch, a kiss, making love, or a bite. Once you remembered, we spent whatever time we could together. It did not matter what we did. You were always killed; it was part of the curse. I begged for your life, and it was granted, but I did not know the cost would be to lose you over and over."

I stood up, shaking. "You called me your curse, but you were wrong. You are mine. I may not have my memories, but I know the person that I am. I was begging you for a reason and you could not get over your own selfish needs. You do not deserve me or any version of me. You cursed me to never know peace. I am constantly being brought back for you. My soul will never have its final rest and that is all on you. You are my curse."

I walked to push past him, but he grabbed my arm to stop me. I pulled it back.

"Larissa, stop. It is different this time. You are different this time. You are the same as the first version of you. There are no slight changes. You *are* Liyana."

"I do not care which version I am. You ruined my life. From the moment I met you, everything has been turned upside down. I am living on borrowed time; I will not stand by and wait for that to happen. I am no longer yours, Nik."

I pulled the ring off and threw it at him. It bounced off his chest. He spun me around.

"You need to remember. I will make you remember." He pushed me against the wall and held me down. "You wanted me to bite you last night. Here it is. You *will* remember our life. To hell with the repercussions." His fangs extended as he moved closer. I squirmed to get out of his reach, but his strength overwhelmed me. I could not push him away and magic would not help.

"I do not consent!" I screamed, knowing that he would not be able to bite me.

He growled but continued to push forward against my wishes. I put my hands on the wall and summoned my magic to make the room shake. I could not use magic on him, but I could on our surroundings. He slammed his fist on the wall as I brought my knee up into his groin. He dropped to the floor; I took this as the time to run.

I fled down the stairs, but he flew and landed before me. He put his hands up.

"Larissa, stop this. I beg of you to stop and be reasonable."

I could feel the magic in my eyes. They were glowing, and everything was heightened.

"If you care for me, let me go. Let me leave right now. I need to be away from you. I just discovered that you cursed me. LET. ME. GO."

He shook his head. "No, I told you I will not lose you again. You can hate me all you wish, but you will stay in this house. I will leave and stay at the penthouse."

I crossed my arms to show my disapproval.

"I will give you the space you require, but in the eyes of the law you are still my mate."

My rage grew as the house shook.

"You can be as angry as you want about the situation, but you cannot deny what we have between us."

He was right, but it did nothing to dispel the anger within me. He turned and made his way for the garage to leave, but he stopped and looked back at me. "I will only be a call away, Larissa. I love you and I apologise for the harm that I have caused you."

I watched him leave and was finally able to exhale, but sadness filled me as he departed. I walked to the kitchen and poured myself a cup of coffee before I sat down on the terrace outside. My phone rang, and I saw it was Roman. I picked up but refused to speak.

"I spoke with Nik," he began. "He told me. Are you alright?"

"How do you expect me to answer that, Roman? You both lied to me, in more ways than one. You lied about knowing my mother and you lied about my entire life. Or lives. Is that the reason you watched me? Was it because you knew who I was already? But if that is the case just..." Tears flowed as I was not able to finish my sentence.

"Larissa," he pleaded as I hung up the phone. The only person I wanted to speak to was Luce, but I could not do that. I had lost my closest friend because of a life that I did not want, a life that I had no choice in. It was horrible. The tears flowed harder. I wanted to be held, but I had no one to hold me. My stomach ached from the pain. I screamed with everything that I had inside me, but it provided little relief.

———

I went to work the next day and kept my head down. I did not want to be there. I wanted to stay home and continue to cry, as I struggled to wrap my head around the fact that my life was simply playing on repeat. I was bound to love the same person that I had in every lifetime.

Did my mother know? Is that why Katrina was keeping my existence hidden? She did not want Nik to find me, and if that was the case, then why? Is that why Elizabeth tried to keep me in the little town? Was it part of her manipulation? These were the questions that hurt the most.

I could barely bring myself to focus on anything. I paid the outstanding bills with the money that Nik sent through; which was more than he originally promised. I knew this was his way of saying sorry, but it was not going to work. A sorry would not fix what I felt. I did not even know what I was feeling. It was strange. I rubbed my forehead as Stacey walked into my office.

"Knock, knock!" she chirped.

I looked up and smiled at her. "Come in, Stacey." I waved her in as she closed the door behind her and sat down opposite my desk. She was quiet as she kept her hands in her lap.

"What is it?" I asked.

"You were not in yesterday, and Mr. Dankworth was moodier than usual. Now today, you are withdrawn and not yourself. Are you alright?"

I put my pen down and the tears started. I could not stop them from falling. I was holding everything in as I had no one to talk to. She asked the one question that will generally make any emotionally unstable person fall apart. She ran over and put her arms around me.

"What happened? Did you guys have a fight?"

I shook my head. "I do not even know where to begin Stace, it is just so surreal. It feels like my entire life has been flipped upside down."

"What has happened?" she asked, her face filled with concern. It radiated from her body.

"I found out that I am Nik's reincarnated lover. I reincarnate every hundred or so years. I feel strangely betrayed, like my life has no other purpose than to live and be with Nik. I wanted more for myself than to fall in love. I wanted to travel and maybe fall in love with different people over my lifetime, but it is impossible when you have already supposedly met your soulmate." I let my head fall in my hands.

Stacey scoffed. "Are you seriously complaining about that right now?"

"About what?" I asked as I glanced up at her.

"You get to fall in love with a God every couple of hundred years, get over it." She moved away. I thought maybe I would have gotten a little more emotion than just flat-out contempt.

"Are you serious right now, Stacey? I am born to be with the same man. I have no choice in my life. It is all predetermined. I am born, I find him, I die, and the cycle repeats. Nik may be attractive but at his core, he is a selfish monster."

I picked up my pen and pretended to shuffle through my paperwork silently to alert her that she could leave. Stacey understood and moved towards the door.

"Sometimes you need to look at the brighter side of life."

I wanted to throw a curse or a spell her way, but I held off and glared at my paperwork until she left the office. My stomach rumbled as I grabbed my purse and headed downstairs to the local café. I smiled at Alina, who was manning the front desk by herself, and buttoned my coat. My phone rang. It was Nik. I did not speak to him for the remainder of yesterday, and I missed his voice. I hated myself for this bond. I answered the phone.

"Hello," I answered softly, not wanting to admit how much I wanted to hear his voice.

He cleared his throat. "I shall keep this brief. Luce and Peter have been spotted in London, and you need to be vigilant."

I turned to see Luce standing before me, her hands alight with magic. Nik and I had our bond, I pushed through fear for him to register.

"Why are you scared? Is she near? Send through love if I am correct."

I did as he asked and pushed all the love I had for him through our bond.

"Get back inside," he ordered, but as I turned to step towards the office, I bumped into a figure. I looked over my shoulder, but I knew from the smell alone that it was Peter.

"Larissa, I will find you. Do you trust that?" His voice was frantic but filled with affection.

"Yes. I love you." I wanted him to know that, despite my frustration with the whole situation.

"I love you, too. With every part of my being."

I did not want to hang up the phone, so I took it away from my ear and walked towards Luce. I put up a protection shield to block her magic, but when she smiled, I realised why. She had already cast her own spell to dampen my magic. Peter was behind me again.

"Do not fight this. Or do. Either way, I will enjoy inflicting pain on you, you filthy blood whore."

CHAPTER 62
YOU CANNOT HAVE WHAT IS NOT YOURS
Larissa

I woke feeling cold. I opened my eyes to see Peter holding a bucket of water near me.

"Rise and shine, blood whore."

My hands were tied behind the back of a chair. The metal was pressed tightly into my skin. I glared at Peter before my eyes fell on Luce. She could not look me directly in the eye.

"Can you not look at me because of your guilt?" She shook her head and walked away.

"You should be thankful to her. If it were up to me, you would be dead already." His words were filled with a hatred that I still did not understand.

"What the hell have I ever done to you?" I glared at him.

"You side with them."

"No, this started before that. You hated me from the start. Is it because I rejected you? Did I hurt your precious little ego?" I asked, trying to stop myself from laughing.

His fist came down hard on my face, my cheek crunched under his blow.

"I would never lower myself to a whore like you."

"I love how you call me a whore when you are dating the town bicycle. Everyone has had a ride on Luce." I chuckled at my metaphor, the laughter coming from my anxiety at being in this situation.

"She still has more class than you," he scoffed.

The swipe did not hurt because it did not feel true. Lucianna had always been petty, and Peter was now just extorting it for his own gain. He was sociopathic.

"Tell me, do you only keep her around because of her skills? She must be mighty useful to your cause. She would be able to disarm certain vampires a lot easier than you could."

He raised a brow. I had tweaked his interest.

"Certain?"

"The older the vampire, the harder it is to harm them with magic. Some are older than our family's magic."

"Yes, but once the full moon arrives, she will cast one final spell and her rightful powers will be returned to her."

"Rightful?" I questioned, knowing he may not answer. He only smiled wickedly and left.

As I looked around the room, it struck me how alone I was. The warehouse was empty and abandoned. I tried to tap into my magic, but it did not work. Luce must have placed another dampening spell on me. I reached to find Nik, but even that was hard to do. I barely felt him. Wherever I was being kept was heavily guarded by magic.

I closed my eyes and whispered, "Please find me, Nik."

A small laugh from the darkness had my eyes shooting open to scan for where it came from.

Luce appeared and sat down. "Pathetic."

"What is so pathetic? The fact that I have a man who wants me without conditions? I assure you, Peter would not look twice at you if it were not for your magic," I spat at her. I would not hold back now.

Her face twitched; she knew it was true. "At least he cares for me and not my blood." She tried to hurt me but it would not work.

I groaned at her. "Just stop, Luce. My relationship with Nik has never been about my blood. He has never drunk from me. What we have is different. We are bound together."

She scoffed. "Bound, now that is certainly true."

It clicked into place. "Wait, you know?"

She smiled, but it was cruel. "Of course I knew. Mother told me about it. She warned me to always keep you safe from them. She spelled the hate into our lives to keep you safe. It was what your mum wanted; she never wanted you to find each other."

"Who knew you were capable of this many lies? I should not be surprised, really. You and Peter are the perfect match," I snarled at her.

She glared at me and her hands lit up briefly. "At least we have true love."

"He is incapable of love." How did she not see that Peter was using her?

"No, *they* are incapable of love." She was referring to vampires.

"Did you not see the lengths he went to protect me? Did you not see the way he looks at me?" I pleaded with her to see reason, but she was too far gone.

"You are a prize to him, nothing more than a piece of meat on his arm." I rolled my eyes at her ridiculous assumptions.

"That is all you are to Peter. He will use you for every drop of magic you have. Mum would not have wanted this for you."

"Do not speak of *my* mother," she hissed, emphasising the word, pointing out the fact that we shared nothing between us anymore. I shook my head as tears fell from my eyes. My sister was now a stranger, possibly even my enemy.

"I cannot believe I mean so little to you. We grew up together, we played together, we slept together. I would hold you when you were scared of thunderstorms or during scary movies and now...we are reduced to nothing." I appealed to her emotions, hoping she would see through the hate that drove her to do this. The hate Peter had instilled.

Her face flinched, and what looked like remorse flashed across it quickly. "It was always meant to be this way, Larissa. Once the full moon arrives, it will be over."

"What is happening on the full moon?" I asked, hopeful she would reveal the truth.

She sighed and clasped her hands together with eagerness. "I will receive my rightful powers."

"What do you mean by rightful powers?" I could not understand her thoughts on this when I remembered Nik's comment—a witch's powers are passed down through the bloodline. I struggled in my chair. She wanted something that was not hers.

"I did not steal your magic!"

"Yes, you did. I never received *all* my mother's magic on the day she died. I deserve them, not you."

I could not believe her thinking. "Luce, Elizabeth stole her magic from Katrina. Her magic was never yours; I am sorry that you are disappointed. Elizabeth was never powerful, but Katrina was."

She growled and bared her teeth. "NO, YOU ARE WRONG! It is mine and I will have it, as is my right."

She stormed from the room and slammed the door behind her.

CHAPTER 63

CURSED TIME

Larissa

WHAT WAS LEFT OF THE LIGHT WAS DISAPPEARING AS NIGHT approached. I did not know if tonight was the full moon or if it was tomorrow. It would be responsible as a witch to keep track of this, but I refused. I wanted a normal life despite the magic that coursed through my veins. My stomach grumbled as another person walked into the room with their face covered. I saw the compass tattoo on their forearm as they walked over and untied the rope. I thought about hitting them, but I was too weak. I rubbed my wrists as they put food on the table in the corner and walked out again. I took slow tentative steps towards the food, worried about it being poisoned or spelled. I would not be able to detect either of them. My stomach grumbled again.

"Fuck it." I grabbed the sandwich, stuffed it into my mouth, and groaned from the satisfaction of finally eating. When I felt a little stronger, I cased the room for any sign of an exit. The walls were concrete or steel, there were two tiny windows that were too high for me to reach, and only one door in or out.

I put my hands on the wall and pushed all my magic forward in hopes of blasting a hole through it. The wall started to shake, but I could not manage any more than that. Luce's spell was blocking full access. I knew I could push harder, but it would use more energy than I currently had. I needed to stay alert and sharp. I heard voices grow outside the door, and I moved towards it to listen intently.

"She has to die." Peter's words were filled with hate.

"Baby, please. Once she is stripped of her magic, she will not be a threat anymore. We can let her go. We don't need to kill her," Luce begged, despite her hatred towards me.

"If she stays alive, it is more dangerous for us. Nik will not stop hunting her. He has more resources than us. You can only dampen the bond between them in small amounts. You are not strong enough to sustain that block. After the spell is completed, I will slice her throat and dance in her blood. The filthy whore deserves nothing more than that."

I closed my eyes. Luce was blocking the bond, but she needed a break. I would continue to prod at that bond until I reached him. If only to keep my brain busy before my inevitable death.

It took a couple more hours before I could feel Nik. I pushed further and closed my eyes. I knew I could transport myself if I ever needed it, but with Luce's dampening magic on my own, it would be harder. I focused on sending my spirit to him as I breathed deeply and uttered the spell quietly. I opened my eyes to see Nik sitting in his office, his hair was dishevelled, and his suit rumpled.

"Nik." My voice was soft and weak.

His eyes moved up slowly before he rushed over to hold me but fell through me instead.

"Where are you? I have been searching for you for days."

I yearned for his touch. Our argument and his lies seemed irrelevant in this moment.

"Luce and Peter have me, but I do not know where I am. There are no windows to see out of. All I know is that it is a warehouse."

He rushed over to his map and started to scour it.

"Nik, stop, please." He looked up, tears were brimming in his eyes. I had to say it, deep down I knew I was not going to survive tonight. I wanted Nik to know that I did not blame him, that despite our arguments, I did love him, and I would continue to love him.

"Please, Larissa, I beg of you, do not say it." I could feel his despair. He had no hope of finding me.

I closed my eyes. "I know you will find me, Nik. I have faith in you. This is not the end of our story."

He walked back over and reached for my face before he pulled back, knowing he could not touch me.

"I love you, Larissa." Tears streamed down his face.

"I love you, Nik."

"I will search for you, till my dying breath. I will find you, Larissa." I let the spell end and returned to the warehouse. Tears were falling down my cheeks. I turned around to see Luce leaning against the door, her face showed sadness.

"I suppose you felt the use of my magic and came in." I cleared my throat as I composed myself.

She sighed and did not move. "I don't want to hurt you, Larissa. I do care for you and after the exchange you had with him, I see that your love is true."

She was not finished, but rather trying to find the right words for what she wanted to say next.

"I don't want to kill you, Rissa, and I don't want to harm you either. Would you be willing to hand over the power to me without the spell? It will cause you no pain and I will let you go so you can be with him."

I shook my head, I could not bring myself to say the word no. I would never give her the magic that belonged to me. Everything I had read within the grimoire stated that magic was passed on to the person it belonged to. Luce would know this, but Peter would have convinced her otherwise. It would be useless to argue with her. She walked over and pulled me into her embrace and held me tight. "I pray it is painless for you."

She moved towards the door. I could hear her nose sniffling from the obvious tears she held in. The door closed and my knees buckled as my cries filled the room. I would die young in this life, as I had in every other life before it. I looked to the sky and held my hands together in prayer.

"Whoever is listening, please spare my life. I deserve more than this end."

I crossed myself and found a spot to sit and wait for my inevitable death. For the curse to be activated once again.

CHAPTER 64

IT ALL CAME CRASHING DOWN

Larissa

THE DARKNESS OUTSIDE THE WINDOW GREW BRIGHTER AS THE moon rose in the sky. I heard shouts outside the door as I stood and waited for them to enter. I expected Luce, not the men in masks who cuffed my hands in iron. The iron would keep my magic contained, and I noticed it was engraved with small inscriptions.

I followed willingly and then I found myself standing before an altar. Luce wore a black gown and spoke a spell over a cauldron. It was all so cliché, I could not help but laugh.

There was a sharp pain in the back of my head. I turned with fuzzy eyes to see Peter behind me, shoving me forward.

Luce glared at Peter. "I told you not to hurt her."

"She was rude to you, babe." He shrugged his shoulders ignoring her pleas.

I rolled my eyes at his attempt to seem loving towards her but even I knew he was not. She looked away and continued with her spell before she pulled out an athame and held it up. She asked for a blessing from the Goddesses.

Luce smiled down at me. I walked over to her, and the floor began to shake. I glanced up at Luce in question, but she shook her head. This was not her doing. I reached for Luce, grabbed hold of her and held her close. My wrists burned from the iron shackles. We may have been enemies at that moment, but I would not allow her to be hurt. There was a bang in the distance as fire erupted from inside the warehouse.

Peter charged at me and held the athame to my throat.

"Finish it, Luce!" he screamed. "NOW!"

Luce could not look away from the fire that was spreading quicker than I had ever seen before.

"LET HER GO!" I turned to see Nik approaching us, his eyes were filled with flames, and relief flooded me. I smiled and then glared at Peter as I brought my knee up to his groin. Peter groaned and dropped the knife. Luce did not care as I ran towards Nik, who pulled off my iron shackles.

"Come, we must leave." He held me close as we rushed to safety. He glanced back at the warehouse and smiled before it burst into flames.

"LUCE!" I screamed and attempted to run back towards the warehouse, but Nik grabbed me and growled.

"She is not worth it." There was a coldness to his words, and I noticed the lack of tingling. I took a step back and noticed that his eyes were still a bright red instead of his beautiful blue. He smiled and it did not reach his eyes, as it normally did.

It was an evil smile. I took another step back.

"What is it, my love?" His voice sounded sweet and tender, but something was wrong.

"You are not Nik."

He smirked. "You are smarter than I expected you to be. No, I am not your precious Nik, but that is of no relevance right now."

He tapped my forehead. "Time to sleep." As I felt the weariness of sleep take over, I tried to fight it. I did not wish to sleep, I wished to know who he was. I wanted to know where Nik was and how this man had his face. But the more I fought it, the harder it was to resist.

"Sleep, dear Larissa," he said before my eyes closed and I fell into darkness.

THE END